MW00355061

LACRIMOSA
OF
DANA

THE OFFICIAL NOVELIZATION

ANNA KASHINA

Dragonwell Publishing

This is a work of fiction based on *YsVIII: Lacrimosa of Dana*, a video game by Nihon Falcom Corporation.

All of the characters, organizations, and events portrayed in this novel are either products of the author's imagination or are used fictitiously.

Copyright © 2023 by Anna Kashina

Cover and interior art by Nihon Falcom Corporation
Cover Design by Clarence Lim

Published by Dragonwell Publishing, Dragonwell, LLC
www.dragonwellpublishing.com

All rights reserved. No part of this book may be reproduced or transmitted in any printed or electronic form without permission in writing from the publisher.

ISBN 978-1-940076-98-0 (hardcover)
ISBN 978-1-940076-88-1 (paperback)
ISBN 978-1-940076-99-7 (ebook)

First Edition

A NOTE FROM THE AUTHOR

Lacrimosa of Dana was my first game in the *Ys* series—and I instantly fell in love with it. Since that day, I have dreamed of writing a novel based on its story and characters. I am very excited to be able to bring this project to life.

This novel is a standalone, self-contained story based directly on the events of the game. I omitted many of the action-based game elements—such as beast raids, secondary side quests, treasure chests, and many monster encounters—to leave more space for character development that sometimes took me beyond what was shown in the game. Followers of the *Ys* lore have a common understanding that the games in the series are based on the journals written by our hero, Adol Christin. As players, we interpret these stories in our own way. This novel is one interpretation of the events that occurred on the Isle of Seiren, and I hope you enjoy this retelling of the tale.

Those who have never played the game can read this book as an independent novel, set in a magical world that broadly resembles an alternate version of the Mediterranean region around the early 18th century. The Romun Empire is a dominant force in this world, and places like Greek, Creet, and Romn have direct parallels to historical places. Distances in Ys are measured in krimelye and melye, similar to the kilometers and meters we use. A rich variety of fish in the Gaete Sea and the rivers that flow into it include boleh, sadina, saman, rowana, and many others. The world of Ys has two moons, but they rise in the sky similarly to ours.

Some say that the events of this novel have rewritten known history, setting the world of Ys on a new course that may eventually bring it closer to our own. But this is only an unverified rumor—and definitely part of another story.

The events described in this book were first recorded in *The Travelogue of the Gaete Sea*, by Adol Christin, an adventurer who left behind over a hundred travelogues and journals waiting to be retold by later generations.

Anna Kashina

Also by Anna Kashina

The Majat Code series:
Blades of the Old Empire
The Guild of Assassins
Assassin Queen

The Spirits of the Ancient Sands series:
The Princess of Dhagabad
The Goddess of Dance

Standalone novels:
Mistress of the Solstice
Shadowblade

Also from Dragonwell Publishing

The Garden at the Roof of the World
The Reality, Mythology, and Fantasies of Unicorns
The Chocolatier's Wife
The Chocolatier's Ghost
The Chocolatier's Journal
Wishes and Sorrows
The Key to All Things
The Blackwell Family Secret: The Guardians of Sin
Ashamed, Desert-Born
Fire and Shadow
Devil's Ways
The Loathly Lady
Sorrow

CONTENTS

Everything originated from an abyss—the boundless sky spreading in all directions. In time, rain fell from the sky, giving rise to the ocean. Fire spewed forth from the ocean, giving rise to the Earth and the Great Tree. By the power of the Great Tree, life was formed, evolved, and set foot on the Earth.

Life is nurtured by the Earth. One day, life must return to the sky through the Great Tree in a great cataclysm known as the Lacrimosa, to clear the way for new life-forms to evolve. From one Lacrimosa to the next, the Great Tree fosters life and rebirth. Thus continues the cycle of evolution.

—from the Eternian Myth of Origin, as recorded in
The Travelogue of the Gaete Sea by Adol Christin.

The Isle of Seiren

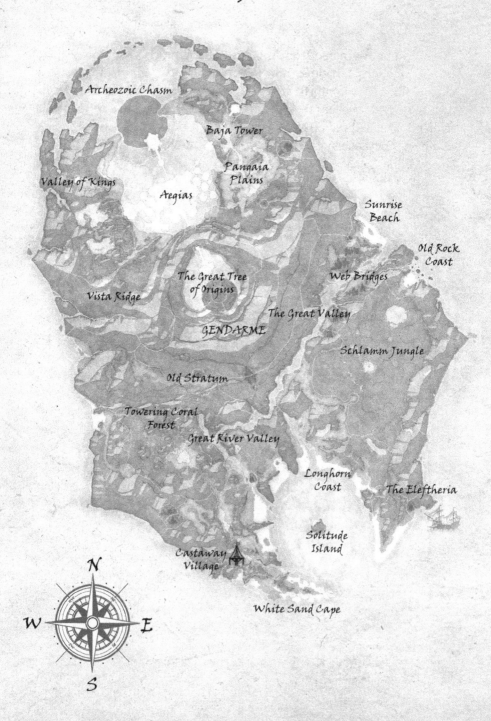

THE LOMBARDIA'S LAST VOYAGE

Adol Christin loved adventure—the thrill of discovering new lands, venturing into the unknown. But some of the challenges he and his friend Dogi faced in their travels had nothing to do with danger and exploration. Finding a ship in the port of Xandria willing to ferry two armed, tough-looking young men across the Gaete Sea proved be one of those.

Adol and Dogi felt lucky when, after too many aggravating exchanges, they finally found a solution to their transportation problem. The captain of the four-masted passenger liner *Lombardia,* about to set sail to Eresia, offered to enlist them as temporary members of the crew. After all the hassle, Adol was looking forward to a quiet journey, with nothing to do but swab decks, coil lines, and enjoy the sweeping sea views.

In hindsight, he should have been experienced enough to realize that this peaceful state of things wasn't going to last.

It all started with the land Adol spotted on the horizon a few days after they left the port.

He had just finished swabbing the quarterdeck and was heading down the ladder when he paused by the rail to steal a look at the view.

Sun blazed in the clear afternoon sky, coating the calm water with a soft velvety sheen. A fresh breeze cooled his face, leaving a subtle taste of salt on his lips. Seagulls soared over the masts, their cries accentuated by the rhythmic splashing of the waves against the hull. One of the birds dipped gracefully into the water and emerged with a silvery boleh squirming in its beak.

Adol peered into the distance. What was that bluish shape, barely

1

visible off the starboard bow? An island? A very large one, by the looks of it. He hadn't realized that the *Lombardia* was scheduled to pass a major destination so early into the voyage. Strange that he'd heard no mention of it after he came aboard. He glanced around for a crewman to ask about it—and froze at the sight of the tall, middle-aged man approaching from the direction of the helm.

Captain Barbaros.

"Adol Christin, is it?" the captain asked.

"Yes, sir." Adol stood to attention, looking at him in surprise. He hadn't expected the captain would remember his name from their brief conversation back at the port. But even more curious was the captain's casual smile, as if stopping to chat with a simple deckhand was part of his normal routine. The twinkle of humor softening his stern, weathered features, the quiet interest in his gaze, made for quite a difference from the other sea captains Adol had encountered in his travels.

"As I recall, you introduced yourself as an adventurer," the captain said. "Do you know of the Isle of Seiren?" He gestured to the distant shape.

Seiren. The name did ring a bell, but Adol couldn't quite place it. "I don't, sir."

"Understandable." The captain leaned on the rail next to him, looking toward the horizon. "The Gaete Sea is home to many islands, treacherous to navigate. But none of them have a reputation as fearsome as Seiren."

"Fearsome, sir?" Adol raised his eyebrows.

"Yes." The captain looked at him appraisingly, as if deciding if he was up to the information. "Every ship that sails too close sinks under mysterious circumstances. Rumors speak of a curse that plagues its coastal waters. Some sailors believe even talking about Seiren brings bad luck."

Oh. That would explain why Adol hadn't heard anything about it from the crew. He met the captain's gaze. "I assume you aren't one of those sailors, sir?"

The captain chuckled. His face lit up with a new expression. Approval? Adol had a strange feeling he had just passed some sort of test.

"Well, we're talking about it, aren't we? And—anticipating your next question—I don't believe in curses. There's definitely a mystery about Seiren, though. No one ever walked its shores and lived to tell the tale."

"No one?" Adol echoed, his eyes glued to the distant shape. "Has no one ever tried to explore it?"

"Oh, they tried, all right. The last attempt I heard of was a Romun exploratory vessel about five years ago. It approached the island in calm weather—never to be seen again. To this day, no one knows what happened."

Wow. Excitement rose in Adol's chest. A ship, vanishing without a trace on a calm day. A mysterious island no one had ever escaped. What could possibly lie out there?

"There must be some explanation," he said.

The captain's smile widened. "Oh, definitely—many explanations, actually. The most popular one comes from the pirates who first discovered the island and declared it cursed ground. They claimed that it was inhabited by Seiren—monsters from Greshun legends, whose songs lure ships to their doom. But if you asked a boring person like me, I would probably speculate that this island harbors an anomaly, perhaps a tide or a current around its shores that draws the ships in if they ever get too close. I would never risk the *Lombardia* by sailing any closer than a few krimelye away, and even that distance is only safe when the sea is calm, like today."

"I wonder what the island's like." Adol didn't actually mean to voice the thought. Nor did he intend to sound so wistful. He glanced sideways at the captain, surprised to see the same longing stir in the older man's gaze.

"Every time I sail these waters," Barbaros said, "I wonder the same thing. No one alive knows the answer to that question. But if you are truly that curious, come out to the deck tonight after the eight bells of the First Watch. We'll be passing Seiren around that time. It will be dark, of course, but this is the closest you'll probably ever get."

Eight bells of the First Watch. Midnight, in land terms. Adol nodded. He wouldn't miss it for the world.

"You may be interested to know," the captain went on, "that I often share this tale with new members of my crew. It seems only fair to alert them to the worst. Many are so terrified that, when we sail past Seiren, they are reluctant to leave their quarters. But I see you come from sturdier stock."

"Thank you, sir." The captain's intent gaze was so captivating. No wonder the crew spoke about him with such fervor. This was probably the only conversation Adol was ever going to have with

3

the man, but he knew he was always going to remember it.

"And now," the captain said, "I must resume my duties—as I'm sure must you. I expect I might see you patrolling at my passenger welcoming party this evening?"

"Not in the saloon," Adol said. "I'm assigned to the decks."

"Oh?" The captain raised an eyebrow. "A punishment already?"

"A favor, actually. I'm not much for parties."

"Interesting." He measured Adol with a thoughtful gaze.

The captain must surely be as aware as Adol was of the perks of patrolling the saloon during a party—such as leftovers from the food trays, or the large flask of grog stashed at the back of the bar. But he didn't comment further, simply gestured dismissal, watching Adol pick up his bucket and mop and descend the ladder to the main deck.

A group of crewmen were hauling crates into the saloon, directed by Katthew, the ship's first mate. Dogi towered at least half a head over the rest, his shirt opened down the front to expose his immense muscular chest. As Adol headed in their direction, Dogi set aside the crate he was carrying and waved. One by one, his companions disappeared through the hatch leading to the cargo hold, but he and Katthew held back.

"Yo, Adol," Dogi called. "Was that the *captain* talkin' to you up there?"

"Yes, it was." Adol looked from Dogi to Katthew, both of them frowning in disbelief.

"What was it about?" Katthew asked.

"That island, mostly." Adol gestured toward the horizon.

"Oh. The Isle of Seiren." Katthew's face slowly drained of color.

"Seiren?" Dogi shielded his eyes with his hand, looking into the distance. "It looks as large as Creet. How come I've never heard of it?"

Katthew threw a nervous glance toward the quarterdeck. "Talking about it is bad luck, especially at sea. I wish the captain took those warnings more seriously."

"Bad luck?" Dogi frowned. "Why?"

Katthew shifted from foot to foot. He looked uneasy. Gosh, was he one of those fearful sailors the captain had spoken about?

"Many say it's cursed," Adol said. "Every ship that sails its waters sinks, and no human ever landed on its shores and lived to tell the tale."

4

"Holy cow." Dogi's face lit up in fascination.

Adol grinned. "I knew you'd be interested. We'll be sailing past it after the eight bells of the First Watch. I intend to be on deck to see it. Want to join me?"

Dogi rubbed his forehead. "I think I might just wander up."

"Just make sure not to take too long with it, you two," Katthew said. "Don't forget, we all have patrolling to do...Which reminds me." He turned to Adol. "Are you certain you don't want a turn at the saloon? Most crew are *fighting* for the assignment. We had to assign shorter shifts so that everyone gets their chance. I could still arrange—"

"No thanks," Adol said. "I prefer the decks. Let others have their fun."

Dogi laughed. "Adol wouldn't want to parade himself in front of the ladies and steal all the attention, see? It could get downright ugly if they all—"

"Hey," Adol protested. "I'm not the one walking around with my chest exposed."

"You would be, if you worked in the cargo hold," Dogi retorted. "The place's stuffy as hell. Besides"—he smirked—"unlike you, the rest of us here have to actually put effort into being noticed by ladies. I figured if I show myself on deck, I'd better—"

"Oh, look at the time," Katthew said quickly. "They're about to ring three bells. Let's all return to our duties, shall we?"

The party in the saloon was still in full swing when Adol finished his rounds. He could hear laughter and the clinking of glasses. Perhaps he should stop by for a glance, but he wasn't about to miss his chance to see the mysterious Isle of Seiren.

As he headed past the open doorway toward the ladder leading to the main deck, he nearly collided with a young lady who sped out of the saloon, looking backward, as if she were being chased. She tried to sidestep him and tripped on the hem of her long dress, grasping his arm for support.

"Careful, miss," Adol said.

"Oh." She steadied herself against him, then drew away abruptly. "How dare you touch me?"

Adol spread his hands to the sides with exaggerated care. "Please forgive me. You looked like you were about to fall." And no wonder, with the kind of dress she wore, its puffy skirt large enough for three. Something in the way she held herself gave him a feeling she wasn't used to dresses. Curious.

She drew herself up. "I am perfectly capable of walking on my own, thank you very much."

Adol looked past her into the saloon. He couldn't see anyone chasing her right now, but he was sure something in there must have disturbed her. "Are you all right?"

"Are you questioning me?"

Her voice had an edge, as if she were about to burst into tears. It probably wasn't any of Adol's business, but he couldn't help taking a closer look. Her sharp-featured face looked drawn, suggesting that she wasn't getting enough sleep, or had cried recently, or both. A thin layer of powder did a poor job of covering the freckles underneath, as if applied half-heartedly. Wisps of blond hair escaped from the elaborate arrangement around her head. A lady in distress, if ever he saw one.

"I am patrolling the decks," he said, "to make sure there's no trouble. If anyone in there is bothering you—"

Her gaze wavered. She surveyed him for a moment, as if deciding whether she could trust him, then stepped back and drew herself up again.

"I am a lady," she snapped. "A common sailor like you has no business talking to me at all, let alone asking personal questions. Now let me pass at once, or I will have you thrown into the brig for insolence."

The threat was so ridiculous that Adol couldn't help a smile as he stepped aside, giving her as wide a berth as possible in the narrow passageway.

"Oh, you find me funny, do you?" she demanded.

"I find you curious," he said truthfully. "And—with no intention to delay you any longer, my lady—my offer stands. If anyone in the saloon, or anywhere else on this ship, is giving you trouble, I will deal with them for you. You have but to say a word."

Again, he sensed a brief hesitation before she scoffed and lifted her chin, marching past him toward the passenger quarters. After a few moments, he heard a distant door creak open and bang closed. Oh well. At least she'd reached her cabin safely.

The ship's bell rang overhead. Eight bells. Time to see the mysterious Isle of Seiren. Adol did his best to put the strange young lady out of his mind as he ascended the ladder to the main deck.

Everything there was peaceful and quiet. A few passengers were gathered near the rail, soaking up the night air. Two crewmen crouched at the mast, coiling lines. The helmsman stood at the wheel, peering ahead. In the darkness, brightly lit windows in the saloon and upper cabins made the ship gleam like a holiday tree.

It was darker up on the bow. In the light of the rising moons, the view out to sea was as good as possible at this hour. Adol leaned over the rail, peering into the gloom off the starboard side.

The dark shape of the island was much closer than earlier this evening when Adol had commenced his patrol below decks. Despite the darkness, he could even make out some of the shoreline, a deep bay framed with a set of jagged rocks on one side and a long sandy beach on the other. The water in the bay gleamed in the moonlight, with a dot of a tiny islet in its center the only blemish on its mirror perfection. The rest of the island lay in shadows, dwarfed by a massive mountain range rising in the distance. From here, it looked like the spine of a giant beast curled up to sleep.

The Isle of Seiren. Strange how in the short time since Adol had learned about this mysterious land, he had come to think of it as a living thing, a magical creature waiting in the darkness to lure ships to their doom. Or perhaps the island was more like a trapped beast, yearning for an adventurer to free it from its curse. Most likely the captain was right, and it was all about weather anomalies and underwater currents, but it was hard not to wonder if there was more to it. Adol wished he could walk on those shores one day.

Dark water swirled and churned around the distant reefs—too far for the *Lombardia* to worry about but definitely dangerous enough for any ship that dared to steer into those waters. Straining his ears, he thought he could just make out the sound of splashing over the jagged tips that poked out of the sea like the claws of a submerged beast.

Wait ... Was the splashing getting closer?

It certainly seemed that way. The waves lapping against the hull had a new tone, as if a large shape were approaching underwater. Adol leaned over the rail, trying to spot the source.

The ship jolted, the impact so strong that Adol nearly fell overboard.

What in the underworld ...?

A door banged in the distance, followed by an erupting concert of voices and the pounding of running feet.

"What's happening?" the captain bellowed on the quarterdeck.

"I don't know, sir! We seem to have run aground!"

"Impossible. We're in open waters."

"Maybe we—"

"Assess the situation at once!"

"Aye-aye, sir!"

The ship shook again, harder this time. A piercing scream cut the air. Adol rushed down the ladder to the main deck, skipping several steps.

The deck was in complete disarray. Sailors ran frantically between their posts, while passengers mixed into a disorderly crowd. Broken rigging rained from the masts. Had something just hit them from above? At sea? Adol looked up but couldn't make out the cause.

With a crack, a long piece of a spar tumbled down the foremast, tangling in the furled mainsail as it fell. He dodged to avoid it and nearly ran into a log that had somehow planted itself across the deck. No, not a log. Wet and leathery, it twitched and slithered, glistening with a sheen of slime that brought to mind the skin of deep-sea creatures.

A giant tentacle?

A chill ran down Adol's spine. He looked up just in time to see another tentacle rising out of the water. Its end looked wide, like a club, covered with suction cups bigger than his head. He drew his dagger, aware of how inadequate the short blade was against an opponent this size. If only—

"Adol!" Dogi rushed out to the deck with a long object in his hand. It gleamed as he flung it toward his friend.

My sword. Adol tossed the dagger into his off hand and caught the Isios Blade by the hilt, its curves settling familiarly into his grip. Just in time. The tentacle descended toward him, seemingly intent on taking him out. He slashed and it retreated, then whipped toward him again. The ship shook.

Adol's attempts to sever the flailing tentacle quickly proved insufficient. Its slimy surface was curiously resistant to steel. Despite a series of mighty hacks, Adol was only able to open a small wound, oozing with greenish-blue slime. A tremor echoed through the ship in response. Blast it. Probably all he was doing was getting the owner of the tentacles really mad—not a good idea, unless he could do some actual damage.

8

He spun his blade, but none of his moves made any difference. The tentacle attacking from the air kept lashing out. The other one, lying log-like across the deck, twitched and rolled in a seemingly concerted effort to knock him off his feet. He had no choice but abandon all finesse. The only effective tactics proved to be hacking and slashing to match the tentacles' moves.

It was hard work, less like sword-fighting than cutting timber, but at last the tentacles slithered back along the deck and disappeared into the inky blackness overboard.

The tremors stopped. The *Lombardia* was moving again, with no interference from below.

Was it over?

Adol slowly exhaled. Focused on the fight, he had almost forgotten about all the people on deck, the crewmen with their daggers out and the panicking passengers. He lowered his sword as people rushed toward him from all sides.

"Nice work, Adol."

"Impressive!"

"You are so brave!"

Dogi emerged from the crowd and patted his shoulder. "Good job. I knew you could handle that thing, Adol."

Adol looked at him thoughtfully. When this was over, he was definitely going to ask how Dogi had managed to get his sword out of the trunk in the crew quarters and make it on deck in time for the fight.

"What were those tentacles?" Dogi wondered. "Some kind of a giant squid?" His gaze trailed upward, his jaw falling open.

"Dogi?"

"Uhh..."

Adol looked up.

More tentacles were rising out of the ocean on both sides of the ship. One, two...five...Adol stopped counting. Too many to handle, even with the entire crew's help. Some reached higher than the masts. They all closed in at once, grabbing the ship in a chokehold.

The deck buckled and tilted under their feet. The ship moaned, listing dangerously to one side. The foremast snapped like a matchstick. The main mast tilted, showering rigging and spars on the panicked crowd below. The entire railing peeled away, followed by a shower of bodies tumbling overboard.

The ship was sinking too rapidly to do anything at all. Waves lapped over the deck, washing off more people. Dogi slipped and fell, sliding down the wet boards. As Adol reached to catch his friend's hand, a piece of rigging struck him from behind. He swayed and let go, tumbling into the dark water.

SHIPWRECKED

Giant birds with long tails circled over a sunlit valley that stretched all the way down to the sapphire-blue sea. A beautiful city in the distance rose out of the morning haze, its domed roofs and ornate towers reaching up to the sky.

A young girl stood on the cliff looking at the view, her long dark hair streaming in the wind.

A girl?

Adol's eyes snapped open, the view dissolving into a blaze of sunlight beating down from the clear sky. Was that a dream? And if so, why did it feel so realistic?

Where in the world was he?

He tried to move, but his body wasn't quite working the way he expected. It took him some time to figure out that he was lying in the surf, sand chafing his skin, cool waves splashing rhythmically over his feet. Smells of kelp and sea rot mixed with the bittersweet aromas of wildflowers carried on the breeze. For the life of him, he didn't remember arriving at a beach. What in the world happened?

The dull pain at the base of his skull messed with his sense of orientation, sending the world spinning every time he tried to get upright. He waited for the dizziness to recede, then clambered up and surveyed his surroundings.

The beach was small and secluded, flanked by a strip of rocks on one side and a grassy hill on the other. A mountain range rose in the distance, tall peaks reigning over the peaceful landscape. To his left, the shore curved into a deep bay, with a small islet in its center.

Wait. Wasn't this the scenery he'd spotted last night from the . . .

Lombardia?

11

Memories snapped back into his head with nauseating force. The fight with the giant tentacles. The shipwreck. Falling overboard after Dogi and grabbing a piece of floating debris to hold on to.

Dogi.

He staggered into the surf, peering out at sea. No sign of the ship or any wreckage that could give any clues about the *Lombardia*'s whereabouts.

With everything that happened, it was a miracle he'd survived. But if he had, then surely others must have survived too. He darted around frantically, but could see no sign of people or even anything man-made, besides a tangle of old fishnets and rotten wood boards stuck in the rocks at the side of the beach.

After a while, he waded ashore, trying to settle his thoughts. Survivors from the *Lombardia* could have washed up anywhere along this coastline. Dogi, at least, had to be out there somewhere. He was a good swimmer—and he always tended to land on his feet. Adol just needed to find him, and all the others. For now, he decided not to think about what the captain had told him, how no one had ever returned after landing on Seiren. That was something to worry about later.

He stumbled toward the pile of driftage at the edge of the beach— old and rotten, definitely not from the *Lombardia*. A rusty metal rod wedged between the rocks caught his eye.

A sword?

Adol leaned over and pulled it out.

An old broadsword—or what was left of one. Part of the blade had broken off, reducing its length to that of a one-handed blade and completely messing up the balance. Its edge was eaten away by rust. No Isios Blade—probably lost forever at the bottom of the sea— but still, better than nothing. He forced all thoughts of the legendary blade out of his head as he tucked the rusty sword into his belt next to his sheathed dagger and made his way up the shore.

The sand at the back of the beach ran into a wide strip of grass and toward a passage between two large boulders, blocked by a fallen tree. A stream flowed down a gully on his right and into the bay. Fresh water. Adol followed it uphill until he found a flat shore with easy access. He waded in and scooped a few handfuls, gulping greedily. The water was clean and cool—it felt like the best drink he'd ever had.

He had to look on the bright side. Just last night, he had been longing to explore the mysterious Isle of Seiren—and now he was doing just that. Strange how one's wishes sometimes came true in the most twisted of ways.

Laxia von Roswell was a proper lady, thank you very much. And a proper lady had to maintain her bearings in every situation—even when shipwrecked on a deserted island. After washing up on the beach, she'd spent what felt like hours rushing around in a vain search for other survivors. Now she felt absolutely exhausted. Her salt-encrusted clothes creaked with sand, chafing in the most uncomfortable places. She needed to wash it all off if she wanted to restore her ability to think straight.

Last night on the *Lombardia*, Franz had infuriated her so much by showing up out of the blue. Being her butler didn't give him any right to follow her everywhere. She probably shouldn't have said all these things to him before storming out of the saloon, but she fully expected to straighten them out in the morning, as well as to give him a proper scolding for disobedience. And now she didn't even know what had happened to him. She refused to entertain the idea that he hadn't made it ashore—but given that, so far, she hadn't found any trace of survivors, she had to at least acknowledge the possibility. The thought brought tears to her eyes, even though crying was absolutely unseemly for a proper lady.

She supposed she should feel grateful that leaving the party early and being in her stateroom when the disaster struck had allowed her to change out of that ridiculous dress into a comfortable pair of breeches and shirt, strap on her rapier and belt pouch, and grab a few necessities, such as a scarf and a life vest. This had made her as prepared as possible when she rushed on deck and into all the chaos. She would never forget the screams, the breaking masts, people falling overboard. What a horror! And now she was alone, possibly the only survivor, with no idea what to do. Tears welled in her eyes again, and she vigorously wiped them away. First things first. A bath.

She found a clean stream and followed it to a secluded glade where a big boulder at its bend marked a wider pond she could use to wash properly. Glancing around to ensure that no predators would disturb her at a vulnerable moment, she unsheathed her rapier and set it within easy reach, then quickly took off her clothes, rinsed them, and spread them over the boulder to dry before stepping into the water.

It felt so good to wash off the crust of sand and sea salt, the cool water soothing her parched skin. She always got sunburned easily, and of course she'd left her creams and ointments on the *Lombardia*, but that was something to worry about later. She knelt, plunging her whole head beneath the water. Then, standing knee-deep in the pool and lifting her face to the sun, she wrapped into her scarf to dry off.

Rocks clattered behind her. A predator? A wild beast? She grabbed her rapier and spun around.

A man emerged from behind the boulder. His eyes widened when he saw the rapier pointed at him. His arm blurred as he drew his sword and knocked it out of her hand in a fluid move too fast for her to follow. Shocked, she stumbled backward, releasing the scarf she was using for cover. It slid down into the water, leaving her stark naked.

The stranger's eyes grew wider still. His cheeks flared scarlet, and the jagged tip of the rusty sword in his hand—how *had* he managed to draw it so quickly?—dipped to the ground.

She screamed, then grabbed her clothes and sprinted for the nearby bushes. She recognized the man—that insolent crewman from last night, who had interrupted her so rudely on the way to her cabin. A swirl of emotions swept through her head. Relief at seeing another survivor of the shipwreck. Annoyance about their previous meeting, when he'd talked to her like an equal and showed much more perception and insight than a simple crewman like him had any right to do... Disappointment that this wasn't Franz.

Deep in the leafy thicket, she hastily pulled on her damp clothing, unsure what to do. Should she keep running? Probably a sensible course of action, considering she didn't know this man at all. But then again, a villain trying to take advantage of her probably wouldn't look so terrified or blush so deeply after catching her at an inappropriate moment. At present, the two of them seemed to be the only survivors from the *Lombardia*. It seemed like a better idea to stay together.

She supposed, worries aside, she should be thankful that it wasn't Franz who'd discovered her. She would never live down the shame of being seen naked by her own butler. Still. Facing that arrogant man was hardly any better. Last night he had acted so boldly around her, as if he considered himself to be superior, and now... Why did men have to be so...so disgusting. Tactless. Domineering. Ogling every woman they came across. A lady was entitled to privacy when taking a bath.

She clung to her anger as she finished dressing. Without the anger, she'd probably burst into tears—with a witness this time, which would be completely unforgivable. Anger helped her to hold it together as she finally allowed herself to face the full extent of her predicament—shipwrecked and stuck alone with an arrogant stranger, on a deserted island notorious for being cursed.

When she finally emerged from the bushes, the man was standing a few feet away, his back decisively turned. She carefully checked her clothes and hair before approaching him.

"I suppose I have kept you waiting long enough," she said. "You may turn around now."

He kept his eyes down as he obeyed. His cheeks were still red. Good. At least he'd learned a lesson. In fact, he looked so embarrassed she almost felt sorry for him, even though she was still reeling from the memory of the incident.

Last night in the dark hallway she hadn't had a chance to see him clearly. Now that she did, the first detail that caught her eye was his distinct hair color—flaming red, gleaming in the sun like fire. She'd never seen anyone with hair this red before.

He looked younger than she'd originally thought—three or four years older than herself, at most. She was good at telling people's age by small signs—like their skin, which always accumulated wrinkles and blemishes over time. This stranger's skin was surprisingly smooth, but his hands, callused from manual work, betrayed experience.

Tall and well-muscled—but not overly so—he held himself with the grace that brought to mind the renowned fencing teacher her father had once invited to Roswell Manor all the way from Romn. She'd already witnessed the ease with which this stranger had disarmed her—a nearly impossible move when wielding a heavy broadsword one-handed against a rapier. How had a swordsman of his skill ended up as a simple crewman on the *Lombardia*?

"We should introduce ourselves," she said. "I am Laxia von Roswell, a noble lady from Garman. And you are a sailor, I presume?" She drew herself up, looking at him down her nose—not an easy feat, considering their height difference.

He finally raised his eyes, their clear blue a vibrant contrast with the red of his hair.

"I'm Adol Christin—an adventurer, actually. I only enlisted as crewman for this one trip."

"An *adventurer*?" Laxia scoffed. "What sort of an occupation is that?"

"One that lands you in all kinds of unpredictable situations." Adol's eyes trailed to her belt. "Is that a book?"

Laxia stepped back, placing a defensive hand over the tome in its waterproof covering, sticking out of her belt pouch. "Yes. Why?"

He frowned. "You fell overboard off a sinking ship carrying a *book*?"

"And my rapier, yes. When I realized we were in trouble, I made sure I was prepared."

His lips twitched in disbelief. "What does a book prepare you for, on a deserted island?"

Laxia drew herself up again. Was this...this *commoner* going to lecture her on priorities? "I'll have you know that this book is the foremost scientific reference on the wildlife of all Gaete islands. Of course, on this particular island a lot of the vegetation seems indigenous, but still, one could gather a lot of useful information about edible and medicinal plants, as well as dangerous predators, and..." She paused as Adol's eyes widened, trailing past her to the bushes behind.

A cloud of bats swarmed out, circling over their heads. Laxia scurried over to Adol's side. The bats looked as big as hawks—larger than any species she knew, armed with sharp teeth.

"I think I can recognize dangerous predators without a book." Adol drew his sword in a deft, easy move. A rusty piece of garbage, even though the graceful way he wielded it made the weapon look better than it actually was.

"Stay behind me," he said.

Oh, the protective kind. Laxia rolled her eyes. She should have gathered that much from his remarks last night. Probably the type who thought all girls were fragile and vulnerable and needed a big strong man to stand up for them, even if the rapier at her belt should have been a hint to the contrary. Well, she'd had enough of that attitude—from father, from Franz, from pretty much everyone around her up to now—and she was going to have none of that from this arrogant crewman who obviously thought very highly of his sword skill.

"No, thank you," she snapped. "I don't need to be protected by an *adventurer*." She drew her rapier just as the bats swooped down, cutting the nearest one in mid-flight. The rest of the creatures clearly thought better of it as they turned around and darted out of sight.

Laxia sheathed her rapier and regarded the leathery shape on the ground. Nausea rose in her throat as she watched its blood ooze into the water of the stream. She crossed her arms over her stomach and looked away.

Adol stepped forward and turned the creature over with his boot. "What does your book say about these? Are they edible?"

"*Edible?*"

He shrugged. "Since we're stranded on this island, we should be thinking of a reliable food source."

"I'd rather starve than eat *these*, thank you very much."

Now that she had a chance to calm down, she felt a bit embarrassed about the way she had behaved. This man, Adol, seemed all right—for an adventurer, that was. And yes, perhaps he was a tad too protective, and a better swordsman than her, but here in the wilderness that wasn't a bad thing. All in all, if she had to be stranded on a deserted island with someone, he seemed like better company than most. She should at least try to make amends.

"Your swordsmanship is rather impressive," she said. "Clearly, it was no accident that you managed to parry my attack."

"Thank you."

Had she seen him grin when he said it, or only imagined it? She hoped the latter, but she wasn't quite sure.

"I...I wasn't complimenting you," she added, just to make sure he didn't get any wrong ideas. "Incidentally, these bats—or a species very close to them that I'm more familiar with—are more intelligent and aggressive than people commonly realize. This area must be their territory. Let us relocate somewhere safer, Mr. Christin."

"Right."

He put away his sword and leaped over the stream. Laxia followed. They crossed the glade toward an opening between the rocks on the other side.

"You seem to know a lot about bats," Adol observed.

"I'm simply speaking from common sense." Laxia lifted her chin. "Let's get one thing straight. Given the circumstances, a temporary alliance is our only rational course of action. But this doesn't mean we will be taking it all the way to easygoing camaraderie. Do we understand each other?"

"Yes."

Once again, she thought she caught a smile sliding over his lips, but his face was straight again when she looked closer. Honestly. Who did he think he was, to act this way around a highborn lady?

"Good. Then I suggest we stop wasting time on small talk." Well, that probably wasn't the friendliest thing to say to the man who might turn out to be her only companion for a while. But she didn't feel settled enough to let go of her anger at him just yet. Besides, what would a commoner like him expect from a lady of Laxia's station? He should be grateful she was talking to him at all. Yes, that seemed about right. Laxia raised her head high as she brushed past Adol and walked ahead.

WATERDROP CAVE

Lady Laxia von Roswell. Adol had barely recognized her in her breeches and shirt, so different from the gown she'd been wearing on the *Lombardia* when she burst out of the party in the saloon. Somehow she seemed much more comfortable in this outfit, as if, despite her high station, wearing dresses wasn't natural for her. She had already perplexed him last night, but now he was finding her even more odd. What kind of a person would take the time on a sinking ship to change clothes and collect a rapier and a book, of all things? And why would the first thing she'd do on a deserted island after surviving a major shipwreck be taking a bath? Too many things about her didn't make sense. Only one was certain—she was going to be a pain to deal with.

Even as this thought crossed Adol's mind, he realized he was being unfair. Laxia had a lot of qualities that would make her a great companion in the wilderness. She was brave, independent, knowledgeable, practical, decent with a rapier. A lot of her snappishness probably had to do with the shock. She'd just survived an unimaginable ordeal—not to mention the fact that he had caught her at such an . . . inappropriate moment. He felt his cheeks flare with heat at the mere memory. He should have been quicker to retreat when he saw her bathing, instead of standing around like an idiot, too dumbfounded to move. Adventuring didn't exactly prepare one for this kind of a situation.

The passage between the boulders brought them into a flat grassy area surrounded by cliffs on all sides that formed roof-like ledges around one side of the open space. A cave mouth gaped on the right. A passage on the left led to the seaside—a small, secluded cove, protected from the open sea by the rising line of rocks.

Adol had a good feeling about this place. A perfect shelter, secluded enough to keep out of the way of chance beasts wandering by, with ledges to serve as a roof in case of rain. They had yet to explore the cave, but assuming it wasn't inhabited by something terrible, it might prove comfortable enough to sleep in.

A strange object at the side of the clearing drew their eyes. It was a giant rock crystal, a pointed triangle rising up from the ground to tower several heads over Adol. Blue and semitransparent, unevenly shaped, it seemed to emit a deep yellow glow. Or was it just the way the sun hit it? Adol couldn't resist touching its smooth reflective surface. Keeping his hand on it made him feel energized. Odd. He'd never seen crystals like this before. Had it formed here on its own?

"What an unusual mineral." Laxia touched the crystal too, then turned away and ran her gaze around the clearing. "That terrace up there looks to be a good observation point. I'll check it out. You survey the lower grounds." Without waiting for a response, she set off along the path leading uphill.

Adol contemplated following her, but stopped himself. The area looked safe enough. The upper terrace she was headed for was surrounded by cliffs on all sides, except for the narrow passage that lay open in plain view. He shouldn't interfere if she wanted to be on her own.

He followed the path to the cove. The water looked deep, transparent enough to see all the way to the bottom. A perfect place to dock a boat—if only they had one. The beach stretched on to his right, eventually running into a pile of boulders rising out of the surf.

Adol stood for a moment, staring at the horizon. Somewhere out there lay Eresia, the Sounion port he and Dogi were headed for. And now . . . He forced the thought away. Dogi was fine, he told himself firmly. They'd survived worse on their travels together.

The ground rose in cascaded steps to a grass-covered terrace, open on three sides to a spectacular sea view. Laxia stood at the edge, almost directly above the beach he'd just explored. Adol approached and stopped by her side.

"Nice view," he said.

She pursed her lips. "This is no time to be taking in the scenery. I did notice, however, that this area is remarkably well fortified. It may prove to be a suitable location for a base camp."

Adol nodded. "I thought the same thing. We should explore the cave, though, just to make sure."

To his relief, the cave appeared uninhabited. The large main chamber led into two smaller ones at the back, separated by rock formations that looked like natural doorways. Each of these chambers had an opening on the far end that let in enough daylight to illuminate the entire space and provided access to a small stream running through a narrow canyon right outside. Low bushes and vines growing along its bank created a natural screen that made the cave chambers cozy and private.

Adol leaned down and scooped a handful of cool, fresh water, looking across the stream to the steep rock cliffs rising in an impenetrable wall on the other side of the canyon. Even Laxia had to approve of this kind of a shelter, a room with its own source of running water and enough protection not to worry about safety or privacy. He checked the area and returned to the main chamber, where Laxia stood looking into a darker passage leading farther into the cave.

They followed the passage into another wide chamber, lit though distant cracks in the ceiling that let in scarce streaks of sunlight. This cavern was deeper and darker than the one they just left. A small stream picked its way through a shallow rocky bed toward the opening on the other side—probably a branch of the one Adol had just seen on the other side. The air here was cool and moist, infused with earthy smells of mold and fungus. Dripping water echoed hollowly in the shadows.

"Let's give this place a name," Laxia suggested.

"A name? Why?"

She shrugged. "As we discover new areas, we would most certainly need to refer to them again, maybe even draw a map to get around the island."

Adol nodded. This actually made sense, even though it felt strange to think so far ahead. He paused, listening to the water dripping in the distance. "How about Waterdrop Cave?"

Laxia hesitated. "I was thinking more like 'The Cave of Dark Echoes', but you're right. It's not even that dark. Waterdrop Cave works."

The path wound through the next cave chamber and eventually veered away from the stream, into a darker area of the caverns. In the gloom, they could make out man-made structures. A wooden platform rose from the damp cave floor, piled with barrels and crates.

A support pillar in its center looked to be made from a segment of a mast. Adol's heart leapt. Were people living here? He quickly stopped himself. Everything here had a stale feeling about it, as if this place hadn't seen any care for a very long time.

At the back of a moldy crate stack, a real treasure awaited. A longsword stood leaning against the wall. Rusted and old, it still had a keen edge and was in much better shape than the weapon Adol had found on the beach. He picked it up and swung it a few times—much better balance too—then slid it into his belt, leaving the old one in its place.

A skeleton slumped against a boulder in the next chamber. Laxia gasped and drew back. Adol bent down for a better look. Its clothing was decayed beyond recognition, except for the remains of a padded leather doublet—light armor, often used by pirates and mercenaries. A rusty cutlass lay across the skeleton's lap. An eyepatch covered one of the empty eye sockets.

"Must be one of those pirates Captain Barbaros told me about, who first discovered this island," Adol said. "The settlement must belong to them too."

Laxia nodded but didn't respond as she hurried on ahead.

The opening at the end of the passage gleamed with sunlight. As Adol looked in that direction, he imagined a human silhouette briefly outlined against the gap. His heart leapt, but the shape disappeared too quickly to see any details.

"Did you see that?" Laxia exclaimed.

Adol nodded.

They rushed through the cave opening onto a small terrace overlooking the sea. Empty. No clues to that shape they had both just seen blocking the sunlight. There was nothing here but a bunch of rocks descending toward the shore.

"Ah." Laxia's shoulders sagged again. "It's just—" She cut off abruptly and walked ahead, stopping at the edge of the terrace.

Adol held back for a moment, then followed. It seemed very unlikely they'd discover a friendly human settlement or a group of survivors from the *Lombardia* greeting them with a fire and a nice warm meal, yet the disappointment of finding nothing but another deserted terrace with a sea view echoed with an emptiness in the pit of his stomach. He stopped beside Laxia, looking into the distance.

"Don't get discouraged," he said.

She sniffled, wiping her face with the back of her hand. "Discouraged? I'm hardly the type. It's just that—"

A cough and a muffled swear echoed behind them. Adol and Laxia spun around to see a large man emerge from a gap beside the cave opening they'd previously overlooked.

Adol stared. "Captain Barbaros?"

"Adol? Lady Laxia?" The captain rushed toward them.

Relief washed over Adol. He felt so happy the captain had survived. Besides, his presence was further proof that there were more survivors. It was only a matter of time until they found others.

"I'm glad you are safe, sir," he said.

The captain nodded and patted him on the shoulder. "I've seen a good spot a short distance down the shore. A calm inlet, accessible through this cave. It seems like a good place to set up camp."

Adol nodded. "Yes, we've just come from there."

"Let's head back then. There's nothing useful out here."

They retraced their steps through the cave and collected driftwood to build a fire and dry kelp to use for tinder. Some of the rocks proved suitable to make a flint. Soon the three of them were sitting around a campfire, sharing fresh coconuts from the local palms and dry meat rations from Adol's belt pouch.

"Seiren's curse has never extended so far away from its shores," the captain said. "I've sailed this route many times before, without any problem. Now I feel responsible. I was the one who put the *Lombardia* in harm's way."

Laxia shook her head. "You couldn't have known this would happen."

The captain looked away.

"Those remains of a settlement deeper in the cave," Adol said. "Do they mean Seiren isn't truly deserted?"

"That was my first hope." The captain looked at the flames. Amazing how much comfort could be brought by a simple campfire. "Unfortunately, the structures we saw look to be over a hundred years old. Clearly, no one has been here in a very long time. That skeleton..." He paused, glancing at Laxia.

"It's all right," she said. "You don't have to worry on my account."

"It certainly looked like a pirate's corpse."

"True," Adol said. "But it could have been a castaway who washed ashore on this island, same as us." Pirate or not, once they settled in, they should give that person a proper burial.

"Could be anyone," the captain agreed. "Many ships have gone missing in this region."

"Is that the fate of all castaways who find themselves here?" Laxia asked quietly.

"No," the captain said. "Sorry to cause you worry."

"I can handle the truth, Captain Barbaros."

The captain's lips twitched. "That you certainly can, Lady von Roswell."

"Laxia. If we are to be stranded together on this island, we might as well drop the formalities." She threw a sideways glance at Adol.

Was she including him too? Perhaps it was best not to push it.

"Some formalities help maintain the routine," the captain said. "But fine—Laxia." He straightened up. "We must not give up hope. We'll find a way off this island if we work together."

Laxia nodded. Adol found himself nodding too. This was the captain's power—to lead, to inspire confidence no matter the circumstances. And he was telling the truth. As long as they worked together, they were going to find a way.

SURVIVORS

We should scout the beach for any useful items that might have washed up from the shipwreck," the captain said. "A lot of the *Lombardia*'s cargo containers were made to be watertight. With the direction of the local currents, they should all be washing up on the beach over there. That should also be the first place to look for survivors." He pointed in the direction of the bay.

"I'll go," Adol said. "You and Laxia should stay here, in case more survivors show up." He hoped they would. On this windless afternoon, the campfire smoke rose tall, straight into the sky. A beacon that people stranded on the island would see for krimelye around.

"I'll go with you." Laxia got to her feet.

"It would be safer if you remained here, Laxia," the captain protested. "After all the hardships—"

Laxia drew herself up. With her slight build, it was odd to see her towering over the captain—or the way the large man receded from her, as if truly intimidated.

"In times as desperate as this," Laxia said, "are you suggesting I sit idle and rest, while there are people out there who need rescue?"

"I merely—"

"Merely what?" Laxia took a breath, probably remembering that a temper outburst was unseemly for a noble lady. "I appreciate your concern, Captain, but it would bring dishonor to House Roswell if I remained here."

"Dishonor?" The captain frowned.

Laxia's gaze wavered. "A servant of mine accompanied me on this voyage and is still missing. I cannot allow someone to search for him on my behalf, when I'm capable of doing so myself. I will accompany this 'adventurer'." She looked at Adol haughtily, then turned around to adjust her belt, balanced by the sheathed rapier on one side and the book in its leather pouch on the other.

The captain's gaze stirred with sympathy. He offered no further objections as Adol picked up his gear and he and Laxia headed out of camp.

"So, who is this servant of yours?" Adol asked on the way.

Laxia pursed her lips in an expression of defiance Adol was already learning to recognize.

"My 'servant' was a story I concocted to persuade the captain," she snapped.

Fine. Adol suspected otherwise, but he knew better than to push it. "Last night when we ran into each other, I couldn't help noticing that you looked troubled. I thought—"

Her abrupt glance cut him off. He expected another sharp retort, but to his surprise her gaze softened.

"If you really must know," she said, "I ran away from home."

"I see."

She heaved a breath. "I know you must be wondering why a noble lady would choose to do a drastic thing like that, but I—I was angry at my circumstances. Too many things in my life have gone wrong. I needed to get away. Alone. But that...that servant of mine found out, and he followed me. He managed to track me all the way from Garman to Xandria and find out I was booking passage on the *Lombardia*, even though I made this decision at the last minute." She swallowed. "Last night in the saloon...I had no idea he was aboard. When he approached me at the party, I felt so angry. I told him I never wanted to see him again. Despite all that, he tried to save me when the ship was sinking. When I fell overboard, he jumped after me. And now..." Her voice trailed into silence.

Adol understood. Her servant was likely dead—or, at best, stranded somewhere on the island. She blamed herself for bringing him to harm, and that guilt was eating her up. This had to be the reason for all her attitude.

"I'm sure he survived," he said. "This is a big island. It might take us a while, but we'll find him, along with every last person from the *Lombardia*." He wanted to believe it. If only he could control these things.

Laxia sniffled, keeping her eyes firmly ahead as they walked on.

"Now then, Mr. Christin," she said at length. "Tell me, who exactly are you?"

"I thought I told you. An adventurer."

"An adventurer. Really?"

Adol raised his eyebrows. "Yes. Why?"

She hesitated. "You certainly know how to wield a sword. That much I will concede. But I've never met anyone so audacious, so frivolous, that he would introduce himself as an 'adventurer'."

Audacious? Frivolous? Where the heck was this coming from? "What's wrong with being an adventurer?"

She scoffed. "You might as well call yourself a 'tourist' or a 'sightseer'. It's not as if adventuring is some sort of life-affirming calling."

Adol let out a laugh. "You seem to have a thing for adventurers."

Her cheeks lit up with color. She didn't respond as she strode ahead.

Adol hurried to catch up.

They made their way through a passage between the rocks and into the low foothills that cascaded over the ridge down to the beach. A wide strip of sand curved toward the line of rocks at the far end that, by Adol's calculation, separated this beach from the one he'd washed up on this morning. The rocks jutted out to sea, obscuring the bay view.

A set of indentations ran across the sand from the edge of the water into the grassy area beyond. Footprints—made fairly recently, so that the sea hadn't had time to wash them away. Whoever made them had to be large and heavy, wearing wide boots that uprooted a shovelful of sand with every step. Another survivor from the *Lombardia*. Adol's heart leapt. He and Laxia sped forward along the tracks.

The trail became less obvious as it led them into a secluded grass meadow just off the beach, surrounded by cliffs on all sides. Adol stopped, peering across the glade into the bushes on the other side. Was there a passage in there, leading deeper into the jungle?

A low roar thundered from that direction, followed by a scream and the noise of a large body crashing through the bushes. A man shot headlong out of the passage. He saw the travelers and sprinted toward them, stumbling as he reached Adol and grasping his arm for support.

"Please help me!" he panted.

An earth-shaking thud echoed from the passage behind him, and a huge beast thumped out into the glade.

Adol gaped.

The bipedal lizard facing them stood to at least two men's height. It had smaller front paws, a long leathery tail, and a maw large enough to swallow a whole sheep, lined with enormous teeth. It spotted the newcomers and let out another deafening roar.

"Are you well enough to run?" Adol asked the man.

"Well, I—yeah."

"Then, go." Adol signaled to Laxia, then drew his sword, backing away toward the opening between the rocks they'd just come from. His companions' footsteps pounded behind.

The creature paused, surveying Adol with its beady eyes, then rushed at him, crossing the glade in a few strides. Its jaws snapped at Adol, its foul breath making his eyes sting. He swerved out of its way, aiming a stab in the nose. His sword barely drew blood. The thing's hide was tougher than it looked. The beast reared and edged back, jerking its head from side to side to size up its opponent.

Adol pressed an attack, showering blows that screeched down the animal's hide without doing much damage. The beast lashed out with its paws, alarmingly quick to adjust to his maneuvers. Dodging its claws, jumping and rolling over the ground to avoid its sweeping tail, made Adol painfully aware he wouldn't be able to keep this up for long. His opponent showed no sign of battle wear. It was only a matter of time—not very much of it—before he would end up as the beast's meal.

"Adol!" Laxia shouted. "What do you think you're doing? Run!"

She dashed to his side, poking her rapier in a set of academic moves taught in sports fencing, which were totally ineffective in a real fight. But they did make the creature pause, probably remembering the painful stab in the nose from Adol's sword. Adol used this moment of hesitation to dart into the gap between the rocks, drawing Laxia with him.

They listened for sounds of pursuit as they ran, but heard nothing. Still, they kept running across the sand and up the hill on the other side of the beach before dropping down in exhaustion.

"What do you think you were doing back there?" Laxia demanded as soon as she regained her voice.

Adol heaved a few more breaths. "Covering your retreat. I thought—"

"You thought you would face that thing alone to give the rest of us time to escape, did you? A beast five times your size. Did I say you were foolhardy? If I didn't, I certainly thought it, multiple times. Well, add reckless to that. And idiotic. I don't know what you normally do on your adventures, but here on this island, we band together. Do you understand?"

"Yes, ma'am." Adol took a step back. He hadn't expected this kind of outburst. He turned to their new companion, who was still panting, doubled over with his hands on his knees.

He looked to be middle-aged, large and bulky, wearing a plain outfit that could mark him equally as a sailor or a lower-class merchant. Adol remembered seeing this man aboard the *Lombardia*—a passenger with seafaring experience, who tended to hang out on deck rather than stay in his quarters below.

Tattoos covering the man's forearms were shaped like wavy lines, a pattern also woven into the knit bracelets around his wrists. A ship's wheel charm hung around his neck on a shell-studded string. Greshun fishermen often adorned themselves this way, to bring good luck at sea. Even the shipwreck couldn't quite wash away the man's natural smell—fish and tobacco, both scents seemingly etched into his tanned skin. His dark, unruly hair looked greenish, as if infused with kelp and algae.

The man steadied his breath and laughed, scooping both Adol and Laxia into a bear hug.

"Thanks for saving my hide," he rumbled. "I dunno who you kids are, but I love ya anyway!"

"Wh-wh-" Laxia twisted and squirmed until she finally managed to pull herself out of the embrace. "What do you think you are doing?"

The man dropped his arms and stepped away. "Sorry 'bout that, li'l lady! Guess I got a little carried away expressin' my gratitude."

"Your words will more than suffice." Laxia turned away, straightening her outfit.

The man's grin was so infectious Adol found himself smiling too. Even Laxia's grunt seemed half-hearted in the face of the man's good-natured humor.

"I remember you from the *Lombardia*," Adol said.

"Yep." The man nodded. "The name's Sahad. Sahad Nautilus. I'm a fisherman from the Greshun region. Nice to meetcha, uh, um ..."

"Adol."

Sahad squeezed Adol's hand in a numbing grip. "And you, miss?"

"Laxia ... Lady Laxia von Roswell."

"Adol and Laxia." Sahad let out a sigh. "Of all the islands in the Gaete sea, we just had to wash up on the Isle o' Seiren. Some rotten luck the three of us have, eh?"

"Four of us, so far," Adol corrected. "Captain Barbaros survived too. We hope to find more. We should head back to camp before that beast catches our scent."

"Camp?"

"Over that ridge." Adol pointed.

"Sounds good to me," Sahad agreed.

Laxia looked thoughtful, her gaze returning to the rocks they'd just run through. Adol wondered if she knew something they didn't about that creature.

"How did you come to encounter that beast?" Adol asked as they walked.

Sahad reached behind his back and drew a weapon. No—not a weapon, exactly. A rusty ship's anchor, with two of its three blades broken off, creating a shape that crudely resembled a large lopsided war hammer.

"Found this on the beach," Sahad said. "Weird, if ye ask me, to find an old anchor, o' all things. Anyway, figured it's better than nothin' if it came to defendin' myself. Somehow, I didn't realize that beast was sleepin' very close by. The sucker blended right into the rocks. As I was practicin' swinging' this thing around, I ended up smackin' it by accident, right in the kisser."

"Well, that would certainly lead to hostilities." Adol hoped the beast, whatever it was, didn't have too long a memory—and that there weren't too many of its kind out in this wilderness.

CASTAWAY VILLAGE

Captain Barbaros was busy building the fire when Adol, Laxia, and Sahad walked into the camp. He straightened, watching them approach.

"Sahad..." He paused. "Nautilus. Right."

Sahad raised his eyebrows. "Ye know my name, Cap'n?"

The captain smiled. "I make it a point to remember all my passengers. Can't well have anyone on my ship I'm not familiar with, can I? So glad you are unharmed."

"Thanks to these kids," Sahad pointed at Adol and Laxia. "If it wasn't fer them..."

"The beasts here are more dangerous than we thought," Adol said. "We need to be careful."

Sahad shook his head. "Don't sound so surprised, lad. The creature that sank the *Lombardia* wasn't ordinary either. I wonder if it was the legendary kraken."

"Perhaps." The captain's face darkened. "The kraken were never mentioned in any chronicles about Seiren, but who knows? The creature that attacked us clearly made its home in these waters. It may well be responsible for the kraken legends."

Laxia shifted from foot to foot. Once again, Adol had a feeling she knew more about the subject than they all realized. But he had learned better than to question her when she had that determined look on her face.

"Anyway, we're still alive," Sahad said. "Let's hope more castaways are gonna start showin' up."

"With a campfire like that, you can count on it," a new voice said. "You can see that smoke from krimelye away."

Dogi. Thank the gods. Adol spun around to face his friend.

Dogi looked unharmed and unperturbed, just like when Adol had last seen him on deck yesterday afternoon—shirt opened down the front, short hair swept back in artful disarray, a merry twinkle in his eyes. His grin made Adol feel weak with relief.

"Adol." Dogi locked his friend in a long hug, then pulled away, surveying him at arm's length. "I see you've picked yourself a new sword, and—oh—a lady?" His gaze fixed on Laxia.

"And who might you be?" Laxia demanded icily.

Dogi responded with an elaborate bow. "The name's Dogi, miss. At your service."

Laxia pursed her lips and turned away.

"I was worried about you," Adol said.

Dogi laughed. "It's gonna take more than some giant tentacles and a sinkin' ship to kill me. After I fell overboard, all I had to do was grab a plank floating by and ride the current till I washed up here. Easy." He winked. "I swear, these things only happen when I'm with you, Adol. Never a dull moment when you're around."

"You're welcome." Adol grinned. Seeing Dogi alive and well lifted a huge weight off his shoulders. It also reinforced his certainty that more people from the *Lombardia* must have survived too. He wouldn't rest until he found them all.

"Dogi and I were getting acquainted while you were gone," the captain said. "He is remarkably handy. With his help, we now have the makings of a proper base camp." He gestured.

Adol looked around. In all the excitement, he hadn't had time to notice all the improvements. The area by the rock wall under the stone ledge now held a stack of neatly piled crates, with a piece of cloth stretched on poles overhead to extend the shelter. Short logs lay at angles around the fire, affording enough seating area for a large group of people. A cleaned and polished cast-iron pot stood at the side, next to the newly carved kettle supports. Further on, a few boards rested across a platform of level rocks to create a makeshift table.

"For cooking," Dogi said. "Or handiwork, if we ever find enough tools. Those pirates weren't much for makin' things, but some of the driftage from the *Lombardia*? Priceless. We have a stock of dry meat rations and potatoes, sugar and spices, cooking supplies, and even bedding in the sleeping quarters. And the crates are still coming—over by the cape, where the current turns them around. Some head straight to our beach. You should go take a look."

Adol looked at his friend with wonder. He and Laxia had only been gone a few hours. When had Dogi and the captain managed to do all this?

"It's been a long day for all of us," the captain said. "The sun will be setting soon. Let's eat some rations and rest for tonight. Tomorrow we might try for a hot meal with our new cooking pot."

W hile the men busied themselves with the fire, Laxia decided to take a stroll around the camp. Watching the thin strip of campfire smoke rising into the clear evening sky reminded her of the field trips Father used to take her on when she was still a little girl, creating a strange mix of irritation and longing that made her feel restless. She supposed it was her own fault that she'd landed in the middle of this impromptu adventure. It served her right, too. She had been selfish, neglecting her duty as the heir to Roswell Manor, abandoning her estate in the face of hardships, dragging Franz into it too. She had to have known that the stubborn man would never stay behind and let her disappear quietly. And now he was gone, and she had no idea if she would ever see him again. Why did he have to jump into the sea after her, instead of taking care of himself?

Dogi said it had been easy for him to escape the shipwreck, but if so, why hadn't Franz showed up too when he saw their campfire? Why weren't more castaways here by now? She wiped her eyes angrily, drawing a long breath. If she wanted to survive, she had to keep it together.

The sun dipped beneath the horizon, night chill creeping up from the shadows under the cliffs. The sea lay still like a mirror, gleaming in the gathering dusk. A chorus of crickets rang from the grass—a cozy, homely sound that made her think of a warm fire and a lovely cup of tea. Back at the manor, Franz always served it just the way she liked it—black and strong, with a thin slice of lemon. She forced the memory away as she made her way back to the center of the camp.

The men sat around the fire. Laxia lowered herself onto the log beside Adol, stretching her legs toward the flames as she tuned into the conversation.

"Are you certain, Dogi?" Captain Barbaros was saying.

The large man nodded. "Yeah. I washed up on the beach just south of here. And I definitely saw another set of footprints in the sand. I would've followed them, but the path to that area was blocked, so I couldn't get through."

Another castaway? Laxia's heart leapt. She lowered her head to hide the emotion.

The captain nodded. "We'll set out first thing in the morning to find him."

"Her, I think. The footprints weren't that big. They could have belonged to a woman."

"Or a child," Adol suggested. "I remember seeing a boy on the night of the party, wandering outside the saloon."

"I remember a little girl running around on deck," Sahad said. "A feisty one. A crewman on helm duty caught her tryin' to sneak into the captain's cabin."

"I hope they're all safe," Laxia murmured. A woman or a child. Not Franz, then, but definitely a person in need of their help. She imagined herself, lost and alone, with the dusk rolling in. What kind of creatures roamed here at night? Hopefully not many of the kind they had encountered today. She had her suspicions about that one, even though to the best of her knowledge these ideas didn't make any sense. Creatures like that couldn't possibly just roam around in the wilderness. She needed to recall more details and consult her book before jumping to any conclusions.

She hoped Franz was somewhere out there now—safe and unharmed, sitting beside a warm fire with a cup of tea in his hand. It was ridiculous to picture him like that on a deserted island after a shipwreck, but the image made her feel a little better. He had to be alive. And when she found him, she was going to give him a proper scolding, just like she'd intended to if this disaster hadn't happened.

"We'll search for this survivor first thing in the morning," she said.

The captain looked at her thoughtfully, as if considering whether to bring back their earlier argument about safety and her place in the search party, then obviously thought better of it.

"You and Adol do that," Dogi said. "Take Sahad too. In the meantime, the captain and I will work on setting out fences and barricades to protect ourselves from beasts. We need a few, at key points around the village."

"Village?" Laxia asked.

Dogi grinned. "Adol tells me you were the one who first suggested giving names to places. We thought we should name our camp. Castaway Village. Do you like it?"

Laxia looked around. Castaway Village. The name felt cozy, implying a settled life she could imagine looking forward to as they went exploring. It would be nice to think of living in a village, if they had to stay on this island for any length of time.

"It's suitable," she admitted.

"Good." Dogi winked, then turned to the captain, and the two men drifted into a conversation about fortifications that involved a lot of drawing on the sand and felt far too tedious to follow.

Laxia was too tired to think straight. Tomorrow was a new day, when they would go out and rescue more castaways. She hoped they were going to find a lot and settle them all into Castaway Village. But first she needed a good night's sleep. After everything that had happened today, she felt absolutely exhausted. She muttered her goodnights and retreated into the cave.

WHITE SAND CAPE

Adol dreamed.

"Come! Back to the barn, everyone!" The girl who spoke was young—maybe twelve or thirteen. She seemed oddly familiar, even though Adol couldn't recall where he could have seen her before.

Bleating and the clonking of hooves filled his ears. A herd of animals trampled toward the open gate. Goat? Sheep? They seemed unusual.

"Yes, yes. You're such good boys." The girl laughed and patted their furry hides. She was wearing a plain tunic, calf-length breeches, and a head scarf that did a poor job of containing her mass of long, dark hair. Work clothes, suitable for doing chores around a farm.

Was she the one who'd appeared in Adol's vision when he'd first landed on the beach? If so, this must be her younger version, an adolescent showing only glimpses of the beauty she would become.

The scenery around her was unfamiliar. A mountain valley descended toward a distant plain, with a thin line of water barely visible on the horizon. The sea? It was so far away Adol couldn't quite tell. Strange birds with long tails circled high overhead. Distant cliffs rising on both sides of the valley flanked the view like an exotic picture frame.

"What's the matter, Dana?" a man's voice said.

In his dream, Adol couldn't turn and see the speaker. Was this because the girl didn't turn either, keeping her eyes on the valley? It seemed odd to think that their actions could be linked somehow, even though they clearly weren't the same person.

Dana.

What an unusual name.

"They're coming for me, Father." She pointed at the road, where a solemn procession of women was emerging from behind a line of low hills on a slow ascend toward the village. Tall and stately, they all wore identical head scarves and long robes, decorated with a pattern of intertwined lines. A symbol of some sort?

"The priestesses from the Temple of the Great Tree." The man's voice rang with disbelief. "Just like in your vision... But how did they even find us?"

Dana finally turned to face him, giving Adol a view of his tall, stooping shape, lined face, gray hair streaming down his shoulders. He didn't look all that old—just aged by hardships before his time.

"When the Maiden of the Great Tree grows old," Dana explained, "she starts looking all over the kingdom for girls with a strong gift of Essence, to be trained as her potential successors. That's why these priestesses are here. They must have sensed my gift. They think that I—"

"Did your visions give you all this information?" He shook his head. "They couldn't possibly be this detailed, Dana."

"They are, Father." She took a step toward him. "I could tell you so much more... Mother was always afraid of this happening, wasn't she?"

The man looked away abruptly. Dana turned away too. The pause stretched for a while as they both looked at the women walking along the road.

"It's fine, Father," Dana said at length. "You don't need to worry about me."

"I need your help at the farm."

Her gaze wavered. "I know. But I—I really want to do this. Just think of it. I am offered a chance to become the next Maiden, the spiritual leader of the realm, equal in standing to the Queen herself. And if not... I can always come back home."

"Years from now."

"But if I succeed," she insisted, "I'll be able to help so many people. I will use all my power to ease pain and suffering everywhere in the kingdom."

The silence stretched as the two of them walked out of the barn and down to the gate, watching the approaching procession.

"Look. The priestess at the front is the advisor to the Maiden herself. See that medallion?" Dana's voice wavered, as if she were afraid to believe her good fortune. "I know the Temple only sends her for someone who is exceptionally gifted. We can't refuse."

"Will I ever see you again?" her father whispered.

Dana didn't respond as he squeezed her arm, briefly closing his eyes. She reached up and hugged him. Then she turned and walked toward the women.

Adol woke up to the sounds of running water and chirping birds. He opened his eyes, trying to remember where he was.

The cave. The lodge at their newly named Castaway Village. He was lying in a hammock Dogi had found among the driftage, next to the sleeping cots they had set out for themselves and other castaways they might find.

The room was empty. Was he the last to wake up? Adol washed up in the stream and hurried out of the cave.

Dogi and Sahad sat near the fire, grilling a fresh catch of fish over the coals. Laxia stood beside them holding a skewer, a content smile on her face. Adol hurried toward them.

"Up already?" Dogi said. "Well, you didn't have to rise so early on our account, Adol. It's not like there're any chores to do around here, or any survivors to look for." He held up a skewer. Adol took it and bit in.

The fish was delicious, its skin crispy with a neat crust of salt, the meat juicy and tender, a touch of herbs accenting its fresh flavor. Had Dogi been carrying his spice pouch when he fell overboard?

"Don't get used to it," Dogi said. "That mix was the last of my private stash. But I'm sure we'll find a way to replenish it as we continue exploring. At least we've found a reliable food source." He nodded at Sahad, sitting at the other side of the fire with a pile of fish bones on the ground beside him.

"There's a lot to say for bein' a fisherman," Sahad said. "Especially when you get stranded at the seaside with no other options. The fish 'ere practically thread themselves on a hook as soon as you cast the line. Can't wait to explore the local lakes and streams." He wiped his mouth with the back of his hand, then gathered his fish bones and threw them into the fire. "I don't know about you two, but I'm ready to go."

He glanced at Laxia. She pursed her lips and carefully set her empty skewer beside the fire, wiping her hands on the grass.

"We should let Adol have some tea first," she said.

"Tea?" Adol raised his eyebrows as Dogi handed him a mug filled with steaming liquid that emitted a tart but fragrant scent.

"A crate from the galley got stuck out in those rocks at the edge of the bay," Dogi explained. "Good that I decided to go out for a morning swim. We have dishes now. And some of the local herbs seem perfect for tea." He winked. "Who said our life in Castaway Village can't be civilized?"

Adol took a sip. Dogi always made his tea too strong, and this was no exception. Still, the brew was refreshing, a mix of mint and citrus and an unfamiliar herb that instantly cleared his head. As he drank, he thought of his strange dream. *Dana.* Her image in his mind was so clear, the events in his dream so real—as if they were memories of actual events.

"Good morning, everyone." The captain walked toward them from the camp's upper terrace. A brightly colored parrot nested comfortably on his shoulder.

"Morning, morning," the parrot said.

Sahad stared. "Huh? Did that bird just talk to us?"

The captain looked at the parrot fondly. "He's a quick learner. I believe he's another castaway, maybe from one of the ships that perished in these waters. Parrots can live for quite a long time, you know. I found him while I was scouting the area this morning. We developed a connection."

The parrot dipped its head a few times, as if confirming the captain's words.

"We were getting ready to go search for survivors, Captain," Adol said.

"Right." Sahad stood up, brushing some twigs off his outfit. Laxia decisively took her place on Adol's other side.

Adol glanced at both of them. It would be curious to have Laxia and Sahad in the same search party. The two seemed nearly as opposite as it came. But they did have complementary skills. Laxia's knowledge and Sahad's anchor-made war hammer would surely come in handy if they encountered dangerous beasts.

Adol thought of the giant lizard that had chased Sahad. They could handle regular predators, but that creature was something else altogether. If this island turned out to have more of those monsters, they would need better weapons before confronting them. He had no idea how they were going to do that.

The small beach where Adol had washed ashore yesterday morning was only a short walk away. The area Dogi had spoken of, south of here, had to lie through that gap in the rocks covered by a large fallen tree. Yesterday, Adol hadn't wanted to attempt clearing it away all by himself. But now he had help, even though he doubted Laxia or her rapier would be of much use for this kind of job.

He drew his sword and hacked at the nearest branch. It broke with a loud crack, settling the entire trunk deeper into the gap. He sighed.

"This could take a while," he said. "We should probably—"

"*We?*" Laxia stared. "By 'we', are you including me? I don't think—"

"Nah, you just sit tight, Laxia," Sahad said. "Me an' Adol will do it."

Yeah, right. Adol rolled up his sleeves, readying his sword. It was a crime to use a weapon this way, but in the absence of proper tools, they had no other choice.

Wings flapped overhead, and a shrill voice cried: "Found red one! Found Adol!"

A colorful bird landed on a rock next to them.

Sahad frowned. "Wait a minute . . . Ain't that the parrot the cap'n was teachin' to talk back at the village?"

"Indeed, it is," Laxia said. "I wonder . . . What is your name, pretty bird?"

The parrot appeared to consider it. "Name?"

Adol stared. He'd heard parrots were smart, but could this bird actually understand human speech?

"Little Paro," the parrot said at length. "Mess. Injure."

Adol, Laxia, and Sahad exchanged glances.

"Maybe something happened in the village," Adol suggested. "Is someone injured? Is it trying to tell us to go back?"

"Mess. Injure." The bird dipped its head a few times. "Little Paro tell."

"Tell?" Sahad frowned. "Are you tellin' us there's a mess and someone's injured?"

The bird shook its head vigorously. "Mess. Injure. Tell."

"I think," Laxia said, "it might be trying to say 'messenger'."

The bird dipped its head, as if excited. "Mess. Injure. Tell." It flapped its wings and rose up into the air.

They stood for a while, contemplating. Should they return to the village and see if everyone was all right? Would they act on the words of a bird? It seemed like a stretch, even though Adol couldn't help feeling worried as they returned to their job of clearing the blockage.

After a half hour or so, they hadn't made much progress. Laxia ended up joining them too, but since her rapier wasn't of any use, all she could do was pull branches out of the way as Adol and Sahad hacked their way through. This was probably going to take the rest of the day. If they didn't manage to finish the job before sunset, the castaway whose tracks Dogi had spotted on the other site of this blockage would be forced to spend another night in the wilderness. If only—

"Hey, Adol," a man's voice called out from behind.

Adol spun around to see Dogi and Captain Barbaros approaching them, with Little Paro perched on the captain's shoulder.

"Our little messenger led us here," the captain said. "He said you needed help."

"Little Paro?" Laxia stared.

The bird let out a long chatter, looking pleased with itself.

Sahad wiped his forehead with his sleeve, leaving a long smudge of mud. "Gotta admit, I'm pretty impressed. Nice work, little guy."

Paro dipped his head a few more times. "Treat. Treat."

The captain smiled, then took a nut out of his pocket and handed it to the bird. "I think Little Paro did a wonderful job as a messenger. We could use his help in situations like this." He picked the parrot off his shoulder and placed it carefully on a nearby boulder before taking off his coat and hanging it on a nearby branch. "Let's get to work, shall we?"

The added help made a major difference. While Adol and Sahad hacked the tree branches, the others cleared the bushes at the sides and dragged away the debris, until the main tree trunk sank down to the ground, leaving a passable gap. Dogi and the captain departed, with Little Paro flying over their heads, leaving Adol and his party to their exploration.

The sandy cape ahead of them extended out to sea, flanking the south side of the bay. The tide was low, exposing sea-etched rocks covered with kelp, barnacles, and shellfish. Between them, small tidepools housed all kinds of sea life. A few seals splashed in the deeper water just off the shore, their dark hides glistening with moisture. They emitted low musical wails when the group passed by. Perhaps these creatures had contributed to the legend of Seiren?

A large rock formation in front rose much higher than the boulders around it. Its bright blue surface looked textured, as if made of coral covered in a layer of vibrant paint. As waves broke against it, water siphoned out of the opening at its top, cascading down its sides and pooling at its base. Sunlight reflecting off the water enfolded the whole structure in a vibrant colorful glow. They stopped for a moment to admire the sight.

"Mesmerizing," Laxia said.

Sahad nodded. "This weird-lookin' rock might make fer a good landmark."

"Let's give it a name," Laxia suggested. "How about Cobalt Crag?"

"*Cobalt Crag?*" Sahad frowned. "Wha' kinda name is that? What does that even mean?"

"Cobalt is clearly the chemical element that gives this rock its blue color. As for the crag—"

"Aren't you gettin' a bit too scientific?"

"You have something against science?"

Adol stepped between them and raised his hands in a gesture of peace. "Cobalt Crag is fine. But we should probably name this whole area too, so that we can refer to it easily." He shielded his eyes from the sun, peering ahead. "I believe this is the cape that marks the south end of the bay. An important point in the island's geography."

"How 'bout White Sand Cape?" Sahad suggested.

Laxia scoffed. "Really?"

"What?"

"That is the best you can come up with for an important island's landmark?"

Sahad shrugged. "Well, it's a cape, right? And it's got white sand."

Laxia only shook her head as she started down the beach again. After a moment, Sahad followed. Adol fell into stride by his side.

"Not that I mind education," Sahad said, throwing a quick glance ahead to make sure Laxia was out of earshot. "It's the attitude them nobles sometimes have that tends to get to me. She's still a young lass, yet she looks so far down on us common folk."

"Give her a few more days," Adol said. "She's already come a long way from the time I met her. Besides, she's not that bad, really. I've seen nobles with far worse attitudes, believe me."

"So have I," Sahad agreed. He trudged ahead, and Adol hurried to keep up.

The path took them around the tall group of rocks to a tiny cove framed by a strip of white sand. A woman stood by the water, look-ing into the distance.

"Gah-haha! Found one!" Sahad exclaimed.

The woman turned around, her eyes wide as she watched them approach.

She looked young, only a bit older than Laxia—and far more timid, if one could judge by appearances. Her eyes were swollen, as if she'd been crying.

"Are you a survivor from the *Lombardia*?" Laxia said.

"Yes. Thank the gods..." The young woman swayed, as if about to faint. Adol rushed forward to support her. She seemed near tears again.

"Come," Adol said. "We'll escort you to our camp."

"Camp?" The woman's eyes lit up with hope. "Are there other survivors?"

"Only a few so far," Adol said. "Captain Barbaros is there. And Dogi, one of the crew."

"Oh." She lowered her eyes. Disappointed? Had she, like Laxia, lost someone in the shipwreck?

"We believe there are more survivors," he said. "And we won't rest until we find them all."

Her lips trembled as she raised her eyes to him. "My name's Ali-son. And I will do everything in my power to help."

RASTELL

I've been talking to Alison," Laxia said. "She's a seamstress from Greek, and her husband, Ed, is among the missing." She cut off abruptly, tearing through a tangle of vines at the edge of the jungle into the open space beyond.

Adol followed, with Sahad panting behind. The edge in Laxia's voice every time she talked about survivors spoke more clearly than words. It's been three days since they found Alison, and they still hadn't discovered any more castaways. With every passing day, the survivors from the *Lombardia* stranded on the island would be facing untold hardships and dangers out in the wilderness. Adol couldn't stop feeling that they were running out of time.

"Perhaps we should camp tonight," he said. "We can save ourselves a lot of walking and get an early start tomorrow."

"*Camp?*" Laxia's eyes widened. "As in, the three of us *sleeping* together?" She looked at Adol and Sahad with horror, as if they were monsters about to devour her.

Adol sighed. Of course, Laxia would object. In her upbringing, ideas of privacy and propriety obviously took precedence over common sense. They'd only made day trips exploring the island so far, and during those she had been acting almost like a normal companion. But it was naïve to think she would change her ways in such a short time.

"Do you prefer to go back to the village?" he asked.

She looked away.

The sun was lowering toward the cliffs, throwing long shadows across the grass-covered foothills. The deep, secluded ravine ahead of them beckoned with cool shade. A glowing blue crystal, similar to

44

the one in Castaway Village, rose out of the grass beside a rock wall, next to a small brook trickling through. The place seemed inviting and cozy, a perfect place to rest. Short of returning to the village, they'd be hard pressed to find a better one. Would Laxia really insist on hiking all the way back instead? If so, there was no way Adol was going to bring her along on another day of exploration.

"Well," Laxia conceded after a long pause. "Much as I'm loath to admit it, returning to the village isn't a good option."

"Thank the stars." Sahad grunted, wiping the sweat off his forehead. His shirt was torn at the collar, patches of prickly balls sticking to the cloth here and there. Seeds of some local plant that Adol had never seen before. His own outfit had a fair share of those too. He looked forward to picking them off as soon as they laid down their packs.

The sun had dipped behind the line of the hills by the time they reached the ravine. While Adol and Sahad built a large leaf tent in a sheltered area beside the tall cliffs, Laxia gathered wood for a fire. Soon they were sitting around the flames, setting out their food supplies.

The night was clear. Both moons shone brightly overhead, like giant lanterns floating in the sky. Stars scattered around like glittering jewels. The air smelled of earth and night lily, a distant chorus of frogs accented by the occasional hoot of an owl. Nights like this were among the many reasons Adol loved adventuring so much. Nothing compared to sitting by the fire after a day of exploring, looking forward to more adventures tomorrow.

"What made you want to become a fisherman, Sahad?" Laxia asked.

"Huh?" Sahad scratched his head. "Well, I guess you could say I didn't have a choice."

"How so?"

"I grew up on Creet. It's an island, so pretty much all we have there is the sea. Doesn't matter how old ya are—if ya wanna eat, ya gotta fish it up yerself. Simple as that."

Laxia looked at him thoughtfully. "I can't even imagine what that must have been like. Wasn't it difficult for you to grow up in a harsh environment like that?"

"Harsh?" Sahad seemed surprised. "I suppose I had my fair share of hardships over the years. The sea—she can be gentle, like a mother. But she can also be violent." He crossed his arms over his chest, rocking gently in his seat as he looked into the distance. His rhythm brought to mind the rocking of waves, gentle and soothing like a lullaby.

"You can't face the sea, in all her majesty, unless you first accept how small you are," Sahad continued. "Once I realized that, I felt like I could face the world fer the first time. Ever since, I've been true to myself, no matter what. I tell it to my little girl too, so she can grow up just like me." He let out a laugh. "But enough heavy talk. Time to hit the hay. Let's get some shut-eye, you two." He stood up and headed toward the tent.

Adol stayed for a moment longer, looking after him. *True to myself, no matter what.* This was what he always tried to be. He understood exactly what Sahad meant.

He couldn't imagine what it was like for Sahad to be stranded here, while his wife and little daughter waited back home. What would it feel like to have a family? The thought twirled in his head as he made it to the tent and sank into sleep—and into another one of his dreams.

Despite the midday heat, the large stone courtyard felt cool, shaded by the giant tree stretching overhead. The girls lined up against the wall—at least thirty newcomers, brought from different areas and provinces to be trained in the Temple. Dana felt so small among them.

An older priestess walked down the line, thirty pairs of eyes following her intently. Advisor Urgunata, the Maiden's right-hand woman in charge of the candidates' training, as they all had been informed upon arrival on the Temple grounds. She stopped at the end and turned, addressing all the girls. Her voice carried easily through the large space.

"Welcome to the Temple of the Great Tree. As candidates to become the next Maiden of the Great Tree, this Temple is your home now. And now that you've all settled in, it is time to start your training."

A murmur rustled down the row of girls.

"There exists a power that allows one to manipulate the laws of nature," the woman continued. "With this power, one can steady the wind, control water and fire, and even foresee the future. We call this power Essence. You are gathered here today because each of you is blessed with the power of Essence. Under our tutelage, you will develop this gift, while also receiving a proper education. When the time comes, one of you will be chosen to become the next Maiden of the Great Tree."

The lined-up girls exhaled in near unison.

"I will have you all remember that the Maiden of the Great Tree stands on equal footing with the Queen of Eternia. Please keep that in mind as you face what lies ahead. And now, let me introduce your first teacher. Chief Guard Dran will instruct you in the basics of swordplay."

"Swordplay?" a tall girl on Dana's left breathed out in excitement.

On her right, a thin girl with greenish hair pursed her lips in disapproval. "How are we supposed to learn about Essence by waving a sword? Useless, if you ask me."

Dana looked from one girl to the other. She could relate to both views. She felt excited about learning swordplay, but would it really help them master Essence? Had the current Maiden learned fighting too?

She watched a tall, lean man enter the courtyard, with a boy of about ten trailing in his wake.

"Chief Dran is the kingdom's top blade," the girl on Dana's left said quietly. "Everyone in the capital knows him. He's won every tournament for the past eleven years. Some would kill for a lesson with him."

"And who's the boy?" the other girl said.

"His son, Rastell. The Chief brings him around in case he needs an extra hand for sparring."

"Sparring? He's just a child."

The tall girl laughed. "Chief Dran's son learned fencing before he could walk, or so they say. Besides, some girls here are probably of a similar age." She looked at Dana.

Dana sighed. The fact that she was shorter than anyone here didn't mean she was younger. She had already turned thirteen, probably similar to the others. She trailed her gaze to Chief Dran, who was walking down the line of girls, pointing and directing them to form pairs on the practice range. His powerful grace made his walk seem like a dance, each move so smooth and precise that she couldn't help but gape. He looked far too young to have a son this age, or to have participated in sword tournaments for over ten years.

He reached Dana and stopped, looking down at her and her two neighbors.

From this close she could see that he was actually older than he'd initially appeared, his tanned face crossed with deep lines, his dark hair faintly streaked with gray. His body looked young, though— pure lean muscle, its fluid lines more perfect than the warrior statues in the Temple's main hall. She realized she was staring and hastily averted her gaze to his son, a skinny boy about her height. Not nearly as perfect as his father, but already showing the beginnings of the same grace.

"You, and you." Chief Dran pointed at the two girls on Dana's sides, sending them off together to the practice area. Dana realized that she was the only one left.

"You'll train with Rastell today," he said. "We'll see after that."

They all got arm-length sticks to practice with, spending most of the morning learning blade orientation and basic blocks.

Rastell proved to be a perfect partner, her match in height, skilled enough to meet her blows and launch attacks without overwhelming her. He was so patient with her first clumsy attempts to mimic Chief Dran's moves, which seemed to come much more naturally to many other girls. A couple of times Rastell stopped and helped her adjust her hold and angle, until she finally understood what was needed.

Dana had seen kids practice this way back in her village but never realized how much the exercise could be aided by Essence. Chief Dran walked around giving instructions until she finally caught the feeling. Her stick felt lighter in her hand, seemingly moving on its own to anticipate her opponent's moves. The exercise became enjoyable as she and Rastell circled around each other.

When they finally stopped for the day, it felt unnaturally quiet on the practice range. Looking around, Dana realized that everyone was watching her and Rastell—even Chief Dran, his face thoughtful as he briefly met her gaze before turning to the rest of the group.

"I will see you again next week," Dran said. "In the meantime, keep up the practice." He walked to the edge of the range, directing the girls to tuck their sticks into a stand along the back wall.

Dana turned to Rastell. "Thank you."

Rastell nodded. "You're very good. I could tell at the start of the day that you've never held a sword before, but you improved so much in only a few hours. You must have very strong Essence to progress so quickly in just one day."

Dana held his gaze. His praise meant more to her than she'd

expected, even though she wasn't sure it was well deserved. Her skill came mostly from her strong gift of Essence. His skill, a far superior one, had to be gained by endless hours of hard work, under the watchful eye of his father, who looked like a tough man to please.

"Until next time then?" she said.

"Sure. I'll look forward to it." Rastell looked at her a moment longer, then turned away to join his father. Dana paused, watching them leave the courtyard.

During their training, Rastell had made her feel so comfortable. She probably wouldn't have done so well with any other partner. She barely knew anything about him, but she felt that she'd just made a friend.

"You were great!" Dana's former neighbors in line approached her. The one excited about swordplay skipped in place, her curiously colored hair mixed of light and dark strands flowing behind her. She looked graceful, like a dancer. "Didn't you just love the lesson? Chief Dran is the best! Oh, I'm Sarai, by the way."

"And I'm Olga," the other, prim one, said. She too looked pleased, different from before. "Dana, right? It looked like you and Chief Dran's son were getting along well."

"He's a great training partner." Dana couldn't help a glance at the gateway the chief and his son had disappeared through.

Rastell had said he was looking forward to another training session with her. She looked forward to it too. In fact, she couldn't wait to see him again.

TOWERING CORAL FOREST

Adol opened his eyes. For a while he lay on his back, staring at the leaves of the tent roof as he thought back to his strange dream.

Ever since he was a child, he sometimes had vivid dreams, in color and so realistic that he could swear he was witnessing real events. But none of them compared to these dreams about Dana. He could see every detail of her world—every sight, every scent, every color. It didn't resemble any place he'd ever visited, or even heard or read about, but he was absolutely sure a world with this level of detail must exist somewhere. Even stranger, inside these dreams he sank so comfortably into Dana's mind that he actually became one with her.

There had to be a reason he had started having these dreams after he'd washed ashore on the island.

Outside, Laxia and Sahad were sitting by the fire, roasting large plant pods over the coals. Their smell reminded Adol of toasted bread. He approached and sat beside them.

"Here." Sahad handed him a cooked pod. "Not sure what they're called, but when I was a kid back on Creet, we used to gather them up on the hills and bake 'em. My wife an' daughter sometimes gather them too, when we're low on grain. They taste all right."

Adol took a bite. The pod tasted bland, but savory—like the toasted wheat pudding served in the villages back north.

"You look tired, Adol," Laxia said. "Are you all right?"

For a moment, Adol considered telling his companions about his dream but decided against it. Now that he was fully awake and out in broad daylight, he could convince himself there wasn't anything unnatural about it.

"I'm fine," he said. "How about you? Did you sleep well?"

"Like a log." Sahad belched, wiping his mouth with the back of his hand.

Laxia looked at him with distaste. "W-well...I managed to get more rest than I expected."

"Gah-haha!" Sahad laughed. "Great to hear you're no longer touchy 'bout campin'."

"We should make more campsites as we explore the island," Adol said quickly, before an argument could erupt. "That way we can cover more ground."

"Right," Sahad said. "Cheers to another day of explorin'."

By now, Adol believed he had a good idea about what this island was like, and what type of scenery to expect when they entered new areas. But as they followed the mountain passage leading out of the clearing deeper into the hills, he found out how wrong he was. Nothing he'd seen so far could possibly have prepared him for the sight that opened to them on the other side of the ravine.

Imagine an ocean reef, planted on dry land. Cover the rising columns of coral with grass, moss, and vines. Plant exotic-looking trees to spread their crowns in between, forming a dense canopy. Add sunlight filtering through, narrow sunbeams piercing the greenery like arrows shot from a celestial bow. Extend this view into the distance, so that the place would seem to stretch forever, without any boundaries. It felt like they were trapped underwater, about to swim into the unknown.

"Wow," Sahad said. "Would ya look at that..."

"A fascinating place," Laxia agreed.

"Looks like a bunch o' coral."

"Perhaps," she suggested, "this used to be a coral reef, when this area was completely under water."

Sahad snapped his fingers. "I know what we should name it. Towerin' Coral Forest."

To Adol's surprise, Laxia offered no objections this time.

A natural path wove down, past a pond formed by a trickling waterfall, into a cave-like tunnel made of the coral formations fused together on top, dimly lit by openings in the roof overhead. Land crabs scattered out of their way, heightening the sense that they were navigating through a real reef.

The cave tunnel widened, opening into a small ravine with a larger pond glistening in its center. Two men crouched near side the pond, one lying down, the other one bent over him. Adol rushed toward them.

The man lying on the ground looked portly and middle aged, dressed in an elaborately tailored suit with a tall lace-trimmed collar. Even in this wilderness his hair looked like it had just been arranged by a barber. A thin moustache curved around his long upper lip. A nobleman—and, by the looks of it, not the easygoing kind.

The man bending over him was dressed in a plain practical outfit with no frills or decorations. A large shoulder bag sat on the ground beside him. He looked resigned, as if his companion's attitude was giving him trouble. From what he'd already seen, Adol could easily believe it.

"Ouch!" the man lying on the ground said regally. "My ankle...It hurts!" He sounded accusing, as if the other man was personally responsible for the pain. "What are you waiting for? Tend to my injury at once!"

The other man sighed. "Please be still."

"Still? I am in agony, you idiot."

"You seem to have sprained your ankle. This is not a serious injury, but just to be safe I'll make a splint."

"Ugh." The nobleman rolled his eyes. "Why did this misfortune befall me? This wouldn't have happened if the ship hadn't sunk." He looked past his companion's shoulder, noticing Adol and his party. "Ah, rescue has arrived. It's about time!"

The other man turned too, watching the party approach. Curious how calm he looked, as if nothing out of the ordinary were going on.

Laxia narrowed her eyes. "Sir Carlan?"

The nobleman drew himself up. "My dear Lady von Roswell. Fancy meeting you here, and in such a company." He looked over Adol and Sahad in distaste.

"You know him?" Sahad asked.

Laxia sighed. "Yes, we met aboard the *Lombardia*."

"Indeed," Sir Carlan confirmed. "Lady Laxia was one of the few passengers on board whose station permitted her to have a conversation with me. Of course, one cannot compare her family to mine, especially with all the scandals—" He cut himself off. "But whom am I talking to? I am a nobleman of the Romun Empire. I am not obliged to converse with the likes of you." He turned away.

Wow. Adol exchanged a glance with Sahad. Up until now, all the castaways they'd met had been agreeable and understanding about the situation. It looked like their luck was about to change, at least in that regard.

"And what about you?" Sahad asked the other man.

A calm half-smile slid across the man's face. "My name is Kiergaard. I'm a doctor, actually."

"A doctor, huh?" Sahad brightened. "That'll sure come in handy, 'specially if we run into that big lizard again."

"Let us escort you both back to Castaway Village." Adol turned to Sir Carlan. "Can you walk?"

Sir Carlan grunted loudly. "Lady Laxia, I desire you to inform your, um, companions that they are not to address me directly."

Sahad looked at him in disbelief. "Not address you directly? But how will you get your sorry ass—"

"How dare you?"

"He can walk," Kiergaard said mildly.

Sir Carlan harrumphed, then scrambled up to his feet. As he took a few steps, Adol couldn't even see much of a limp. What a character. He hoped this man wasn't going to turn into a problem for the villagers.

"Lady Laxia," Sir Carlan said. "You may lend me your shoulder."

"What?"

"Your shoulder, so I can lean on it."

"Why?"

"To escort me to this so-called Castaway Village, of course. I cannot make the trek on my own, for I have injured my ankle, you see."

Laxia turned around helplessly. She didn't seem too keen to oblige. Sahad's eyes narrowed, but Adol preempted a response by stepping between Laxia and Sir Carlan, shielding her.

"Let me help you, Sir Carlan," he said.

The nobleman drew himself up, as if preparing for an outburst. But at that moment a newcomer emerged from the tunnel opening they'd just come through.

Dogi. Adol let out a sigh. How did the man always know when to show up? Adol thought he could guess in this case, as he saw a colorful bird dive from the branches above and land on Dogi's shoulder.

Laxia beamed. "Dogi. What are you and Little Paro doing here?"

"I happened to be in the area. Taking care of a few things." Dogi ran his eyes around the group, meeting Adol's gaze.

Following our tracks. Adol felt guilty. They should have discussed the possibility of camping before they left the village. Dogi and the captain were bound to get worried when Adol and his party didn't return for the night.

"Found Adol!" Little Paro croaked. "Found Red!"

Sahad's shoulders slowly relaxed. He pointedly avoided looking at Sir Carlan.

"I can escort you both," Dogi offered. "I'm headed back anyway." *Now that I've found you and made sure you're all right,* his reproachful look said as he glanced at Adol again.

"But," Sir Carlan protested "I don't wish to be escorted by a hulking brute like you."

"These guys need to focus on searching for other castaways," Dogi said calmly. "The only way we're getting off this island is if we all help each other." He crossed his arms over his chest, towering over the nobleman. "So would you please cooperate?"

Sir Carlan's beady eyes darted from Dogi to the parrot and back. "Hmph, fine. Let's get this over with."

He lifted his chin and marched past Dogi toward the opening of the tunnel leading back to where they'd come from. By now everyone watching could appreciate his walk—haughty and confident, not even the slightest limp.

"So you don't need me to carry you?" Dogi called after him.

"I'm perfectly capable of walking on my own, thank you very much," Sir Carlan snapped.

"What a relief," Laxia said quietly.

Sahad nodded. "That stuffed shirt seems like a real pain in the ass."

"I'd better follow him before he comes to harm." Dogi turned to Kiergaard. "You comin'?"

"Yes. But first, I wanted to inform you that there's a third castaway—a rather spirited young woman. We washed ashore in the same area, but as Sir Carlan and I decided to venture inland, she chose to stay behind. Never even told us her name." He threw a tense glance at the cave, where Sir Carlan had just disappeared.

"I wonder why," Sahad said under his breath.

"We'll look for her," Adol assured. "Where is this spot, exactly?"

"On the other side of this forest." Kiergaard pointed. "I asked her to stay put until we came for her, but I've been very worried."

"Understood," Laxia said. "We'll head out there at once."

Kiergaard bent down and picked up his bag, slinging it over his shoulder as he took off after Sir Carlan and Dogi.

"How fortunate that he's a doctor," Laxia said. "I imagine he'll be very helpful to us."

Adol nodded thoughtfully. Something about Kiergaard seemed off, but he dismissed the thought. Castaway Village could certainly use a doctor, not to mention another able-bodied man.

"Sir Carlan, on the other hand . . ." Laxia went on.

Sahad snorted. "Don't even mention him. I have a feelin' we're all gonna get tired talkin' about him before long. Let's just get through this weird-lookin' forest and find that shore."

The path took them past a small lake into a denser jungle. It took a while of picking their way over rocks, through knee-deep ponds, and into a maze of vine curtains draping down from the tree canopy, until they finally found themselves back at the seaside. Adol paused at the edge of the jungle, enjoying the cool sea breeze.

This beach was much more secluded than the others they'd visited so far. The only way here was through the forest they'd just navigated across, or by sea. A large pile of rocks rose like an island in the middle of the sand. Probably the same origin as the landslides around the island, here long enough to trap some earth and even sprout serious vegetation—like a very tall palm tree rising in its center. It looked unlike any other tree they'd seen so far, its wide bottle-shaped trunk tapering sharply at the top, crowned by a lush bundle of long, fleshy leaves.

"*Metavolicalis*," Laxia said.

"What?" Adol blinked.

"A primitive palm species." She nodded, as if finding this tree had confirmed a theory in her mind. "They are believed to be extinct."

Adol ran his eyes up the massive trunk, covered by scales that resembled a snake's. He'd certainly never seen a tree like this before.

As they skirted piles of boulders to make their way toward the water, they spotted a woman standing at the edge of the surf, peering into the distance. The castaway Kiergaard had mentioned.

Tall and athletic, she wore a leather bodice over a plain linen dress, with a tool belt strapped around her waist. Her hands were large and callused, as if they'd seen some hard work. Not a noble then. Adol felt ridiculously relieved as he strode toward her over the sand.

"Who are you people?" she asked by way of greeting. Her voice was low and rough, as if she'd spent too much of her life giving orders or trying to act even tougher than she looked.

"We're from the *Lombardia*," Laxia said. "We've come to rescue you."

The woman nodded calmly. "Right. You haven't, by any chance, encountered two men out there in the jungle? One, a doctor, the other—the stuffiest, most pompous—"

"Yes, we have," Adol said. "The doctor, Kiergaard, directed us to come and find you here. They are both on their way to our Castaway Village now."

"Oh." The woman nodded with an expression that held an equal measure of relief and disappointment. Clearly she didn't relish the idea of seeing Sir Carlan again.

"It's going to get dark in a few hours," Adol said. "We should head back too."

She narrowed her eyes, looking him up and down. "I remember you from the ship. You were the one who fought that monster before we went under, weren't you?"

"Yes." Adol felt surprised. It had been so chaotic on the ship, it was a wonder she recognized him.

Her eyes trailed to his sword. "A shame for a swordsman of your stature to carry around this piece of junk. Found it on the beach or somethin'?"

"In a cave near our camp." Adol missed the Isios Blade, not that it mattered to the conversation. He was sure the woman wasn't trying to be offensive. She must be this direct with everyone.

"I'm sure you know how to use it, but"—the woman sighed—"you can't fight at your full potential with a dull, poorly balanced sword. And you." She turned to Laxia. "That rapier's got a flashy hilt, but I bet it needs work. If I had to guess, that thing hasn't seen real combat in years."

Laxia paused, clearly struggling between affront and surprise. The surprise won—such a change from the noble lady Adol had first encountered a few days ago.

"You can tell at just a glance?" she said.

The woman only shrugged. "Your weapon," she said to Sahad, "is garbage. Literally. You're gonna injure yourself if you keep swingin' that thing around."

Sahad scratched his head. "Gah-haha. Now that ya mention it, my back's been achin' more lately."

"You seem to know a lot about weapons," Adol noted.

She let out a short laugh. "I would hope so, being a weaponsmith. The name's Kathleen, by the way. Good to meet you."

Adol nodded. A weaponsmith. How lucky. Perhaps they could build a forge, so that Kathleen could help make their weapons more effective against the local beasts. He thought back to the monstrous lizard that had chased Sahad. Having a weapon that could actually hurt that creature would make Adol feel a lot safer during their rescue operations into the wilderness.

HUMMEL

Thick vapors rose up from the swamp, gathering into a milky fog that made it difficult to see. The air here smelled of mud and decay—a heavy, musky scent that didn't fully match the local vegetation. Laxia twitched her nose as she peered ahead.

It took her too long to realize that the giant shape looming in the fog ahead wasn't a boulder. Boulders didn't rise and fall so rhythmically, as if breathing. They also didn't normally sprout crests of fleshy spikes she had originally taken for leaves of an exotic plant. A clump of roots protruding across the path began to look suspiciously similar to a claw. As her mind gradually worked through these details, she arrived at the inevitable conclusion that they were looking at a sleeping creature.

She was about to alert her companions, when the loud crack of a branch underfoot cut through the silence. *Sahad.* The fisherman smiled guiltily, but it was too late.

The beast stirred and raised its head. A beady eye focused on the intruders.

"Man, that thing is huge," Sahad whispered.

It was. In the fog, it was hard to guess the creature's true size, its monstrous lines distorted by the rising vapors, but its overall shape bore an alarming similarity to the giant lizard they'd previously encountered back near the beach. As it rushed toward them, it seemed to grow, as if the swamp itself had spawned it to terrify them. Its roar shook the air, flattening the leaves of the nearby bushes.

They turned and ran for their lives.

Another roar echoed behind. Massive footsteps pounded in pursuit. Adol pointed to a narrow passage between two giant boulders, and they sprinted toward it, squeezing through onto the beach.

They didn't stop running until they reached the water. Only then did Laxia realize that the jungle behind them was quiet, and no one was chasing them anymore.

They panted, crouching against the rocks, looking back at the passage they'd just come through.

"I—" Adol heaved a few breaths. "I think we're out of the beast's territory."

Sahad gulped. "I—I thought we were done fer. That beast looked like the one that was chasin' me when I ran into you guys. 'Cept bigger, faster, and madder."

"On the bright side," Adol said, "we finally made it to the other side of the bay."

They looked around. The campfire smoke from Castaway Village rose steadily up into the sky a few krimelye away. It almost seemed that they could walk along the beaches—or swim, if Laxia could find a suitable flotation device—to get back to the village from here. The idea that there could be another way out of here made her feel better. These giant lizards clearly avoided the seaside. Even though she couldn't swim, anything seemed better than returning to the swamp and into the beast's territory again.

This beach was larger than the ones close to the village, a wide strip of sand curving away into the distance around the bay. A stone arch rose in in front of them like a gateway that separated the stretch of the beach they stood on from another, longer stretch beyond. The light of the setting sun painted the rocks into dramatic red shades, spilling grotesque shadows over the grass-covered foothills.

As Laxia peered in that direction, a movement caught her eye on the other side of the arch.

A man, walking away along the sand?

Franz. She rushed forward and paused, her shoulders sagging in disappointment as she realized her mistake.

The stranger definitely wasn't Franz. His build was slighter but more athletic, as if his daily occupation involved a lot of physical activity. Or maybe this impression came from the way he moved, with the prowling grace of a predator scouting hostile territory. *A man up to no good.* Laxia wasn't sure where this thought had come from. One had every right to walk with caution on a deserted island teeming with dangerous beasts. But watching this man made her think of the dark alleys and disreputable establishments she had always been warned about, places where a proper lady would never go.

The stranger's outfit and gear matched this impression—especially the musket rifle with a bayonet slung across his back, a wicked weapon that required great skill to handle. His clothing looked rogue-like too—all black, girded with a wide leather belt that held a sheathed dagger and a gunpowder horn, along with an ammunition pouch. The outfit clung to his slender form with deliberate elegance, as if specially tailored to accent his graceful lines. Odd. What kind of a rogue would care about his own appearance enough to pay a tailor for a custom-made suit?

And why was he walking away so decisively, as if deliberately ignoring their presence?

"Excuse me!" she called out.

The stranger stopped but didn't turn. His pose betrayed irritation, as if Laxia had interrupted something very important.

"Hello?" she called.

The man hesitated, as if deciding whether turning around was worth his time, then resumed his walking.

Laxia gaped. Had this man just *ignored* her? Wasn't he interested in their help? Or did he, like Sir Carlan, consider Laxia and her companions unworthy of addressing him?

Perhaps he was deaf? Injured? Confused?

She glanced at Adol and Sahad who paused a few steps behind her with thoughtful looks, watching the stranger's retreating back. Their idle poses told her they weren't about to act. Oh well. She, for one, wasn't going to stay behind when they'd just found another survivor. This man clearly needed their help, even if for some reason he wouldn't admit it.

She raced after the stranger. This time, she passed him and turned around to face him, blocking his path. He stopped in his tracks, looking at her with the resigned expression of someone who would rather be anywhere else than facing her right now.

Up close, he looked even more showy. Ridiculous, really. He couldn't have possibly picked that black silky shirt with a cutaway collar just to accent the paleness of his smooth skin—or to let his blond hair sweep over it so dramatically. Nor would anyone in his right mind tan his black jacket, brush out his pants, and polish his boots for a beach stroll on a deserted island. Yet Laxia couldn't shake the impression this stranger must have done just that. How else could he possibly look so perfect, as if he had just stepped out of a bath and donned a freshly pressed suit? Even his hat, flat and wide-brimmed, seemingly designed for the sole purpose of casting a mysterious shadow across his face, looked as if it had just left a hatter's stand.

His gray eyes studied her calmly, with no trace of the surprise, shock, or relief anyone in their right mind would show when approached by fellow survivors on a deserted island. Unbelievable. Laxia could only explain it by trauma, perhaps a concussion suffered during the shipwreck. She lifted her chin, determined not to be swayed by the man's strange behavior.

"Were you a passenger aboard the *Lombardia*?" she asked.

The man measured her up and down with his gaze, as if deciding if she was worthy of an answer. "What if I was?"

She heaved a breath. "So glad we found you. We were passengers too, and now we are all stranded on this deserted island."

"Not my problem."

"What?"

The man shrugged, then stepped around her and resumed his walk.

Laxia gaped after him, at a loss for words. Of all the insolent, conceited, impossible people she'd ever met, this stranger definitely won the prize.

"Hey," Adol called out, striding up to Laxia's side. "Where do you think you are going?"

"That's my business," the man said, without turning or stopping. "No offense."

"Oh, really now," Laxia said. "You could at least tell us your name."

"Hummel Trabaldo." He stepped onto the path leading up the hill and proceeded without another word until he had disappeared from view.

Laxia moved to chase after him, but Adol placed a hand on her shoulder. "Leave him be."

"But he—"

"He's an adult," Adol said. "I assume he knows what he's doing."

Sahad let out a short laugh. "Well, this island ain't that big. I'm sure we'll run into him again."

Laxia nodded. In all fairness, she couldn't care less what this odd man was up to. And of course, Adol and Sahad were right. Whoever he was, he seemed to know what he was doing. And they were indeed likely to run into him again—if those lizards or other beasts didn't get him first. She wasn't going to waste any more time thinking about him.

"It's getting late," she said. "We should look for a place to make camp."

Sahad chuckled. She grinned in response, remembering her little tantrum a few days ago when Adol had first suggested camping together. Life on this island was changing her so much, in such a short time. Surprisingly, she found herself enjoying the new Laxia she was becoming.

A passage under the stone arch led to a secluded grotto, protected by rock walls on all sides. A perfect shelter. They wouldn't even need a tent to sleep here.

They built a fire. Sahad took out a small kettle he carried in his backpack and filled it from a spring nearby, bringing it to a boil and dropping in some fragrant leaves for a bedtime tea. Darkness descended outside. Laxia pulled her knees up to her chest, looking across the campfire at the night sky. The moons were not visible yet, but stars lit it up just as well, distant and bright.

She thought of the strange man out there, all alone and apparently content with it. Hummel Trabaldo. What was he doing right now? Was Franz somewhere out there too, sitting by a fire? And if this island had such limited space, how come they hadn't run into him yet?

The last thing she saw when she lay down was the view of distant palm trees outlined against the starry sky. Waves rustled gently, breaking on the shore. Their sound was soothing as she drifted off to sleep.

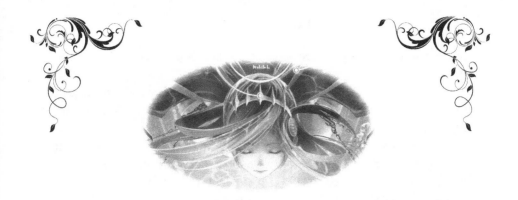

THE GREAT TREE GARDEN

Dana stood in the Temple hallway, hesitating. The door ahead was open a crack, letting in a stream of daylight. A low keening sound carried from outside—a bird that needed help. This garden was off limits to trainees, but she couldn't bear to leave the poor suffering creature out there.

Her eyes darted to the empty passage behind her. She needed to hurry. If she were discovered here by Advisor Urgunata or one of her minions, she would be severely punished. She felt certain her little adventure was going to end that way, but the thought didn't stop her from walking through the doorway.

The deep shade of the Great Tree of Origins fell over her. Its rich, lush canopy blocked out the sky, its trunk so wide at the base that it would take two dozen trainees holding hands to encircle it.

It took her a moment to realize that this entire garden had no other plants. Everything here was the tree—its roots, its branches, garlands of leaves and flowers descending down to create a deep and cozy shade, like a cradle of life.

Here in the garden, where nothing stood between her and this majestic creation, she felt a unity with nature that she had never experienced before. The tree seemed sentient, watching her with every leaf, every bit of its skin-like bark.

The little bird sat at the base of the tree, its foot tangled in a net of creeping vines. A swallow, its slim body dark gray, its beady eye fixed on her intently as if aware that she came here to help. Its wing hung limply—broken? Oh dear. Dana could use her Essence to heal the creature, but not here in this inner sanctum where the Maiden herself prayed in seclusion, joining with the Tree in meditation. She needed to get it somewhere safe, where she could work without being disturbed.

She freed the bird from the vines and tucked it gently into the fold of her robe. The bird kept very still, its tiny heart pounding rapidly against her skin.

As she raised her face for a last look at the Great Tree, she felt disoriented. The world spun out of focus and then coalesced again into a different plain of view. Or was it she who had changed?

The bark of the Great Tree suddenly seemed transparent, like water. Peering through, she saw a vast space, stretching out of sight. A glowing sphere floated it its center, and inside the sphere...

A woman slept peacefully, curled up in a bed of woven strands of light. Her long hair streamed down her shoulders, covering her like an exquisite blanket. Her face looked young, unblemished, but somehow Dana knew that this woman was more ancient than anyone she'd ever known, perhaps more ancient than the Tree itself.

She narrowed her eyes. A woman, sleeping inside the Great Tree? This couldn't be true. Why—

"Oh dear, are you a candidate? You're not supposed to be here."

The voice startled Dana out of her trance. Turning, she felt her eyes widen as she recognized the newcomer.

The Maiden of the Great Tree.

"Y-your Eminence," she stammered.

The Maiden approached, leaning heavily on her walking cane. She looked so old, her skin dry and wrinkled, like parchment. Long, silvery-white hair fell down her back. But despite the frailty, Dana could feel her power too. Her heart fluttered as rapidly as the baby bird's under the old woman's penetrating gaze,.

Dear spirits, she's going to be so angry with me for disturbing her sanctuary. Despite the thought, Dana stood her ground. The vision of a woman sleeping inside the tree consumed her. It didn't make any sense, but no matter how impossible it seemed, it rang true in her mind. She had to know more.

"Is there a woman sleeping inside the Great Tree of Origins?" she blurted, then mentally kicked herself. She should have phrased it more carefully, not just sputtered it out like this. The Maiden would probably think she was crazy.

It certainly looked that way, judging from the way the old woman froze, wide-eyed. She didn't hurry to respond, her silence sending Dana into a new fit of panic.

"I—I'm sorry. Please forgive me, Maiden. I shouldn't have asked such a strange question."

The Maiden stepped closer, plying her cane with a shaking hand.

"What is your name, child?"

"Dana."

"Listen carefully, Dana. Do not speak of what you just saw to anyone. It could undo the world itself."

Dana didn't remember how she made it out to the Temple's hallway, straight into Advisor Urgunata's path.

Looks like Cleric Sienna finally released you from her sermon." As usual, Sarai didn't walk but danced into the room, her mass of hair sweeping behind her.

Dana smiled. "Sarai! Did you come to pick me up?"

Sarai winked conspiratorially, leaning forward and lowering her voice. "I didn't come alone. The grouch is with me too."

Oh. Dana watched Olga step into the doorway, her thin-featured face folded into a perpetually grumpy expression. Her downward look made Dana feel even smaller than she already was.

"Oh, Olga!"

Olga pursed her lips. "Don't 'Oh, Olga' me. I swear, you're such a troublemaker." Her eyes narrowed. "Let's see." She lifted one finger. "In the time we've been training here at the Temple, less than a year, you've snuck out too many times to count—including that little detour to the black market that sent Advisor Urgunata into a fit." Another finger rose. "You entered Cleric Sienna's room without permission and destroyed things, claiming it was research."

"It *was* research."

Olga continued as if she hadn't spoken, raising a third finger. "And just now, you ditched the trial ceremony to sneak into the Great Tree Garden. Need I continue?"

"No." Dana hung her head. Olga was right. Her curiosity, her urge to help others, kept getting the best of her. If she didn't stop causing trouble, their superiors would lose patience and send her home. The mere thought of leaving this place, abandoning her hopes for successful training, filled her with dread. When had she become so committed?

"Come," Sarai said. "I think Dana has had enough lecturing for today. They're about to serve dinner. Let's go."

"Right." Dana swept to the door, glad for this change of topic, but Olga stopped her with an abrupt gesture.

"Forgetting something?"

"Huh?" Dana wasn't sure what she meant.

"The baby bird you're hiding under your clothes. I bet you snuck into the garden to save it." Olga pointed an accusing finger.

"H-how did you know?" Dana edged back, cradling the fluffy bundle under her tunic. The little creature was surprisingly quiet. Probably scared to death, poor thing. She needed to get it to a safe place outside, where she could use her Essence to heal its wing and set it on its way.

"So what are you waiting for?" Olga prompted. "Hurry up and take care of it. Sarai and I will save a seat for you in the dining hall."

"R-right." Dana turned and rushed down the hallway. She felt overwhelmed. Olga could be a grouch sometimes, but she always supported Dana, no matter what. She was so lucky to have friends like Olga and Sarai.

Another surprise waited for her outside. Rastell was standing on the stone walkway near the Temple entrance. His face lit up with a smile when he saw Dana.

"Rastell?" Dana skipped down the steps toward him. "What are you doing here?"

He glanced around nervously. "Father's inspecting the guard stations at the Mountain Gate. I heard you were in trouble. Are you all right?"

Warmth washed over her as she met his gaze. "You came here because you were worried about me?"

"They said Advisor Urgunata put you in seclusion."

Dana shook her head. "Not really, thank the spirits. She just sent me to Cleric Sienna for a really long lecture."

"What did you do?"

Dana reached into her tunic and brought out the little bird. Its dark feathers gleamed in the sun. It looked at Dana sideways with its small beady eye, then darted a nervous glance at Rastell.

"Stand back. You'll scare it." Dana held the bird in an open palm, reaching with her other hand to channel Essence. She could feel the power coursing through her into the bird's wing, mending the injury. The swallow chirped and flapped its wings but didn't hurry to fly away.

"I think it likes you," Rastell said.

Dana laughed. One of the things she missed about home was taking care of animals. "Let's see if it likes you too."

He held out a hand, and she put the little bird into it. It sat there for a moment, then spread its wings and took off into the sky.

They stood side by side, watching it circle around the Temple's main building and fly into the shade of the Great Tree. Dana hoped it wouldn't get into trouble again.

"I have to go to dinner," she said. "The clerics won't be happy if I'm late. I think I caused enough trouble for one day."

Rastell nodded. "I have to go too. Father doesn't like to wait. See you at practice tomorrow?"

"Yes, definitely."

For a moment, she stood on the long walkway, watching him retreat toward the distant building of the Mountain Gate. He turned and waved to her. She waved back, then hurried into the dining hall.

WATCHTOWER

Adol sat up and looked around, shaking off the remains of his dream. By now, sharing Dana's mind, learning more about her life, had become a part of him. He wasn't sure if this girl even existed in real life, but he had come to look forward to their dream closeness, falling asleep to become submerged in her world—which felt almost as real as his own.

The rising sun hovered just above the horizon, throwing long shadows across the beach. Laxia stood at the edge of the grotto, tying up her hair. Across the cold firepit, Sahad stretched his arms and yawned.

"Good mornin'!"

Laxia looked at him with reproach. "I probably should have mentioned it earlier, but you shouldn't yawn in front of people."

"Huh?" Sahad blinked. "Nobles don't do that?"

"No one does that. It's just common sense." She glanced at Adol. "Don't you agree?"

Adol shrugged. "It's no big deal."

"Really?" She frowned. "And to think I mistook you for someone civilized."

Sahad snorted. "Bein' a noble lady sounds pretty tough."

Laxia paused. For a moment it seemed to Adol that she was gathering strength for another temper fit. Then, unexpectedly, she burst out laughing.

The three of them couldn't stop laughing all through breakfast as Laxia and Sahad recalled some of the nobles' rules of behavior that indeed seemed ridiculous. No belchin'. No fartin'. No scratching, yawning, or stretching. No serving your own food or drink—and *certainly* never serving others. No pointing fingers. No slurping. No staring, unless you deliberately wanted to offend. With all these restrictions, being a lady did indeed seem pretty tough. In Sahad's words, it must be a picnic for Laxia in Castaway Village. Laxia heartily agreed.

After breakfast, they left their shelter and continued exploring.

This beach skirted around the bay toward the mouth of another river streaming from the mountains down a deep canyon. There was no way to cross it here, so they turned uphill, following the path they'd seen Hummel take yesterday.

After ascending a few terraces, they reached a flat area open on all sides, affording a good view of the valley. A tall observation tower rose in its center.

They stopped.

The tower made clever use of a dead tree standing at the edge of the cliff, dried out but sturdy enough to support a wooden ladder and a covered observation platform on top. It looked much newer than any of the pirate settlements they had discovered so far—and well maintained, as if someone had been using it regularly.

"Ya think that Hummel guy made this?" Sahad asked.

Adol shook his head. "I don't think so. He's been here as long as the rest of us. He wouldn't have had the time."

"Let's take a look," Laxia suggested.

Adol grabbed the ladder and tested it for strength. It seemed solid enough.

The observation platform at the top of the tower was big enough to hold all three of them, with room to move around and view the island in different directions. A roof made of boards and topped with dry palm leaves stretched overhead, sturdy enough to withstand a storm. A stout rail made it safe to walk around the platform without worrying about falling over the edge. Adol paused for a bird's eye view of the bay. The islet in its center looked bigger from up here, most of its area covered by a large tree perching on top of the rocks. The campfire smoke from Castaway Village rose steadily into the sky at the far end of the bay. The swampy jungle they'd crossed on the way here spread in between, a patch of lush greenery suffused by the vapors rising from the water.

He turned back to the central beam, covered with notes nailed directly to the wood. They looked like pages torn from a journal or a diary, all written in the same hand—even and bold, with a flourish at every capital letter that looked both distinct and sophisticated. Some of the notes were faded and splotched, probably damaged by rainwater. Others looked more recent.

"Been here twenty days already," Laxia read aloud. *"Figured I should start searching the island instead of waiting to die. I believe this is the south side of the island."*

"Check this one out," Sahad said from the other side. *"While walkin' through the valley, I was attacked in the fog by a creature I'd never seen before. A fantastic beast, it reminded me of stories I'd heard before..."* He frowned. "The next part's all smudged. I think it says Pri...Pre..."

"Primordials." Laxia kept her eyes on the torn page.

"Primordials? What's that mean?"

"Obviously, based on context clues, it must refer to some kind of ancient species."

Adol recognized the snippy tone. She clearly knew something she wasn't revealing. They needed to have a conversation about that soon, but for now pressing her any further didn't seem productive. Luckily, Sahad didn't seem to notice as he moved to the next note.

"Afterward, I tried to go to the northern region o' the island, but the path was too difficult to traverse. Huh?" Sahad frowned. "Looks like whoever wrote this note signed it 'T'. What kind of a name is that?"

"Probably an initial," Adol suggested.

"I wonder if this T fella's still alive."

Adol wondered too. Judging by the craftmanship, by the careful handwriting on these notes, he guessed this T was educated and skilled, a survivor, stranded on the island like the rest of them, with a talent to find resources and use them to his advantage. A person they definitely wanted to meet. They should do their best to find him.

From the top of the tower, they had a better chance to survey the terrain ahead. It looked rough. The road they had been following picked its way through the rocks to the edge of the canyon, where a recent landslide had destroyed a section of the hill, creating an impassable gap. Another road branched east into a narrow valley. A large stretch of the jungle lay to the southeast, with a beach barely visible beyond.

They descended the tower and continued up the path that climbed steeply into the hills. It narrowed as they gained altitude, picking its way between the rocks that creased the side of the canyon, so deep they had trouble seeing the river below.

The path ended abruptly at the edge of the cliff. They stopped, peering across the canyon.

"It looks like there used to be a way to cross here," Adol said. "This path seems to continue on the other side."

"Well," Laxia said. "There isn't a way to cross here anymore."

Adol looked up the mountain. If they wanted to explore the entire island, they had to find a way to climb it. This canyon in front of them formed a decisive boundary that separated them from this goal. Maybe if they followed the valley eastward, they could find another route?

"Fine with me," Sahad mumbled. "Don't see why we need to go that way at all." He edged away from the chasm.

The path veered away from the edge of the cliffs, winding into a narrow valley. As they entered the area, Laxia, who was walking in front of Adol, stopped so abruptly that he nearly ran into her. His eyes widened as he realized what she was staring at.

Hummel stood under a large tree dead ahead, facing them.

"Hey, wh—" The words froze on Adol's lips as Hummel swung his rifle off his shoulder and aimed it at the approaching party.

A gunshot rang through the air.

It took Adol a moment to realize no one was hurt. Another moment to register the echo; the flapping of birds startled by the sound; the thud of a heavy body falling to the ground behind him.

Adol spun around.

A dead wolf lay in the grass, fangs bared, paws still extended for a leap. Hummel's shot must have caught the beast just as it pounced. If he hadn't done it, someone in the party would have been injured or killed.

Adol slowly let out a breath, inwardly cursing himself for not having heard the wolf's stealthy approach. If not for Hummel . . . The man was clearly someone to be reckoned with. Adol had seen rifles before but had never encountered anybody who could use one with such speed and accuracy. No wonder Hummel had rejected their offer of help and companionship. He clearly believed he didn't need anyone's help. And maybe he was right.

"You startled us," Adol said. "But—thanks."

Hummel flicked the rifle back into its sheath behind his shoulder, watching the party calmly. He didn't look like he was about to speak.

"You could have warned us before you fired," Laxia snapped.

"Yeah," Sahad agreed. "I was so scared, I almost wet myself. Ye could've said somethin' when you pointed that thing at us."

"True." Hummel's lips twitched. "And you'd have been down one arm before I'd taken a shot."

Laxia opened her mouth for a retort, then closed it again, her gaze trailing to the dead wolf.

"I'm coming with you, by the way," Hummel said.

Laxia's eyes widened. "E-excuse me?"

"We're headed the same direction." Hummel slid his gaze to Adol, as if prompting him for a response.

Adol met his gaze. Despite the oddness of Hummel's behavior, he had a good feeling about the man. Hummel fit so naturally into his surroundings—the only person they'd met on this island so far who looked entirely in his own element. They could use a man like this—as well as that handy rifle of his—on the exploration team.

"Welcome aboard," Adol said.

Hummel nodded then stepped up to the party as if the question was settled once and for all. Laxia looked at him sideways but didn't offer further objections as they resumed their walk up the path.

The narrow gorge that opened in front of them behind the next bend of the valley looked almost too picturesque to be real. A raging stream carved its way through the rocks, their lines flowing like elaborate abstract sculptures, highlighted by the swirling water that gathered at the base to plummet down the canyon in a powerful waterfall.

A cave entrance gaped ahead. In the reddish light of the setting sun, its uneven edges threw grotesque shadows over the glade.

"A cave. It could lead to the other side of the valley." Hummel looked at Adol as if expecting him to lead the way.

Adol considered it. Hummel was probably right. According to the map sketched by Captain Barbaros, there should be a beach—possibly harboring some castaways—somewhere at the end of this path, likely unreachable along the shore. But venturing into a dark cave this close to dusk seemed like a bad idea. They didn't know how far the cave stretched or what creatures might live inside.

"It's getting late," he said. "Why don't we camp here for the night and explore the cave tomorrow?"

Hummel proved to be invaluable when it came to camping. The way he carved tent poles and kettle supports using his wicked-looking belt knife seemed almost like a show, each move so fast and precise that Adol couldn't stop staring. With Hummel involved, it seemed like no time at all before they all sat down around the fire, eating their rations and enjoying the warmth.

"So, what have you been up to on this island, all by yerself?" Sahad asked.

Hummel kept his head lowered. Under the brim of his hat, Adol couldn't see his face. What kind of a person would keep on his hat at night, sitting beside a campfire?

"I'm a transporter," Hummel said at length. "Ever heard of those?"

"Transporter?" Sahad raised his eyebrows. "Oh, I see. Mail? Packages?"

"Anything. Contraband. Dead bodies. It's all the same to me."

"Dead bodies?" Sahad's eyes widened.

Laxia nodded as if this information connected the dots in her mind. "Transporters are heavily involved in the criminal underworld." She looked at Hummel with distaste. "Many people utilize their services to transport all manner of illicit material."

"You don't say." Sahad looked fascinated. "So, what's a transporter like you doin' on a deserted island?"

Hummel lifted his face just a bit. Firelight washed over his jawline and licked his cheek, but left his eyes in shadow. "Wouldn't be professional to answer that."

"Professional?"

"As a transporter, I live by three unbreakable rules: never breach a contract, never ask questions, and never open the package."

"Huh, I see."

Hummel's lips twitched. "Relax. I have no intention of harming any of you."

Sahad grinned. "Oh, good. I feel much safer now."

He finished his tea, stood up, and made his way into the tent. The rest of them rose too, kicking down the fire and settling down to sleep.

WEB BRIDGES

I brought you something," Rastell said.

He took a bundle out of his shoulder bag and carefully unwrapped it, placing its contents on the ground next to Dana. A fruit, larger than the palm of her hand, its bluish skin emitting faint fragrance.

"A dragon-tree fruit," Dana breathed out. "A ripe one. They're so expensive at the market. Where did you get it?"

A quick smile slid across Rastell's lips. "They grow along the road leading out of town. The low-hanging ones have all been picked, but I managed to climb up and get one while Father was making rounds. You once told me you liked them."

"I do." She smiled too. She'd mentioned it a long time ago, when they first became friends. How had he remembered?

She reached over to the fruit. Its leathery skin was cool to the touch. Somehow these fruits had a way of keeping cold even on a hot day, making them so coveted as a refreshment.

"Do you want me to peel it?" Rastell took out his belt knife.

She shook her head. "Back in my village, we eat them whole."

"With the skin?"

"It tastes good, actually. Adds tartness. You should try."

He shrugged and slid the blade over the fruit, splitting it in half in a smooth motion that reminded her of swordplay. Of course, Chief Dran's son would be good with any weapon he touched. They'd been training together for over two years now, but she still had no hope of achieving the same perfection.

Sitting in the tree shade near the brook at the back of the Temple gardens made her feel as if they were having a picnic—a forbidden picnic that would surely be interrupted if someone like Advisor Urgunata caught them. The thought made their little escapade seem like even more fun.

A vision hit her without warning. Flames. A thick wall of all-consuming crimson fire. No, not crimson...Scarlet? She gasped and dropped the precious fruit, jumping up to her feet.

Rastell was on his feet too in a split instant. "What's wrong?"

"A forest fire."

"Where?"

"No time to explain." She grasped his hand, and they ran back to the Temple buildings. "I must find Sarai and Olga. Go get your father. Tell him I had a vision. The fire will consume the Temple if they don't prepare. He'll know what to do."

"What? When?"

"Soon. I—I don't know." She didn't wait for a response as she darted up the stairs into the library, where she'd left Olga and Sarai earlier this afternoon.

Her friends were still there, bending over an old lithograph at the far corner, away from the other trainees. They lifted their heads as she entered, their smiles fading when they saw the urgency in her gaze.

"Come with me," she said. "Now. I'll explain on the way."

Wordlessly, they rushed out of the hall after her. A few heads turned as they passed, but no one took any special notice. By now, everyone expected Dana, Sarai, and Olga to sneak out on all kinds of crazy ventures.

"A forest fire?" Sarai panted as they ran. "Are you sure?"

"Yes. I had a vision."

"What color?"

"Scarlet. A really clear one."

"Scarlet?" Olga stopped dead in her tracks.

"Yes. Come, there's no time to..."

"Dana." Olga's voice rang with reproach. "You know full well what a scarlet vision means. An event that cannot be changed. A clear one means it's going to happen very soon." She turned. "We're going the wrong way. We need to go back and warn the others."

"No." Dana shook her head firmly. "Rastell and Chief Dran are already doing it. And if we go back, we won't be able to change a thing."

"We won't be able to anyway. It's a *scarlet* vision, remember?"

"We can't avert the fire, true—but we can make a difference to the outcome. Just trust me, all right?"

Olga and Sarai exchanged glances. After a moment, they set off again, trudging through the muddy ground.

A majestic building dominated the forest clearing ahead, rising directly out of a large lake. Ancient trees perched on the hillside around it, water streaming over their roots into the pond. The reservoir... The amount of water it held, if unleashed all at once, should definitely be enough to stop the fire.

"Help me release the water," Dana said.

"You must be mad," Olga protested. "Do you want to flood the whole valley?"

"Not if we also control it using our combined Essence," Dana insisted. "We can adjust the floodgate near the Maiden's sanctuary, can't we?"

"Floodgate? But—"

Dana tossed her head impatiently. "Olga, Sarai, listen to me. I need your help. My Essence is not enough to do it alone."

"Dana's right," Sarai said. "It could actually work."

"You are both mad," Olga grumbled, but she was already raising her hands to summon Essence, joining Dana and Sarai.

Adol woke up with too many questions in his mind. Who was this Dana, and why did he keep reliving these vivid episodes from her life, in which his consciousness merged with hers? Why did these dreams cut off so abruptly, right in the middle of the action? He sat up, staring into the depth of the empty tent.

A forest fire. Had Dana, Olga, and Sarai managed to avert it? Had everyone in the Temple survived? He longed to know more. The idea that whether, and when, he would see the continuation of this story was out of his control made him feel frustrated.

Even though he'd slept the longest—again—he didn't feel rested. He couldn't escape a feeling that the scenes he was experiencing, as well as the timing of his awakenings, were deliberate, as if some unknown powers had already determined how much information he was to be given each time. These dreams were also becoming more and more realistic. It felt more difficult each time to transition to his own reality. Was he really dreaming about Dana? Or was he actually part of her? The questions were too big for his mind to enfold.

Everyone was sitting around the fire as Adol stumbled out of the tent and washed his face in the spring, shaking off the hold of his dream. Laxia edged sideways to give him room. Sahad handed him a ration and a mug of warm tea.

"I took a peek at the cave while you were sleeping." Hummel's calm expression didn't exactly hold disapproval, but Adol felt he was being judged anyway for his tardy rising. He should probably tell his companions about his dreams, but he didn't feel ready to share—especially with Hummel. He barely knew the man.

"What did you find?" he asked instead.

"The cave opens into another gorge on the far end, with a lot of tunnels veering into the mountains. If we follow that gorge, we should find another beach—probably a secluded one with no access from anywhere along the shore."

"How far exactly did you scout to determine all that?" Laxia demanded.

Hummel shrugged, sliding another glance at Adol.

Adol returned his gaze calmly as he finished his meal.

"Let's make it to that beach then," he said. "I hope we find more castaways there."

Laxia couldn't quite put her finger on what gave her a creepy feeling as they made their way through the shallow cave. It felt as if they were being watched, as if something terrible was following them. It made no sense, with the way the cave chamber stretched only a short way, with plenty of daylight shining in from the gaps in its tall ceiling. After a while she managed to convince herself she was imagining things.

The view of the gorge on the other side was dramatic. Tall rocks framed a powerful stream that rolled down a series of rapids toward the distant gap blazing with a strip of sea blue. The beach. It would only be a short way if they could travel directly down the stream, but plunging into the deep, rapidly flowing water would be suicide.

A series of large boulders protruding from the river were stitched together by gossamer bridges that gleamed in the sun, making it difficult to discern what they were made of. Ropes? Unusually white ones—and fuzzy, as if woven of the finest quality wool.

The party skirted a few rock ledges and stopped in front of one of them.

Up close, the bridge looked much sturdier than it had from a distance, each of the tightly woven strands composing it thicker than a finger and slightly sticky to the touch. Laxia bent down, feeling around the expertly woven cradle that provided both footing and handrails to walk across safely.

These didn't look like any man-made structures she had ever seen. Perhaps they were some sort of indigenous plants no one had ever heard of? A new species of fungi? Much as Laxia wanted to believe this, she knew better. Only insects and spiders were capable of producing this kind of thread to weave their webs and cocoons—and judging by the thickness, it seemed highly unlikely that these threads could have been placed here by a tiny, harmless creature. She was still recovering from the shock of encountering the giant spiders on the outskirts of Xandria, but even those fist-sized monsters wove only hair-thin threads, their nets incapable of trapping anything larger than small birds. The spider that made these . . . She cut off her thoughts, peering down the gorge at several more web bridges running across in strategic places that would enable crossing the river to the other side.

"I don't like the look of these webs," she said at length.

"Yeah, me neither," Sahad agreed heartily. "Don't know 'bout y'all, but I don't look forward to meeting the creature that made 'em."

Neither do I. Laxia glanced at Adol. He was looking at the bridges too, but if he was worried about them, he certainly wasn't showing it. "Maybe we should turn back."

"Back?" Adol frowned. "The beach we're trying to reach is just ahead. If there are castaways out there, they will definitely need our help."

"Right." Laxia nodded. If her fears were correct, any castaways trapped on that beach would have no way of getting out without falling into the clutches of whatever monstrous creature had woven these webs. It could be Franz—or someone far less capable, like Alison. It wasn't like Laxia to turn back at the first sign of danger. When she'd fallen overboard on the *Lombardia*, Franz had jumped after her without hesitation. Would she do any less for him? She glanced at Hummel, who slung his rifle over his shoulder, staring at the gorge ahead. At least they had a ranged weapon. Any creatures lurking out there should be vulnerable to bullets, shouldn't they?

The web bridge proved even sturdier than it looked, bringing them safely across to a large boulder rising in the middle of the gorge, where another set of bridges led them all the way across to a cave opening downstream. There seemed to be no way around the cave, so after hesitation, they all drew their weapons and entered a long tunnel, dimly lit by clusters of glowing crystals along the walls.

Nothing monstrous crossed their path, except for a few coconut-sized spiders that scurried along the walls into the dark crevices and tunnels. While they looked absolutely terrifying and disgusting, none of them seemed eager to attack, and after a while Laxia managed to convince herself that she had overreacted. These spiders, though uncommonly large, even compared to the Xandrian species, did not seem aggressive. Could they have made all these webs? Well, possibly, if their silk glands worked differently from any spiders she knew. After all this time on the island, though, she shouldn't be that surprised at unusual traits among the local species. In fact, these thick threads could prove quite useful as building material, if they were to collect some and bring them back to the village. In one of the chambers they entered, threads covered the entire floor, like a carpet, making them very easy to pick up.

She was about to suggest it when Sahad, walking in front, ran into a thick cable planted right across the path.

"Ouch," he said. "Whose dumb idea was it to put this rope out 'ere, as if—"

The shadows in front of him shifted, forming a shape that emerged into the glowing crystal light.

A scream froze on Laxia's lips.

She had been expecting a spider, true. A monstrous, terrifying spider, possibly gigantic enough to consider them prey. But even the worst of her imagination couldn't have formed *this*.

The creature towering over Sahad looked larger than an elephant. Its bulging body filled the cave tunnel ahead, its head adorned with too many pincers that clicked threateningly as it advanced. A set of dark eyes—at least half dozen of them—fixed menacingly on the intruders. Its legs . . . gods, each was as thick as a tree trunk, covered in stiff bristles and ending in a sharp point long enough to impale a cow.

"Gah—" Sahad edged back, eyes fixed on the creature as it raised its pincers over him.

"Bloody hell," Hummel whispered.

Adol sprang forward, sword in hand, pushing Sahad aside. He whirled his blade so fast that in the semidarkness Laxia couldn't see it at all. A crack echoed through the cave, and the creature reared from Adol's blow, then rushed forward, pouncing at him with all its weight. His shape blurred as he swerved out of its way.

Laxia shook off her stupor and grabbed Sahad by the arm, pulling him away from the action.

Adol had the creature's full attention as he edged deeper into the cave. Laxia knew what he was doing. Drawing it away from the party. He'd made the creature really mad, too. One of its pincers lay twitching on the floor, greenish goo oozing out of the stump. The monster still had plenty of others, though—not to mention stingers that looked like a vastly enlarged rear end of a wasp.

Over the short time she'd known Adol, she had grudgingly progressed from an acknowledgment that his sword skill was better than her own to a reluctant admission that he may be an even better swordsman than her renowned teacher from Romn. But as she saw him moving right now, she realized that in all this time she had never seen the full extent of his capabilities.

His fighting style didn't resemble anything she knew. It was of course impossible to translate the knowledge she'd learned in a training hall into a battle against a giant arachnid, but even with that limitation she could tell that she had never even heard of anyone fighting like this. It was as if he blended all the sword styles that ever existed and synthesized them into a new skill no human could possibly possess. When he danced around the creature, attacking it from opposite sides in the span of seconds, slashing and stabbing as he dodged and rolled to avoid the creature's blows, he looked like a god of swordplay—if there even was such a thing.

But even all that skill would probably not be enough to win the fight. The dark horror that attacked Adol seemed supernatural too. If Adol's skill was godlike, this creature must have come straight from the underworld, spawned by the dark forces as an opponent capable of defeating him.

She knew she would be completely outmatched if she joined the fight, but she didn't have a choice. Adol needed all the help he could get, and she wasn't one to stand back when her friends were in trouble. She drew her rapier, edging forward in a hopeless attempt to find a gap that could make any difference to his attack.

A click of a cocked gun echoed behind her. *Hummel.* No. He was going to hit Adol if he started shooting in this cave. His bullet would ricochet and kill them all. But she didn't have time to voice the warning as a gunshot thundered through the cavern.

The creature reared again, and Laxia saw that one of its eyes was now missing, blown away by the bullet. Hummel's aim was impeccable, but even that wasn't enough. Losing an eye only seemed to make the creature angrier as it lunged at Adol, who had to roll between its legs to avoid being impaled.

Don't just stand there, idiot, move! Gathering all her strength, Laxia rushed forward, aiming rapid stabs at the bulging body, so large that it blocked half of the cavern ahead of them.

The creature whirled toward her, fixing her with its remaining eyes.

"Laxia, no!" Sahad roared, dashing forward with his hammer in hand. He swung it, but it bounced off the creature without doing any obvious harm. A spiked appendage lashed out in his direction, but Adol stepped out of the shadows and severed it with a mighty blow. Hummel fired another shot, and the creature edged back, just enough to allow Laxia and Sahad to dodge its flailing pincers.

Time blended into a continuous stream. Screams—some of them Laxia's own; pounding blows; screeches of steel; gunshots banging one after another. The creature emitted a high-pitched chitter that momentarily nailed her to the spot in a fit of guttural panic. She no longer even tried to aim her rapier as she stabbed at everything in sight, bristles, pincers, eyes, a huge body moving faster than a creature this size had any right to be capable of.

She kept screaming and stabbing even after her senses told her that the creature was no longer moving. Several voices were shouting her name. Someone grabbed her arms, pulling her away. She kept kicking, trying to twist free, stabbing with her rapier until strong hands pinned her arms to her sides and pried the weapon out of her hand.

"Laxia," Adol's voice said by her ear. "Stop. It's dead."

She heaved a few breaths. Her legs gave way and he pulled her up, supporting her against him. She leaned into his chest, grabbing on to him until the world stopped spinning and she was able to comprehend her surroundings again. Sahad, leaning heavily on his hammer. Hummel, slinging his rifle back into the strap at his back in a smooth move that seemed almost tender. Adol, holding her against him as if she were a little girl that needed comfort. She wanted to pull away, to tell him that he had no right to hold a noble lady with such familiarity, but words stuck in her throat and then poured out in a flood of uncontrollable sobs.

It took her a while to steady herself, sniffling, wiping her eyes with both hands before she finally found the strength to disengage from him and stand on her own.

Throughout this battle, Adol had drawn most of the heat to himself. He'd almost died, saving them all. How could he possibly still be so calm?

There were so many things she wanted to say to him. How impressed she was with his bravery, with his incredible sword skill. How ashamed she was that she had frozen, instead of fighting by his side from the start as a proper teammate should. She probably would have made no difference even if she had—but what good was she, if confronting an unexpected enemy drove her into a fit of hysteria, rendering her useless when everyone needed her to be at her best?

Shakily, she raised her eyes to Adol. He held her at arm's length, hands on her shoulders, leaning down so that their faces were level.

"Are you all right?" he asked.

She nodded. Her eyes drifted to the hulking shape humped in the depths of the cave. Even though the spider's head was sliced off and some of its legs were severed or broken, she couldn't stop feeling that it was about to come alive and attack them again.

"I'm sorry," she said. "I—I'll do better next time."

"You did great." Adol smiled and squeezed her shoulders, then dropped his hands away. Hummel handed over her rapier.

It took Laxia a few tries to sheathe it. Her hands would probably never stop shaking again.

"That beach we're headed to," Hummel said, "should be right through that passage ahead. Let's go out there and take a break."

POISON

Adol kept close to Laxia as they walked. She seemed better now, even though she stumbled once or twice and didn't snap at him when he reached out to support her, a clear indication that she was still very shaken. He didn't blame her for the way she'd reacted. He had felt terrified too when the creature crept out of the shadows and nearly devoured Sahad. The fight had been a close one. Even with everyone's help, it was a miracle they'd been able to defeat the creature.

In all his travels, he had never encountered this kind of monster. The incident was another stark reminder that searching for castaways, getting everyone out alive, wasn't all about exploration and discovery. This place was full of real dangers, and even his sword skill may not be enough to face them all.

The path out of the cave climbed over a low stone ridge and down to a secluded beach, surrounded by rocks on all sides. By Adol's calculation, this must be the easternmost point of the island. As they suspected, impassible cliffs surrounded the beach, making the cave tunnel the only means of access.

"This beach must see some amazin' sunrises," Sahad said. "Too bad none o' us are ever here to enjoy 'em."

"How about we name it Sunrise Beach then?" Adol suggested as he took out his map sketch.

Everyone nodded.

The first thing they saw when they approached the water was the giant skeleton of an unknown beast that lay in the surf, half-buried in the sand. Its spine rose out of the water like a rocky crest. Inadvertently, Adol remembered the giant lizard that attacked them before.

Was it another one of those? Probably not. It looked much larger—another species that could well turn out to be even more hostile. He hoped none of them had a habit of frequenting this area. After the fight with the giant spider, he wasn't ready to face a creature like this.

He was considering whether he should bring that up when Laxia stopped abruptly, pointing.

"Look, someone's there!"

There surely was. A young woman knelt in a crevice between rocks, vigorously rubbing two pieces of wood against each other. She looked too busy to notice the newcomers.

"That's not how you light a fire," Hummel said as they approached.

The woman jumped up, a frown on her face quickly relaxing into a relieved smile.

She looked to be a few years older than Adol, dressed in an ornate outfit with a flat cap, an embroidered vest, and knee-length pants. Merchants in Xandria often wore outfits like this, showy and practical at the same time.

"You scared me," the young woman said.

"We apologize." Adol glanced at Laxia, who was surveying the area with a dazed look. Still in shock and in no shape to handle any more hardships for today. He noted the disappointed frown that creased her face when she realized that the woman was alone. Of course she had hoped to find her servant here. Adol wished with all his heart that they would do so, and soon. Laxia could surely use the support.

"Might we assume you were a passenger aboard the *Lombardia?*" he asked the young woman.

She sighed. "Yes, I was. I hope you're the rescue party. It's about time. This ridiculous shipwreck has already delayed me for days."

"We *are* the rescue party," Adol confirmed. "But not off the island, unfortunately." He explained the situation.

The woman's face fell. "A deserted island. Just my luck. How in the world am I supposed to do business if there aren't any customers?"

Business? Customers? Adol frowned. This woman seemed curiously unconcerned about their predicament.

Hummel was already crouching down, his hands moving with amazing speed over the prepared wood pile. In moments, a flame flickered over the kindle, sending a wisp of smoke into the air.

"Wow," the woman said. "You're really good at this. I had a heck of a time lighting the fire every day. You have to teach me that trick some time."

"It's called a flint." Hummel flicked in it his hand, then tucked it into his belt pouch like a magician putting away his wand. "Any piece of metal and rock would do, really, if you also set the kindling correctly. I assume you have a source of fresh water?"

"There's a spring over there." The woman pointed.

Soon they were all sitting around the fire sharing rations, the boiling kettle emitting the fragrant flavor of the herbs they used for tea. Laxia leaned against the rock at her back, sipping from her mug. Adol felt relieved to see her relaxed again, her shock finally receding.

"My name's Dina, by the way," the woman said. "And if I may say so, you all look a bit disheveled for a rescue party."

"We ran into a problem on the way here," Adol explained. "You haven't tried to venture inland, have you?"

"I went as far as a cave tunnel over that ridge," the woman said. "It looked very creepy. I hate dark spaces, so I figured if I fended for myself here, rescue would come eventually. You surely took your time with it though. I hope that village of yours isn't far away."

"A few hours," Adol said. "We should get going soon if we want to make it all the way back before dark."

He frowned as he noticed Sahad leaning against the rock next to Laxia, pale in the face. Shocked? With all the excitement, he'd never checked on the man after the fight was over. It was really a wonder they had all come out of it with no more than a few bruises and scratches.

"Sahad?" he said. "Are you all right?"

"I . . . " The large man shifted position. "I don't feel s' good. My shoulder . . . It hurts."

Adol moved over and knelt by his side, folding away the collar of Sahad's shirt to expose a large puncture wound. The skin around it was already turning leaden, oozing with pus.

"Poison," Dina said. "He looks like he's been stabbed with a poisoned stiletto. I saw this happen once in a market in Sounion, when a local nobleman—" She broke off under Adol's gaze.

"Not a stiletto," Hummel said. "A stinger. That spider jumped out at Sahad first, remember?"

Dina edged away. "Did you say ... spider?"

"Long story." Hummel knelt down on Sahad's other side, looking over his head at Adol. Laxia scurried away to a spot next to Dina, green in the face.

"We need to drain out the poisoned blood," Hummel said.

Adol nodded and pulled out his dagger, holding it over the flames to sterilize it, then up in the air to cool it off. Sahad followed his movements with a mesmerized look.

"What are ye goin' to do?" he whimpered.

"We'll cut the wound open," Adol explained. "So that the blood can run out until it's clean. This is the only way to prevent the poison from spreading too fast." He turned to Hummel. "Ready?"

Hummel nodded, locking his hands over Sahad's arms to hold him in place.

"I—Wait—Aaaahhhhh!" Sahad screamed as Adol sliced through the wound.

"Are you all right?" Adol asked.

Sahad nodded. His breath came in shallow gasps. He looked feverish.

"What you really need," Dina said, "is an antidote."

"Good to know," Hummel said through clenched teeth. He slowly released his grip and sat on his heels, watching the sickly liquid streaming out of the wound.

"No, really," Dina insisted. "I heard these could be prepared if you crush digitalis leaves with a few drops of juniper extract. There are some specific ingredients I could probably figure out if I had some poison from the creature that stung him. Most of them are common enough. For example, purple lichen that grows on these rocks would repel bees and cure bee stings, and some of the extracts I have here in my bag can surely—"

"Are you a doctor?" Adol asked.

She let out a short laugh. "Me? No. I'm a merchant. But I do know a thing or two about potions and repellents. Before traveling to Xandria, I used to run a shop over in Romn—and I would never sell a potion without knowing the exact recipe, mind you. Saves a lot of money, if you can mix your own. Got a lot of happy customers, I did."

"Glad to hear it," Adol said. He nodded to Hummel, who rummaged in his bag and pulled out a clean piece of cloth. A bandage would be a good idea, once the poison ran out. He hoped Sahad was strong enough to counter the rest.

"In any case," Dina said. "You mentioned a spider, did you? If you could get me some of its venom—"

"We're fresh out, I'm afraid," Adol said.

"Actually—" Laxia sat up straight. She looked as pale as Sahad. "That's not true. That creature's still out there. I think I should be able to locate its poison gland."

Adol looked at her hesitantly. He knew exactly what she was suggesting, and how much this was costing her. The thought of going back to that cave and dissecting the corpse of the horrendous creature that had nearly killed them all made him feel nauseated. It had to be a thousand times worse for Laxia, after the meltdown she'd had back there. Yet none of them would hesitate if it meant saving Sahad's life.

"Let's do it then." He turned to Sahad. "Can you walk?"

"He looks to be in no shape," Dina protested. "I can stay behind and keep an eye on him, if you want."

Adol shook his head. "Too dangerous. We need to get out of this gorge while we still have some daylight left."

"I—I think I can make it." Sahad shakily got to his feet, leaning heavily on Adol's arm.

It didn't take long to retrace their steps to the large, dim cavern. Dina let out a muffled swear as she saw the giant shape slumped by the wall. Several small spiders scurried around it, but they retreated out of sight when the party approached.

"We'll need the head," Laxia said. "You didn't blow it off completely, did you?" She was looking at Hummel, who shifted uncomfortably in place.

"I wasn't exactly focused on preserving it at the time," he admitted.

"Well." She leaned forward and used her rapier to sift through the debris around the body. Adol supported Sahad, looking around tensely. In all the excitement, it hadn't really occurred to him until now that the giant spider may not have been living alone. If one or more of its relatives chose this time to descend on the party in force, it would probably mean the end of them.

"Here," Laxia said triumphantly. She straightened out, holding the monstrous spider head by the sides, carefully to avoid the bristling stingers and pincers. The sight made Adol's skin creep. He couldn't believe Laxia could touch it so calmly.

"Why don't we bring it with us and dissect it in a safer place?" he suggested.

"Bring it? How?" Laxia stared at her hideous trophy.

"Here." Dina rummaged in her bag and brought out a large, folded sack. "Put it in. It will be nice and snug." She held the sack open. Laxia hesitated, then dropped her burden inside.

"Now let's move," Adol said. "We don't have much time before it gets dark."

On their way back through the caves and over the web bridges, Dina talked incessantly about trade, commerce, and all kinds of gossip she'd heard at different markets throughout the realm. It made for a good distraction. Sahad wasn't doing too well. Once or twice he stumbled and sank to the ground, so that in the end Adol and Hummel had to drag him along between the two of them.

By the time they reached their old campsite near the cave entrance, Sahad looked feverish and half-delirious. They lay him down on the grass and Adol kept by his side, watching Dina and Laxia lay out the spider head on a flat rock, next to a set of bottles and pouches from Dina's bag. Hummel busied himself with the fire.

Here in broad daylight, the creature's head looked even more hideous. Crowned with four dark eyes on top—one blown off by Hummel's bullet—and a row of smaller eyes along the bottom, it seemed to glare at them with reproach. A set of pincers, stingers, and mandibles in different sizes and shapes bristled around the rim, with a few of them sliced off. In retrospect, Adol felt glad the light in that cave had been dim enough not to see all these details.

Laxia looked remarkably composed as she took out her book and spread it on the grass, leafing through the pages until she found the correct diagram.

"This is where the poison flows out." She held out her belt knife, slicing around one of the stingers. Dina reached over, handing her an empty bottle.

"Pour the poison in here," she said. "Whatever is left after we're done will fetch a fair price when we finally get back to civilization."

What an optimist. Adol sat back on his heels, watching Laxia remove a greenish sac and puncture it with her knife point to let the poison drip into the narrow opening of the bottle. Dina took it reverently and measured out a drop, sniffing thoughtfully.

"We're in luck," she finally said. "This kind of spider venom can be countered with a fairly simple concoction." She mixed ingredients in a small mortar, adding pinches and drops from different pouches and bottles to produce a sticky greenish paste that emitted a strong medicinal smell.

"Here." She handed it to Adol. "Spread it over his wound. And bandage it well. He should be feeling better by morning."

Adol woke up earlier than usual to the smells of roast meat and campfire smoke. Laxia and Dina were still asleep, but Sahad and Hummel were already out, so Adol hurried to join them by the campfire.

Sahad sat leaning against the rocks at his back with a mug of tea in his hand. He still looked pale, with dark circles under his eyes, but seemed worlds better than last night. He smiled when he saw Adol and moved over to make room for him.

"How are you feeling?" Adol asked as he sat down.

"Hungry," Sahad said. "I feel I could eat a cow. Look what Hummel was able to catch with one of his rope traps."

"Rope traps?" Adol looked at the two rabbits, neatly skinned and sprinkled with spices, sizzling over the coals.

"I set some out last night," Hummel said. "Figured after all the excitement, it wouldn't hurt any of us to have a good breakfast."

Adol nodded. Once things had settled down, he definitely needed to learn some of Hummel's wilderness tricks.

After a delicious breakfast, they quickly packed up and set out on the road back to the village. Sahad still walked unsteadily, but even with frequent stops they were able to make it to Castaway Village early in the afternoon.

Adol and Hummel settled Sahad on one of the cots in the medical area Kiergaard had set up, which everyone had started referring to as the clinic. While they were busy, Dina wandered around the village. She looked impressed as she surveyed the fortifications, the watchtower Dogi and the captain had built in their spare time, the sturdy work bench under the rock ledge next to the clinic, and the well beside the lodge that used a clever pulley mechanism designed by Dogi to direct the water from the stream into the common area close to the fire. Dogi followed her closely, with a look of suspicion on his face as she found her way into the supply area and began a silent inventory of the stacked goods.

"Not bad," she announced at length. "I think I have enough here to work with."

"Work with?" Adol blinked.

"I told you I was a merchant, didn't I? I'm going to set up shop—right here." She pointed at the space in front of the crate stack under a deep rock ledge.

Dogi frowned. "A shop? What're we supposed to do with a shop? We're all castaways on this island, and none of us have any money."

She shrugged. "What difference does that make? We can switch it up. How about an item-for-item exchange? A perfect system, in the absence of real money." She turned to Captain Barbaros, who was watching from a respectful distance. "How about this. I will be your new supply manager. I will oversee the exchange and distribution of materials, so that they are all used in the most efficient way. In my spare time, I will be scouting the beaches for driftage and useful supplies. Everything extra that I find—collectibles, items of value that can't be used for the village's needs—are mine to keep. Deal?"

"As long as we don't locate the items' rightful owners," the captain corrected.

Dina nodded, but she seemed a bit disappointed. "Fair enough."

ATTACKS

Advisor Urgunata wasn't particularly tall. But in her anger she seemed gigantic as she towered over the three girls, her face pinched into an angry frown.

"The sanctuary is destroyed," she thundered. "All because you unleashed a flash flood to put out that fire. Not once in the history of this Temple has an incident of such magnitude ever occurred." Her eyes fixed on Dana. "And to make matters worse, Dana, you had Olga and Sarai, two of our most exemplary trainees, acting as your accomplices. I expected better from them, at least. I'm afraid I have no other choice but to put all three of you in seclusion until the Maiden herself decides your fate."

Dana shrank away from the accusing gaze. She felt terrible for dragging Olga and Sarai into this too. Except that she'd needed their Essence to accomplish her plan. And now they were all in so much trouble because of her.

"I know an apology won't make this right," she said miserably. "But . . . I'm very sorry."

"I'm sorry too. You've been showing such promise. But after this—" Urgunata stopped abruptly as she heard the shuffle of approaching footsteps.

A chill ran down Dana's spine as she recognized the newcomer— her frail form, her cane, her flowing white hair. *The Maiden of the Great Tree.* Their situation was already bad enough, and it was about to become so much worse.

The Maiden leaned heavily on her cane as she stopped in front of the group. Her clear eyes ran over the three girls with cool appraisal.

"Dana, is it?" the Maiden said. "Of course. I should have known.

I still haven't forgotten our little encounter. And these are your inseparable friends Olga and Sarai, I presume?"

Wait. Was that a smile forming on the old woman's lips?

Dana swallowed, unable to draw her gaze away. She should be begging for her friends right now, but the smile on the old woman's lips held her back. Were they still being reprimanded and punished? Or...

"Well done, girls," the Maiden said.

Urgunata gaped. "Y-your Eminence...?"

"You've summoned them here to reward them, haven't you, Urgunata?"

"I..."

"Had these children not taken action," the Maiden went on, "the Great Tree and the Temple would have been in grave danger, perhaps even destroyed. Thanks to them, all we have to do is mop the floors and put this incident behind us. The hallway was due for a cleaning anyway. And yes, the sanctuary needs to be rebuilt, but that's been coming for years, hasn't it? One could say these flood waters did us a favor by sparing us the demolition work. A worthy alternative to seeing everything here burn down, don't you think?"

Urgunata took a step back. "Y-yes, of course, my lady."

The Maiden nodded. "I shall see to it personally that Her Majesty knows full well what transpired here today. I'm certain she will be very impressed with our three most talented trainees."

Urgunata's hands trembled as she bowed her head. "As you wish, Your Eminence. The destruction they caused is inexcusable, but—"

The scene faded.

When Adol woke up, it took him a few moments to remember where he was. The leaf tent they'd built last night at the edge of a new jungle area they were about to explore, a few hours' walk from Castaway Village. He lay staring into the ceiling for a while, watching the dance of the sun patches filtering through the wavering tree canopy onto the tent roof.

The previous night, Sahad and Laxia had gotten into a heavy argument when they ventured into the area, wet and muddy to the point that made it difficult to find an area to set up camp. Laxia wanted to call it Schlamm Jungle, in honor of an explorer who had pioneered research on wildlife habitats and symbiotic species. Sahad, annoyed about all the sinkholes that had thoroughly soaked his pants and boots, proposed Ol' Mudhole as a name. In the end, Adol and Hummel had sided with Laxia to break the tie, and Sahad had refused to talk to them all evening.

Outside the tent, the rest of the group was already finishing breakfast. This had become a habit by now, everyone greeting Adol with knowing looks as he woke up late and came out to a fully cooked meal. Today it consisted of roasted partridges served on a bed of palm leaves with a garnish of baked roots and fragrant herbs. Apparently, Hummel had been out on an early hunt before surprising everyone with his unexpected cooking skills. Was he trying to make amends with Sahad for last night? Probably not, but the fisherman did look unusually content as he sat beside the fire.

"Look who's awake," Sahad said.

Adol didn't respond as he sat down beside him, leaning over to take his share. The birds tasted delicious, cooked just right. Hummel and Dogi would probably rival each other once they all returned to the village.

He was finishing his meal when a gruff-looking man emerged from the jungle and stopped at the edge of the glade, staring at the party.

Tall and broad-shouldered, he had a square jaw, a heavy forehead, and a look of suspicion that seemed to be permanently etched into his stern features. His hair was trimmed very short, military style. His jacket gleamed with polished brass buttons bearing an elaborate dragon design, his leather breeches tucked into his tall, tightly laced boots. The field uniform of a Romun military officer, defaced by mud and seawater after the shipwreck but still recognizable. A long scar crossed the stranger's cheek all the way up to the eyebrow.

"Military police, right?" Adol asked.

The man frowned. "And how would a civilian like you know that?"

Adol shrugged. "I've met a few in my day. I take it you're from the *Lombardia*?"

The man didn't bother to respond. His eyes darted around the group. "Is this all of you?"

"No," Laxia said. "There are more survivors back at Castaway Village. Captain Barbaros is there too."

The man nodded. "A good man, the captain. And you are?" He measured Adol with a heavy glare.

Adol introduced the group. He didn't like the scrutiny in the man's gaze, but it didn't seem like the best idea to erupt into an argument. Besides, the others seemed fine with it. Only Hummel appeared tense, avoiding eye contact. Back in civilization, transporters and Romun military police must be natural enemies, Adol guessed.

"I'm Euron," the Romun said. "Catch you all later." He turned to leave.

"You are not joining us?" Laxia called out in surprise.

"Not now. I'm in pursuit of a dangerous criminal." Before anyone could respond, he disappeared into the bushes.

"Boy, I tell ya, that guy is somethin' else," Sahad said after a pause.

"He's a professional." Hummel's voice held quiet approval as he looked after Euron. Despite the dense undergrowth, no movement or sounds could be detected from that direction. Adol remembered how Euron had first emerged, so quietly that no one had noticed him until he was already standing in the glade. Clearly, the man was very good at stealth, a quality that probably ranked very high in Hummel's book.

What was it that he'd said about a dangerous criminal? Military paranoia? It had to be. It seemed unlikely that a criminal would end up on a deserted island. Still, Adol kept wondering about it as they packed up the camp and moved on.

"This is really annoying," Laxia said after a few minutes, pulling her foot out of her boot, then her boot out of the mud. She hopped on one foot to put the boot back on.

"That's exactly what I was talkin' about," Sahad grumbled. "*Schlamm Jungle.* Yer Schlamm, whoever he was, wouldn't be happy to hear 'bout this, I tell ye."

"Professor Schlamm is already dead," Laxia said.

"Whatever. Ol' Mudhole's what it is." Sahad turned away and trudged on ahead.

Adol didn't comment, but deep inside he felt Sahad had a point. The swampy jungle was really annoying to move through. It seemed like such a relief when they finally made it to the firmer ground on the other end, where sunlight peeking through the leaves heralded an open space ahead. Another beach? Adol hoped so. After a few hours in this place, he missed the open air.

This was the smallest beach they'd discovered so far. Rocks rose out of the water just off the shore, a row of natural wave breakers that made the water here still, like a lake. Fish darting under the surface were visible as clearly as if this were an aquarium.

"I'd call it Old Rock Coast," Sahad suggested. "Nothin' but old rocks everywhere."

"Not true." Hummel pointed with his eyes to a spot behind the nearest rock formation. Peering in that direction, Adol imagined he saw movement.

A person?

Inadvertently, he remembered Euron's words about a dangerous criminal. Had they just found him?

"Hey!" Adol called out.

After a moment, a timid voice spoke from behind the rocks: "D-don't come any closer! I'm—I'm armed!"

"He sounds terrified," Hummel remarked.

"Please, leave me alone!" the voice begged.

Adol frowned. That didn't really sound like a criminal.

"Please don't be afraid," Laxia called out. "We're castaways from the *Lombardia*."

They waited out another pause. Then a young man emerged from the rocks and approached them cautiously.

Skinny and slightly built, he was dressed in an old-fashioned worn green vest and breeches covered by an oversized naval coat and girded with numerous straps and pouches probably designed to carry all kinds of tools. A frayed tie held together the collar of his mud-stained shirt that must have been white once but had seen lots of misuse. Despite his earlier threat, Adol could see no weapons on him, not even a dagger at his belt. He ran his nervous gaze over the party and fixed it on the jungle behind them, as if expecting someone else.

Definitely not a dangerous criminal—unless, of course, he was very good at pretending.

"Why in the world were you hidin' from us?" Sahad demanded.

The man straightened his vest nervously. "There's this scary-looking man chasing me. I don't know what he wants, but I barely managed to get away...Oh, where are my manners? My name's Licht. I was on the *Lombardia* too."

Licht. Adol tried to guess the man's origins. His speech was educated, both in the word choice and in the way he rolled his syllables, as if mindful about preserving every sound. This kind of speech came only with years of schooling—like Laxia's, except that this young man also seemed much more timid than a noble. Added to his highly practical outfit, probably a highly skilled professional of some sort? Adol introduced the party and explained the situation.

"Castaway Village," Licht said. "This man isn't from there by any chance, is he?"

Sahad scratched his head. "A scary-lookin' man? I don't recall—"

"I think he means that Romun military officer we saw at the entrance to the forest," Hummel remarked. "Euron. He was looking for a criminal, wasn't he?"

"A criminal, eh?" Sahad fixed his eyes on Licht. "Did ye do somethin' bad?"

Licht shook his head. "No, I'm not a criminal, I swear! I have no clue why he was after me. I just—"

"Either way," Laxia put in, "I'm sure, if we meet him again, we can clear up this misunderstanding. Why don't you come with us to the village, Licht?"

Licht had serious trouble keeping up as they retraced their steps through the jungle. Obviously whatever extensive education he'd received hadn't included any physical training. A wonder he could have given a slip to a man like Euron.

Only after they reached the village did they realize that Hummel was no longer in their party. Adol had no idea when the man had slipped away. He had no time to wonder, because he saw Dogi rushing toward them with a concerned face.

"Adol! Man, am I glad to see you." Dogi nodded to Licht but didn't comment on the new arrival.

"What's happened?" Adol asked.

"Captain Barbaros was attacked. He's hurt pretty bad."

"Attacked?" Sahad frowned. "By beasts?"

"By a person, or so we think."

Adol blinked. The only people on this island were the castaways, most of them gathered here, at the village. They all looked up to the captain for leadership and guidance. Surely none of the castaways would possibly do Captain Barbaros any harm.

"Where's the captain?" he asked.

"In bed. Doctor Kiergaard says the injuries aren't life-threatening, but—"

Adol didn't listen to the rest as he swept past Dogi into the lodge.

The captain was sitting up, leaning into a pile of pillows at his back with Doctor Kiergaard in attendance. Bandages covered his upper arm, chest, and leg. He looked pale, but the familiar sparkle of humor twinkled in his eyes, showing that his spirit hadn't suffered because of the incident.

"Captain..." Laxia's lips trembled as she knelt at his bedside.

Adol glanced questioningly at Kiergaard.

"He's lost a lot of blood," the doctor said. "Don't stress him out." He patted Adol's shoulder and stepped past him out of the cave.

The captain pulled up to settle into a more upright position. Adol rushed forward to support him, but the captain stopped him with a gesture.

"How did this happen?" Adol asked.

The captain sighed. "To be honest, I'm not quite sure. I was out patrolling the village when I heard a voice call out to me near the shore. The moment I turned to face it, something sliced into me."

"Something?"

"It felt like a knife. Except that I never saw any weapons. Very peculiar. I can only guess I might've lost consciousness for a moment." The captain shook his head, as if embarrassed.

"Did you recognize the voice?"

"No. The only thing I'm certain about is that it belonged to a man. And this is another peculiar thing. I know everyone in the village pretty well. But this voice—"

"Anyone could have deliberately altered their voice not to be recognized," Laxia pointed out.

"True." The captain looked uncomfortable, as if the mere suggestion of a deception pained him almost as much as the fact of the attack itself.

"I assume you didn't have a chance to take a good look either," Adol said.

"No. He was wearing a long robe, and I only saw him from behind...I can't believe I was taken by surprise."

"I found the captain lying on the ground," Dogi put in. "I called for help, and Kiergaard and I brought him here. That's when we noticed this note on the table."

"A note?"

Dogi held out a crumpled piece of paper with words written unevenly in bold red ink:

I WILL RIP YOU ASUNDER. EVERY LAST ONE OF YOU. — NEMO

"Nemo?" Sahad frowned. "We don't have anyone that goes by that name."

"Not that we know of," Dogi agreed.

"It's not a real name," came a voice from the door.

Euron. Adol saw Licht edge backward when the Romun strode into the room, but the newcomer didn't pay him any notice as he reached over and took the note out of Dogi's hands, holding it carefully by the edge as he examined it.

"Not a real name?" Laxia asked. "What do you mean?"

Euron looked up. "'Nemo' is a Romun word. It means 'nameless'."

"Why would anyone want to call himself 'nameless'?" Sahad wondered.

"A criminal would. In this case, a serial killer. In the Romun capital, he is known as the Nameless Ripper. His victims fit no known pattern. He kills men and women, always with a bladed instrument. And at the scene of his crime, he always leaves a note that he signs as 'Nemo'."

The captain nodded. "I've heard the rumors. The Nameless Ripper has the Romun capital trembling with fear. You don't believe that—"

"Yes, I do," Euron said. "It's him."

Dogi shook his head in disbelief. "What are the odds of a famous serial killer ending up on this island?"

Euron crossed the room and settled into a chair. He looked at ease, as if he'd always lived here. "Higher than you think, unfortunately. I've been pursuing the Nameless Ripper for a while now. I got a tip from my partner that a man who fit Nameless's profile was preparing to board a ship."

"Not the..." Laxia paused, wide-eyed.

"Yes, the *Lombardia*. As soon as I got that tip, I wasted no time securing passage. I was supposed to rendezvous with my partner on board, so we could take down Nameless together, but... Well, you all know what happened."

"Y-y-you're sayin' we were on the same ship as some psycho serial killer?" Sahad stammered.

"That's right. Worse, now we know for sure that Nameless is still alive, somewhere on this island. Hell, he could already be in Castaway Village."

"N-no," Laxia whispered.

"What's this Nameless guy look like?" Sahad said.

Euron looked away. "Unfortunately, I don't have a physical description. I was supposed to find out from my partner after we boarded the ship, but—"

A scream from the outside interrupted his words.

Adol rushed out. The others followed.

The camp looked quiet. Smoke rose from the campfire. Dina, shifting boxes at her trading outpost, looked up at them and spread her hands with a puzzled expression. No one else was in sight.

"I'll take the beach," Euron said. "You take the hill."

He ran off without waiting for a response. Adol rushed in the opposite direction, with Laxia and Sahad in his wake.

A short way up the hill, Sir Carlan lay on the ground, clasping his leg.

"Sir Carlan!" Laxia exclaimed. "Are you all right?"

"Do I look all right?" Sir Carlan snapped.

Adol felt relieved as they knelt around the nobleman. At least the injury wasn't bad enough to affect Sir Carlan's temper.

"He's bleeding," Sahad said.

"It looks like a blade wound. Just like…" Laxia's voice trailed off as she met Adol's eyes.

"Can you tell us who did it, Sir Carlan?" Adol asked.

The nobleman shook his head. "It happened too fast. It was a person, that's all I could tell. He swept away before I could do anything."

He. At least that part matched the captain's story, even if it wasn't much to go by. Adol leaned down and hooked the injured man's arm around his neck.

"Hold on to me," he said. "We'll get you to Doctor Kiergaard."

The doctor himself was already rushing toward them, followed by Dogi and Euron. Together, they lifted Sir Carlan up and carried him to Kiergaard's clinic.

NIGHTTIME CONVERSATION

By the evening, Captain Barbaros felt well enough to join everyone at the campfire. He still looked pale and had a slight limp, but it was reassuring to see him up and about.

"I can't stand this any longer," Sir Carlan complained. He also looked much better but continued to nurse his injury, reclining near the fire with Doctor Kiergaard in attendance. "If this murderer is among us, I demand that he reveal himself." He looked at Licht, who shifted uncomfortably under his gaze. "The newest member of our fold certainly seems suspicious to me."

"Really, Sir Carlan," the captain protested. "This is uncalled for. Licht arrived here after I was already injured."

"No matter." Carlan lifted his chin. "He could have easily snuck into the village, attacked you, then pretended to—"

"No, he couldn't have," Adol said. "It takes hours to get here from the jungle where we found Licht. We were with him all the way. He couldn't possibly have been in two places at the same time."

Sir Carlan pursed his lips indignantly. From across the fire, Licht nodded to Adol with gratitude.

"We'll find the culprit, I assure you," the captain said. "I will lead the investigation myself."

Sir Carlan crossed his arms on his chest. "You do that, Captain. As for me, I refuse to spend another second trapped on this island with a murderer."

The captain sighed. "Getting off this island is a priority for us all, Sir Carlan. At present, however, we do not possess the means to—"

"Rubbish." Sir Carlan tossed his head impatiently. "Didn't the musclehead build a boat already?" He pointed his chin at Dogi.

"Why not use it to sail off the coast and hail a passing ship?"

Dogi's lips twitched as he looked into the fire.

The captain shook his head. "The Isle of Seiren is so feared by sailors that no ship would dare to venture into its coastal waters. You would need to sail far out into the open sea to even have a chance at hailing a passing vessel. It would be suicide to sail that far out in such a tiny boat."

"Do you have a better idea then?"

"Not at the moment, no."

"I thought so. And I'd say it's time for us to act. We'll never escape this island if you keep rejecting every proposed solution. Besides, Captain, it's your fault the *Lombardia* sank in the first place. If anyone should venture out to sea to get help, it's you."

"Sir Carlan," Laxia protested. "You shouldn't—"

"It's all right," Captain Barbaros said. "Sir Carlan is entitled to his opinion, just like everyone else here. On my side, I—"

He didn't have a chance to finish his sentence. A roar shook the evening air. It seemed to come from very close by. Alison screamed and drew closer to the fire. Everyone else jumped up from their seats.

"Sounds terribly familiar, doesn't it?" Sahad reached for his weapon.

"Do you mean . . . ?" Laxia's voice sank to a whisper.

"The monster that attacked me before. Yep, I'd recognize that sucker anywhere."

"Here at camp?"

Adol was already running, drawing his sword on the way.

The giant bipedal lizard occupied the sea overlook, planted on the camp's mid-level terrace near the seaside. It surely looked like the beast that had chased Sahad before. Adol had no idea how it had been able to get past the barricades unnoticed by anyone. He didn't have time to wonder though. The beast attacked on sight, lunging toward him with its jaws open, as if intent on swallowing him whole.

Adol barely had time to duck. Teeth snapped beside his ear, so close that he felt whish of air on his skin. He twisted around and raised his blade, aiming for the creature's nose—a strategy that had worked for him once before—but the beast must have learned its lesson. It swerved away from the sword tip, the edge of the blade sliding harmlessly down its scaly neck. Curses, this beast's hide was tougher than chainmail. Added to its dagger-like claws and teeth, it made Adol feel badly outmatched.

Other villagers joined the battle, stabbing and swinging, throwing rocks, but all these attacks proved equally ineffective. Their blows seemed only to anger the creature.

Just when Adol thought they were done for, a gunshot rang from the distance, echoing through the terrain. The beast shuddered and reared, and Adol saw a thin streak of blood ooze down its cheek.

A lone man stood on the camp's upper terrace above the action, aiming a rifle.

Hummel.

Another shot banged. The beast turned and ran, trampling down the rocks, across the main area, and out of camp.

From across the distance, Adol saluted Hummel with a fist to his hand in front of his chest and received a nod in return.

Adol, Dogi, and Euron spent the next hour inspecting the barricades for possible breaches and tightening a few loose boards. None of them had any idea how the creature was able to get so close without anyone noticing, but for now, there seemed to be nothing else to do, so they returned to the fireside to join the other castaways, huddled around with concerned looks. Sunset flared in the sky, blood-red and ominous. Or was it just the mood?

"First the Nameless Ripper," Sir Carlan complained. "And now this. What is wrong with this wretched island?"

No one responded as they sat around, staring into the flames.

"What was that lizard thing?" Euron wondered.

"We've met a couple of them as we explored," Adol said. "Or maybe it was the same one. I wonder if it followed us here." It was an unnerving thought. He hoped these creatures weren't *that* intelligent.

"So there's at least one, maybe more of these giant aggressive lizards, and we don't know a thing about them?" Dogi said.

Adol turned to Laxia. She looked at him defiantly.

"What?" she snapped.

"I think it's time you told us what you know."

"What makes you think I know anything about this creature, Mr. Christin?"

Adol waited. After a moment, Laxia's gaze wavered.

"Very well," she said. "I think that creature is almost certainly a

Primordial."

"A Primordial?" Sahad frowned. "Somehow the name rings a bell."

"T's watchtower," Adol reminded. "One of the notes mentioned Primordials, remember?"

"Oh, right. So what are these Primordials, anyway?"

Laxia looked hesitant, as if the topic were somehow personal to her. "Long ago, before the human race came into existence, enormous creatures of unimaginable power ruled the Earth, before going extinct. These creatures are known as Primordials. Though diverse in form, their defining traits are their reptilian appearance and ferocious disposition."

Sahad narrowed his eyes, as if it took effort to absorb the information. Laxia did have a tendency to use fancy vocabulary when she felt unsettled.

Sir Carlan scoffed. "You bated our breaths for this nonsense? I'm disappointed in you, Lady Laxia. Common folks blabber out all kinds of tales. We, the nobles, should know better than to repeat these things."

"I've heard of Primordials too," Kiergaard said. "According to reports, fossils of these giant creatures have been found deep underground. Certain academic circles within the Romun Empire have recently begun more research into the matter."

Sir Carlan grunted and looked away. Clearly, Kiergaard had risen in the nobleman's hierarchy after successfully treating his leg wound.

Sahad looked at Laxia in wonder. "How do you know all this? Are you some kinda expert on these Primordial beasts?"

Laxia lowered her gaze. "Yes…um…I won't bore you with the details, but I'm well-versed on the subject."

Sahad nodded eagerly. "Finally, some good news. Since ya know 'bout 'em, ya can help us figure out how to fight 'em off. Ain't that right, li'l lady?"

"I don't know how much help I can truly provide on this topic."

Dogi shook his head. "Damn. First a serial killer, now Primordials. That's two too many things we gotta worry about right now."

"I grow sicker and wearier each day I'm forced to breathe the same air as you all," Sir Carlan announced loudly. With a grunt, he scrambled to his feet and limped off in the direction of the lodge.

Dogi scratched his head, watching the nobleman's retreating shape. "What a pain in the ass that guy is."

Adol could have sworn he saw the captain grin, just for an instant.

"The sun is beginning to set," the captain said. "Adol, let's gather some volunteers and take turns keeping watch tonight. Please try to get some rest, everyone. No one is to wander off by themselves. Make sure you're always with someone."

Laxia stopped by the ladder and glanced up the village watchtower. The structure looked even more impressive in the dark, taller than a ship's mast, supported by a bundle of logs held together with waxed ropes, nails, and sticky tree sap. From down here, the observation deck at the top seemed tiny, even though she knew it to be large and sturdy enough to hold at least three people.

Adol was up there, taking the first watch. She was aware she was violating the captain's orders by venturing out of the sleeping quarters on her own, but she needed to speak to him alone, and it seemed like she would never get a better chance.

She felt dizzy as she started up the ladder. She had never been all the way at the top and hadn't realized how much the structure swayed, even though the night was a still one, with almost no breeze. The ladder creaked and moaned under her feet. Only her certainty that this tower could easily withstand the combined weights of Dogi, Sahad, and Adol, who sometimes occupied the observation platform together, kept her going.

By now she'd long stopped being surprised how bright the nights were on this island. The sky blazed with myriads of stars, the light of the rising moons reflecting off the water to coat the landscape in a suffused gleam. The dying embers in the campfire down below emitted a mysterious glow. The tall mountain peak loomed in the distance, a dark silhouette against the night sky. Farther on the horizon, a pale streak still lingered, harboring the remnants of the daylight.

She pulled herself up over the edge of the platform.

Adol was sitting with his back against the tower's central support, gazing at the sea. He reached over and helped Laxia to climb all the way up, shifting to make room for her.

"Ugh. This is quite a difficult climb, actually," Laxia said. Now that she had made it, the situation seemed awkward. She hoped Adol wouldn't get any wrong ideas. Starting the conversation was harder than she'd expected as she settled beside him, keeping a conscious distance from the rail running around the edge of the platform.

The structure swayed slightly. Or was she just imagining it because of the sway of the waves? From here the water looked closer than it did from down below, as if they were on a ship again, sailing in open sea.

Blazes, how did Adol manage to look so easy and relaxed sitting at this height on such stiff boards?

"Today was rather eventful," she said at length. "I'm having a difficult time falling asleep. And ... I thought—" She swallowed. Why was it so difficult to talk? "I couldn't think of anything else to do at this hour, so ... Here." She handed him a loosely wrapped bundle. Adol opened it to reveal a small pie, topped with seafood.

He raised his eyebrows. "Did you make this?"

She lifted her chin. "Yes. Even though, I have to admit, I've never prepared this dish before, so I can't vouch for its flavor."

"It looks pretty tasty."

"Really?" She surveyed it critically. "I thought the end result would look more appetizing than this. Go ahead, eat it."

"Thanks." Adol broke off a piece and chewed thoughtfully. "It's quite good, actually. Would you like some?"

She didn't feel that hungry, but it didn't seem fit for a cook to refuse her own dish, even if this whole concept of cooking was new to her. Back in the Roswell Manor, they had their own cooks—and cooks for the cooks too, at the height of their family's power.

She took a small piece and nibbled on it. The pie was surprisingly good, even if, in retrospect, she should have worked more on the presentation.

"Anything on your mind?" Adol asked. He finished the pie and put down the wrapping, shaking the crumbs off his hands.

"Hummel." It wasn't the topic Laxia had come here to discuss, but it would do as a start. "He hasn't returned to the village with us after we found Licht. But then he showed up just in time to take a shot at that Primordial—only to disappear again right after the fight. Why do you think he's acting so strangely?"

Adol shrugged. "If I were to guess, he probably has an issue with Euron. A Romun military policeman has to stand high on the transporters' blacklist, if there is such a thing. Besides, he probably prefers to camp in the wilderness rather than fall into other people's routine. I'm sure he'll join us again at some point."

"I hope you're right. However good he is with that rifle, it isn't safe to be alone out there."

Adol looked at her sideways. "You came all the way up here to talk about Hummel?"

She coughed to hide her embarrassment. "I—I was interested in your opinion about him—but, no. I came here to tell you how I know so much about Primordials."

Now that she had broached the subject, it seemed ridiculous that she would go through all the trouble of cooking for him, climbing all the way up the tower at night with a serial killer lurking around, just to talk to him about her past. But she needed to get this off her chest, and Adol seemed to be the only one who would listen—not laugh at her or challenge her, but just sit next to her in quiet companionship. If only Franz were here. But she knew wishing for impossible things never helped.

"My father is—*was*—an archeological scholar who specialized in the study of ancient species."

Adol nodded. He didn't say anything, and Laxia was grateful for it. His silence made it easier for her to proceed.

"As a child, I often visited his laboratory, and he would have me accompany him on his excavations." She swallowed. "I loved and respected my father. He was my whole world."

Her voice trailed into silence. Images flowed in her head. The library at Roswell Manor. Smells of dust and parchment. Giant tomes scattered over the massive wooden table in the center of the room. *Father.* Perhaps she shouldn't be speaking about him in the past tense. He may still be out there somewhere, for all she knew. But as with Franz, no amount of wishing was going to bring him back.

"What happened to him?" Adol asked quietly.

Laxia swallowed again. These lumps in her throat were getting quite annoying. "The year I turned sixteen, my father grew so obsessed with his research that he abandoned his house and lands. In response, his people began rioting throughout the countryside."

She remembered it so well, that day when she and her brother had to address the crowd of peasants at the manor's gate. Father was nowhere to be found. Sixteen and frightened witless, Laxia had no idea what was going to happen.

"The rioting finally ceased when my brother assumed control of House Roswell," she said. "But the loyalty our house once commanded had already been lost. Soon after, the other noble houses successfully unseated my brother. It drove my mother ill. And just three months ago, House Roswell was forced to relinquish its titles and lands." She'd lost everything in those three months. Perhaps running away from home to look for Father hadn't been the best thing to do under the circumstances. And now, because of her recklessness, she had lost the last person who always stood by her no matter what, loyal until the very end.

Franz.

With all the time that had passed since the shipwreck, any hopes of finding more castaways seemed remote. She had to accept the possibility that he was dead, that she was never going to see him again. Tears filled her eyes. She blinked them away.

"My father taught me many things," she said. "When he left us and traveled gods know where to continue his research, I blamed him for everything that had befallen our family. My brother's despair. My mother's death. Even his research. And today..." She swallowed. "I never imagined the things he taught me could actually prove useful. Though this is hardly the time to feel this way, I think...I've found somewhere I belong."

"I know how it feels."

"You do?" She felt genuinely surprised. Adol always seemed so balanced, so confident.

Yet, she had decided to talk to him tonight because she considered him the only person here who'd understand, hadn't she?

"It's a great feeling, to belong," Adol said. "When you achieve it, you get clarity. You know what you want to do."

She nodded. "If I manage to escape this place, I will search for my father."

"I know you'll find him."

Laxia heaved a breath. For a while she kept her silence as she sat next to Adol.

She didn't notice how the sky turned dark, glowing with myriads of stars. Looking at the starlit landscape, it was so easy to forget all her concerns and worries.

"I owe you an apology," she said.

Adol turned toward her. In the darkness, she couldn't read his expression, but she sensed surprise in the set of his shoulders, in the way he cocked his head. She smiled, comfortable in the knowledge that he probably couldn't read her expression either—but more importantly, that even if he could, he wouldn't judge.

"Though my father was a noble," she said, "he was a carefree and welcoming man. As an adventurer, you remind me of him. You even resemble him somewhat. I think this may be why my behavior toward you has been so, um . . . unseemly, at first. So . . . I'm sorry."

This time she definitely saw him grin.

"I didn't mind at all."

"Please, you don't need to be so kind. I was forcing you to bear the brunt of my resentment toward my father." She stood up. "Now then, I'm going back to rest. Thank you for letting me confide in you. Good night, Adol."

She scrambled down the ladder before he could respond, letting out a sigh of relief when her feet touched the ground. The camp was still quiet, no serial killers lurking around as far as she could tell. On a peaceful night like this, it was easy to convince herself they had imagined it all. She made her way into the lodge, curled up in her bed, and fell asleep.

INVESTIGATION

Adol woke up from a dreamless sleep to find Sahad standing over his hammock.

"Ya finally awake, Adol?"

"Is something wrong?" Adol sat up and glanced around the empty room.

"Looks like that stuffed shirt Carlan vanished on us."

"Oh." Adol jumped out of the hammock and leaned over the stream for a quick wash, then followed Sahad out of the cave.

The captain and Dogi stood by the fire, talking.

"About time," Dogi said as Adol approached.

"What happened?"

"We don't know," the captain said. "But judging by the fact that Sir Carlan's belongings are missing, I am assuming he left of his own will."

"Just like he said last night," Dogi confirmed. "Couldn't stand our company any longer."

Euron strode up to them from the direction of the beach.

"The boat," he said. "It's gone."

Dogi and Adol exchanged glances.

"You don't think—?" Dogi began.

Adol peered into the open sea. Trying to escape the island in a small rowboat was suicide, even for a seasoned sailor. A man like Sir Carlan, with no seafaring experience, in less than perfect physical shape, wouldn't last a day—not to mention that the monster that sank the *Lombardia* was likely still out there, lurking in search of easy prey.

"Let's climb the watchtower and take a look," he said.

109

Dogi nodded and followed him to the ladder. Sahad climbed after them too, the rigging croaking under their weight.

It proved easy to spot the boat from the observation platform. It looked so tiny as it bobbed on the waves just off the coast, Sir Carlan no more than a dot at the stern, pushing the oars with fierce determination.

"Wow." Sahad shielded his eyes with his palm. "He really did go out to sea."

"He's rowing really hard," Dogi said.

"Can't believe he's rowin' that boat all by himself," Sahad agreed. "He's got more guts than I figured him fer, but still, what he's doin' is foolhardy."

"If he goes out too far," the captain said from the ground, "the water's going to get really choppy. He'll capsize in a boat that small."

They descended the ladder and joined the captain at the fireside. More people had gathered by now, everyone looking unsettled.

"We must bring him back," the captain said.

Nods from around the fire didn't look overly enthusiastic.

"How are we supposed to do that when he took our only boat?" Dogi asked.

"Well," Sahad said. "With the direction he's goin', he'll have a real tough time rowin' against that wind. It's blowin' toward the shore. We might be able to catch up with him at White Sand Cape."

The captain nodded. "Let's do it then, before he gets too far."

"I'll go." Adol rushed to the village exit, Laxia and Sahad trailing behind.

With the way now familiar, it took them no time to get to the rocky sand cape where they had found Alison. The boat bobbed on the waves a few hundred melye away. Sir Carlan was rowing furiously against the wind, but the boat wasn't moving very much.

"Ahoy!" Sahad shouted.

The nobleman's shoulders stiffened. He stopped rowing for a moment, then resumed without turning his head. Adol could see his lips moving, as if he were muttering to himself, but the wind carried the sounds away.

"Sir Carlan, please!" Laxia called. "You must return to shore!"

Sahad shook his head. "No good. Doesn't look like he can hear us."

Adol heaved a sigh and pulled off his sword.

"What are you going to do?" Laxia asked.

"Swim out to get him," Adol said. "As far as I see, it's our only choice."

"We could try to reason with him."

"No use. Even if he can hear us, he's probably determined not to listen. Besides, he may need help controlling the boat. It looks like he's using all his strength, but he's barely moving at all." He bent down to take off his boots.

"Hey, Adol," Sahad said hoarsely. "You seein' what I'm seein'...?"

If you mean a stubborn idiot in a boat who wouldn't listen to reason— Adol looked up and froze.

A giant tentacle rose out of the water. Another one cut through the surface on the other side of the boat.

Before Adol could move, more tentacles rose all around the boat. The water churned, the outline of a giant body taking shape just under the surface. Adol hadn't realized a creature that large could come so close to shore. He froze, seized by the kind of mind-numbing horror he hadn't experienced in a very long time.

Sir Carlan saw the tentacles too, but to Adol's surprise his face showed irritation rather than fear. He raised an oar, swatting at the approaching tentacles as if they were a swarm of annoying flies.

Was he unaware of the danger he was in? Or was this man braver than Adol had ever given him credit for?

"Sir Carlan!" Laxia screamed.

A giant triangular head emerged from the water. It looked like a tail end of a squid. An enormous squid. It also had eyes, huge yellow disks that surveyed the boat with cold malice.

The creature looked otherworldly—slimy, moldy, barnacled. Ancient. Evil. Its yellow eyes studied the boat with an expression that left no doubt the creature was sentient—a monster that enjoyed causing pain, watching people squirm and fight for their lives with no possible hope. It wasn't out hunting for food or protecting its nest. It was playing.

What in the world could anyone do against a creature like this?

Adol had to admire Sir Carlan's spirit. Instead of cowering in fear, the nobleman stood up in the boat and raised his oars, facing the creature. He was shouting in anger, but they couldn't hear the words.

A tentacle hovered in the air over him. Then it smashed down. Shattered pieces of wood flew into the air as the boat dipped under the surface and out of sight. After a few moments, the water settled again. No debris—and no body—ever came back up.

Waves radiating from the wreck reached the shore, splashing over the rocks lining the cape. The creature looked at them for a moment as if coolly taking their measure, then submerged. A giant shape, like the hull of an underwater ship, slid past and out into the open sea.

After a while, the oars and a few broken planks floated into view. They stood for a while, staring.

"Do you think he . . . it . . ." Sahad's voice trailed into silence.

Adol swallowed. No one could have survived such an encounter. There was no possibility that Sir Carlan could still be alive.

The only consolation was that Sir Carlan had disappeared instantly. Whether the creature had devoured him or targeted him merely as a warning for anyone daring to traverse these waters again, he hadn't had time to suffer. Adol clung to this thought as he pulled on his boots and strapped his sword belt over his waist.

"Let's return to the village," he said.

The castaways spent most of the day searching for Sir Carlan, to no avail. It felt more like a duty to the deceased rather than a real rescue mission. After what had happened to the *Lombardia*, the idea of one man in a small boat surviving a similar encounter seemed remote.

Their evening meal felt like a vigil as they sat gloomily around the fire.

"Now we know for sure what we're up against," the captain said. "The creature that sank the *Lombardia* is still out there." He turned to Laxia. "Is there anything you know about this kind of creature, by any chance?"

Laxia swallowed. "That monster—it might be a Primordial."

"Really?" Sahad said.

"In prehistoric times, the ocean was full of giant cephalopods. The tentacles, the shape of the head, the near-human eyes, all suggest we are dealing with one of those. It is reasonable to assume that this monster must share characteristics with its modern-day cephalopod cousins. That means its eyesight will be remarkably sharp, and it can likely travel at great speeds using pulsatile jets . . ." She paused, noticing Sahad's dumbfounded expression.

"So what you're saying," Dogi summed up, "is that if we don't deal with that thing, we're never getting off this island."

"I suppose so, yes," Laxia admitted.

Dogi shook his head. "Man, things just keep goin' from bad to worse."

Euron sat up straight, as if he'd just noticed something. He stood abruptly and headed over to the supply area, where he tore loose a piece of paper that had been pinned to one of the wooden supports. He brought it back to the fire.

"What is it?" the captain asked.

Euron held the note out for everyone to see.

ONE PIG DOWN. —NEMO.

The words were written in rusty red ink. Adol didn't remember seeing such ink among their supplies.

"Blood?" Licht asked nervously.

"I think so," Euron confirmed.

"When did he leave this?" Dogi wondered.

They exchanged glances. Everyone in the village was here, and they had all been together for the past hour or two. Who could have possibly left that note?

"I wonder," Adol said. "Why does this Nameless think he can take credit for Sir Carlan's death? Unless, of course, he somehow commands that giant Primordial."

Euron shrugged. "I suppose, in his view, Sir Carlan was so scared that he stopped thinking straight and ended up getting himself killed. Which means he must truly believe, in some twisted way, that Sir Carlan died by his hand. But this is not our real problem right now."

"It isn't?" Laxia asked.

"No. The real problem is, Nemo is part of this village. I'm afraid he's one of us."

Alison whimpered. She huddled up to Laxia, who looked horror-stricken too. Others around the fire exchanged uneasy glances. One of these people, the castaways that had banded together to survive, was a serial killer. The thought didn't fit into Adol's head.

"He's already claimed one victim," Euron went on. "If we don't act fast, I guarantee the body count will get higher."

"We must continue to investigate," the captain said. "But first we must reinforce the village. In the very least, we should be feeling safe from Primordial attacks while we are solving our internal problem."

Everyone nodded. This made lots of sense.

Adol spent another dreamless night. He had to admit to a feeling of disappointment when he woke up and lay in his hammock for a few moments, staring at the ceiling. He had come to look forward to his dreams of Dana's life.

After a quick wash, he emerged from the cave into the morning light, half-dreading news of another disaster that might have befallen the castaways while he was asleep.

The first person that caught his eye was Hummel, standing near the fire with a nonchalant look.

"Hummel," Adol called out as he approached. "You're back."

Hummel nodded, trailing his eyes to a freshly reinforced barricade at the village entrance, then toward the beach, from whence Laxia and Sahad were approaching, each carrying a bundle of sadinae on a string. They acknowledged Hummel with sideways looks, then bent down to arrange the catch over the coals.

"Anything wrong?" Hummel asked.

Sahad glanced up. "Depends on what ye mean by wrong. Let's see where to begin. We have a serial killer on the loose. Captain Barbaros got attacked. And Sir Carlan—Sir Carlan died while ya were gone."

"Oh. Sorry to hear that."

"Are you now?" Sahad's eyes narrowed. "Why did you disappear while we were comin' back to the village the other day? Where did ya go? An' what were ya doin' while you were away all this time?"

Hummel looked at him calmly. "Sorry, I can't divulge that information."

Sahad straightened up, towering over the other man. "How d'we know you're not the culprit behind all these attacks?"

Hummel's lips twitched. "You could just ask me, couldn't you?"

"Fine. Are you?"

"No."

"Wait a moment, Sahad," Laxia put in. "Hummel can't be the culprit. He was with us when we found Licht. Even though he didn't return to the village with us, there's no way he could have attacked Captain Barbaros."

Sahad hesitated. "Well, if ya swear you're not the culprit, I guess it's fine. But why did ya disappear all of a sudden?"

Hummel shrugged. "Isn't it obvious? I was done working with

114

you."

"*Done workin' with us?* What's that supposed to mean?"

"This crime you're trying to solve is your business," Hummel said. "My business lies elsewhere and has nothing to do with you. So why force an unnecessary collaboration?"

Sahad blinked. "Well, ya got a point, I suppose."

"In any case," Adol put in. "Hummel's back now. How about you help us investigate?"

Hummel held a pause.

"I'll keep my eyes open," he conceded.

"You do that," Adol said. "I'm going to talk to Captain Barbaros."

The captain looked almost completely recovered. He and Euron bent over a worktable next to Dina's supply station, spreading fragments of the island's map over the wooden surface. Little Paro, the captain's faithful outdoor companion, perched on a ledge nearby. It took Adol a moment to realize they were applying sticky tree sap to the sturdy cloth backing to glue the pieces together. The name "White Sand Cape" caught his attention. Apparently, these handy names they had been giving to places as they explored were now becoming official.

"Found anything?" Euron asked as Adol approached, with Laxia and Sahad beside him.

"Hummel's back," Adol replied. "But we haven't done much investigating so far. I have a question for the captain."

The captain looked up at him.

"The day you were attacked," Adol said. "You mentioned someone calling out to you from a distance, right?"

"Yes."

"And then you said you were cut with a blade."

"That is correct."

Adol shook his head. "This doesn't add up. The person cutting you had to have been close by—unless he somehow was able to throw several daggers and then retrieve them without you noticing."

The captain hesitated. "True. He was at least a few melye away from me."

"Adol's right," Sahad said. "That's pretty far away for someone to cut ya."

"Yes, it is." The captain nodded slowly. "I don't recall. It happened so fast, I thought perhaps I was misremembering things."

"There has to be an explanation," Adol said.

"Perhaps," the captain suggested, "it wasn't a blade he attacked me with. Maybe...a whip?"

"A whip a few melye long, with a sharp tip?"

"You're right," the captain said. "It doesn't add up."

"Let me go question others," Adol said. "In the meantime, see if you can remember any more details."

The captain nodded. Euron looked thoughtful, but he didn't say anything as Adol and his party moved on.

Licht was sitting at the table in the common room chatting with Alison, who was sewing at her station in the corner. Adol lowered to the bench next to him. Laxia and Sahad took seats on the other side. Licht edged to give them room, looking around the group nervously.

"You chose a heck of a time to join Castaway Village," Adol said. "Things were a lot quieter here before you arrived."

"Suspicious, all I can say," Sahad mumbled.

"Licht couldn't be the criminal," Adol reminded. "Like Hummel, he was with us when Captain Barbaros was attacked."

Sahad only shrugged.

"I've been thinking," Licht said. "Sir Carlan was the first fatality, and the killer seems to take it to his personal credit. Why make such a deal out of Sir Carlan's unfortunate incident?"

"Well..." Sahad hesitated. "It's probably 'cause his death came in kinda handy, when all of us were already scared witless. At least I was." He glanced sideways at Laxia and Adol.

Or because Sir Carlan was the one the killer felt the most annoyed with. Adol didn't voice the thought. In Sir Carlan's case, this could have been a motive for pretty much anyone in the village. Besides, one didn't speak badly of the dead. In his last moments, Sir Carlan had shown true courage and spirit. That was how they should all remember him.

"Exactly." Licht nodded. "The killer had us all scared, and Sir Carlan's death came just in time to reinforce that."

"What do you mean?" Laxia asked.

"I believe," Licht said, "the Nameless's true goal—at least for now—is to sow dread and paranoia among us. Maybe that's what Nameless really enjoys—playing mind games with his victims."

Like the giant tentacled Primordial. The thought came out of nowhere, sending a chill down Adol's spine.

"And now that Sir Carlan's dead," Licht went on, "the village's morale has never been lower. The Nameless is probably gloating right now as he's watching us questioning each other, looking over our shoulders every time we venture anywhere on our own." He looked at Alison, who lowered her needlework, staring at him with a pale face.

"You seem to know a lot about people," Adol observed.

Licht let out a laugh. "Me? Not really, no. It's just that in my line of work I have cause to observe many different kinds of people."

"Your line of work?" Now that the topic came up Adol suddenly realized that, in all the excitement since Licht's arrival in the village, none of them ever had a chance to learn anything about the man.

"I am a medical resident," Licht said.

Sahad frowned. "A medical resident? What's that mean? What do residents have to do with medicine?"

"He is training to become a doctor," Laxia explained.

"Oh, I see."

"The attending physician aboard the *Lombardia* asked me to cover for him," Licht went on. "He had a last-minute emergency and couldn't make the trip. When I agreed, I never imagined I would end up in this situation."

"You could say the same of everyone here, really." Laxia rose. "We should probably go on with our investigation, Adol."

Their next stop was Kiergaard's clinic, where the doctor sat at his workbench grinding leaves between two curved rocks. He showed no surprise at the party's approach.

"We noticed a curious thing," Adol said. "Captain Barbaros tells us his attacker was a good distance away, yet the wounds he received seemed to have been made by a blade."

"True." Kiergaard nodded.

Curious how he seemed so calm, as if the discussion were purely academic.

"Do you think another type of a weapon could have made these kinds of cuts?" Adol asked.

"I am not sure." Kiergaard hesitated. "If you speak of curious aspects of this incident, I myself found it interesting that neither the captain's nor Sir Carlan's wounds appeared life-threatening. Quite odd for a famous serial killer to attack his victims with so little effect, don't you think?"

"Odd indeed," Adol agreed. "Unless the attacks were merely warnings." Or the killer's main purpose was to sow panic, like Licht had suggested. For some reason, he didn't feel like saying this out loud.

"Coming back to your original question," Kiergaard said. "Blade or not, I'm afraid all I can tell you about this weapon is that it's very sharp. Sorry for not being of more help to your investigation."

Adol was about to move on when Laxia leaned forward, peering at the doctor.

"What's that on your neck, Doctor?" she asked.

Adol looked. Only now did he notice a red spot, partly hidden by the collar of Kiergaard's shirt.

"Don't tell me you were attacked too?" Laxia said tensely.

Kiergaard laughed. "Oh, this? Don't worry. It's just the remnant of a bad sunburn I received a while back."

Sahad laughed. "Gah-haha! Had me scared fer a minute there."

"Before I ended up here," Kiergaard said, "I was staying in a country called Altago. I spent much of my time outdoors, doing medical work in the sun."

"The kingdom of Altago?" Laxia nodded. "I heard many stories about it from my father. It's said to be a mysterious land, where giant beasts roam. Have you heard of it, Adol?"

Adol had. In fact, the mention of Altago had set off an alarm bell in his mind. He returned to the clinic and sat down on the patient's bench.

"Tell me more about Altago, Doctor," he said.

"Now?" Laxia frowned.

"Why not? As an adventurer, I'm always interested to hear stories about mysterious lands. Giant beasts, did you say?"

Laxia's frown deepened. "Now is not the time for—" She paused as Adol fixed her with a sharp glance.

Kiergaard looked at them both, his lips twitching into a thin smile. "I'm happy to share stories about all I've seen and heard. But shouldn't you focus on solving this case first?"

"I agree," Sahad said. "You'll have plenty o' time to gab with Kiergaard later, Adol."

Adol sighed. During his time on this island, he'd come to appreciate his companions, but sometimes he wished the three of them were a little bit better at communication. He really wanted to stay behind and question Kiergaard some more. But the moment was lost, leaving him no choice but to move on for now.

"Sure," he said. "Later then."

THE NAMELESS RIPPER

Laxia was having trouble keeping up with Adol's purposeful stride as he led the way past the barricade to a small glade outside the camp.

"Where are you going?" she demanded. "Didn't the captain ask us to stay inside the village until the investigation is complete?"

Adol stopped abruptly and turned to face her. "I'm looking for a quiet place to talk."

"Why?"

Adol looked around. "Let's cross the brook." He pointed toward the rock where he and Laxia had first met, weeks ago. It seemed like ages.

"Fine." Laxia brushed past him in that direction. She had no idea what this was all about. She had never seen Adol act so strange. Was he going to scold her for reminding him that they had more pressing concerns than listening to Doctor Kiergaard's adventure tales? Wasn't that the point when the conversation turned south? Well, she had merely stated the simple truth. Besides, she was part of this investigation too. She had every right to make suggestions.

She noticed a faint glint in the grass as she strode by but didn't even turn around to look. Probably a smooth rock catching the sun.

"Laxia, *stop!*" Adol shouted from behind.

She paused mid-step.

A thin streak of metal shot out of the grass, brushing her neck as it swept past.

Laxia cried out as her skin erupted in pain and clasped her hand to her neck. When she drew her fingers away, they were covered with blood.

Something had just cut her. Something thin and sharp that had shaved off a strip of skin and would have cut much deeper if Adol's cry hadn't stopped her in time. If she had taken another step...

"Don't move." Adol approached carefully and crouched in the grass beside her.

Laxia touched her neck again, then pulled out her handkerchief and pressed it to the wound. The bleeding was slowing. The injury didn't seem that bad. She should be feeling lucky—except she couldn't help the nausea rising in her throat. A sharp object had just sprung out of the grass and cut her. How was this possible?

She looked at Adol crouching over the ground, eyes darting left and right.

"Over there." He pointed. "Near that tree." He crept in that direction, then knelt in the grass and picked up a thin strand of metal wire.

"Sharp," he said thoughtfully. "And long. But not a blade."

"What happened?" Euron rushed across the glade toward them.

Wordlessly, Adol held out the wire for him to see, then pointed at Laxia.

Euron frowned as he saw Laxia's injury. His frown deepened as he examined the wire.

"Do you know what this is?" Adol asked.

"Yeah." Euron searched beside the tree, then rose, holding out a small contraption made of hooks and springs tied up to a wooden board. "I thought so."

"What is it?" Laxia asked shakily.

"A trap," Euron said. "Romun guerilla warfare units set them with military-grade steel wires, stretching them across paths and around the perimeter of field fortifications. One end of each wire goes here." He pointed at a small hook on a spring, sticking to the side. "The other can be attached loosely to any branch or rock, usually at knee height. It's hard to spot, especially in thick grass. Tripping over the wire causes it to shoot out, ripping a poor bastard to shreds." He looked at Laxia. "You're lucky that head of yours didn't go rolling into the grass."

Laxia let out a breath. A chill in the pit of her stomach simply wouldn't go away. A military wire trap had nearly decapitated her. Her mind was having serious trouble dealing with this information.

"Both the captain and Sir Carlan received their wounds from a sharp object," Adol said, "without a person coming near them. A steel-wire trap would do the trick, wouldn't it?

Euron stared thoughtfully at the contraption in his hand but did not respond.

"Which brings us to the next obvious question," Adol went on. "Could the Nameless Ripper be part of the Romun military?"

Good point. Laxia stepped up to Adol's side. They both looked at Euron. He stared back at them grimly.

"I guess this makes me a suspect," Euron admitted. "However, if I was Nameless, why would I reveal it to you that this is a Romun military trap?"

Adol shrugged. "I don't know. Maybe because you saw me holding a steel wire in my hands after Laxia almost got sliced by it?"

"I could have simply pretended I knew nothing about it."

"For the moment, maybe. But if anyone at camp heard about this and could expose you—"

"Stop it, both of you." Now that the conversation had turned back to logic and deductions, Laxia felt a bit less shaky. The image of her head rolling through the grass still bothered her, but with effort she could manage not to think about it all the time.

"It does us no good to keep accusing each other," she said. "Let's just keep this wire as an important clue, shall we?"

"Right." Adol rolled it up and put it in his pocket under Euron's heavy gaze.

"I swear," Euron said. "I'm getting real sick of this Nameless crap." He turned and strode away.

"Adol," Laxia said when he was gone. "When you took us out here, what was it that you wanted to talk about?"

"Altago," he said.

"Oh, yes. The adventure tales you were so keen to hear."

Adol tossed his head impatiently. "It wasn't about the tales. I wanted to confirm something after Kiergaard mentioned having visited the kingdom of Altago not long ago."

"What's wrong with visiting Altago?"

"Altago's at war with the Romun Empire. You can't just come and go as you please. You'd have to be a top government official. Or a member of the Romun military."

They stood for a moment, contemplating the information.

"Are you sure about that?" Laxia said. "Doctor Kiergaard isn't an official. And he's not a soldier either. He's just a doctor... A doctor in the military, maybe?"

Adol shook his head. "He mentioned no such thing, I'm sure of it. In fact, he always claimed ignorance when Euron talked about the Romun military."

"We should go talk to the captain at once," Laxia said.

When they returned to camp, the captain stood beside the fire with Dogi and Euron. The three men paused their conversation, watching Adol and Laxia stride toward them.

"Adol, Laxia," the captain said. "Euron was just filling me in."

Adol took the steel wire out of his pocket and handed it to the captain. "We believe this wire—or one very much like it—is responsible for your wounds, Captain."

"Yes." The captain turned the coil around thoughtfully in his hands. "Euron also mentioned that setting such traps is a special skill of the Romun military. I understand that you and he—"

Adol locked his eyes on Euron's. "I apologize. You are no longer my suspect. At least not the primary one." He pointed at the field clinic—now empty, with Kiergaard nowhere in sight.

"Doctor Kiergaard?" The captain blinked. "But he—"

"He mentioned a recent trip to Altago." Adol glanced at Euron again.

Euron frowned. "Altago?"

"Yes. Dogi and I have wanted to visit Altago for ages. But as I understand, the place is off limits to everyone . . . unless you are a member of the Romun army."

"True," Euron said slowly.

"Let's find the doctor," Dogi suggested, "and question him ourselves, shall we?"

"Let me check something first." Euron strode into the medical area and rummaged around the supplies.

"What are you looking for?" Laxia asked.

"This." Euron turned and held out a spool of coiled steel wire.

They all stared in disbelief.

"But that—that's—" Laxia began.

"It's the exact same wire as the one used in the trap that nearly decapitated you." Euron turned to the captain. "I'd say this is evidence enough."

The captain's face darkened. "Indeed it is. Let's apprehend Doctor Kiergaard before he claims another victim."

The doctor stood on the mid-level terrace of the camp, looking out to sea. He seemed quite calm. Approaching him, Adol suddenly had doubts. How could this quiet man possibly be a killer?

"Hello, Adol." Kiergaard turned. "Something the matter? Has someone else been hurt?"

Adol paused. He finally realized what had always seemed so strange about this man. His smile never reached his eyes. As his lips stretched now, his eyes looked cold and calculating, watching Adol without a hint of humor.

"Over here!" Adol called.

One by one, members of the search party rushed into the glade and stopped beside Adol.

"Nice weather we're having today, Doctor Kiergaard." Euron folded his arms over his chest. "A bit like Altago, isn't it? Except more humid, of course."

Kiergaard's smile widened. "Is that what gave me away?"

"That," Euron confirmed, "and a coil of steel wire we found among your things, as well as the one you set as a spring trap outside camp. Quite elaborate, I'd say. Must've taken you a lot of time."

"Leisure time, really." Kiergaard chuckled. "Officer Euron. You never got the chance to rendezvous with your partner on the ship, did you? Not before he met his rather unfortunate end. Suffocation, was it? Right in his cabin, with no witnesses, of course. A blade would have been more appropriate, but these things do tend to get quite messy."

Euron's face twitched. "You bastard."

"How could you do such terrible things, Doctor?" Laxia's voice caught as she stared at him, wide-eyed.

Kiergaard laughed softly, looking over the gathering with cold calculation. "Consider it a favor, my dear lady. Before I showed up, you castaways were perfect strangers to one another. But look at you now. Your bonds and trust in each other flourished—all for the sake of survival. Beautiful. Would anyone else have been able to achieve it all in such a short time?"

"What the hell're ya talkin' about?" Sahad demanded.

"Don't listen to this lunatic," Euron said. "He's a serial killer."

"Come quietly, Doctor Kiergaard," the captain said. "This is a deserted island. There is nowhere for you to run."

"Hah!" Kiergaard stomped the ground, and metal wires shot up everywhere around him, cutting him off from his pursuers.

Laxia screamed.

"The world needs one such as I to exist," Kiergaard said. "So, respectfully, I must now take my leave." He grasped a rope coiled in the grass nearby and used it to swing off the cliff to the camp's lower terrace.

"Damn," Euron snapped. "He's prepared an escape. Don't let him get away."

Adol and Dogi were already running. The captain whistled, and Little Paro landed on his shoulder.

"Paro, follow Doctor Kiergaard and report his whereabouts."

"Roger!" the bird croaked.

"Good boy. We're counting on you."

Little Paro flew low, a green and red beacon Adol and the others had no trouble following as they ran out of camp. The chase brought them to the beach, close to the place where they'd first found Sahad. Kiergaard's tracks made a clear path across the sand, toward a large object lying in the gap between two boulders ahead.

A body?

Adol felt a chill in the pit of his stomach.

"Found girl! Found girl!" Paro squawked.

"A girl?" Laxia frowned.

Sahad pointed, eyes wide. "Look..."

It was indeed a little girl, curled in the sand with her eyes closed. A few crabs scurried around her as if measuring her up for a meal. They scattered as the group rushed toward the spot, the captain at the front.

"Wait!" Adol called.

But it was too late.

Wires shot up out of the sand around the body, visible only as gleaming streaks in the sunlight. The captain grunted and sank to his knees.

"Cap'n!" Sahad screamed.

The captain folded down to the sand, next to the girl. His clothes were already soaked, blood rapidly spreading around him. This trap had been set differently—not to warn or sow discord but to kill anyone who approached the girl. And now...Adol swallowed as he knelt in the sand next to the captain.

"Captain," Laxia sobbed.

Euron rushed up and crouched over the girl. "She's alive. Drugged, I think."

Laughter echoed over the beach and Kiergaard appeared on top of a tall rock above them.

"I knew I made the right choice, capturing that lost little urchin," he said.

"He used that kid as bait," Sahad growled.

"We need to treat the captain's wound," Laxia urged.

Kiergaard laughed again. "I wouldn't waste your time. I'm all but certain his femoral artery has been sliced clean through. Even if you treat his wound right away, his odds of survival are grim, at best."

The captain stirred. "Adol, please. Capture him." His eyes rolled and fluttered closed.

Kiergaard rubbed his chin. "Drowsiness is a well-known symptom of exsanguination. That makes two victims now ... if you bother to count that idiot Carlan, of course. And now I shall take my leave." He bowed theatrically then stepped away along the rocks and disappeared from view.

Adol exchanged glances with Euron, who was using his belt as a tourniquet to apply pressure to the captain's leg with brisk, expert moves. It didn't seem to slow the bleeding in the least.

"Go after him, Adol," Euron said. "I'll stay with the captain."

Adol nodded and sprang to his feet, darting after Kiergaard.

A small glade opened ahead—the same glade where they'd first discovered Sahad. Kiergaard stood in the center, waiting. Adol drew his sword as he approached.

"I knew it would be you to come after me, Adol," Kiergaard said. "I could see it in your eyes, the passion burning deep inside you. And when I first met you, I could tell at that exact moment. You are a worthy target."

"So you have your sights set on Adol now?" Laxia said, coming up to Adol's side with Sahad in her wake.

Kiergaard shrugged. "I didn't expect the castaways to survive long on this island. I thought they would fall prey to beasts once despair set in. Or fight amongst themselves after all semblance of order had broken down. But I was wrong." He looked at Adol. "You, the captain, and the village, have given them hope. Everyone has begun to work for the common goal of escaping this island. It's just so beautiful."

Adol stepped forward, but Laxia placed a hand on his shoulder.

"Be careful. This place might be trapped."

"It would be so tragic," Kiergaard went on, "if something terrible were to happen to you or the captain. The entire village would fall apart without its leaders, sending everyone to their doom." He smiled. "Why, the mere thought makes me quiver."

"What about that stuffed shirt Carlan?' Sahad demanded. "And that little girl too. You've done terrible things no man should ever do, Doctor."

Kiergaard straightened up. "Who are you to tell me what I should and should not do? As one who bears the burden of evil, I took the only normal course of action."

"The burden of evil?" Adol stared. In his life, he'd never yet witnessed this kind of depravity.

"Yes," Kiergaard said gravely. "I am the counterpart to a paragon of righteousness such as yourself, Adol—an ultimate arch-nemesis, quintessential to bringing balance and harmony into this world."

"Big words, from a small man."

"Small?" Kiergaard's eye twitched, the first indication that he wasn't as calm as he let on. "Hardly. People can only advance when they have land to tread on. Progress cannot be made without two diametrically opposing forces. Good and evil. With these concepts, we give meaning to society and history. Do you think the world as you know it would still exist without evil? And yet the existence of evil is seen as a blight, to be purged without hesitation. Does that not seem irrational to you?"

"You're insane," Laxia said.

"Never thought I'd meet anyone who was rotten to the core," Sahad agreed.

Kiergaard shook his head. "I never expected this conversation to result in mutual understanding between us. After all, the conflict between good and evil is inevitable."

"So, in the end, we must fight," Adol said.

Kiergaard held his arms to the sides. "In the name of evil, I will rip my name into history. Come, the doctor will see you now."

Thin metal lines shot out of his sleeves, lashing out across the glade. Sahad and Laxia fell back, but Adol dodged, darting forward between the wires, jumping and rolling over the ground. He reached Kiergaard and used the flat of his sword to knock the man's legs from underneath him, then straddled him and held the blade to his throat.

He thought the fight was over, but he had underestimated his opponent. Kiergaard twisted, throwing his weight sideways and out of the lock. Rolling over, he kicked aside Adol's blade and jumped to his feet a few paces away.

"I don't intend to stay around and wait to be captured. Nice knowing you, Adol." He sprinted away across the glade.

"No! He's gonna get away!" Sahad rushed forward, pulling to an abrupt stop as a steel wire sprung across his path. "Whoa!"

Adol heaved a breath. "He probably has this whole glade wired up."

"Damn." Sahad shook his head. "How prepped is this guy?"

From the distance, Kiergaard laughed. "Next time will be much more fun. Now then—"

The ground shook with the fall of heavy footsteps. A giant bipedal lizard burst from the passage behind Kiergaard.

The doctor screamed and darted away, but the creature caught up to him in a few strides. Its large triangular head smashed down, its jaws closing over Kiergaard with a sickening crunch. The monstrous lizard didn't pay any notice to the others as it turned and trotted away, the doctor's body dangling out of its mouth.

"I think I'm going to be sick," Laxia said weakly.

Sahad scratched his head. "At least this took care of our problem, once and for all."

Adol heaved a breath. He shouldn't be feeling relieved that Kiergaard was dead. No man should meet such a terrible end, eaten by a giant Primordial beast. But the doctor had killed so many people, terrorized the villagers, attacked Sir Carlan and Captain Barbaros and that unknown little girl on the beach...He had tried to plot the end for all of them. Adol shook off his stupor and sheathed his sword.

"Let's go to the captain," he said.

The captain was lying in the sand, next to the little girl. Both looked unconscious, but now that the urgency was over and Adol could take a better look, he realized the girl was merely asleep, while the captain...He met Euron's gaze. The Romun shook his head briefly. Adol knelt in the sand beside them.

"Kiergaard?" Euron asked.

"Dead. A Primordial ate him."

Euron raised his eyebrow but didn't comment.

"Adol." The captain's voice was no louder than a whisper.

"Captain." Adol reached over and took his hand. "Hold on. We'll take you back to the village. Licht is a doctor. He'll treat your wound."

A faint smile touched the captain's pale lips. "Too late, I'm afraid ... It's just like the Nameless said. My wound ... It's fatal. The curse of the island has caught up to me. No one can possibly ... "

No, don't speak like this. But the words didn't leave Adol's lips. He knew a bad situation when he saw it. No use to sugarcoat it.

"I need you to do something for me, Adol," the captain said. "One last promise."

"Anything." Adol was surprised to realize how deeply he meant it. In the short time he'd known this man, he'd come to think of him almost as a father—kind and caring, a strong leader everyone looked up to. It was unthinkable to be losing him like this.

"You must get everyone off this island ... " The captain heaved a shallow breath. "Alive. I know you can do it, Adol."

"I promise," Adol said solemnly.

The captain smiled. "Thank you ... Their fate is in your hands now." His eyelids fluttered shut.

Adol could almost see the captain's life slip away, his body becoming a shell that no longer held a spirit. The captain's hand went limp in Adol's grasp. Gently, he set it down onto the man's chest, over the capacious heart that would beat no more.

A few raindrops fell from the sky, as if nature itself were mourning the captain's passing.

Adol sat on his heels in the strengthening rain, watching the captain's still face. He barely registered the movements around him— Laxia sobbing, Sahad sniffling and wiping his eyes with his sleeve, Euron staring ahead with a blank face, a blood-soaked piece of cloth clutched in his hand. Dogi and Licht hurried in from the direction of the village carrying stretchers, their faces expressionless as masks as they lowered to the sand beside the body.

Most of the day turned into a blur as the villagers dealt with the aftermath of the damage. Carrying the captain and the little girl back to the village. Scouting the area for steel-wire traps that might have been left behind by the Nameless Ripper. Digging the grave on the camp's highest terrace above Castaway Village with the best view of the sea. Feeling numb and empty doing all that, knowing that from this day on, life in Castaway Village would never be the same.

The rain turned into a steady downpour as they held a small funeral, laying the captain to rest. One by one, with tears in their eyes, they bid farewell to the man who had been the pillar of strength to their island community. One by one, they departed, returning to the lower levels of the village and to their daily tasks.

Little Paro was the last one to stay. As Adol left, he saw the parrot sitting on the gravestone, looking into the sky.

Did he have tears in his eyes too?

ARBOREAL AWAKENING

Dana Iclucia, I name you the new Maiden of the Great Tree. May you guide your subjects with wisdom, using the gift of your divine Essence.

The words of the anointment ceremony kept echoing in Dana's head. It's been two days since her inauguration—and weeks since she'd learned that she was going to be the one—but she still couldn't get over her disbelief. She, Dana Iclucia, the girl who always got into trouble and caused so many problems for her superiors, had been named the spiritual leader of the realm, equal in standing to the Queen herself. Barely out of her teens, she didn't feel old enough to fill the shoes of the previous Maiden, who was now off to enjoy her well-deserved retirement, or to shoulder this kind of a responsibility. But being chosen had always been her dream, and now that it had come true, she was going to do everything in her power to help her people.

The main Temple hall looked magnificent—a giant domed space inlaid with elaborate patterns of terracotta tiles. With the anointment ceremony over, the place had been cleared of all extra decorations, leaving only a ring of sculptures that sat on pedestals around the center of the hall, each depicting a mythical creature from Eternian lore. A small group of handmaids stood on the side of the long walkway leading to the center of the hall, their plain green dresses a welcoming patch of normalcy among all the pomp. Their gazes followed Dana as she walked toward them.

They probably didn't realize that the place where they stood, near a columned gallery at the side of the hall, had a unique echo. Anyone underneath the central dome could hear every word they said, as clearly as if they were nearby.

"Dana, the new Maiden," one girl said. "Can you believe it?"

"A breath of fresh air," another girl responded earnestly. "Looks like our seniors finally got something right."

"I don't know." The girl next to her cast a disapproving glance at Dana's distant shape. "I never expected a troublemaker like Dana would be chosen."

"But Dana—"

"It should have been Olga. Everyone assumed it would be her. But then the old Maiden—"

"Hush, you two. She's coming."

The handmaids paused their chatter and bowed in formal greeting. Dana nodded in response. She didn't mind their doubts. She had been just as surprised to be chosen. But their reverence, the way all conversations paused at her approach, were among the many things she was having trouble getting used to in her new station. The idea of people bowing to her was difficult to accept.

A tall, thin girl of about her age stood waiting in the center of the hall, a page of finely written text in her hand. Handmaid Alta, her handler for today. Of course, the Temple seniors would never leave Dana unattended for her first major ritual as the Maiden of the Great Tree—the inaugural ceremony of Arboreal Awakening.

"Your schedule, Lady Dana." Alta spoke with her eyes lowered, a novelty from only two days ago.

Dana sighed. "You can look at me directly, Alta. And thank you for keeping me so organized."

Alta's eyelids trembled as she slowly raised her gaze to Dana's face. Her eyes were blue. Strange how, in only two days, Dana already felt in danger of forgetting it.

"Your Eminence," Alta said. "I hope you are enjoying the ceremonies?"

Dana shook her head. Alta knew her well enough not to ask a question like this.

"I'm doing my best," she said truthfully.

Alta's gaze wavered, the only sign of sympathy Dana was probably going to get all day. "We will be departing for the Great Valley shortly, Maiden. Everyone's gathering near the Mountain Gate. Advisor Urgunata told me make sure to escort you, but..." She glanced over her shoulder, as if afraid of being overheard. "We still have plenty of time. If you'd rather make your own way there..."

Dana nodded gratefully. Being alone for a few minutes to gather

her thoughts was something she'd been craving since her inauguration.

"Thank you, Alta," she said. "I'll meet you out there soon."

She took a long way through the Temple hallways. Secretly, she hoped to run into Sarai and Olga. She hadn't had a chance to be alone with her friends since the inner council of the Temple seniors had shocked everyone by announcing Dana as the Maiden's successor, so she didn't even know their reaction to the news. Did Sarai approve? Was Olga upset about not being selected? Dana felt bad for her friend, who everyone—including Dana—had assumed would be chosen. But none of it mattered now. It was done, and she was going to perform her duties to the best of her ability.

She made her way to the exit but stopped at the sight of a little girl in one of the side passages—about eleven or so, dressed in a short off-the-shoulder tunic that draped loosely around her slim form. Her hair had a curious tint—pink, as if sprayed with strawberry juice.

Dana paused, looking at the girl curiously. A new trainee? Not likely. Her outfit looked nothing like the Temple clothing. A pilgrim? A bit too young to travel here alone. Besides, this area was off limits to visitors, yet the girl seemed at home in the maze of service passages, as if strolling through her own backyard.

"Can I help you?" Dana asked.

"Ah!" The girl giggled. "I've been caught!" Curiously, she didn't look in the least bit worried, as if being caught in a restricted area of the Temple was a hilarious game.

"Are you playing hide-and-seek?" Dana asked.

"Well." The girl pouted. "No one here to play with, really. I was just curious how long it was going to be before someone noticed me. You win this one, Lady!"

Dana sighed. It was indeed lucky that she had been the one to find this girl—not, say, someone like Advisor Urgunata. "If you get caught playing in here, a really scary lady will get mad at you."

The girl pursed her lips. "Oh, fine." She looked at Dana sideways. "At least I got to meet the Maiden everyone's been talkin' about. I guess I'll head back for today."

"You know who I am?" Dana felt surprised. She wasn't wearing any of her official regalia, or even a proper Temple robe, for that matter. In this outfit, no outsider should be able to recognize her.

The girl laughed. "Good luck on your trial, Lady Dana!" Before Dana could ask any more questions, she turned and skipped away along the hallway, humming a song on the way. *Seren Garden*. Dana's heart quivered. Mother used to sing it to her when she was little. Had this girl learned it from her own mother too?

Only after the girl disappeared behind the bend of the hallway did Dana realize that she had forgotten to ask the girl if she was lost and needed help finding her way out. She hurried after her, but the child was gone.

Two clerics stood beside an open doorway, arguing.

"I still can't believe the Council chose Lady Dana," one of them, whom Dana recognized as Cleric Sienna, said. "After all the problems she's caused. She's bound to mess things up. Lady Olga is much more—" She broke off as she saw Dana, color rising into her cheeks. Her companion bowed and hurried out of sight.

"L-Lady Dana?" Cleric Sienna looked miserable. "I—Please forgive me."

Dana smiled. Cleric Sienna was a zealous woman who worked closely with Advisor Urgunata. It stood to reason that she would disapprove of Dana being chosen. No surprise there.

"It's all right," she said. "Everyone around here is talking about this. To tell you the truth, I'm just as surprised as you are. And..." She stepped closer. "It would really help me do a better job if more people were as honest as you."

"Th-thank you, Your Eminence." Sienna looked stunned as Dana walked by.

Outside, Cleric Cecile was waiting at the start of the passage leading off to the Mountain Gate. Clearly, Alta's lenience had been discovered, and the Temple seniors had chosen a more reliable messenger to ensure Dana was delivered safely to her destination. She hoped Alta wasn't in trouble.

"Lady Dana," Cecile said. "Advisor Urgunata asked me to make sure we go over the details of the ritual."

"Of course she did." A wonder how the Temple seniors, who ultimately chose Dana as the supreme spiritual leader of Eternia over a bevy of highly suitable candidates, couldn't trust her to memorize a simple ritual.

Cecile bowed, falling into stride by Dana's side. They were short on time now, which left no room to slow down for a conversation.

"You did remember to bring the sapling, my lady, did you?" Cecile asked.

Dana nodded, peeking into her shoulder bag where the tiny plant sat comfortably in its pack of soil. As the Maiden, she would always have to carry a few of them around in her bag, but today she brought just one, the first one she'd ever plant in her new role.

"Good," Cecile said. "After you and your followers arrive at the start of the path, you must travel down the Great Valley all by yourself. When you reach the bottom of the valley, you will see the hallowed grounds. You'll recognize the area by its fertile soil, as well as by the prayer trees that have been planted by your predecessors. Choose a good spot, separate from the others. These trees grow slowly, but they do need space."

Dana nodded. After all these instructions, she felt as if she knew the place already.

"As soon as you finish planting the prayer tree sapling," Cecile went on. "You will offer a prayer and then receive a vision of Eternia's future." She heaved a breath, steadying her voice. The guardhouse of the Mountain Gate loomed ahead of them. "With your excellent foresight, I'm sure you will receive a wonderful vision. Best of luck to you, Your Eminence. Blessings of the Great Tree be upon you."

"Thank you, Cecile," Dana said. "I appreciate your guidance."

She felt tempted to ask about Olga and Sarai but didn't do it. By now it was clear that her friends were deliberately avoiding her. She sighed as she ascended the steps toward the gate's city overlook.

The waiting crowd looked fit for a holiday gala, not for a mountain hike. Clerics, priestesses, members of the royal family, and higher-ranking citizens, were all dressed in elaborate garments, accompanied by servants carrying packs with refreshments, umbrellas, and water jugs. Dana supposed all these comforts were essential so that no one would pass out from the heat, enabling them all to focus on the spiritual side of the mission. Yet she couldn't help wishing she could travel the trail alone, without all the pomp. She glanced again at the tree sapling, a tiny sprout peeking from its pack of soil inside her shoulder bag. It was hard to imagine this fragile thing would grow into a mighty tree one day.

She smiled as she spotted a group of her recent fellow trainees at the side, Olga and Sarai in their midst.

"Olga! Sarai!" Dana hurried over, then stopped abruptly as the entire group bowed to her.

"Your Eminence," Olga said. "We are honored to bear witness as you perform the Arboreal Awakening."

"Thank you for allowing the former Maiden candidates to be part of this," Sarai added.

Dana's heart sank as she looked at her friends in disbelief. Was this how things were going to be from now on?

Like the rest of the group, Olga and Sarai wore ceremonial robes, adorned with the Temple symbols. Their elaborate hair arrangements made them look so official. Dana's choice of regular clothing for this ceremony made her feel even more distant from all of them. They both kept their eyes lowered as they stood in front of her.

"It's me," she said. "Dana. Remember? You can stop acting so formally."

Olga drew herself up, even though it seemed impossible for her to stand any straighter. "With all due respect, Your Eminence, you are not the same as before. You have pledged yourself to the Great Tree of Origins. We must all conduct ourselves in a more dignified manner, as befits our stations."

Dana looked at her curiously. Only Olga could make such a humble statement sound like a reprimand.

"True," she said.

Sarai's gaze wavered. "I hope it goes smoothly. Just remember, if you need anything, we won't be far."

Warmth washed over Dana as she met her friend's eyes. At least Sarai hadn't changed toward her. Of course, unlike Olga, Sarai probably didn't consider herself undercut by Dana's appointment as the Maiden.

"Thank you, Sarai," she said.

The Temple clerics joined their Essence to instantly transport the entire party to the large clearing on the southern slopes of the mountain. The path to the hallowed grounds wound away on its far end.

Doubts overwhelmed Dana as she looked over the crowd lining up in the glade to face the sacred path. Would the sapling take root? Would she receive a vision? Would it foretell prosperity and peace for the Kingdom of Eternia? She tried to catch Olga's and Sarai's gazes, but they were both looking away, blending with the waiting crowd. Dear spirits, was being the Maiden always going to feel this lonely?

Well, here goes. She turned her back to them and faced the hallowed grounds, raising her arms, feeling the sounds behind her die down into absolute stillness. The weight of everyone's gazes felt almost like a physical burden. Another thing she was going to have to get used to—being the center of attention, her victories and defeats

136

always in the public spotlight. She raised her voice, filling it with power that reverberated deeply over the hollow space.

"I am Dana. I have answered the call of the Great Tree of Origins and offered myself to become its appointed Maiden. I stand ready to undergo my trial, so that Eternia may receive blessings everlasting. O Great Tree, O Maidens past, please let your strength wash over me. Let the Arboreal Awakening commence!"

Silence lingered for another long moment. Then the crowd rustled behind her with murmurs of approval. It was as if something important had just happened. Dana set her foot on the path that wound down the rocks toward the hallowed grounds.

The path looped through a narrow crevice and over a rocky slope, descending steadily. Wind howled past as she picked her way, threatening to blow her off balance and into the gorge below.

Ahead, a flat area spread in a near-perfect circle, surrounded by a partially destroyed stone wall, crumbling away under a heavy layer of ivy. Prayer trees rose here and there, planted by other Maidens. The largest one in the distance looked many centuries old, but the closest one seemed recent, still a youngling—probably planted by Dana's predecessor.

A certainty she didn't fully understand guided her to the edge of the circle, where a narrow canyon separated the area from the foothills beyond, cascading to the distant sea. She dug a small hole and lowered the prayer sapling into it, then knelt beside it and concentrated, calling in the Essence.

The vision consumed her without warning. She saw a meadow overlooking the sea, much closer to the water than the one she was kneeling in. Butterflies fluttered over a lush carpet of grass and flowers. A bird circled high above in the clear blue sky. Calm sea stretched toward the horizon. Such a peaceful image.

Just as suddenly, the day shifted into night. The moons shone through a ripple of dark clouds. Thunder rolled overhead. Rain lashed her face—or was it the sea? She tasted salt on her lips. A wave rose up to meet her, rolling over her, dragging her away. The land disappeared, water closing over her head. She kicked toward the surface, but the sea was more powerful, dragging her down again, tumbling her as she sank into the depths. The world submerged into darkness.

D ana...? Are you alright?"

Dana gasped and opened her eyes.

She felt as if she were still drowning, as if she couldn't possibly draw a breath. As the vision cleared, she saw faces watching her in concern. Olga... Sarai... *Dear spirits, did I just have a blackout?* She blinked, forcing her mind back to reality.

She was in the mountain glade again, standing at the entrance to the sacred path. She didn't remember getting here from the hallowed grounds.

"What did you see?" Cecile demanded.

Dana heaved a few breaths, steadying her voice. "A... a beautiful sunlit meadow. The sea..." She paused. In truth, she had no idea what she'd seen. But now, with all eyes on her, she had no right to express doubt, to alarm all these people who gathered here in a celebratory mood to hear the good news.

"I saw a vision of a calm, beautiful ocean," she announced.

A pause. Then members of the royal family started to clap, and the rest joined in.

"How wonderful," a senior priestess said. "A calm ocean is a symbol of peace and prosperity. Surely Eternia will know peace in your time, Lady Dana."

Dana kept her smile, hoping her face betrayed none of the confusion she felt. What *was* that strange vision? And why did it feel as if she had just witnessed a true event, one that would definitely come to pass?

PLANS

Vivid as Adol's dreams had been before, the one last night had felt different. That vision of drowning had seemed so... familiar. Had Dana somehow dreamed Adol's experience from the shipwreck?

The thought, both wondrous and terrifying, wouldn't leave his head. Could Dana be dreaming about Adol the same way he was dreaming about her? Did their minds somehow bridge a gap between two realities? For a while, as he sat in his hammock, that other world felt far more real than his own.

His dreams about Dana were becoming too vivid to ignore. He could no longer discount them as crazy. There had to be a connection between Dana and this island—and Adol's arrival here had somehow triggered it, placing him right at the center of those events that felt too much like Dana's true memories. He couldn't escape a feeling that only by solving this mystery would he be able to escape this place. But where would he even start?

Outside the cave, the little girl they'd rescued from Kiergaard was standing near the fire. Quina. Small and skinny, she had bushy hair that simply wouldn't stay down despite any amount of combing, a sharp tongue, and an incessant drive to play tricks on people. According to Licht, Kiergaard must have kept her sedated since finding her after the shipwreck, but luckily the drugs didn't appear to have had any lasting damage. By now, she seemed just fine—a relief, considering what this poor child had been through.

"Adol," she sang when she saw him. "Adol off the starboard bow! Full speed ahead!" She ran straight at him, so that Adol had to swerve to avoid the collision. "Whoa, you're good. I didn't think you'd evade my deadly ramming attack."

Adol leaned down so that their faces were level. "Nice ramming."

She laughed. "I know, right? At this rate, I'll be makin' my raid battle debut in no time."

"Alright," Dogi rumbled, approaching the fire. "Settle down, Quina."

"Oh, barnacles. It's Dogi! See ya 'round, Adol!" She winked, then turned and ran away.

Dogi sighed as he watched her retreat. "It's been one week, and I'm already having trouble keeping up. I'm glad she's recovering well though."

Adol nodded. Quina had been unconscious when they saved her, so that thankfully she had been spared witnessing any part of the tragedy. Being used as bait to kill the captain had been yet another despicable act of the Nameless Killer. Adol didn't want to rejoice about anyone's death, but Kiergaard surely had it coming. He felt relieved the doctor wasn't around anymore.

Despite all the pinecones they kept finding in their beds, despite having to climb rocks and trees around camp to rescue Quina from the most unlikely places, it was good for all of them to have a child like her running around. The mood in the camp had been low since the captain's death, and a child's laughter brightened the atmosphere. They couldn't sit around and mourn forever. They needed to plan, so that they could keep their promise to the captain and get everyone off this island.

"We should discuss our next moves," Adol said. "Why don't you get the map? I'll go find Sahad and Laxia."

"Right." Dogi turned and walked off.

Sahad wasn't hard to find. He was fishing up on the rocks at the side of the beach, humming to himself. A large saman and a few boleh were flapping in a net hooked up in the shallow water next to him.

"We're gathering up near the fire to plan," Adol said.

Sahad nodded. In deft moves, he folded up his fishing gear then used his knife to gut and string the fish. It took him no more than a couple of minutes, a task that would have taken Adol half hour at least.

"Have you seen Laxia?" Adol asked.

"I think she's visitin' the cap'n."

They both glanced upward at the camp's upper terrace. Many castaways had taken to this habit lately, going to the captain's grave, sitting quietly beside it. Even in death he provided the villagers with strength and comfort, a leader they would always carry in their hearts.

"I'll go get her," Adol said.

A small garden spread over the upper terrace. Sister Nia, a young nun they'd rescued early on in one of the nearby caves, had taken charge of the area, and she had truly transformed the place. A flower bed in the center housed a tasteful array of colorful blossoms, lined around the edge with an elaborate pattern of rocks matched by color and shape. A long wooden bench made of log segments and wooden boards they'd found among the driftage stretched along the cliff at the back, a perfect spot to sit around and enjoy the view. The place felt holy somehow. Adol wasn't religious, but he couldn't find another word to describe the feeling of peace and tranquility that enfolded him every time he came here. The captain's grave couldn't have been positioned better, just off the garden, in a flat space at the highest point of the camp with the best view of the ocean.

Laxia stood by the captain's headstone, looking out to sea. She turned when Adol approached. Her eyes looked moist.

They stood side by side for a moment, watching the flowers planted over the captain's grave wavering in the breeze.

"It feels like we've been rudderless for the past week," Laxia said quietly. "I took for granted just how much we'd all come to depend on the captain."

Adol looked into the distance. He more than understood how Laxia felt. How was it possible that despite their weapon skills, despite the resourcefulness their team had shown in scouting the island and rescuing castaways, none of them had been able to do anything to save the captain? They could have discovered the Nameless sooner. They could have learned more about steel-wire traps. They could have stopped the captain from rushing in pursuit of the villain, held him back to prevent him from being harmed. They could have...He swallowed. He felt personally responsible for failing to do any of these things. But it was useless to think about it now.

"We have to keep moving forward," he said.

"Yes." Laxia nodded. "I know. It's just so hard. I guess I shouldn't be the one speaking. I've always been so sheltered, with you, the captain, and the other castaways protecting me this whole time."

"We've all protected each other."

Laxia shook her head. "Not equally. You remember how frustrated I used to get when we first arrived here? That's because I couldn't accept being uprooted from my sheltered life of privilege. In hindsight, I'm really embarrassed by my former conduct."

Adol regarded her. Of course he remembered. But he also knew that the Laxia she spoke about was gone for good.

"You've changed," he said.

She coughed to hide her embarrassment. "Not enough. From now on, I'd like to start making my own decisions, so I can accept responsibility for my future. I don't want to be the one who needs protection. I want to protect others, just like the captain."

"Gah-haha," a voice rumbled behind them. "Couldn't've said it better myself."

Adol sighed. Just like Sahad to ruin an emotional moment. And yet, the older man's presence was comforting. They could all use a dose of Sahad's down-to-earth wisdom and practicality.

"Remember that sayin' I once told you?" Sahad said. "You can't face the sea unless you first accept how small you are. You feel it now, don't you?"

Laxia nodded.

"We're going to be all right," Adol said. For the first time in a week, he really felt this way.

Sahad nodded earnestly. "Yeah. We've all got each other. Dogi, Euron, an' the others too. The cap'n may be gone, but we're still part o' his crew, and we are stronger together than anything this island can possibly throw at us. We all gotta survive, so that we can fulfill the cap'n's last wish."

A faint half-smile touched Laxia's lips. "Yes... You're right."

"Enough talkin'," Sahad said. "Dogi must be wonderin' what's takin' us so long."

After a last glance at the captain's grave, they left to join Dogi at the fire.

To get off the island," Dogi said, "we're gonna need a few things. First, a ship big enough to traverse the open waters and carry all of us."

Sahad scratched his head. "You'd need an expert shipbuilder with detailed blueprints to pull that off. Unlike the cap'n, all I know 'bout ships is how to steer 'em."

"The ship is only a part of it," Laxia said. "That marine Primordial is still out there, remember? Unless we drive it back somehow, big ship or not, we'll meet the same fate as Sir Carlan."

"It seems to me," Adol said, "that we still have a lot to discover here on the island."

"True," Laxia said. "We still have no idea what lies across these mountains in the center of the island. For all we know, the lands beyond may be even more extensive than the southern part."

They all looked. On this clear day, the peak seemed even taller, a giant edifice of stone ascending almost vertically into the clouds.

"The captain and I discussed this," Dogi said. "And I did a lot of scouting to see if there was a way north. The sea around these cliffs is impassable. The only way is to scale that mountain. But even before we can attempt it, we'll have to cross a very deep valley that lies in between. You've seen it, haven't you?"

"We did," Adol confirmed. That area up from T's watchtower, where a landslide had likely destroyed the path across the gorge, leaving an abyss so deep they couldn't see the bottom. He could think of no way to cross it without serious climbing gear—impossible with the resources they had.

"I still say we don't bother," Sahad said. "It could just be barren land out there."

"Or there could be more castaways," Adol said. *Not to mention unexplored mysteries that may give some clues about Dana's world.*

"True," Laxia agreed. "We should try harder to find a way up that mountain. Why don't we explore the area around that gorge?"

"Well, I suppose we could." Sahad looked at the distant peak again. "Man, that mountain...It sorta reminds me o' Euron. A real hardass, always standin' at attention."

"If it reminds you of an uptight military man," Laxia said, "perhaps we should call it 'Gendarme'."

"Right." Sahad didn't look too sure, but he didn't offer any objections.

A BRIDGE FROM THE PAST

The gap across the gorge up from T's watchtower looked impassable—too wide to bridge, as Adol originally hoped they could do. But something about the area felt different today from the way he remembered it. He couldn't escape a feeling he'd seen this place very recently, possibly from a different perspective.

That grove of ancient trees surrounding the meadow on the other side . . . Were those . . .

Prayer trees?

He peered across the gorge.

The meadow over there formed a near-perfect circle, creased by a line of rocks that could have been a low stone wall once, a very long time ago. The trees rising around the ruin were spaced evenly, as if planted with a conscious effort to give them enough room to grow.

Adol's skin prickled.

This couldn't possibly be the hallowed grounds he'd seen in his dream about Dana's Arboreal Awakening, could it?

The more he looked at it, the more convinced he felt. The layout of the space, the path climbing away from it on the far end . . . If he closed his eyes, he could almost see Dana kneeling over there, bent in prayer over a tiny sapling peeking out of the soil.

That one?

The tree had surely grown from the way he'd seen it in Dana's time, probably millennia ago. But no matter how much it changed, Adol felt certain it had to be the one, planted closest to the edge, as if deliberately placed here to fulfill a purpose. Its main trunk was dead—likely charred by a lightning strike a very long time ago—sending its lower branches curving along the ground. They stretched over the chasm toward Adol, as if extending a helping hand.

A pile of rocks at the bend of the path concealed the rest of the view, but as Adol raced in that direction, he *knew* it in his heart what he was going to see.

A bridge, solid and broad, formed by the protruding tree branches that had reached all the way across and wedged themselves into a rock formation on this side of the gap.

How in the world was this possible?

"Look," Laxia whispered.

Sahad whistled. "Fancy that. I don't remember seein' this bridge before. I guess we must have somehow overlooked it."

Adol didn't say anything. He *knew* they couldn't have possibly overlooked something like this. Neither could Dogi, who had specially scouted this area to look for a path into the mountains. It seemed impossible for this ancient tree to have grown out here in the two weeks that passed since they'd last ventured this way. Yet that had to be exactly what had happened. The sapling Dana had planted during Arboreal Awakening in that exact spot had somehow spanned time and space and appeared here straight from her distant era to provide a means for Adol and his companions to cross the gorge.

He felt as if he were in one of his dreams again, two realities converging into one. There was no way Dana could have done this deliberately, to make sure they could explore the northern side of the island. But try as he might, he couldn't come up with any other explanation.

Sooner or later, he had to tell his companions about his dreams. But first he needed to come to terms with the idea. And that meant discounting everything he knew to be possible and abandoning rational thought.

The abyss below looked like a bowl of mist, flanked by steep cliffs descending out of sight. He tried not to look down as he edged across the chasm to the ground on the other side.

Laxia stepped off the bridge in his wake and patted the mighty tree trunk. "Fascinating. According to modern knowledge, these trees should have been extinct for ages."

"Same as the Primordials, huh?" Sahad looked up at a giant winged creature circling high overhead.

Laxia gaped. "A ... *Pterosaur*? How in the world ... ?"

Adol kept silent, watching the flying Primordial. He'd seen one just like it before,, a giant bird with a long tail. in a vision when he'd first landed on the island. Could crossing this gorge have taken them a step closer to Dana's world? His heart raced as he set on the path leading away from the gorge and up into the mountains.

The path wound around the prayer trees and up a narrow canyon toward the rocky cliffs. Following it, Adol continued to feel as if he'd been here before. How else could he explain the way the sights waiting for them behind each twist of the path looked exactly as he expected? That rock wall, creased by a series of protrusions and gaps that made the entire formation look wrinkled. The passage between the tall cliffs ahead, so narrow that the wind whistled as it blew between them, threatening to knock the travelers off their feet. In his dream, Dana had walked this path in reverse—and of course, nothing here looked exactly the same—but he felt almost relieved when the road finally opened into an unfamiliar area, a small grassy meadow squeezed between boulders on one side and the rock face on the other.

Two rhino-sized lizards stood here, munching grass. Fat and scaly, they had large heads decorated with tall spiky crests and thick horns protruding off the tips of their heavy snouts.

"More Primordials," Laxia said with fascination. "A herbivore species. Can you believe—" She rushed forward, but Sahad held her back.

"They're not botherin' anyone," he said. "Maybe we should take it as a hint, ye know?"

Laxia seemed disappointed, but she offered no objections as they skirted the clearing and continued uphill.

The path climbed a set of ledges, clinging to the steep stone wall. A sheer drop on its other side opened directly into the abyss. The view of the island spread beyond, all the way to the sea. From here, the lands below seemed so tiny, peeking through the blue haze like a toy landscape in a craftsman's shop.

Adol took mental notes as they walked. That area off to the southeast of the bay was new, as yet unexplored. Shallow hills down there surrounded a ravine with a large lake, its edges fuzzy with reeds and swamp grass. Beyond it, a jagged line of rocks ran up to the seaside. Another beach? Could be. It didn't look very accessible, but they should at least try to explore it after they returned from Gendarme.

After a few more bends, they unexpectedly emerged onto level ground. A meadow spread ahead, its thick carpet of grass sprinkled with colorful flowers.

It looked so out of place halfway up the mountain, a peaceful oasis in the middle of the rough terrain. A spring trickled down the side of the meadow, gathering into a pond of crystal-clear water. A cluster of trees and bushes beside it rose protectively around a small cabin, tucked into a cozy crevice between the rocks.

A cabin?

Adol stared.

"Am I seein' what I'm seein'?" Sahad asked hoarsely.

"I don't know about you." Laxia's trembling voice betrayed a conscious effort to sound reasonable. "I see a cabin. It appears to be well maintained."

True. If one were to be rational about it, the mere fact of a cabin here shouldn't be that surprising. After all, they had already found traces of a pirate settlement, and even a recently built watchtower. It was the fact that this cabin looked so solid and well cared for that set Adol's mind racing.

Someone had to be living here right now.

They approached the cabin and knocked on the door, but no one answered. Peeking through the windows, they could see a small, neat room set with cozy furniture. It appeared empty.

"Perhaps we should check it out?" Laxia asked hesitantly.

Sahad scratched his head. "I dunno. Would the owner mind it if we just walked in?"

They both looked at Adol, as if the decision was up to him.

"Let's just make sure we don't disturb anything," he said.

The door was not locked. The room inside was comfortably arranged to make the best use of the limited space. Two beds lined one wall, with a small stove placed between them in the exact spot that would enable both occupants to make the best use of its warmth. A stack of shelves on the other side held neatly arranged supplies, dishes, and even a teapot, complete with a set of elegant but mismatched cups. Another small shelf by the window housed a few books. A vase with a bouquet of fresh flowers, tastefully arranged from the varieties they'd seen in the meadow outside, decorated the table. This one detail left no doubt that someone was living here right now. These flowers had to have been picked just this morning.

They spread around the room, surveying the furnishings. Adol stopped by the stove. Still warm, confirming that it had been used very recently. It was also skillfully built, its neatly stacked stones fused by clay, its chimney molded into the ceiling to leave no gaps for smoke to escape. An expert's job, as far as Adol could tell.

"Who do you think lives here?" Laxia asked. "Another castaway from the *Lombardia*?"

"Two castaways," Adol corrected, looking at the beds. Both had definitely been slept in, one more recently than the other. "And if I were to guess, no one from the *Lombardia* would have had the time to build this kind of a house and craft all these items in the few weeks we've been here. This stove alone must've taken a while."

"Someone from previous shipwrecks then?"

Adol didn't respond, his eyes trailing to one of the books on the shelf by the window. It looked like a journal, or a diary. He picked it up.

"I don't think you should read that without permission, Adol," Laxia protested.

"I'll make sure to apologize when we meet the owner." Adol flipped the pages. Laxia and Sahad edged over to join him.

"This handwriting looks familiar," Laxia said.

"I know. Wait—" Sahad snapped his fingers. "Oh, yeah. The T fella."

Right. There was no mistaking the hand—a special flourish at the capital letters, distinct enough to remember. So this was where T lived. Adol couldn't wait to meet this person.

"Curious." Laxia craned her neck over Adol's shoulder, looking at the page. "This notebook appears to contain information about Primordials."

"What's it say?" Sahad asked.

"*Some of them make nests in caves and tend to be aggressive and territorial. Their flesh is harder than I imagined. Conventional weapons can't even pierce it. Still, there might be a way to harm them by using—*" She paused. "The rest of this page has been torn out. I wonder why?"

"There's a lot of books here," Sahad pointed out.

"Judging by their state, they must have all washed ashore." Laxia ran her eyes over the spines. "This one is about medieval knights...A guide to serving tea. And these..." She paused, her cheeks lighting up with color. Looking at the spines, Adol recognized a set of romance novels, popular a few years ago.

They debated waiting around for the cabin's owners to return home but eventually decided against it. Who knew where they had gone, and for how long? Besides, there was only one path from here leading to the areas uphill they hadn't yet explored. If they followed it, there was a good chance they'd meet the cabin's inhabitants on the way.

As they continued up the mountain, Adol couldn't stop thinking about that diary passage they'd just read. Primordials. Clearly, the mysterious T had problems with these creatures too. Without weapons that could harm them, heading up a mountain rich with Primordial species seemed like a very bad idea. What chances would the party have if they encountered one of them on a narrow mountain path—or worse, in one of the caves these creatures apparently favored as nesting grounds, such as the one gaping directly ahead? The path ran inside, with no apparent way around.

"Did that diary say Primordials lived in caves?" Sahad asked tensely.

"It did," Laxia confirmed.

"I don't know 'bout you," Sahad said. "I feel like we've had enough explorin' for one day. The sun will be settin' soon. Maybe we should camp in that meadow and wait for that T to come back an' tell us what was on that missin' diary page."

Adol peered into the narrow cave opening. It was probably a reasonable idea to pause and try to figure out a way to defeat the Primordials before venturing any further. But doing so might delay them for days. He didn't like the idea. Crazy as it seemed, he felt certain Dana had planted that prayer tree sapling to enable them to cross into this area. Whatever waited for them over that mountain had to be really important. With his dreams about Dana getting more and more intense, he had a feeling they were running out of time.

"I think I see light up ahead," he said. "This cave probably stretches only a short way to connect to the path on the other end."

Sahad adjusted the hammer over his shoulder. He and Laxia exchanged hesitant glances.

"I'll scout," Adol said. "You two wait here. If it looks dangerous, we'll turn back and set up camp."

"All right," Laxia said. "Just be careful."

Adol nodded, then drew his sword and edged inside.

The low passage widened a short way from the entrance, opening into a large vaulted cavern that stretched deeper into the shadows. Most of the floor here was covered with shallow, crystal-clear water. A streak of daylight shone from a distant opening on the far end, throwing reflections that made the place look like a giant ballroom gleaming with a smoothly polished floor. Adol could hear no sounds except his own footsteps as he waded knee-deep toward the center of the cave.

He was about to call Laxia and Sahad and tell them it was safe, when he heard a clatter of rocks in the depths of the cave, followed by a roar that echoed loudly under the vault. He hadn't realized the cave ran so deep in that direction. He spun around just in time to face a huge lizard rushing out of the shadows toward him.

It looked like a twin of the one that had devoured Doctor Kiergaard and attacked the village not so long ago. Or was it the same one? He peered at its face, trying to spot a scar from Hummel's bullet, but in the shadows it was hard to tell.

He'd previously faced this creature out in the open, with plenty of room for maneuvers and multiple escape routes. Here in the cave, the space felt much too confined. Running through water slowed him down and severely limited his ability to dive and roll over the ground—the tactics extremely useful against the deadly claws and long leathery tail that proved to have an inordinate reach. He barely had time to jump over as the tail swept across his feet, raising a wave and splattering water into his face. His blade bounced off the creature's hide without doing any serious damage.

"Adol!" Sahad shouted from the passage behind.

"Run!" Adol snarled, diving forward between the creature's legs as it tried to grab him with its front paw. The limb looked tiny compared to the creature's size. But each of its claws was as long as a dagger—and just as sharp. It reached for him again, forcing him to back into the cave wall.

Sharp pain erupted in his chest as the claw swept across, but he managed to maintain his footing. The wound seemed superficial enough to ignore, so he pushed the pain out of his mind, slashing out in a complex set of moves that would have given him advantage against any normal opponent, but proved completely ineffective in this case. The creature kept him firmly on the defensive, snapping with its teeth and sweeping with its tail and claws as it backed him into a crevice between tall rocks. He searched for a gap, but the creature seemed to anticipate his moves, shifting to match him every time.

Screams echoed through the cavern as Laxia and Sahad rushed at the creature, hacking and stabbing. The Primordial didn't even turn, focused on Adol with a determination that made the fight seem almost personal. Did it recognize its opponent from before? Was it intelligent enough to judge that Adol was the main threat that needed to be dealt with to defeat the others? Probably not, but it didn't really matter to the outcome.

Adol feigned a lounge, then shifted his weight, aiming for the brief opening on the other side. The creature swept across to block him, bumping Sahad out of the way. Its paw lashed out, slamming Adol hard against the rock wall.

His head exploded with pain, air draining out of his lungs. Whispers filled his ears, blending into a chorus that echoed and amplified under the cave's vault. Voices—more of them than he remembered—including a shrill, high-pitched shriek that sounded more like a battle cry.

His hand unclenched on its own. His sword clattered over the rocks and into the shallow water.

His vision darkened.

ELDERSPHERE

The Maiden of the Great Tree was entitled to many privileges that set her apart from other inhabitants of the Temple. But the only one Dana truly appreciated was having her own room, next to the main hall and the entrance to the Great Tree Garden. The room probably didn't need to be so large and elaborate, but it was easy to get used to the luxury. The bed was soft and comfortable, even if far too excessive for one person. The sturdy wooden table had enough room for spreading dozens of books and maps, and still leaving enough space to set out a meal without disturbing all the working disorder. A bookshelf in the corner sported a selection of the kingdom's rarest volumes, some of them hundreds of years old. A prayer niche by the far wall glistened with ornate stone carvings, no less elaborate than the ones in the main hall. The room even had an escape hatch, assessable by pulling a secret lever at the side of the bookshelf—as well as its own spring that trickled directly from the wall, gathering into a stone basin that could be used for washing, drinking, or just splashing on her face for refreshment. Here, in the center of the Temple, there was no possibility to have a window with a view, but transparent panes overhead admitted enough light to make the room feel bright and serene, a refuge from all the bustle outside. After another day of celebrations, Dana felt she truly needed it. She headed directly for the stone bench beside the spring and curled up with her knees to her chest, enjoying the peace.

She couldn't stop thinking about the vision she had received at the Arboreal Awakening. Day turning into night. Clear skies erupting with a thunderstorm. Waves, dragging her underwater. Drowning. She felt it as clearly as if she had physically experienced it. She wanted to believe this was an omen of Eternia's prosperity and peace, but it was a difficult stretch to manage.

A knock on the door interrupted her thoughts. So much for solitude.

"Come in," she called.

The door opened to admit Sarai, dressed in a green cloak over an ornate tunic, with the Temple emblem over her throat—the same outfit she'd worn at the ceremony. She held a large elongated box that she set on the floor beside the door before walking across the room toward Dana.

"Pardon me, Your Eminence." Despite the formal greeting, Sarai's smile looked warm. Just like the old times, when they sneaked out after hours to do something forbidden.

Dana jumped up from her seat and rushed toward her friend. "Sarai! What are you doing here at this hour?"

Sarai hesitated, her smile slowly receding. "I...I came to say goodbye."

"Goodbye?"

"I'm afraid, yes. I'm leaving first thing tomorrow."

Dana's heart fell. The unsuccessful Maiden candidates were offered a choice—to stay at the Temple and assume other posts, or to return to their families back home. Most chose to stay, but a few left, to pursue different paths. Dana had never had a chance to talk to Olga and Sarai about these choices, but she'd always assumed they would remain by her side. In fact, she had decided to offer Olga the position of the High Priestess, the second highest authority in the Temple, and she was considering Sarai as an eventual replacement for Advisor Urgunata. Sarai, leaving...She paused, unsure what to say.

"It wasn't exactly my choice," Sarai said. "I would have loved to stay at the Temple and help you, but...My family asked me to come home. I cannot possibly refuse."

Family. When Dana joined the Temple, she'd known she was never going to see her family again. Her whole life was here. She tended to assume the same was true for others, but now that the subject came up, she realized she knew absolutely nothing about Sarai's life before she came to the Temple. How come her closest friend had never spoken about her family at all? And why hadn't she ever asked?

She swallowed. "I understand. If your family wants you to come home, then you've made the right decision. I'm going to miss you, though." *Will we ever see each other again?* She didn't voice the question.

Sarai held her gaze for a moment then turned away to pick up the box she had set on the floor when she entered. "I have a gift for you to remember me by."

"A gift?" Dana raised her eyebrows. In the Temple, they didn't really have any possessions. What could Sarai possibly give her? "You don't have to—"

"Please, I insist." Sarai set the box on the table. "Open it."

Tentatively, Dana reached out and removed the lid.

Inside were two crescent swords.

She gasped, her eyes drawn to the intricate workmanship.

Thin and razor-sharp, the swords seemed almost too perfect to be real. Even without touching them, she could tell that the curve of the blades, creased by long notches and grooves, and the fluid lines of the hilts that begged to fit perfectly into her hands, had been forged by a master craftsman. A blend of lightness and strength, force and balance—weapons fit for a queen. How had Sarai come across this kind of a treasure?

"I named them for you," Sarai said. "Eldersphere. Befitting for the Maiden, don't you think?"

"Are they..." Dana's breath caught.

Sarai smiled. "Yes, they are. Pure orichalcum, strong enough to fell Saurians."

"But...Wasn't orichalcum all mined out?"

"A stratum of ancient rock was recently unearthed near the Great Valley. It contains deposits of pure orichalcum of exceptional quality."

Questions swirled in Dana's head. How could Sarai possibly afford blades like this? Why was she giving them away? How did she know about a new orichalcum deposit even Dana hadn't heard about?

"I—I can't possibly accept such a precious gift," she said.

Sarai put a hand on her shoulder. "You don't have a choice. These blades were custom-made to match your height and build. They're yours. I wish you many happy training sessions with these, in memory of all the good times we had. Perhaps you can even steal a match with Rastell some time."

Rastell. They hadn't seen each other for at least a year, since Rastell had started training to become an elite guard, like his father. The Maiden candidates had moved on too, their lessons with the Chief Guard replaced by others that focused more on meditation and controlling their Essence use. Dana wasn't sure when she and Rastell would see each other again. She had moved on—as she was sure he had. But the idea of crossing blades with him on the training range brought memories back. If only they could do it someday.

She couldn't draw her eyes away from the crescent swords. Custom-made to match her height and build. Sarai of all people knew how being a head shorter than most of her peers was a huge disadvantage during their sparring sessions. With blades like these...

"Go on, try them," Sarai prompted.

Dana lifted the swords out of the box.

The hilts fit into her hands fluidly, as if they had always belonged there. As she swung the swords, she felt lighter, her entire being blending with the blades into a single creature of air. She had never known metal could be so light and so powerful at the same time. She felt as if she'd grown a pair of wings.

She turned to Sarai, who was watching her breathlessly.

"Thank you," she said.

Sarai inclined her head. "With your skill, it would have been a crime not to get you the kind of blades you deserve. Besides, it's only a small token. I really wish I could have stayed here with you." She stepped forward and covered Dana's hands with hers.

They stood like this for a moment, eyes closed, heads bent, one of the ways they'd learned to share the Essence, more intimate than an embrace.

"I've always wondered what makes you so determined," Sarai said. "You've always been more willful than most. I don't expect that side of you to change any time soon."

Dana forced a laugh. "Olga says I need to change the way I behave, even the way I talk. I'm trying really hard to be better, but it's so difficult."

Sarai shook her head. "Olga means well, but she's wrong in this case. Don't allow anyone—or anything—to change what you are. No matter what happens in the future, always be true to yourself."

"Sarai..." Dana's breath caught. It was going to take her a while to come to terms with losing her best friend. She hoped Sarai was going to find happiness with her family, whatever awaited her. Most of all, she hoped they were going to see each other again.

RICOTTA

Laxia felt absolutely terrified. As she leaned over Adol, lying unconscious on the cave floor, she had to remind herself that this continuous bleeding from the nasty gash on his chest was only possible for someone alive, with a steady heartbeat. The thought wasn't as comforting as intended, but it was better than the alternative.

Adol had always been the strong one, who took care of others. In the short time she'd known him, she'd never seen him lose a fight or fail at any task he put his mind to. And now . . .

"That wound doesn't look too good," a voice said beside her.

Laxia turned. In all the excitement, she hadn't had a chance to take a good look at the strange young girl. Too much had been going on when she showed up out of nowhere and drove the beast away with gleaming throwing darts that seemed to be made of pure fire. She looked to be about twelve, dressed in a colorful outfit patched together from different pieces of cloth, her high pigtails decorated with leaves and berries tucked into the hairbands. Definitely not a castaway from the *Lombardia*. Laxia would have remembered someone like her.

"He might have a concussion too," the girl went on. "Father says if someone hits his head and passes out, a concussion is likely."

They both looked at Adol. Laxia swallowed. She'd seen the beast grab Adol and slam him hard against the rock. It was a miracle he was still breathing.

"We'll have to move him," the girl said. "That beast might come back, and I'm down to my last dart."

Laxia glanced at Sahad, standing a few paces away.

"I can carry him," Sahad said. "He ain't that heavy."

Adol's eyes fluttered open. He blinked several times, as if having trouble focusing. "I'm fine."

His voice was barely a whisper. Laxia never heard him sound so weak. Her lips trembled, and she covered them with her hand.

The new girl leaned over Adol. "Do you think you can make it back to my cabin? It's very close, but the path's kind of steep."

"Move over, li'l squirt." Sahad reached down, but Laxia put a hand on his arm.

"Wait. He needs to move by himself first, to make sure nothing's broken."

"And if it is?"

"We don't want to make it worse."

"Worse?" Sahad frowned. "I ain't no doctor, but it already looks pretty bad to me."

"It's no big deal," Adol said. He winced, trying to lift up. It took him several attempts. Sahad glanced sideways at Laxia and reached over to help.

The gash on Adol's chest looked bad. Blood oozed steadily, soaking his torn shirt. Watching it, Laxia felt a weakness in the pit of her stomach. Dealing with messy injuries wasn't her strong suit. But she couldn't afford to show weakness. They needed to get Adol out of here and bandage his wound before he lost too much blood. She searched around for Adol's sword, while Sahad lifted him up to his feet and walked him carefully toward the cave exit.

"Let's take it slowly," the new girl said. "My cabin's just around the corner. It's very safe, no beasts ever bother us in there ... Oh, by the way, I'm Ricotta. Can't believe I finally found more humans."

Ricotta chatted incessantly as they walked, waiting patiently as Sahad helped Adol down steep climbs and over narrow ledges that made the path treacherous even to a healthy person. Listening to her made for a welcome distraction.

By the end of the short trip, Laxia learned a lot about the girl. She loved books, flowers, and brightly colored rocks she sometimes found on the beach. She used to go there frequently to look for driftage, but a recent landslide had destroyed the path. Her father had built this cabin and took care of her. He was going to build a bridge to restore access to the beach too. He wasn't her real father, but she didn't have any other family, so she considered him her real father anyway.

Words poured out of her effortlessly, so that they didn't even have to prompt her with questions. She wasn't sure how old exactly she was, but she could talk to animals and understand their language, and soon she was going to grow into a beautiful young woman with an hourglass figure all men would swoon over. Laxia wondered if that last bit had to do with all the romance novels they'd seen on the shelf in her cabin.

Ricotta took charge as soon as they arrived in the cabin, starting a fire in the stove and bringing pails of water from the spring outside. Sahad lowered Adol to the floor beside the wall and stripped off his blood-soaked shirt. The bleeding wasn't getting any better.

"We need to cauterize the wound," Adol said through clenched teeth.

"Cateu—what?" Sahad blinked.

"Cauterize." Laxia swallowed. Nausea rose in her throat. She knew about cauterization from the guide to field medicine her father always brought on exploration trips. Pressing hot metal to the wound was a very effective way to stop the bleeding and kill infection. It also caused excruciating pain. Would Adol be able to take it in his condition?

"I don't think—" she began, but Adol wasn't listening. He still looked dazed, but his hand was surprisingly steady as he pulled out his dagger and handed it to Sahad.

"I need it red-hot," he said. "Put it in the stove for a few minutes. I'll do the rest."

Laxia swallowed a lump, watching Sahad take the dagger from Adol and hold it over the fire. Out of the corner of her eye she could see Ricotta in the back of the room, standing very still, eyes wide. Had she seen this done before? The fear in her eyes suggested it. Laxia marveled at the way Adol looked so calm, the only one here with his wits about him. He didn't even flinch as he took the dagger from Sahad and pressed it to the wound without a second's hesitation.

Only by knowing Adol so well could she tell how much pain he was in. His face was already pale from all the blood loss, but as he leaned into the wall at his back and closed his eyes, it turned grayish, ghostly. The moments ticked endlessly as he held the dagger steadily in place.

She had to force herself not to look away, not even when he finally removed the blade, leaving behind a long, angry burn. The wound was no longer bleeding, but it probably hurt even more than before.

Healing was certainly going to take a very long time.

"I wish we had something to ease the pain," she said quietly to Ricotta. "Perhaps I could go outside and look for an aloe plant?" At least it would soothe the burn, assuming she could find one at this elevation.

"I have poppy milk," Ricotta said. "Father always keeps some around in case one of us gets seriously injured." She leaned over Adol. "Want some?"

Adol kept her gaze for a moment, then nodded.

Despite the poppy, the throbbing in Adol's chest wasn't easing at all. He drifted in and out of sleep, conversations from the table reaching him through the fog in his head.

That dream about Dana he'd had while unconscious kept bothering him. He couldn't stop feeling its timing was not a coincidence. It had told him something important, something relevant to his current situation. But in his dazed state, he couldn't quite place what it was.

Laxia, Sahad, and Ricotta were drinking tea, the clatter of cups from the mismatched tea service echoing unnaturally loud in his head. Curiously, their conversation wasn't nearly as clear, even though in this small room there should be no problem hearing every word. He didn't think he had a concussion, but that would certainly explain this hollowness in his head that made his thoughts loop around and blend together until he couldn't remember where the information was coming from.

His mind was pulling out bits and pieces, merging the conversation at the table with everything he'd learned from Ricotta's chatter on their way back from the cave. Her father, Thanatos Beldine—the mysterious T—had traveled up the mountain about a month ago to observe the Primordials and was still missing. Those gleaming darts Ricotta had used to drive away the beast back in the cave were his invention, made of some mysterious metal only Thanatos knew how to work. *The metal.* Why did Adol keep feeling that this one detail was the most important one?

He drifted off and came to again to see Ricotta holding up a small throwing dart. The sun was setting outside. The poppy was wearing off, clearing his mind just enough to sharpen the pain.

In the gathering shadows, the dart in Ricotta's hand seemed to glow, as if emitting a light of its own.

"May I see it?" he said.

They all stopped talking, turning to him with concerned looks. Ricotta lit a lantern and brought it to the bed.

"Are you feeling all right?" she said.

"Better." He knew he didn't sound too convincing, but she didn't object when he pulled himself up, wincing as he settled with his back against the wall. If only he could find a position that would make his wound hurt less. He tried to distance himself from the pain as he took the dart from Ricotta, twirling it in his hand.

It looked quite plain, a short wooden shaft with a few feathers strapped to it by a piece of waxed cord. But the tip...He brought it closer to his eyes.

He hadn't imagined the glow. He'd seen this metal before—strong and light, gleaming faintly from within.

Dana's crescent blades, the gift from Sarai, were made of metal exactly like this.

Sarai had told Dana that this metal could be used against Saurians. Had they been referring to Primordials?

"Where did your father get this metal?" he asked.

"In an old cave," Ricotta said. "A few hours' walk from here. We used to go there often, but then the bridge father built to reach that place collapsed, so we haven't been there in a long time. That's why we are running out of darts. I was hoping when father comes back..." She paused.

Adol glanced at Laxia and Sahad. Through his daze, he hadn't caught all the conversation about Ricotta's father, but he'd heard the part where he'd gone missing after traveling to the north side of the island. If they found a way to cross the mountains without falling victims to Primordials, they would be able to rescue him, if he was still alive.

"If you could help us get more of this metal," he said, "we'll use it to make new weapons, so that we can go look for your father."

"Really?" Ricotta's face lit with such hope that Adol's heart quivered. What was it like for her, living out here all alone, venturing out with her last few darts to look for her father, knowing that he may never come back?

"I promise," he said. "If you can lead us to that cave, we—"

"Adol," Laxia protested. "You're in no shape to go anywhere."

"I'll be better tomorrow. I just need some sleep."

"Yes, and after you do, the only place we're going to is back to the village."

"Right." Sahad nodded. "Maybe Dina can make him a healin' potion. And Licht—he's a doctor, isn't he?"

"A medical resident," Laxia corrected.

"Same thing. I'm sure he can patch Adol right up."

"Your village?" Ricotta asked.

"Down by the beach," Laxia explained. "There are many castaways living there."

"Many?" Ricotta's eyes widened. "Can I go there with you?"

"Ye don't expect we'd leave you here all by yourself, do you?" Sahad rumbled.

"We're not going anywhere," Laxia said firmly, "until Adol's well enough to make the trip. Besides, it's getting late anyway." She glanced out of the window, where the beams of the setting sun pierced the distant clouds, painting them into bold, fiery strokes. "Can we stay here tonight, Ricotta?"

"Yay!" Ricotta beamed. "Of course you can! Some of you will have to sleep on the floor, but I have enough bedding to settle everyone in. We'll have a sleepover and go to your village first thing in the morning and get Adol patched up and go to the cave and make more darts and go find Father!"

ORICHALCUM

Adol didn't remember most of the trip back to the village. Dizziness and throbbing in his chest made the steep descent an effort that took most of his energy and attention. He considered it an achievement when everyone finally stopped giving him sideways looks and asking how he was feeling all the time.

Ricotta's chatter provided a good distraction. Her knowledge of local plant and animal species impressed even Laxia, who kept referencing her book as Ricotta pointed things out. They also learned about a giant shoebill that mentored Ricotta when she was little, and a large ape she referred to as Master Kong, who had taught her to fight.

The sight of the tree bridge growing across the chasm made Ricotta pause. She gaped at it for a while, then insisted on crossing it back and forth several times, just to make sure it was real. Adol felt dizzy watching her run over the chasm, so small on the backdrop of the deep gorge with mist rising from its depths. He crossed slowly, much less certain of his footing than he had been when they first used this bridge on their ascent yesterday.

The party made another lengthy stop at Ricotta's father's watchtower so that she could climb up to check for new notes and any clues on his whereabouts. Thankfully, she didn't feel in the least bit discouraged to find everything the same as when she'd been here last time. Instead, this apparent failure only reinforced her certainty that he was waiting for them on the other side of the island. Adol hoped with all his heart that she was right.

Only when they finally arrived in Castaway Village did the girl suddenly become quiet. She stopped abruptly at the entrance, looking around with wide eyes. Her gaze absorbed everything—the watchtower, Euron's workstation, Dina's supply stand, people sitting around the burning campfire.

Just as quickly as she had stopped her chatter, she started up again, louder and faster than before.

"What's that tall structure?" She pointed. "Why's the fire burning? Why are these people gathered here? Why—"

"Whoa," Sahad said. "One question at a time, squirt. That tall structure is our watchtower. We built one, just like yer dad, to spot danger and look out for ships. As for the fire..." He paused with a thoughtful look. "This is the village center. People gather here to eat, talk, an' whatnot. On the mainland, they got cities what have even more people an' buildings than this."

"Cities?" Her eyes widened. "I've read about those!"

Sahad laughed softly. "Don't take my word fer it, though. I've never actually been to a city before."

Ricotta laughed too as she looked up at him. "Let's visit one together some day, deal?"

"Deal."

Adol marveled at their energy. After the hike, he felt ready to collapse. He glanced around, wondering if anyone would notice him just sneaking quietly into the lodge, but at that moment, Laxia, who had been holding back at the entrance to the village, came up to his side. She looked a bit misty-eyed as she watched Ricotta and Sahad by the fire, greeting the other villagers.

"Sahad is so good with children," she said. "They almost look like father and daughter."

Adol nodded. "Well, he *is* a father to a little girl. That makes him a natural, doesn't it?"

"Not necessarily." Laxia lowered her eyes briefly. "Anyway. After we settle Ricotta in, we should—" She paused as Adol swayed and grasped her shoulder for support. "Adol? *Adol?*"

Licht proved to be one hell of a doctor. When Adol came to, lying in one of the beds in his field clinic, the throbbing in his chest had receded and his head wasn't swimming anymore.

His eyes trailed to Dogi, sitting by his bedside with a concerned look.

"I've never known you to be so reckless," Dogi said. "I'm feelin' I should go with you next time—to keep you out of harm, y'know."

"It was an accident," Adol said. "Not going to happen again."

"If you say so." Dogi ran his eyes over the bandage covering Adol's chest. Adol looked too. Clean and dry, it was laid so expertly he could barely feel it. Licht must have used some salve to stop the pain. At times, Adol could almost forget anything was wrong with him at all.

"At least the ladies are all swoonin' over you again." Dogi pointed with his chin to where Laxia, Alison, and Ricotta were gathered near Dina's stand, all four of them looking in his direction. He smiled and waved at them. Ricotta giggled, and they all turned away, chattering among themselves.

"That's what you really did it for, isn't it?" Dogi said. "All the attention. I mean, just look at them. You didn't need to give them any excuse, did you?"

Adol laughed. He was glad the incident was over, and he and Dogi could just sit around joking about it.

"We should go talk to Kathleen." He reached into his pocket and brought out Ricotta's dart. "This metal can kill Primordials, and we might just have found a way to get more of it."

Dogi looked at the dart with interest. "That would be nice. But you're not talkin' to anyone or goin' around mining any metal until Doctor Licht allows it. In fact, he put me here to make sure you don't run away while he's inside getting supplies. Hospital rules." He turned, watching the doctor walk toward them from the lodge.

Licht didn't talk as he set out his medicine bag, then opened Adol's bandage and examined the wound—all closed and dry, as far as Adol could tell. The doctor felt Adol's forehead, then rubbed a salve into his skin and closed the bandage again.

"I know what you are wondering about," he said. "And yes, you can get up and walk around the camp if you feel well enough, but no exploration for now. Your wound is healing well, but I'm not so sure about that nasty bruise on your head. I'd like to observe it for a while. If there are no complications, you may resume your exploration in day or two. In the meantime, if you feel any dizziness or pain, come back at once, do you understand?"

"I'll make sure he does," Dogi said.

Adol got out of bed. He still felt a bit lightheaded, but he was sure it was going to wear off in no time. He'd dealt with worse injuries before.

Kathleen kept turning Ricotta's dart over in her hands as she listened to their story. When they were finished, she placed the dart on her anvil, looking at it thoughtfully. They waited, but she didn't say anything.

"Kathleen?" Laxia prompted after a long pause.

Instead of answering, Kathleen raised her hammer and struck the dart.

"Hey!" Sahad protested. "What're ya doin'? That's the only one we've got."

"Relax." Kathleen lowered her hammer. "Take a look."

They all leaned closer. The dart's shaft had been crushed under the blow, but the tip still looked exactly the same. The anvil, on the other hand, had a dent where the hammer had struck, as if the dart had the power to penetrate iron.

"I guess I should have taken my grandfather's stories more seriously," Kathleen said thoughtfully.

"What're ya talkin' 'bout?" Sahad asked.

Kathleen's gaze drifted. "There's an old story that's been passed down in Greek, about a certain metal. Tougher than diamond and never rusts. But I figured it was just a tall tale."

"Tougher than diamond and never rusts," Ricotta echoed. "I've read about diamonds. That sounds about right."

Kathleen gave her a strange look. "This metal is said to have a faint glow, like the color of sunlight, and a shimmering surface. They call it—"

"Orichalcum," Adol said softly.

Kathleen nodded. "You've heard these stories too?"

"Not exactly." At least not from anyone in this world. This was it, the last bit of information he was trying so hard to recall. In his dream, Dana and Sarai had called this metal orichalcum—a word that meant nothing to him at the time. His heart raced. Was this one detail proof enough that Eternia was a real place?

"Anyway," Kathleen said. "Many people have visited my family's forge in search of orichalcum. I never thought it actually existed."

Sahad frowned. "So if we made weapons outta the stuff..."

"You might be able to fight off Primordials, yes," Kathleen said. "However, we'll need a lot more than this."

"That's the problem," Laxia said. "Ricotta doesn't remember where exactly her father mined the metal."

"Well." Kathleen shrugged. "You'll need to find her father then."

If he is still alive. Adol saw the thought reflected in Laxia's and Sahad's faces too, but no one voiced it.

"Ricotta's father was last seen a month ago, heading to the northern regions of the island," Laxia said. "The mountains are swarming with Primordials. Unless we find a way to fight them—"

"In this case," Kathleen said, "it appears that we're at an impasse."

Adol lifted his head. "We might find orichalcum in an old stratum."

Everyone looked at him in surprise.

"Old stratum?" Laxia frowned. "Where did you come up with that?"

"I..." Adol took a deep breath. "Would you believe me if I said it came from a dream?"

"A dream?" Kathleen raised her eyebrows.

"Yes." He glanced at Laxia and Sahad. "Ever since I got to this island, I've been having these dreams, about a girl named Dana. The dreams follow her life—in sequence, from the time she was a child to the point when she's become a—a very important person, in a kingdom called Eternia."

"Eternia?" Kathleen frowned. "Never heard of it."

"Right." Adol saw Laxia's lips twitch in disbelief. Kathleen was grinning too. He didn't cherish the mockery, but now that he'd mentioned it, there was no way back. "These dreams are much too realistic to ignore. They show real events, I'm certain of it." He looked at Laxia and Sahad again. "Remember that tree that grew across the chasm to provide a bridge for us?"

"Yes." Laxia shook her head. "So?"

"It wasn't there the first time we explored that area, right?"

"We must have somehow overlooked it..." Laxia turned to Sahad, but the fisherman didn't say anything.

"We didn't. Just a day or so before we went out there, I had a dream about Dana planting that tree as a tiny sapling, right in that spot. I don't know how, but she must have done it way in the past so that it would grow to aid us in the present." He paused, the rest of the party watching him wide-eyed.

"Adol," Laxia said. "I'm sure I don't need to explain to you that dreams don't work that way. You can't even *see* real events you have no prior knowledge of, let alone have these events *influence* the present. There must be another explanation."

Adol tossed his head impatiently. "Why don't you just humor me for a while. There's more. When I was attacked by that Primordial, when I hit my head and passed out, my last thoughts were about finding a way to defeat those creatures so that we could find a way across the mountains. And while I was unconscious, I had this dream—or vision, if you will—where Dana and her friend Sarai talked about orichalcum, the metal that could defeat Saurians, and these deposits . . . in an old stratum recently discovered near the Great Valley . . ." He trailed to a pause under everyone's intent gazes.

"Saurians?" Laxia asked.

"They could have meant Primordials."

"They also could have meant something completely unrelated." Laxia shook her head. "What am I even saying. 'They' don't exist, Adol. Information from your dreams can't possibly be real."

"Actually," Kathleen said, "if orichalcum really existed, looking for it in an old stratum makes lots of sense."

"It does?" Adol looked at her in disbelief. A moment ago, Kathleen had looked ready to burst into laughter. She was the last person he'd expected support from.

Ricotta beamed. "Stratum? You must mean strata. I know what that is! It's made with bread, eggs, and cheese! I bet it tastes really yummy!"

Laxia laughed. "No, Ricotta. We're not talking about the casserole."

"You're not?" Ricotta looked disappointed.

"Strata," Laxia explained, "are layers of hardened dirt piled on top of each other."

"It's like layers o' really old rock what got fossils in 'em, right?" Sahad said.

Ricotta brightened. "Now I remember. That cave father used to take me to had lots of fossils. Some of them were so giant. I got scared of them when I was little. That's why he didn't bring me along every time."

Everyone exchanged glances. Adol took out his sketch of the island's map and spread it on the anvil next to the dart.

"It must be in this area that we have yet to explore." Laxia pointed. "Near the foot of Gendarme."

Adol frowned. The way she was pointing to led through the bog with the roaming Primordial that had nearly made them its lunch on the day they'd first met Hummel. Not the best place to go to without proper weapons.

"However," Laxia went on, "I have strong reservations about risking our lives to follow this kind of lead. No serious clues could possibly be gathered from a dream." She looked at Adol sternly, as if reprimanding him for even bringing it up.

"Dream or not," Kathleen said, "I say it's worth a shot. Besides, exploring new areas in search of castaways is one of our goals, isn't it?"

"Well, it is, but—"

"You haven't been to that area yet, have you?" Kathleen insisted.

"No."

"Alright then," Sahad joined in. "Let's explore it. What d'ya say?"

Laxia pursed her lips. "Fine. We'll go search for that cave as soon as Licht says Adol is fit enough to do it."

"You do that," Kathleen said. "And while you're gone, I'll work on my furnace to make sure it can handle higher temperatures to melt orichalcum."

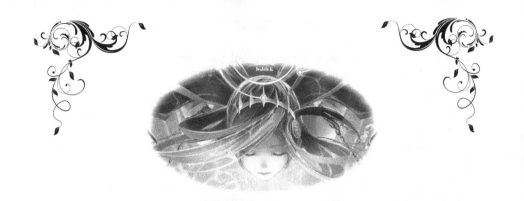

OLD STRATUM

Through the rising swamp vapors, Laxia could barely make out the looming boulders and cliffs rising on the far side of the bog. Being here again brought bad memories of the time they had accidentally woken up that sleeping Primordial. With Adol still weak from his wound, would they be able to escape if they ran into one of them this time?

"According to the map," Adol said, "the cave should be up ahead. Does this area look familiar, Ricotta?"

Ricotta shook her head. "Sorry . . . I don't remember that well."

Laxia looked away. Adol was probably the only person she knew who could get away with admitting he'd gotten information from a dream, and then have everyone follow him anyway. This quest for orichalcum made no sense whatsoever. The only reason Laxia was going along with it was the fact that this trip took them into a yet unexplored area of the island. She had more or less given up on finding Franz, but deep inside she knew she would never stop looking.

"It seems," she said, "the only way to go is forward."

They cautiously made their way through the bog, feeling out the solid areas among the treacherous muddy ground. Shadows darted in the murky swamp water, scattering as they approached. Fish? Laxia hoped so, but she also couldn't help recalling all the aquatic Primordial species she read about, including large and predatory ones. She felt relieved when they finally reached the end of the swamp and climbed out onto dry ground.

After a steep climb, they emerged on a grassy plateau. A river flowed on its far end, fast and deep, and so transparent that one could trace the underwater boulders all the way down.

"An' how're we supposed to cross that one?" Sahad wondered.

Ricotta ran ahead, stopping at the river bend. "There." She pointed. "The bridge. Father built it. But then a storm destroyed it. That's why we ran out of darts."

A bridge? Laxia rushed after her, with Adol and Sahad in her wake.

Ricotta was right. Two tall wooden supports stood on the riverbank, with thick ropes tied to them trailing down into the flowing water. As Laxia stepped closer, she saw a set of wooden planks connected to the ropes, wedged against underwater boulders, and a pair of matching bridge supports rising on the other side of the stream.

A suspension bridge, sturdily built once but destroyed by the weather.

"Well." Sahad scratched his head. "If we don't fix it, we can't go any farther."

"True." Laxia turned to Ricotta. "How did your father manage to build it in the first place?"

Ricotta shrugged. "I'm not sure. I wasn't here when he did it. But I remember he said he was going to build it because explorers like him always find a way."

"Explorers?" Laxia echoed.

Sahad grinned at her.

Annoyingly, Laxia felt a blush creep into her cheeks. Sahad was a simple soul, but sometimes he was too darned observant.

"What?" she snapped.

"Ain't her dad bein' an explorer kinda like how Adol is an adventurer?"

"Not even remotely," she retorted. "For one, 'explorer' is a broad term that applies to a variety of people. Some venture into unexplored lands on their quests of discovery. Others travel the world to learn new things. All in all, explorers are always challenging themselves. Whereas an adventurer, in my opinion, is just someone who acts with reckless abandon." She looked away.

Sahad shrugged. "Sounds like the same thing to me. Adventurers, explorers, they all travel around discoverin' new things. Like Adol here." He patted Adol on the shoulder, then winked at Laxia.

A retort froze on Laxia's lips as Ricotta nodded earnestly. "That's right. Father washed ashore here while he was traveling to go on an expedition elsewhere."

"An expedition?" Laxia felt glad at this chance to change the subject.

"Yes. That's what he said, anyway. I found him unconscious on the beach."

"*You* found *him*?" Laxia blinked. "I thought he was the one who found you."

Ricotta frowned. "Why would you think that?"

"I don't know, I just assumed..."

"Wait a minute," Sahad said. "How long have ya been on this island?"

"My whole life," Ricotta said. "At least as far as I remember. Father said I must have been born somewhere else, since my parents weren't here, but I—"

Laxia's eyes widened. "You've been here for as long as you can remember?"

"Yep." Ricotta smiled. "That's why I was so happy to find Father, and why I'm happy you guys came here. I used to think I was the only human in the world."

"Ricotta..." Laxia paused. What could she possibly say to this little girl, who had been braver than any of them to survive here all by herself? Compared to that, how could they still engage in these petty squabbles, about adventurers, explorers, and old wounds that really had no meaning when measured up against a single human life?

"I hope we can reunite you with your father very soon," she said quietly. "Let's repair this bridge and move on."

Adol wasn't very hopeful about their chances to fix the bridge, but once he and Sahad waded waist-deep into the water to catch the trailing ends of the ropes broken by the storm, they quickly realized that the ropes were still usable. All they needed was to extend and reinforce the knots, then lift the trailing sections out of the water, and re-tie them to the sturdy wooden supports wedged deeply into the riverbank. The result probably wasn't as good as when the bridge had been originally built, but it could hold their weight, and that was all that mattered. Besides, they could always come back and reinforce it later on, if needed.

The rickety wooden planks shifted and creaked as they made their way across. Once or twice, Adol wondered if the ropes were going to hold, or if the whole construction would give way, sending them tumbling into the deep stream that rolled rapidly over the massive boulders rising underwater. Laxia looked green in the face, her hand clenching the rope railing so tightly that her knuckles turned white. Had she once said that she didn't know how to swim? Adol couldn't quite remember. Even for a good swimmer this kind of a current would pose a challenge. He felt relieved when the entire party crossed safely and set out along the path on the other side.

The path wound along the river, very close to the water. They could see fish playing in the stream—a kind he hadn't seen before, with red lustrious scales that shone like gold when they flipped close to the surface.

"That's rowana," Sahad said. "A delicacy back home. Their meat is white, so juicy and tender it melts in your mouth. We should fish here some time."

Adol only nodded. He'd long learned to trust Sahad's fishing advice.

The path brought them to a gaping cave mouth—the origin of the river they were following that flowed out of the deep shadows in a powerful stream. Rocks rose like teeth across the cave opening, with water torrenting in between. The path climbed steeply up and away from the riverbank, winding into the rocky foothills and up to a wide grassy plateau that stretched to a grove of pine trees on the far end.

"I've been here before," Ricotta announced. "We must be on the right track. Oh, look! Is that a person?" She pointed.

It was. A well-dressed young man paced back and forth beside the trees. His long wavy hair fell down to his shoulders from underneath an elaborate hat. A large emerald brooch adorned his expertly tailored outfit. Another nobleman, by the looks of it, probably wearing the same clothes he'd donned for the party aboard the *Lombardia*.

The man didn't seem all that surprised to see the newcomers. He stopped his pacing and crossed his arms over his chest, watching them approach.

"Would you look at that," he said. "Finally, I've found some survivors."

You found? Adol looked at him in disbelief.

"Wait a minute," Sahad said. "Isn't it the other way 'round? We're the ones who found you."

The man lifted his chin. "How dare you contradict me?" He scoffed. "What disrespect. Typical commoners."

172

Great. Looks like we've got ourselves Sir Carlan junior. Adol kept a serene expression as he returned the man's gaze.

"Why are you so rude?" Ricotta asked.

"Rude?" The man frowned. "I thought I was being rather gracious, talking to people so far below my station. By the way, my name is Austin. I am a nobleman from Gllia. I urge you to remember my name, for I will go down in history as a great artist."

"Oh, an artist, huh?" Sahad grumbled. "Just what we need. I'm sure your skills would be very useful to the castaways."

"Useful?" Austin blinked. "I certainly hope so. I'm a painter, sculptor, poet, and playwright. Only the medium of music has eluded me so far."

"If I'm understanding you correctly," Laxia said, "you're not a musician, basically."

"Well, no. Isn't this what I just said?"

Adol looked at Austin curiously. The man seemed completely unfazed by the fact that no one here was impressed by his skills. Well, at least this nobleman's temper wasn't as bad as Sir Carlan's had been. The older man would have been shouting by now.

"We are exploring this area," he said. "After we're done, we can escort you to our Castaway Village, where other survivors from the *Lombardia* live. It's much safer there than out in the wilderness all by yourself."

Austin regarded him haughtily. "Castaway Village, eh? I assume you mean that place, with the constantly smoking fire." He pointed to the ribbon of campfire smoke rising above the jungle canopy in the distance. "No need to escort me. I've been watching that smoke for weeks, wondering if it was a sign of some human presence. Now that I know what it is, I can find my own way, thank you very much."

"There's a bog at the end of this path," Laxia said. "Dangerous beasts may be lurking out there."

"Nonsense." Austin waved his hand dismissively. "I am perfectly capable of defending myself. It was only the annoying broken bridge that kept me trapped on this side of the river. I would have swum across, but I detest getting myself needlessly wet. I expect since you've made it all the way up here, you must have finally fixed it, haven't you?"

He didn't wait for a response but turned and walked down the path they had just climbed and disappeared around the bend.

"Glad we've *finally* fixed that bridge," Sahad echoed after he was gone. "Wouldn't want his excellency gettin' himself needlessly wet, would we?"

"Is he gonna be all right?" Ricotta said.

Laxia looked worried. "I hope so."

"He'll be fine," Sahad said. "He survived here all this time without help. I'm sure he'll manage."

They found the cave they were looking for on the other side of the meadow, its mouth tucked neatly into the rock wall. Inside, it wasn't as large or deep as many of the others they'd explored on this island—and it surely looked different.

The walls here were lined with fossilized bones embedded into the rock. A distant opening in the ceiling filled the cave with suffused light, making Adol feel as if they had stepped into a history museum.

"Primordial fossils." Laxia looked fascinated. "This cave appears to consist entirely of exposed strata. I've never seen so many fossils before."

"I bet your father would have loved to see this," Adol said quietly.

Her shoulders tensed. "Yes, seeing this would certainly make him dance with joy...Just thinking about how he'd react annoys me to no end."

Ricotta looked at her sharply. Adol could relate to her reaction well. One needed to know Laxia to understand the torment she felt about her father—the man she loved and admired, who had taught her everything she knew and then abandoned his duty and drove their family to ruin all because of his love for creatures that had gone extinct millennia ago. Annoyance was a mild reaction, considering. But a person like Ricotta, who never had a real family, wouldn't understand.

Moving forward felt like navigating through a forest of bones that blended into stone, an organic union of Earth's ancient creations. Glimmering veins of metal surfaced here and there, but only after they descended to the lower levels of the cave did Adol realize that the light filling this chamber wasn't a reflection of the sunlight peeking in through the cracks in the roof.

A thick metal vein running along the wall glowed from within, filling the cave with its faint, suffused gleam.

Orichalcum.

The entire cave chamber was threaded with the skeleton of a giant creature that seemed to have dived, in times immemorial, from some long-evaporated ocean all the way down to the cave floor. The creature's spine lined the wall, its skull with an open maw frozen in stone greeting them at the bottom. The living version of this Primordial could have easily swallowed their entire party. Did creatures this size still roam the island somewhere?

"A Sauropod," Laxia said with fascination. "The largest of the known Primordial species. I don't believe a specimen of this size, or this intact, has ever been discovered."

Sahad scratched his head. "I bet it was quite a sight back in the day, when it was still alive."

"Yep," Ricotta confirmed. "That's what I thought too when I first saw it. I was so scared I cried. Good, this means we've found the right place!"

It didn't feel right to disturb the fossil, so they searched the sides of the cave and found a glowing orichalcum deposit that avoided any skeletons and bore unmistakable scars from mining tools. Ricotta's father, Thanatos, must have mined this spot before—and there was plenty left for the taking.

The metal was surprisingly light, yet also amazingly strong. No tools could damage it as they chipped away the rock around it, freeing slabs of ore that they stuffed into their packs. Before long, their bags were full. It was time to return to camp.

As soon as they found themselves in the open air again, Sahad stopped and turned to the whole group.

"It looks like Adol's dream was right." He was looking at Laxia as he spoke.

She hesitated, then nodded. "I admit it. I still have no idea now if this is possible, but Adol's dream provided clear details about the existence of orichalcum deposits in this area. We can no longer dismiss these dreams as mere coincidence."

Adol's skin prickled as he looked up at Gendarme looming over them. He felt even more convinced that the answers they were seeking lay on the other side of the mountain. And now, with the discovery of orichalcum ore, they had the means to defeat the Primordials and travel over there.

THE SUMMIT

Contrary to the routine Adol woke up early the next morning—and with no dreams of Dana to distract him from the pressing task. He hurried to Kathleen's smithy, where he found her standing in front of her anvil looking at a glowing chunk of orichalcum ore. In the light of the rising sun, it glittered with all the colors of the rainbow.

"Never thought I'd actually work orichalcum with my own hands," she said.

"Did we bring enough?" Adol asked.

Kathleen shook her head. "Not for forging an entire new set of weapons. But I think I can use this amount to enhance your existing weapons with orichalcum instead. That way they'll have an effect against any Primordials you encounter."

"How long will it take?" Adol asked.

She grinned at him. "Quite a slave driver, aren't you?"

Adol made an innocent face at her.

She laughed. "I know you're in a hurry. I am too." She picked up the piece of orichalcum with her tongs and turned it around. "I would say about three days should do it."

"Three days it is," Adol said.

Kathleen's hammer rang incessantly, morning to night. Adol couldn't help craning his neck to look at her work each time he walked by. She shooed him away every time she noticed him peeking, until it became a sort of a game between them.

Without their regular weapons, Adol and his party couldn't travel very far, but they did venture into some of the areas they'd spotted from Gendarme and rescued two more castaways.

Reja, the young boy of about Ricotta's age Adol remembered seeing aboard the *Lombardia*, had managed to survive because of his unlikely helper—a pikkard, a small and furry kind of livestock that had an uncanny sense for edible vegetables. At Castaway Village, Reja and his new pet took charge of farming and vegetable stocks.

The other castaway, Miralda, had fared even better, building herself a campsite in the heart of one of the side valleys. An able cook, she added energy to the group and a lot of new dishes to the menu, even though Adol would have preferred it if Miralda were a little less flirty. He had never blushed so much or served as a target for so many jokes from Dogi and Sahad.

When, on the third day, Kathleen's hammer finally stopped ringing, Adol had to stop himself from running to the smithy. Laxia, Sahad, and Ricotta got there just ahead of him, their awed expressions speaking without words.

Laxia picked up her rapier and swung it, cutting the air with a drawn, silken whisper that made the weapon seem almost alive.

"So this is what it feels like to wield an orichalcum-enhanced weapon," she said with wonder.

"Amazin'," Sahad agreed, weighting his war hammer in his hands.

Kathleen smiled as she handed Adol his sword.

For a moment, Adol felt as if he were back in his dream again. That feeling of a sword hilt sinking fluidly into his hand, of a blade forming a natural extension of his arm, stronger and lighter than it could possibly be . . . He couldn't help doing a few lunges and twists, answered by the whistling and applause from all the villagers in sight.

"Not bad, eh?" Kathleen said.

"Your skill is amazing," Adol said earnestly. "We are so fortunate to have you with us."

"What about a weapon for me?" Ricotta asked.

"You?" Kathleen raised her eyebrows.

"If I'm to travel with them, I need one too."

"Oh, no." Kathleen shook her head. "You're not traveling anywhere. You're much too young to—"

"We're going to look for my father," Ricotta said. "If you think I'm going to stay behind—"

Kathleen looked at Adol helplessly. Ricotta glared at him too, with a determined look.

"Well . . ." Adol began.

Ricotta squared her shoulders. "Have you forgotten that I was the one to defend you against that Primordial? The one who showed you what my darts could do? If not for me, you wouldn't even be holding these weapons right now. Besides, I've lived on this island all my life. You could all use my help."

Adol hesitated. "It's all true. If you want to come with us, Ricotta, I won't stop you." He looked sideways at Laxia, who seemed like she was going to object but receded under his gaze.

"Do you have experience with any particular weapons?" Kathleen asked Ricotta.

"Aside from darts, you mean?"

"We can't well send you off on a long trip armed with nothing but darts. Besides," Kathleen looked at the small pile of leftover ore, "it would be a better idea to use the remaining orichalcum to reinforce other villagers' weapons. In fact, I've been working on some in my spare time." She pointed to the shelf at the back of the smithy.

Ricotta stepped up to the shelf and ran her eyes over it, then reached into the back with a triumphant squeal and pulled out a pair of small clubs.

"Clubs?" Kathleen asked in disbelief.

"Yes." Ricotta weighted them in her hands, then spun them with the skill that made Adol feel guilty about the way he questioned her earlier.

"You're good with them," Kathleen observed.

"I always liked clubs." Ricotta looked excited, twirling them as she talked. "I used to have coconut maces I made myself, but coconuts crack too easily if you hit something hard, so Father made me a pair of clubs and taught me how to use them, but they broke too when I—" She paused and lowered her hands, a shadow running over her face. "He was going to make new ones, but then he disappeared."

Kathleen reached over and took the clubs from her. "Let me tweak them a bit so that they fit your grip better. I think I might also coat them with orichalcum spikes, so that you could fight Primordials just like the rest of the team. You four go and prepare for departure. I'll have the clubs ready for Ricotta in the morning."

"Thank you," Ricotta said earnestly.

Adol couldn't help feeling uneasy as they climbed the trail past

Ricotta's cabin and entered the cave where they'd been attacked by the aggressive Primordial. If the beast was still there, this was going to be the first battle test for their new orichalcum weapons. He hoped he was ready for it.

He felt relieved when they waded through the knee-deep water in the cave's main chamber and exited through the passage on the other side without encountering any monsters. The large Primordial clearly wasn't home—or was staying away this time.

The path on the other side of the cave became narrower and steeper, a trail of uneven rock ledges clinging to the cliff face that ascended step-wise into the mist. Keeping away from the edge was no longer possible, so they all did their best to cling to the rock wall as they walked single file.

"I'm having trouble breathing," Sahad panted.

"It's natural," Laxia explained in an uneven voice. "This high up in the mountains, the air is thinner."

And colder. Adol nodded. They all were gasping for air, shivering in the rising breeze. Only Ricotta looked fresh as a rose, chatting away as they walked.

"I know a breathing technique." She drew deep breath, exhaling as she sang: "Hee, hee, hoo! Go on, try it."

"I don't think it's going to help," Laxia huffed.

Ricotta only shrugged as she hopped up the trail.

They were above the clouds now, a white fluffy sea stretching in all directions, hiding the ground from view. Sunlight blazed so brightly that they had to shield their eyes. The path ran along the top of a narrow ridge and looped up to the peak before descending to the island's other side. The north.

"We're pretty damn high," Sahad said.

"Almost at the summit." Laxia pushed away from the rock and started along the path.

"Watch out!" Ricotta warned. But Laxia was already too far to hear her.

A giant bird swooped overhead. No, not a bird. A flying lizard, similar to the one they'd seen at the bottom of the mountain. A Pterosaur. Was that what Laxia had called it?

Laxia was halfway across the ridge now, an easy target for the winged Primordial. Adol pushed past Ricotta and Sahad and rushed after her. But he wasn't fast enough.

The flying reptile circled down. Up close, it looked much worse than it did high above—all sharp talons, toothy mouth, spikes running down its back and rimming its leathery wings. It aimed its talons, as if about to scoop Laxia off the trail.

She seemed ignorant to the danger as she strode on.

"Laxia!" Adol shouted.

She saw the Primordial just in time. Her eyes widened as she dodged the swooping talons, whipping out her rapier. As the creature turned around for another pass, she stabbed it. Adol couldn't see where the blow landed, but the creature shrieked and swerved aside, telling him that the stab had reached its aim. He drew his own sword as he covered the last few steps and stood next to Laxia to face the attacking Primordial.

The path was too narrow to fight side by side, leaving Adol with only a limited range. But his blade, infused with orichalcum, felt so different. Each blow sliced into flesh, causing the creature to scramble and rear, retreating into the air. Laxia seemed even more successful, each of her stabs answered by a shriek and a shudder of the giant flying body. The creature's wings raised wind as it thrashed against their blows, threatening to knock them off the path.

With a last long wail, the Pterosaur retreated, taking off into the sky. Adol sheathed his sword, watching it fly low over the sea of clouds and disappear behind a jagged line of distant peaks. He heaved a few long breaths.

"Well done," he said.

Laxia met his gaze. She looked dazed. "Our weapons . . . What a difference."

"Told ya!" Ricotta yelled to them as she and Sahad hurried up the trail. "Father has it all figured out. These Primordials better watch out now!"

"Right," Sahad rumbled. "Can't wait to try mine." He hefted his hammer in his hand.

On a cloudy day like this, Adol didn't really hope for a good view of the island's north—nor did he expect to notice anything from this distance that could give him any clues about his dreams. Yet, as he stepped to the edge of the summit overlook, he couldn't help feeling that he was about to see something important, something that would change his life forever.

The clouds chose this exact moment to part, allowing him an unobstructed view.

His first feeling was relief. There didn't look to be anything unusual down there—just another piece of land stretching out to the sea, perhaps larger than the island's southern side he was so familiar with by now, but similar in its landscape. Clusters of rocks rose here and there, interspersed with splotches of jungle greenery. A large plain spread on their right, running into distant foothills.

Closer to the mountain, wild vegetation clung directly to the cliffs, climbing up halfway then spreading into a giant meadow paved with large leathery leaves. A waterfall, tall but thin, cascaded directly over it—probably a source of water for all these plants. A forest of rocks stretched below it, with more greenery in between. Another Towering Coral Forest? Possible, but in the afternoon haze, with clouds floating in and out of the way, it was difficult to make out details.

It took Adol a moment to notice the unusual features. Rows of jagged rocks and protruding cliffs down below looked oddly regular, as if deliberately placed down there. Winged shapes circling over them didn't look like birds. Primordials? So many more here than on the island's southern side. Inadvertently, Adol thought back to the vision he'd had when he first washed up on the island. *Giant birds with long tails.* After the recent encounters, he finally knew what they were.

"Astounding," Laxia exclaimed. "Look at all the Primordials. It's like we're seeing prehistory with our own eyes."

"Can't wait to meet them all." Was that sarcasm in Sahad's voice?

"I think I see ruins out there." Ricotta said.

Now that she mentioned it, Adol had to acknowledge that some of the regularly spaced rocks, as well as those distant ones he'd taken for another Towering Coral Forest, did indeed resemble man-made structures. If he squinted his eyes just right, he could almost imagine...

A city?

"Call me crazy," Sahad said. "But all o' them structures look like buildings."

Adol felt a strange pang in his chest. Now that the topic had come up, he could no longer pretend that the rocks they were looking at were natural. In fact, the view down there was beginning to look more and more familiar. He'd *seen* it before—not from this angle, and not in such a ruined state, but...

His heart raced. Was his mind playing tricks on him, blending reality with the world of his dreams? Suddenly, going down there, seeing this place up close, became the most important thing in the world.

"Look over there," Ricotta exclaimed. "It's a big tree!"

Adol turned.

She was pointing at the meadow halfway up the rock cliff Adol had been looking at before.

Just like with the city, Ricotta's words shifted the image in his mind. Perhaps it had been denial when he'd first laid his eyes on it, but now that his mind shifted into a different state, he clearly saw that the large patch of greenery he'd previously taken for a meadow was actually the crown of a tree, so large that even the city below it seemed dwarfed by comparison.

The Great Tree of Origins.

Adol clasped his mouth shut, afraid he'd say something stupid. They needed to go down and see it first. Only then could he have his questions answered, possibly at the expense of his sanity.

"Huh? That thing?" Sahad narrowed his eyes. "Ya sure that's just a tree? That sucker's big enough to be its own forest."

"We can't exactly determine what it is from up here," Laxia said.

"True." Adol swallowed. "Let's continue onward."

"Wait for me," a new voice called behind them.

Hummel.

Adol turned, watching the man approach.

"You?" Laxia said in disbelief. "Where have you been all this time?"

Hummel measured her up and down with his gaze. "Doesn't matter, does it?"

"Doesn't *matter*?" She paused as if at a loss for words. "We *needed* you on the exploration team. We were attacked by Primordials invulnerable to anything except your bullets. Adol almost got killed. We—"

Hummel's eyes trailed to Adol with a silent question.

Adol shrugged. "It wasn't that bad."

"Not that bad?" Laxia heaved an exasperated sigh. "Adol, as the leader, you need to resolve this matter at once. He can't just disappear like this, without a word, and then pop out of the blue and expect us to—"

Leader, huh? Funny how Laxia only said things like this when she wasn't sure what to do. Adol met Hummel's gaze. "Welcome back."

Hummel inclined his head in acknowledgment. "Thanks. It's good to be back."

He meant it, Adol realized. Hummel's eyes held a smile as he spoke, as if he considered himself part of the team. Not such a loner after all. Adol felt better with Hummel in the party.

"That is *not* what I meant!" Laxia protested.

Ricotta stepped past her to Hummel's side. "My name is Ricotta. Nice to meetcha!"

She raised her palm. Hummel held out his own gloved hand, and she high-fived it. The bonding was so unexpected that Adol stared. Dealing with children wasn't something he'd expected Hummel to be good at.

"By the way," Hummel said. "I went to the village and had Kathleen reinforce my bayonet with that orichalcum lot you found. She also prepared special ammunition for my firearm. I should be of more help against Primordials now."

Laxia's eyes widened. "How did you know to do it? Wait...Have you been *following* us?"

Hummel shrugged. "Only when necessary."

"*Necessary?*"

"Hey, Laxia, what're ya worried fer?" Sahad said. "He's handy in a fight. Good at campin' too. It would be nice to have another set o' hands from here on out."

"Fine," Laxia said. "It would be pointless of me to say anything else, I see." She lifted her chin and walked off down the path.

THE LOST WORLD

The trail wound steadily down the north slopes of the mountain. The ground here was less rocky, descending in shallow grassy terraces toward the greenery below. At some point it brought them into a cave—thankfully, Primordial-free—its floor covered almost entirely by a lake that looked very deep. The trail edged precariously along its slippery shore. Light shining in from the entrance reflected off the surface and scattered around the ceiling, making it feel as if they were submerged too, navigating deep underwater.

At the cave exit, a tall waterfall streamed down in a steady curtain, water collecting into a giant stone basin down below that protruded directly from the rock wall—perfectly positioned to nurture the giant tree below.

Up close the tree looked even larger. Its lush crown sprouted enough greenery to shade an entire section of the slope, creating an oasis of peace and tranquility sheltered from the rest of the world. Dear gods. No wonder ancient Eternians worshipped it. It was difficult for Adol's mind to enfold the idea that this was indeed the tree he'd learned about from his dream, but he didn't doubt it anymore.

The path here was more pronounced, as if at one point it had been carved deliberately to make for easier passage. Following it made the descent so much faster. They'd started from Ricotta's cabin only this morning—and now, by sunset, they already reached level ground on the other side of the mountains.

A peaceful meadow stretched out before them, with one of the island's blue glowing crystals rising at its end. In Adol's mind he came to associate these crystals with safety, calm areas that made for perfect camping spots. This meadow definitely looked like one of those, stretching from the rock wall on their right to a stream on their left that cascaded down a deep valley toward the distant plains. Its tall bank made for a perfect observation point of the valley down below.

Adol's breath caught as he stepped to the edge of the overlook.

The ruins they'd seen from the mountain spread right below them, a series of domed buildings rising along the stream, connected by long stone walkways built at the water level. The moss-covered structures looked ancient and in bad disrepair, but he recognized the place immediately.

The Temple of the Great Tree.

He could no longer deny this, or look for alternatives in his mind. This was the place where Dana used to live at the time shown to him in his dreams. That altar in the garden was where she knelt in prayer before the Great Tree, asking for guidance and strength. Those walkways were the ones she, Olga, and Sarai traversed countless times as they ran chores and devoted themselves to their studies. Even the pile of boulders hiding in the deep tree shade beside the stream looked familiar—the place where Dana and Rastell sometimes sat, sharing treats and catching up on the city gossip. This couldn't possibly be the same trees as those that grew here in their time, but it felt as if some supernatural power had spanned millennia to preserve this place as close as possible to its original state.

Adol could name each of these buildings and areas—the living quarters, the dining hall, the training grounds at the back of the compound where the girls learned swordplay and channeled their Essence through exercise. Looking at the ruin felt far too overwhelming. It didn't fit into his mind. After all those dreams about Dana, he was seeing her world with his own eyes, ruined and forgotten, but unmistakably real. It *proved* that she had really existed, that all the events he had witnessed through her eyes had really taken place.

One way or another, these dreams, and Dana's actions far in the past, had guided him here. The implications of it all simply refused to fit into his mind.

The sun dipped behind the distant hills as they finished setting up camp and gathered around the fire for an evening meal. It was so quiet here. Even the crickets hushed their song in the shade of the ancient tree.

"So, Adol," Sahad said. "This place—it's the one from your dreams? I've no idea how, but it seems exactly like you told us."

"Not exactly," Adol corrected. "In Dana's time, this place wasn't in ruin. It was lively and beautiful, and..." He paused. How could he possibly find the right words?

Laxia shook her head. "It doesn't make sense. If Eternia truly existed, it would be recorded in history books, or at least mentioned in ancient chronicles. I studied history in great detail, and I'm fairly certain that isn't the case. There has to be another explanation."

"Such as?" Hummel prompted.

She didn't respond.

"If Eternia wasn't real," Ricotta said, "how could Adol possibly know all these things?"

"It's Dana," Adol said quietly.

The conversation paused.

"What do you mean, Adol?" Laxia said tensely.

"Dana. She's communicating with us from the past. Guiding us here."

Laxia sighed. "I know you believe this, Adol. But such things couldn't possibly—"

"How else would you explain it though?" Sahad joined in. "First, that tree that grew outta nowhere to help us cross the chasm—Don't give me that look, Laxia. We can pretend all we want, but we both know the tree wasn't there before. Then, orichalcum. And now—"

"There must be a rational explanation," Laxia insisted.

Adol looked away. Deep down, he could relate to her disbelief. But Laxia wasn't the one who had visited Dana's world, an experience so vivid that it couldn't be explained within the boundaries of reality as he knew it.

"There *is* no other explanation," he said, perhaps a bit more forcefully than he intended. "Dana *wanted* us to come to this temple, see?"

"But *why*?" Laxia was beginning to look desperate.

"That's what we are going to find out," Adol said firmly. "Tomorrow."

He wrapped himself in his blanket and lay down, watching the stars overhead. They looked familiar too, the same stars Dana had looked up at so many times.

He hoped he was going to dream about her tonight.

A messenger from the royal family?" Dana asked. "That's unusual. Did something happen while I was away?"

Handmaid Alta lowered her eyes, twirling her fingers nervously. "I told the messenger that you were away on a pilgrimage. But she insisted it was urgent, so the High Priestess took care of it."

Olga. Of course, she took care of it. Probably glad that I wasn't available. Dana felt guilty thinking this way of her old friend. Still, Olga seemed to enjoy her power a little bit too much sometimes. They needed to have a talk.

"Could you summon the High Priestess, Alta?" she asked.

Alta bowed, obviously relieved to find herself out of the spotlight. "Certainly, my lady."

"No need for that, Your Eminence," Olga said from the door. "I am already here."

Dana turned, watching her friend approach.

Olga looked stately in her formal High Priestess outfit. Her stern expression made Dana feel like a child all over again. It took her a moment to compose herself and remember that she was now in charge.

She glanced at Alta, who kept her eyes determinedly down as if afraid to draw attention. "You are dismissed."

"Yes, my lady." Alta looked relieved as she bowed and retreated, showing a visible effort not to break into a run.

Now that she and Olga were alone, Dana fully expected an argument. Olga was bound to be unhappy about Dana sneaking out again, not being around to receive an important messenger. And Olga would have a point, even though Dana was determined not to be swayed into feeling guilty again. Her outings, walking around in plain clothes and talking to citizens, were important. She wouldn't be able to do her job as the spiritual leader of the kingdom if she didn't understand her people.

Contrary to her expectations, though, Olga kept her silence. As Dana looked closer, she realized that Olga was genuinely nervous, and that her prim posture was just a façade to hide it.

"I've never seen you so flustered, Olga," she said. "What's going on?"

"The messenger from the royal family. Have you been told?"

"Yes, just now."

Olga nodded. "She came bearing a message from the Queen. Her Majesty has decided to abdicate the throne due to old age."

Dana's eyes widened. Queen Elaine was wise and generous, well loved by her subjects. She had ruled Eternia since before Dana was born. Of course no one expected her rule to last forever—but to abdicate? Now? The Queen wasn't really that old, probably younger than Advisor Urgunata.

"Do you know why?" she asked.

Olga shrugged. "Like I said, due to old age—that's all we've been told."

"Any idea who will succeed her?"

"No, but mercifully we won't have to be guessing for long. The messenger brought an invitation for a private audience with the new queen before she is revealed to the public. We must depart at once."

Dana loved visiting the capital. Nothing could compare to Aegias's majestic buildings, its lush gardens, the waterways feeding all the lakes and fountains around the city. The stone highway that led into the capital from the Temple brought the visitors directly to the palace plaza, where the Stupa—a tall crystal focusing Essence for the entire kingdom—rose into the sky. The air here crackled with power, making Dana feel calm and energized.

The base of the Stupa was enclosed in a separate building that also served as the entryway into the royal palace, adorned with statues of mythical creatures from the Eternian chronicles about the foundation of the kingdom. Dana knew of no other place where history, myth, and reality came together in such harmony, as if time in this plaza flowed differently from anywhere else. She stopped for a moment, running her eyes up the tall Stupa crystal gleaming against the sky.

"It seems that we have plenty of time before our audience," she said. "It's in the evening, isn't it?"

"True." Olga's eyes hovered on her thoughtfully. "Why would you bring it up though?"

Dana grinned. "How can I fulfill my duty as Maiden of the Great Tree without knowing the lives of the people?"

"Really, Dana?" Olga frowned. "You know how important today is. Can't you stay put, just this once?"

"But now is the perfect time," Dana insisted. "With the people about to receive a new queen, I want to know what's on their minds. Even if I only catch a glimpse, I still think that glimpse is worth knowing. I'm sure the new queen would appreciate it if I were to discover something of concern."

"Huh." Olga hesitated. "You've actually thought this through.

Very well. Just make sure to be at the palace before dusk."

Dana smiled. "Thank you, Olga."

The High Priestess shook her head. "I was planning to confine you to a guest room once we arrived at the palace, but I'm sure you would just tie some sheets together and climb out the window."

"Oh, I'm sure I wouldn't do *that* again."

"Right. Of course." Olga's lips twitched. "A well-behaved Maiden like you would never resort to such childish tricks, would she?"

"Nothing gets past you, huh?"

"I'm sure I don't need to worry about you—but please stay out of trouble."

"I will," Dana assured her.

After Olga departed, Dana stood around by the Stupa for a while, watching the citizens walk by. Did they know they were about to get a new queen? Dana wasn't sure how much had already been announced. She ran her eyes around the plaza.

Her heart leapt as she spotted a familiar face.

Rastell.

It had been at least three years since they'd last seen each other, both of them swept into too many new duties as their paths diverged. Chief Dran didn't come around to give lessons anymore, making it impossible for her and Rastell to even run into each other by chance. Now that she saw him, she realized how much she missed him. It all came back at once. Their sparring sessions. Their escapades. The feeling of calmness and comfort she always felt around him.

"Rastell!" she called, waving to him.

His eyes widened as he saw her. He wove through the crowd toward her.

He'd grown a lot over the last three years—no longer a child, his likeness with his father becoming more and more obvious. He moved like his father too—graceful and fluid, like a prowling Saurian.

"Dana!" He halted in front of her, his smile slowly shifting into an uncertain frown. "I mean . . . Maiden. Your Eminence." He bowed.

"Blessings of the Great Tree be with you." The formal response popped out before she could think. She said it a lot these days, especially to those who bowed to her. With Rastell, though, the entire exchange seemed wrong. She met his gaze. "What are you doing here, Rastell?"

"Well." He glanced toward the palace entrance. "My father's on duty guarding the inner palace, but they won't let me though to see him."

"Why not?"

His smile looked resigned. "They think I'll distract him. They still believe I'm a child."

A child. He definitely wasn't, not anymore. She wasn't sure how she felt about the change.

"It's an honor to be guarding the inner palace," he went on. "As a guard in training, I'm not yet worthy."

"Oh?" She knew guarding the inner palace was an honor, but surely Rastell would be eligible by now. Even though they hadn't met in person, she had followed his career with great interest. His superiors and peers uniformly praised him as one of the best. "I didn't realize it was such a long process."

"Only for those striving to be the best. It takes a lot of extra training to be entrusted with protecting the Queen..." He paused, color rising into his cheeks. "And the Maiden."

She held his gaze. The information made sense, but the way he said it made it feel far more personal than that. *Protecting the Maiden.* Was he working on a way to be allowed to spend time with her?

They'd drifted so far apart in the last few years, their backgrounds now an impassable gap that set them on two widely different paths. There was only one thing they still had in common. Neither of them was allowed to form personal bonds. Even a friendship was a complicated issue now. Why couldn't they go back to the good old times?

"I will look forward to that day, Rastell," she said quietly.

His blush deepened. Her cheeks warmed too. He'd grown so much in the past three years. As a boy, he always used to look at her with this admiration, but it felt very different coming from a young man.

"Everyone is talking about you, Maiden," he said. "They praise your gift, the way you use it to help your people."

She smiled. "I try my best, Rastell. We all do, don't we?"

"I hope—" he began, but a shout from the palace gate interrupted him.

"Rastell! Your father's assembling all trainees on the inner grounds."

Rastell's smile faded. "I have to go. My apologies, Your Eminence."

She reached over and touched his hand. "It was good to see you,

Rastell. I hope we'll run into each other again soon."

He held her gaze a moment longer, then bowed and turned away, rushing toward the palace. She stood on the plaza, watching. He had definitely inherited Chief Dran's grace. In time, he would probably earn the title of the kingdom's top blade too.

She hadn't asked him how far along he was in his training, or how long it would take until he could be assigned to the Temple. Years, most likely. So many things could happen in that time. But just like the day they first met, she couldn't wait to see him again.

People around the city were in good spirits. The harvest was plentiful this year. Merchant Barossa claimed to have fresh stores of Oceanus meat, even though Dana could easily tell that it was nothing but sliced squid. Merchant Mussdan at the lower market plaza was already selling coronation memorabilia honoring the new queen. Dana shook her head as she watched Mussdan's wife, a stately matron jingling with massive amounts of jewelry, directing servants at the stall while Mussdan himself stood nearby talking to a younger merchant, Orlet. How in Eternia did Mussdan get the wind of things so early that he had time to stock up on these trinkets before the news was even officially announced?

A tall old man with long white hair was sitting on the bench in one of the small gardens in the upper city. Council Darius, Queen Elaine's closest advisor. Rumors had it his relationship with the Queen extended beyond work, but Dana was never prone to gossip. She approached him with a smile on her face.

"Council Darius," she greeted. "Are you out here relaxing again instead of working?"

"Maiden." Darius stood up and bowed to her, but she gestured, and he lowered to his seat again. "I would relax inside the palace if a moment's rest could be found there. What brings you to the capital, my lady?"

As if you don't know. Dana kept her smile. "Aegias is my favorite place in the world, Council. Do I need an excuse to visit?"

"Of course not, my lady, but...Wandering around the city by yourself is rather unusual for the Maiden. As your ally in relaxation, should I be concerned?"

"Please don't worry," Dana assured him. "I have High Priestess Olga's permission this time."

Darius cocked an eyebrow as he gestured to the bench beside him—a silent invitation to gossip she couldn't possibly refuse. She sat down. For a while they both kept their silence, enjoying the view of the gardens and the bay beyond.

"The news of Queen Elaine's abdication took us by surprise," Dana said at last.

Darius shrugged. His eyes were fixed on the row of the aqueducts connecting the city's waterways to the palace and the harbor. For a while, Dana wasn't sure he was going to respond.

"Everyone wants to enjoy some rest in their old age," Darius said at length. "Queen Elaine was looking for an able successor she could feel comfortable leaving the kingdom to. She found one sooner than she expected, that's all."

"I'm glad to hear this, Council. It's not a trivial task for anyone to fill Queen Elaine's shoes."

Darius glanced at her sideways. "I think you'll be pleased with the Queen's choice, Maiden. The princess is highly deserving of this position. Just the right person we need to handle the unrest in the north."

"I look forward to meeting her," Dana said.

"You might be interested to know," Darius went on, "that it was the princess herself who came up with the idea of this private meeting before she is introduced to the people. Normally we wouldn't extend this courtesy of an early preview, even for the Maiden. But the princess felt it would be very important for both of you, so that you could start on the right foot."

"It was a wonderful idea." Dana looked at him thoughtfully. "Is there anything else you could tell me about her, Council?"

Darius kept his eyes on the distant mountain view. "The princess had a rather unique upbringing. She survived a very serious illness when she was a child. After that, she studied abroad until very recently. In fact, she returned right around the time you assumed your position as the Maiden."

"What's she like?"

The Council appeared to consider his answer. "She's young, but very wise—not unlike yourself, in fact. Queen Elaine is understandably concerned about this change—but I think she can relax, knowing her successor is so capable."

"I can't wait to meet her," Dana said.

"In that case..." Darius shot her a side glance. "You'd best be on your way. You don't want to be late for your audience."

The Council was right. It was almost time. Dana could barely contain her curiosity as she bid him farewell and returned to the palace gate.

She had no time to stop anywhere else, but as she passed through the Stupa building and emerged onto the breezy terrace on the other side, she couldn't help but pause for just a moment to enjoy the view.

The terrace lay in deep shade, so that the sunlit gardens around it seemed even brighter by the contrast. To the right and left, wide-leaved palms cast their lush shade over the ponds and fountains of the water gardens. Straight ahead, the Aerial Corridor—a stone walkway leading to the palace—ran above the aqueducts that fanned out from the water gardens all the way to the sea. The palace itself sat on the far end, the focus of all these stone beams, like the sun with its many rays. A symbol of Eternian power and an architectural marvel, clearly outlined against the sky.

Even the clouds churning over it looked deliberately placed, ornamental. The Pearl of the Gaete Sea, as the poets all over the kingdom referred to the palace in their songs. No matter how many times Dana saw it, she would never stop admiring it.

The breeze picked up, gently ruffling her hair as she walked along the Aerial Corridor. This walkway alone had been a subject of so many fables. At least half of them also featured the small garden halfway across, where an elaborate array of flowers rose out of a large ornamental stone urn in the center. Dana heard that the royal gardeners replanted these weekly to make sure the Queen could enjoy a fresh arrangement as often as possible. Dana wasn't sure if this was actually true, but in all her visits here she'd never seen the same flowers twice. She inhaled a full breath of fragrance as she passed by.

Olga was waiting near the guard post in the palace entrance hall, with several servants hovering a few paces away. The grand space, decorated with ornate stone mosaics in different shades of jasper, ran up to the rows of elaborately carved columns along the sides. Through the open doorways, one could see more elaborate hallways leading into the depths of the building—and more servants scurrying around. The palace décor looked magnificent. Dana always felt sorry for the tourists and other visitors who had to admire the palace from the outside but never had a chance to see the interior.

"Finally." Olga let out a sigh. "I was beginning to get worried."

Dana only smiled as she headed up the stairs into the throne room, with Olga falling into stride by her side.

Another servant, this one dressed in formal royal livery, hurried up to them from the inner doorway.

"Your Eminence, High Priestess, I do beg your pardon." He turned to Dana. "The Princess wishes to meet you both alone, before your audience with the Queen... She is arriving now."

Before any of them could respond, the thud of a door opening and closing echoed under the colonnade at the far end of the room.

The Princess. Prepared for a formal greeting, Dana folded her hands Temple style, freezing in mid-bow as she recognized the approaching woman.

"*Sarai?*" She stared at her best friend.

They hadn't seen each other since Sarai had left the Temple over three years ago. In all that time, she hadn't changed at all—the same blend of energy and grace that had always made her stand out among the trainees, the same mischief twinkling in her eyes. Even the heavy robes she was wearing couldn't weigh down her steps, light, as if she were floating over the floor. Seeing her cross the large hall in a blink of an eye without losing any of her majestic presence—the way only Sarai could—made Dana's mind drift back to those happy times.

"Dana, Olga, I'm so glad to see you!" Sarai extended her hands, and Dana seized them in greeting, both of them skipping around as they used to do when they were girls.

"What are you doing here, Sarai?" she asked.

Sarai frowned. "I'm here for our audience. Hasn't the servant just told you?"

"But we... The princess..." Dana's voice trailed to a halt. "*You?*"

"Yes." Sarai laughed at her stunned expression. "Me. I am the princess, Dana. Next in line to become the Queen of Eternia."

Dana gaped. Even Olga seemed at a loss for words as they both folded their hands again and bent down in a formal bow.

THE PATH TO THE RUINS

Y ou're up early, Adol," Laxia said.

Adol kept his eyes on the ruin as she approached and stopped beside him at the edge of the overlook. They stood side by side for a while, looking at the view.

"My dream woke me," he said.

"Did you dream about Dana again?"

He nodded.

"As far as I can tell," Laxia said, "that ruin down there appears to be completely uninhabited. It's also in a lot of disrepair. Based on that, we must conclude you're dreaming of past events that may—or may not—have transpired here centuries ago."

Past events. Yes, except that these dry, logical words couldn't possibly relay what it felt like, seeing this place so vibrant and alive just a short time ago and then waking up to this desolate view.

"Probably," he said.

Laxia glanced behind her in the direction of the camp. "Others are getting up. We should eat and get going."

Adol nodded. He took another moment to absorb the view before following Laxia back to the campsite.

The descending trail wound down between the river on their left and the towering rock cliffs rising on their right. Around the next bend, it brought them to a tall wall on the Temple side, its stonework remarkably well preserved. An ornate gate built into it was tightly shut, leaving no possibility to get through.

The Temple's Mountain Gate. Even in this era it still looked grand, the tall arched gateway angled elaborately at the top, the doors themselves carved with dragon heads, half-hidden under a heavy layer of lichen. In his mind's eye, Adol could envision what lay beyond—the city overlook on top of the outer guard house, a grassy meadow inside the gate favored by both pilgrims and the Temple's inhabitants as a gathering place with a view. Curious how these walls had withstood whatever cataclysm had reduced so many of the buildings on the Temple grounds to useless piles of rubble.

The locked gate left no way to access the Temple grounds from here, or to use the city highway leading from the Temple directly into the capital. This obstacle meant a detour around the valley that could delay them for days, putting off the answers Adol was yearning for. His heart fell as he thought about it.

The path descending from here into the valley was well preserved, paved with stone steps and flanked with a low railing that had partially crumbled away but could still be traced all the way down. Ruins now rose all around them—walls, towers, and passages on the outskirts of the city, connected by stone stairways cascading down the shallow slopes. In Dana's time, these settlements had spread all the way to the East Gate and the Towal Highway, but Adol hoped they wouldn't need to travel that far. The path they were following should lead them to a closer gate station in between that flanked the city on the southeast.

From here they could see the entire city, an ornate lace of buildings and towers spreading over the valley with its focal point—a giant stone pillar in the middle of the ruins—rising into the sky. The Stupa, the channel of magical energy people in Dana's era called Essence. In this era, it was no longer glowing, but it still stood much taller than all the buildings.

The path took them out of the ruins into a small forest, dominated by an unusual kind of trees. Their scaly trunks resembled palm trees in shape, but their crowns looked unlike anything Adol had seen before. Flat and evenly shaped, packed densely with a twined nest of branches, they were filled with water that stood level inside the circles of wavering leaves—treetop reservoirs, never to be accessed by people. A tangle of exotic plants grew in their shade—the outskirts of the jungle creeping down the mountains toward the plains beyond.

They had to hack their way through the dense growth to enter the jungle, but inside the tree shade, the vegetation wasn't actually that thick. The air here was infused with moisture, moss and ivy spreading along the ground.

"There's something in that thicket," Ricotta suddenly said, pointing into a dense patch of leafy growth ahead.

"I heard it too," Laxia said. "It could be a Primordial."

The leaves rustled, and a tiny creature leapt out of the greenery.

It was a Primordial all right, but not like any Primordials they'd seen up to now. This tiny bipedal lizard rose about knee-high. It had a blue hide, large sad eyes, and a tall red crest that adorned its head like an elaborate bonnet.

They all stared.

"Oh, how cute!" Ricotta exclaimed.

"Cute?" Sahad looked at her in disbelief. "It's one o' them lizards."

"Yes, but such an adorable one," Laxia joined in. "Just look at those eyes."

The creature jumped up and down excitedly, then darted off into the bushes.

"I'm going to catch it!" Before anyone could stop her, Ricotta took off after the little beast.

Sahad scratched his head. "It's cert'nly popular with the ladies. Seems harmless, I guess."

Just then the grass in front of them rustled again, and about half a dozen of the small blue lizards hopped out. They gathered around the group, jumping up and down and squeaking as if trying to communicate.

"Oooh," Laxia cooed. "How cute. I wouldn't mind taking one home with me."

"I feel the same," Hummel said.

Adol looked at him in disbelief. The statement seemed so odd from a rough guy like Hummel.

The blue lizards continued squeaking as they scattered away.

"Looks like they're wanderin' off." Sahad turned his head left and right, his smile dissolving into an alarmed frown. "Where'd the squirt go?"

"She ran off that way." Laxia pointed. "To try to catch that Primordial."

"Well." Hummel looked into the forest ahead. "She's gone now."

"Wait a minute," Sahad protested. "This isn't safe. We gotta find her right away."

They hurried down the path.

A cave opening greeted them around the next bend. One of the tiny blue lizards was standing at its entrance. As soon as it saw them approach, it turned and ran off into the cave as if inviting them to follow.

Sahad stopped. "It's another one of those critters. Should we follow it, you think?"

"Too dangerous," Hummel remarked.

"I believe we have no choice, if we want to find Ricotta." Adol drew his sword and headed inside.

The dark passage curved deeper into the cave, with faint light coming from its end. A distinct lived-in smell filled the air—musk and dried grass that reminded Adol of the grass beds they often made when camping. As they walked, Adol couldn't help reflecting on the fact that this cave looked much bigger than the size of a dwelling he would expect for the tiny cute Primordials they were following. In their rush, they'd failed to consider the possibility that these creatures were young offspring of a much larger species, one that might well feel threatened by visitors entering their lair. But it was too late to turn back. Besides, if Ricotta was really in here, they had no other choice.

The passage brought them into a large, airy room, thankfully empty, and much more inviting than he had originally feared. An opening on top let in sunlight. A small pond in the corner looked very deep. The walls gaped with holes, big enough for the tiny Primordials to hide in but not for anything larger. Adol felt relieved, at least for the moment.

The floor was covered in soft, lush grass. Here and there piles of dry leaves formed nests, padded with straw and ferns along the edges. Many of them held clutches of grayish leathery eggs, each the size of a large coconut—except for the nest by the back wall. Instead of eggs, Ricotta lay curled up inside it. She wasn't moving, but Adol could see her chest heaving, as if she were in a deep sleep.

"Hey, squirt!" Sahad rushed forward.

Ricotta's eyes flew open. She frowned, then focused, as if just recognizing them. "Huh? You guys? Where am I? What happened to all the yummy food?"

Laxia sniffed the air. "Poppy. Do you think someone might have drugged her deliberately?"

Now that she'd mentioned it, Adol could also detect the sweet lingering scent, more pronounced as they neared Ricotta. Could the little blue creatures have deliberately drugged her? It seemed unlikely. The lizards couldn't possibly be intelligent enough to lure

Ricotta here, then drug her and leave her in this nest . . . as food?

He raised his sword. "Let's get out of here."

"Too late," Hummel said. "We have company."

A swarm of blue creatures crept out of the holes in the walls and surrounded them, chittering excitedly.

Laxia smiled. "Ah, the little ones."

"Watch out, Laxia!" Ricotta warned.

"Hmm?" Laxia blinked, but before she could react, the creatures shrieked and advanced, joined by two similar-looking creatures several times larger that just appeared from the cave's opening.

The parents?

"Was this a setup?" Hummel slung the rifle off his shoulder.

"It's all my fault!" Ricotta whimpered. "Sorry, you guys." She reached for her clubs, strapped behind her back, and edged toward Adol.

Laxia frowned. "Are you saying these Primordials are intelligent enough to set a trap?"

"Let's talk about this later." Hummel aimed at the larger Primordial coming at him.

A shriek echoed through the cave, and all the Primordials attacked at once. Hummel fired, and the larger creature in front of him reared, a wound on its neck oozing blood. Adol swiped at it with his sword, slicing across its hide. The creature fell back, but the other large one took its place, lashing at Adol.

The little blue lizards were surprisingly effective at jumping and biting, hanging on with teeth and claws. Sahad had a few of them attached to his shoulders and back, the swing of his hammer too wide to dislodge them. Ricotta used her smaller clubs to knock them off, but the creatures just kept coming.

Adol quickly gave up the idea of defeating them. It seemed more realistic to try and fight their way to the exit, but even that would be difficult. Most members of the party were cornered, stuck fending off the tiny jumping lizards. Hummel had given up shooting and was using his rifle as a pike, but it didn't help much.

It took Adol a while to notice that the creatures' incessant chitter had a pattern to it, as if carried by a deeper rhythm. He looked around to locate the source. That lizard at the edge of the pack—not one of the parents, but somewhat larger than the others—emitted low-pitched hums that led the chatter of the others. A leader?

No, an attack coordinator.

Adol sprinted toward it.

The blue lizards redoubled their attack as soon as they saw his maneuver. He no longer bothered knocking them off as they bit into his shoulders and legs, dangling off him to add extra weight as he fought his way across the cavern. He reached the humming creature and lunged at it, piercing it with his sword in one decisive thrust.

A collective wail went up from the creatures around the cave. All the action stopped.

"Run!" Adol shouted.

Everyone darted for the tunnel leading outside. The wail behind them rose to a higher note, but no lizards followed them. The party burst out of the cave and ran until they had left the place far behind.

They paused in a small glade to tend to each other's scratches and wounds. The digitalis leaf extract Licht had packed for them did wonders for the pain and bleeding. In no time, the party was back on the road, picking their way through the jungle outskirts toward the plains.

After a few more bends, the road opened up to another spectacular view. A vast grassy plain stretched all the way to a line of low foothills in the distance, with the sea gleaming beyond. A river coiled across like a carelessly thrown ribbon that widened here and there to form lakes and ponds and cascaded down the rocks in picturesque waterfalls. Groups of trees grew along its banks. The ruins of the city rose to the west, separated from the plains by another chain of low foothills.

"It is quite possible," Laxia said, "that this scenery is a glimpse of the ancient world, the way it was before humans came into existence." She paused. "Why this island, though?"

Adol wondered too. But he knew they may never get an answer to this question.

The path down the hill eventually tapered to flatter ground lined with lush grass that reached above the knees, with fragrant yellow flowers scattered throughout. They continued to follow the trail to a deep, clear lake filled by the river they had seen from above.

A tall, colorful crest stuck out of the water. Another kind of exotic plant? Before any of them could approach for a closer look, the crest moved.

The party jarred to a halt.

"Something's coming out of the water!" Ricotta shrieked.

The creature emerged spectacularly, raising waves that erupted in a shower of rainbows as they broke against the rocks near the shore. It was magnificent, its long neck rising higher than the nearest palm trees, its deep emerald hide painted evenly with black-rimmed yellow spots. Its tall crest was purplish-pink, running all the way up its spine to the top of the head that featured triangular ears, a sharply pointed nose, and large, dramatically slanted eyes that looked straight at the newcomers.

There was no use trying to run. The creature would catch to them in a few strides. Adol doubted even their orichalcum weapons would help this encounter in any way.

"A Sauropod," Laxia said quietly. "Even their fossils are exceptionally rare. I can't believe we're actually seeing a live one."

"That's not what I'm concerned 'bout at the moment," Sahad said tensely. "We can't possibly fight this thing. There's only one, though. Maybe..."

Before he could finish, two more creatures rose up majestically from the water.

"Oh." Sahad gulped. "How many's that now?"

Three. Not a chance in hell. Adol hesitated, hand on his sword hilt.

One of the creatures stepped forward and lowered its long neck to stare at the group.

"Guh," Sahad whimpered.

Hummel cocked his gun. "Primed and ready."

"Wait, Hummel," Laxia whispered. "Don't shoot. You'll just make things worse."

"Worse how, exactly?"

The creature stared at them for another tense moment, then reached over their heads to bite a chunk off a palm. It chewed with gusto, losing all interest in the travelers.

A herbivore?

Adol slowly relaxed. They all exchanged relieved glances.

"Let's be mindful not to provoke these creatures," Laxia said in a shaky voice.

She glanced at Hummel, who shrugged as he slung away his rifle and moved past her onto the trail.

The plains proved to be rich grounds for Primordial species. In addition to the tall Sauropods that stayed mostly in the water, there were plenty of rhino-like herbivores, as well as more aggressive bipedal species that tended to take chase if the party got too close. Luckily, fending off a few of these attacks with orichalcum weapons proved to be enough to thwart such attempts, as if the creatures could somehow communicate and warn each other at a distance.

They circled the lake with the giant crested Primordials, bearing closer to the foothills.

A surprise waited for them at the edge of a small lake in a more secluded area of the ravine—a pile of ashes and coals, arranged in a neat circle near a flattened grass patch.

"A campsite?" Laxia said in disbelief.

"A recent one, by the looks of it," Hummel added.

Sahad scratched his chin. "Ya think yer father might've made this, Ricotta?"

Ricotta shook her head. "My father's campsites are different. I can tell by the ashes."

Adol could see disappointment in her gaze.

"Then whose is it?" Hummel wondered.

"Another castaway?" Laxia sounded wistful as she said it.

They checked the area but saw no tracks anywhere in the vicinity.

"The person who camped here could be anywhere by now," Hummel said. "We should move on. Maybe we'll find them on the way."

The path took them to a bridge across a stream, with a long waterfall cascading down the cliff on the left. The ruins spread ahead, over the entire valley. Looking down along the path of the stream, they could see a large domed building up in the distance flanking the east boundary of the city, and a much taller tower in the foothills beyond, tilted to one side, as if it had started to fall but changed its mind midway. It must have been sturdily built to be standing in that position for such a long time. Centuries? Millennia? Adol had no idea.

They were almost at the ruins, but another obstacle waited up ahead. The road they were following ended abruptly at the edge of the cliff. An ancient landslide must have destroyed the section of the path descending into the city. Short of jumping to their deaths, they could see no obvious way to get down there.

A blue glowing crystal rose at the edge of the overlook. They stood beside it for a while, contemplating.

"Maybe we should take a break, yeah?" Sahad said. "We haven't had a chance to rest since we got off Gendarme. I don't know about y'all, but I'm pretty bushed right now."

It was true. Hard to believe it was only a couple of days since they'd left Castaway Village.

"This spot seems quiet," Hummel said, "and we've got a great view of the ruins from here too."

"Yes," Laxia agreed. "We should set up camp here for the night and look for a path down into the ruins tomorrow."

Adol nodded. He hoped there *was* a path to get down there. The ruins seemed curiously resistant to letting them approach any closer. But he didn't voice his doubts as he dropped down his pack. It had been a very long day. Camping here was a good idea.

THE SHIMMERING CRYSTAL

"Finally, we can relax for a bit," Sahad said as they gathered around the campfire. In the darkness, the ruined city below the cliff was all but invisible. Sitting with his back to it, Adol could actually manage not to think about it all the time.

Laxia hugged her knees to her chest. "We haven't had a moment's rest since we arrived on the north side of the island."

"Tell me about it," Sahad said. "Those giant Primordials in the water scared the crap outta me. It's good that they're actually pretty calm."

"I was rather surprised by those cute Primordials that captured you, Ricotta," Laxia said. "Did they actually drug you?"

Ricotta shook her head. "They had those yummy fruits piled up in the nest, and they seemed to want me to eat them, so I took one... Come to think of it, it did taste like poppy."

"You think they infused the fruit with poppy on purpose?" Hummel asked.

Sahad shrugged. "That would certainly make for easy huntin', wouldn't it? Drug your meal with some yummy fruit and wait for it to go to sleep, right?"

Laxia frowned. "The current research does not indicate that any Primordial species had such high intelligence. Perhaps this is the providence of evolution."

"Evolution?" Sahad blinked.

"It's the process by which a species' traits and characteristics transform over generations."

"Whaddya mean?"

"Take the Primordials, for instance. They are thought to have been no more intelligent than your average beast. But each parent produces offspring of its own, and only the fittest of them survive. The Primordials we saw could have developed intelligence through that process. And that process, we call evolution."

"Is that really possible?" Hummel said.

Laxia shrugged. "Well, to be fair, it's not proven. But it is the most popular theory among researchers."

"Is it sorta like how a child learns words and starts talkin'?" Sahad asked.

"That's growth. Not evolution. Characteristics passed on through evolution are inherent from birth."

Sahad turned around and looked at Adol. "Do you understand any of this?"

"Sort of," Adol admitted.

Sahad laughed. "Man, I don't get it at all. Laxia must be some kinda genius."

"I—" Laxia began, then stopped. "Ricotta? What's wrong?"

Ricotta sniffled and turned away, but Adol, who was the closest, saw tears standing in her eyes. She wiped them hastily as she turned back to the fire.

"Maybe yer lecture bored her to tears," Sahad suggested.

"It's not that." Ricotta swallowed. "It's just...Spending time with you guys has been so much fun. And when I got captured by those Primordials... You guys came to save me."

"That's what family do," Sahad said.

"*Family?*"

"That's right."

Ricotta looked at him, wide-eyed. "I have a father. But he wasn't there when I was born. And...all the families in my books have lots more people in them. But I..." She swallowed again. Her gaze trailed off into the distance.

"Well, yeah," Sahad said. "We are a real family. Let's see. Laxia over there, she's basically yer big sister."

"Laxia?" Ricotta blinked. "My big sister?"

"That's right." Laxia smiled.

"Adol an' Hummel, they're sorta like yer two big brothers."

"Adol and Hummel? I get two big brothers?"

Hummel inclined his head. "I accept."

"And since you already got a dad," Sahad went on, "I suppose that makes me..."

206

"Her granddad?" Adol grinned.

"Hey," Sahad protested. "I may be older than you kids, but I ain't that old yet."

"I want Sahad to be Sahad," Ricotta said. "Cuz you're nice and funny, just like Father."

"Ya think so?" Sahad looked at Ricotta, and they both laughed.

"It's getting pretty late," Laxia said. "We should rest up for tomorrow."

"Tally ho!" Ricotta exclaimed.

Before drifting off to sleep, Adol stole a last look at the edge of the cliff, where the blue crystal stood glowing softly against the night sky. He hoped he'd have another dream of Dana to guide them into the ruins.

Adol woke up feeling disappointed. Laxia looked at him expectantly when he got up, but he only shook his head. No dreams to guide them today. They'd just have to find a way forward on their own.

Adol was finishing breakfast when he heard an odd high-pitched sound, a pulse so shrill it felt almost painful. It hovered in the air and disappeared just as suddenly.

He set down his tea, darting his eyes around in search for the source. To his surprise, the conversation around the fire continued, as if nothing was going on.

Did nobody else hear it?

"...is a dead end," Laxia was saying. "Let's try to find another way into the ruins."

"I think..." Sahad began.

The sound filled the air again, a high note coming and receding in waves. It felt worse this time. Adol clasped his hands to his ears.

"What's the matter, Adol?" Laxia's voice seemed to be coming from afar, even though she was sitting right next to him. Adol heaved a breath as the sound faded, replaced with chirping of birds and a rustle of grass wavering in the breeze.

"The crystal," Hummel said.

They all looked at the blue crystal at the edge of the cliff.

It didn't look like the same as Adol remembered from last night. Its surface was rippling, as if made of water, not solid stone. The glow filling it from inside seemed more intense, as if trying to break the surface and reach out.

The reasonable part of Adol's mind warned him to keep away, but he simply couldn't help himself. It felt as if an alien power drove him to the edge of the cliff where the crystal was now glowing continuously, filling the air with a strange hum. Ignoring his companions' warning cries, he reached over and touched it.

Waves of light and sound enfolded him. His vision faded, and he sank into a void.

Dana woke with a gasp. It took her a moment to realize she was in her room, lying in bed.

Had she just had another vision? Or was it only a dream? Red hair, like fire... Who was that man?

A knock on the door interrupted her thoughts.

"Dana, are you awake?" Olga called from outside.

"Yes. Come in!"

Olga frowned as she stepped into the room. "Are you all right? Your look pale."

Dana forced a laugh. "I just had a strange dream."

"A dream?"

"Yes. Why?"

Olga shook her head. "It's not like you to look so troubled."

"Um, well... It might have been a vision," Dana admitted. "I'm not quite sure."

Olga lowered into a chair, staring at her expectantly—the look Dana knew all too well.

She sighed. "I was a red-haired swordsman."

"I'm sorry, what?" Olga blinked.

"I know how strange it sounds. For one, I shouldn't have been able to see my own appearance if I truly was this person. But somehow— I was him, but I also saw him from aside. He—I—was on a journey with a group of travelers, and we arrived at some dilapidated ruins. I had no idea where I was, at first. But then I recognized the layout of the ruins, and the insignia engraved on the buildings. That's when I realized I was looking at the ruins of Aegias. I— I'd love to be certain it was just a dream."

Olga nodded. "You want to go to the same location as the swordsman in your dream."

"Yes."

"Then go."

Dana met her friend's gaze. She felt guilty for all the resentment she'd felt toward Olga, for all the times she and Sarai had giggled behind her back. Olga did take her duty a bit too far sometimes. But she was loyal and caring—and now more than ever Dana realized how much it meant. Apart from Sarai, there was no one else she could confide in with such ease, no one she could trust with anything, including her life.

"You'll cover for me, right?" she said.

Olga rolled her eyes. "Do I have any other choice?"

"I'd like you to be on board with it."

Olga shrugged. "You vowed to help Queen Sarai bring peace and prosperity to Eternia. Together, you are ushering in a new golden age for our country. With all that, I don't think we can simply ignore this kind of dream."

"Olga..." Dana paused. "Thank you."

Olga looked gruff, but Dana knew it was just a facade. "No need. I'll catch up with you once I've finished making the necessary preparations."

"The swordsman was in the outskirts to the east," Dana said. "Overlooking the capital."

"Understood." Olga nodded. "Please be careful."

Normally, Dana would have used her secret escape hatch accessible through the bookshelf in her room. But since Olga approved of Dana's foray, she didn't need it this time. She exited through the door instead, keeping her head high as she walked through the hallways to the Temple entrance.

At the exit from the Mountain Gate, she ran into Advisor Urgunata, who was talking to a resigned-looking cleric.

"This is the document I spoke of earlier." Urgunata waved a piece of parchment in the other woman's face. "You should use it as a reference for next month's ceremony. Everything must proceed as—" She broke off as she noticed Dana approaching. Both she and the cleric bowed, folding their hands respectfully.

"Maiden," Urgunata said. "Do you have plans somewhere today? You look like you're about to leave."

Suddenly Dana felt like a little girl again, caught sneaking out of the Temple at an unusual time. "Y-yes, well..."

"Actually," Olga's authoritative voice rang in the hallway behind. "We need the Maiden to personally attend to a matter that has arisen elsewhere."

Dana let out a breath. "High Priestess Olga ..." She paused. How did Olga always know when and where to show up?

Urgunata bowed her head. "I understand. I see you are very busy right now. Please forgive my impertinence."

"No, it's quite alright." Dana smiled.

Olga stepped between them smoothly. "I would be happy to discuss the details of next month's ceremony. Please, Lady Urgunata, let's go inside."

As soon as the they left, Dana let out a breath she hadn't realized she was holding. No matter how high her position, she was never going to feel at ease around Urgunata.

Halfway down the paved roadway leading around the city outskirts down to the plains, she stopped again when she heard a voice.

It was a strange one, quiet yet persistent, as if sounding inside her head. The words were unfamiliar—yet, after she concentrated, the language changed, as if the speaker had sensed her thoughts and shifted from a foreign tongue to Eternian speech. *Help ... me ...* Dana rushed forward toward it.

A blue shimmer hovered in the center of a small secluded meadow. An Essence mass? It shifted in and out of focus, so it took her a minute to notice a small glowing ball in its center, slightly brighter than the rest.

Dana frowned. Was this ball the one begging for help? She'd never seen a talking ball of Essence before, but she could think of no other alternative.

She reached out with her mind, linking it with the blue shimmer. After a moment, she felt a pull, and the small glowing ball popped into view.

Freedom! The voice in her head echoed with laughter. *How wonderful! I feared I would fade away.* The ball bounced up and down, then hovered in mid-air, giving Dana the odd impression that it— whatever it might be—was staring at her.

Oh, forgive me, the mysterious voice said in her head. *My name is Jenya, Spirit of Life. I thank thee for saving me!*

A spirit?

Some of the ancient texts in the Temple library spoke about those ethereal beings, the embodiment of Essence itself, but Dana never fully believed it. Even if the spirits did exist somewhere in other plains of reality, it seemed nearly impossible for them to cross their paths with mortals. They seemed of no more consequence than sunlight or air—always present but never substantial enough to give them any extra thought. She had no idea spirits could ever appear in a visible form—let alone talk. One might as well imagine having a conversation with the wind, or flowing water.

How did one even address these creatures?

She bowed. "Greetings. My name is Dana Iclucia."

The spirit laughed, a delicate tinkling sound gradually shifting from Dana's mind into the outside world, as if hearing Dana speak aloud had made the spirit adjust its own manner of speaking. "Dana Iclucia... 'Tis quite remarkable for one of thy kind to observe us. Thee must be very powerful."

"I'm..." Dana paused. It seemed boastful somehow to mention her title to this spirit, who probably cared nothing for the affairs of people. "I'm honored to meet you, Jenya, Spirit of Life."

"'Tis rare that we are afforded the chance to converse with mortals," Jenya said. "As a token of my gratitude, I shall grant thee my protection."

A tingling sensation washed over Dana and she sensed a new power course through her body. She felt warm, full of energy and strength.

"May it serve thee well someday, Dana Iclucia." Jenya fluttered in the air, bobbing up and down. "Hohoho... The power of my kin is tickling at me. I'm afraid I must leave thee now. I bid thee farewell, Dana. Till next our paths cross again."

The light flickered and darted away, gone in the blink of an eye.

Dana stood still for a while. She wasn't quite sure what had just happened, but she knew for certain that her connection to Essence had become stronger than ever. She hoped she could put Jenya's gift to good use.

It took her another hour or so to reach the blue crystal at the ledge overlooking the city, the spot where the red-haired swordsman and his party had stood in her dream, looking at the ruins below. She patted the crystal's smooth surface, feeling the Earth's Essence trapped inside it reverberate with energy and warmth. These crystals, placed around the realm by ancient Essence Maesters, provided safety and protection, as well as convenient travel points. Surely nothing could harm this land as long as these crystals stood intact, their network channeling energy directly from the Stupa.

For reassurance she looked at the view of Aegias, so peaceful and beautiful as it spread over the valley all the way to the distant sea. She hoped what she'd seen had been nothing more than a dream. But she knew no amount of hope could alter the truth. She had to find out, so that she could face the reality, no matter what it was.

She finally remembered the swordsman's name. Adol Christin. Such a peculiar name—not from this era at all.

Without warning, her view shifted. A definite vision this time, of herself standing in this exact spot, looking down at the city. The crystal next to her was still intact, but the city lay in ruins, moss-covered and abandoned, as if no one had lived here for a very long time.

Exactly how she had seen it in her dream.

"Dana!"

The vision shattered. Dana shook off her trance and turned to watch Olga hurrying up the mountain path.

Suddenly she knew exactly what she needed to do. She reached into her bag and took out a tiny tree sapling, similar to the one she'd planted during the Arboreal Awakening. She always carried a few around in her pack.

She dropped down to the ground and dug a small hole to tuck in the plant, then used her Essence to call in water and nutrients to help the tiny tree grow. Jenya's power must have helped, and she was grateful for it.

By the time Olga reached her, the prayer tree already took root, peeking out of its cozy hole toward the sun.

A DELIVERY

Adol! *Adol!*"

Adol opened his eyes to see Laxia leaning over him, a frown of concern etched into her face.

Dear gods, did I just faint?

"Are you all right?" Laxia said.

"Yeah, I think so." He sat up and glanced around. The crystal. The Earth's Essence, solidified. Now he knew what these crystals were. A source of energy for those who could channel their Essence, like Dana.

"What happened?" he asked.

"You touched that crystal," Ricotta said. "And then you fell down." She raised her hand to point, and froze, eyes wide.

"What's wrong?" Sahad asked. Then he too paused, staring. "What the . . . ?"

Adol turned.

A giant tree towered before them, rising out of a spot right next to the crystal. A tree that hadn't been there before.

"It—it looks like this tree just grew here in the blink of an eye when we were distracted," Laxia stammered. "Now its roots are forming a bridge. But how . . . ?"

It didn't seem possible. Where before they had faced only a sheer cliff, a massive tree root now extended smoothly downward, forming a path to walk along. Just like before, when they'd searched for a way to Gendarme . . .

Dana.

How had she known to plant this tree in her timeline, so that it would grow over all these centuries to aid Adol in proceeding into the ruins of her city? It didn't make any sense. But the vision he'd just experienced *proved* that this was exactly what happened.

"Did you do this, Adol?" Ricotta asked, wide-eyed.

Adol heaved a long breath. He felt as stunned as the rest of the party, even though he had been a close observer of the events. "I think Dana did." He tried his best to explain what exactly he'd seen Dana do.

Laxia shook her head. "I'm sorry, Adol. This is very difficult to process."

"Sounds crazy," Sahad agreed. "But after seein' this tree show up outta nowhere, it's kinda hard *not* to believe."

"True..." Laxia rubbed her chin. "Perhaps this is indeed the same phenomenon that occurred in the Great Valley."

"It doesn't matter," Hummel said. "We have a path now. Let's go."

The tree root formed a perfect bridge down into the ruins. In fact, its curves and bends seemed deliberate, guiding them to the exact spot they needed to reach, right in the center of the ruins.

Up close, the buildings didn't seem as well preserved as they'd appeared from up above. Broken walls gaped with holes. Partially collapsed staircases led nowhere. Piles of stone rubble littered the ground between the buildings, covered heavily with ivy and moss. The only thing that fully matched Adol's dream memories were the waterways that still ran through the city, flowing down into the harbor.

Ricotta ran ahead and climbed up a large pile of rocks that looked like a fragment of a building toppled over. "I've never seen anything like this before. Buildings are so tall up close!" She turned to the group. "Laxia, is where you live even more amazing than this place?"

"I'm not sure," Laxia admitted. "I'm hard pressed to recall a single building in Eresia as magnificent as these must have been back in their time. How could ruins this ancient be so architecturally advanced?"

"You think my father's here?" Ricotta jumped down from her perch and fell into stride by Laxia's side.

"It's certainly possible," Laxia said. "As an explorer, I doubt he would pass on the opportunity these ruins present. He might have entered this area and gotten trapped, looking for a way out." Her voice trailed off at the obvious question of how Ricotta's father could have found a way into these ruins without the aid of Adol's magical dreams, but no one raised it as they continued on.

They entered a large—and familiar—plaza. In his mind's eye, Adol saw it in its former splendor. Merchant Mussdan would have his stalls right over here, filled with all kinds of exotic and colorful goods. His rival, Orlet, would set up his counter on the other side of the fountain, now all dried up, selling much more moderate fare. And right over there . . . Adol stopped himself. The memories he was having still didn't make any sense, no matter how well they matched the layout of this ruined city.

Sahad, walking in front of him, halted so suddenly that Adol almost ran into him.

"What is it?" Laxia asked.

Sahad pointed to the ground ahead.

Footprints?

They looked as if made by large, muddy boots—still fresh, suggesting that their owner must have passed by here less than an hour ago. They exchanged glances and rushed forward to follow the tracks through the archway ahead, which stood surprisingly intact among the wreckage around it.

Adol remembered this area too. The craftsmen district. In his mind's eye, he saw it bustling with activity as people milled around, displaying pottery, paintings, musical instruments, and, more importantly, Essence equipment—magical artifacts that possessed useful powers. The tracks led across the plaza through a gateway ahead. They rushed in that direction.

"That building over there doesn't look like it was destroyed by natural weathering," Laxia noted. "It almost looks like it was caught in a powerful impact."

It sure did. In fact, a lot of buildings in this area looked as though they had been blown apart after being hit by powerful flying objects.

"There's also something unusual about these houses," Laxia went on. "Notice the placement of the windows and the size of the doors."

"What about them?" Sahad asked.

"They look too big for humans, don't they?"

She was right again. Despite his height, Adol could barely peek into the first-floor windows of the building ahead. The empty doorway towered over him, as if made for a person much taller than him.

"Maybe whoever used to live here was taller than most folks?" Sahad suggested.

"Not just here," Hummel said. "The other buildings are the same."

"Could this mean the inhabitants of this city were significantly larger than us?" Laxia asked.

Adol wasn't sure. The Eternians in his dreams looked human in every respect. Dana always seemed conscious about her height, a head or so shorter than average among her peers. But he had no idea how they all measured up to present-day people.

The tracks they were following led them up a flight of stairs to another familiar area. The palace plaza, with the Stupa building looming ahead. They stopped, looking up at it.

"Now, that is one ridiculously tall buildin'," Sahad said.

"It makes my neck hurt just to look up at it," Ricotta agreed.

"This is the Stupa." Adol's mind was in another era again. He was with Dana, standing here looking up in awe at the grandeur of the structure. Even without the magical glow that had surrounded the Stupa in Dana's time, Adol felt the same awe now.

"What was this building used for?" Laxia asked.

"The tall monolith inside," Adol explained, "used to channel the energy for the city."

She nodded. Odd how after all the disbelief, they now accepted him as a guide, as if the idea that he had been here before didn't surprise them anymore.

"Looks like the tracks we're following lead inside," Hummel said. "Let's check the place out."

Adol's skin prickled as they entered the circular chamber surrounding the base of the Stupa. It looked much better preserved than other areas. The raised pedestal surrounding the monolith in the center looked exactly as he remembered. Even the stone tablet embedded into the wall looked intact, covered with writings Adol found illegible. Around it, animal statues formed a circle. In fact . . .

"Hey, look at these statues." Hummel pointed. "Some of them look exactly like Primordials."

They did. How could Adol not have realized this before?

Laxia shook her head. "Not possible. Primordials were extinct long before humans first appeared. There's no way for craftsmen to have fashioned these likenesses with such accuracy."

"Well, they look pretty accurate to me," Hummel said. "Whoever made these statues definitely knew exactly what Primordials looked like."

No one else commented as they circled the base of the monolith and proceeded to the gallery on the other side. The Aerial Corridor.

Adol stopped.

The walkway was still here. Even the aqueducts running on each side were in place, as well as the water gardens and the cliffs on the sides of the bay, framing the view. The only thing missing was the royal palace itself. In its place, the sea formed a giant whirlpool, its churning water shrouded in mist that foamed and swirled over the bay. Through its opaque curtain, Adol could see a massive wall of water inside the whirlpool falling endlessly into the abyss.

He felt vertigo as he watched it. A whirlpool like this shouldn't be possible by any laws of nature he knew.

Nor should dreams that spanned millennia and eras.

But who could possibly say what in this world was real anymore?

"The walkway ahead of us is gone," Ricotta said weakly.

Sahad nodded. He also looked a bit shaken. "Yeah. Doesn't look like anyone's here either."

"Boo!" a voice said from behind them.

Laxia screamed.

A large man stepped from behind a stone pillar.

He looked wiry and muscular, his deeply tanned face framed by unruly graying hair. Closely trimmed beard traced his jaw neatly. A small golden ring glinted in his left ear.

"Father!" Ricotta rushed forward and launched herself into his arms.

The man's expression turned tender as he held her close, surveying the rest of the group over the top of her head.

"Thanatos Beldine, I presume," Adol said.

The man nodded. "And you are?"

"They're my new friends," Ricotta announced. "More like family, really. It means they're your family too, right? Sahad is so funny. Laxia—she knows everything. And Hummel...you should see the way he uses that rifle. As for Adol...his sword skill...They're all so nice. Oh, Father, I have so much to tell you! Where have you been all this time?"

Thanatos looked at her fondly. "Sorry for disappearing on you. You see, that morning when I went out, a Pterosaur scooped me up. It flew me all the way to the northern region."

"A Pterosaur?" Laxia's eyes widened.

"How the hell are ya still alive?" Sahad wondered.

"I was lucky," Thanatos admitted. "It dropped me somewhere among these ruins when it caught sight of bigger prey. I guess lady luck hasn't left me for a younger man just yet. I was looking for a way to return, but the cliffs around here are impassable. How did you manage to get down here?"

"Long story," Adol said.

"I was worried sick," Ricotta complained.

Thanatos laughed. "So was I, worried sick about you. But look at you now." He glanced at the group. "Your new friends seem alright by me."

Ricotta laughed too.

It was nice to see the two of them together. Adol could sense the close bond they shared.

"So, you're T," Hummel said quietly. "Thanatos Beldine. Right." He stepped forward and reached into his pack, bringing out a small, neatly wrapped package.

Thanatos blinked. "What's this?"

"I have a delivery for you," Hummel said.

Dazed, Thanatos unwrapped the package. Inside was a tightly sealed jar and a rolled-up scroll. He looked at the jar in disbelief. "These...are my favorite pickles. But how did you—"

"You seem surprised."

"Shouldn't I be?"

"Let me jog your memory." Hummel reached into his pocket and took out a small note.

Thanatos unfolded it and ran his eyes over the few lines. "Hmm, that's right..."

"Well, then."

"What does it say?" Ricotta asked.

Thanatos handed her the note. She read aloud:

"If you're reading this, send a jar of pickles and the blueprints for a ship to the Isle of Seiren. Signed: *Thanatos Beldine."*

"I wrote this message a few months ago," Thanatos explained. "That day, I went down to the beach to look for driftage, and I found this bottle—it still had some rum in it, but only a few sips. Enough to make me tipsy, I guess. After I finished it, I really felt like having some pickles, so just to pretend it was possible, I wrote the note, put it in the bottle, and cast it out to sea. But I never thought..."

"You never thought a transporter like Hummel would find it and take it seriously," Laxia said. "Or that he would go out of his way to deliver these things to you."

"I only did it for laughs. Who could have thought—"

Hummel kept his gaze. "There was a jewel in the bottle as payment. As a transporter, I could not refuse this delivery after receiving it."

"Oh, yes, the jewel." Thanatos looked at the note again, then at the package in his other hand. "You have quite a sense of humor."

"I fail to see what's so humorous about this," Hummel said coldly.

"Wait a minute," Laxia said. "Did it escape you all what has been mentioned just now?"

"You mean, the pickles?" Ricotta asked. "Yum! I read about them. Can't wait to try one. If Father likes them this much—"

"The blueprints for a ship."

They all stared at the rolled-up scroll in Thanatos's hand.

"Oh," Sahad said.

"Exactly. The one thing we desperately need." Laxia turned to Hummel. "You had those blueprints with you this whole time, Hummel. Why didn't you say anything?"

Hummel crossed his arms over his chest. "A transporter must never reveal the contents of a package to anyone but the intended recipient. Trust is the foundation of this line of work."

Laxia shook her head. "Let me get this right. You booked passage on a ship, with full intention of landing on a cursed island no one ever escaped from, without any plans on how to get off it? Do transporters regularly do foolhardy things like that? Or was it some sort of a suicide mission?"

"Well, I—"

Laxia stepped closer. Somehow, she managed to tower over him despite being shorter by almost a head. "Did you count on the shipwreck, on us being around to help, on all the survivors from the *Lombardia* banding together? Did you ever even think this through in any detail?" She paused, clenching and unclenching her fists. "I know you're not going to answer any of that. Transporter's code and all. I'm not going to dispute that, but... I'm just so irritated by how irritated I am right now."

Thanatos laughed. "Relax. You can have these blueprints." He held out the scroll. Adol reached over and took it.

"Thank you," he said. "This isn't going to solve all our problems, but it will definitely benefit us... assuming you and Ricotta are interested in leaving this island too."

"Really?" Ricotta jumped up and down excitedly. "We can?"

Thanatos patted her shoulder. "Now that we have such good friends and building a ship is actually possible, I really hope so."

"You should come with us to our Castaway Village," Adol said.

"Their village is so beautiful, Father," Ricotta said. "The people there are so nice."

"I believe that. But how are you planning to get out of these ruins?"

"The same way we got in," Adol said. "We'll show you, after we finish exploring this area."

There was a lot of the city still left to discover, but Adol's mind was set on only one place. The Temple of the Great Tree. He wasn't sure why it was important to visit that place before all others, but he knew he wouldn't be able to rest until they did.

Having spent so much time wandering among the ruins, Thanatos could now provide directions even better than Adol, who had to recall the scenery from Dana's timeline. Together, they had no trouble following the highway that connected the city and the Temple, all the way to the Mountain Gate. But just short of reaching the outer buildings of the compound, they came across another obstacle. A section of the road in front of them had collapsed, leaving a large gap. Pieces of rubble littered the ground below, the abyss too steep to cross without special gear.

"Another dead end," Hummel said. "We just seem to get lucky with those, don't we?"

"Look," Ricotta pointed.

A blue Essence crystal rose at the edge of the gap, emitting pulses of light that made its surface ripple, like water.

"Touch it, Adol," Ricotta prompted.

Adol hesitated. He knew what she was thinking. Last time they'd reached an impassable obstacle, touching a similar crystal had transported him into Dana's era, where she'd planted a prayer tree sapling to help them along. Would the same thing happen this time too? It seemed worth a shot. He reached over and touched the crystal.

The surface of the stone vibrated under his hand, and he sank into a void.

SANCTUARY CRYPT

Dana opened her eyes to see Olga staring at her intently. They were still standing at the hilltop overlooking the city. Dana's hands tingled with the Essence she'd just released to help the sapling grow.

Had she just blacked out?

"Did it work?" Olga said.

Dana straightened up and rubbed her hands to clean off the dirt, forcing her mind back into the present. *Adol.* She nodded. "Yes. Adol has successfully reached the capital. A root from the prayer tree sapling I planted became a path for him to walk on."

Olga frowned. "I can't believe you actually used a sacred prayer tree in this manner. You always surprise me with your unorthodox approaches to problem-solving."

Unorthodox. Only Olga could describe it that way. "I don't know about 'unorthodox', but at least now I know for certain. Adol and his companions are traveling through the ruins of Aegias. I don't know how far into the future he is, but the remnants of our kingdom surround him." She looked at the city spread below, in all its beauty. It was difficult to imagine this place reduced to the lifeless ruins she'd seen in her visions, no matter how far into the future. There had to be a way to avert that fate.

"I don't want to accept this," Olga said. "But all civilizations, no matter how much prosperity they enjoy, must come to an end some-day. Not even Eternia can escape that fate, it seems."

Dana tore her eyes from the view. "The real question is when that fate will arrive."

"Perhaps we should inform Queen Sarai," Olga said hesitantly.

Dana shook her head. "I think it's too soon for that. There's still so much we don't know."

"'So much we don't know'? Dana, don't tell me you're suggesting..."

Dana let out a laugh. "Nothing gets past you, Olga. I can learn more by observing Adol as he advances in his exploration. Besides, I'm the only one who can help him by planting prayer tree saplings. I need you to cover for me while I'm gone, so I can find out what happens to Eternia."

"Same old Dana, I see." Olga sighed. "Fine. I'll do what I can."

"Thank you, Olga," Dana said earnestly.

Olga looked at her curiously. "Where will you go first?"

"Adol is making his way toward the Temple of the Great Tree."

"He's what?"

"In his era, it's ruined just like the rest of the city, but I want to make sure he reaches it safely. So I think I'll head toward the outskirts south of the capital."

Olga gave her a resigned nod. "Understood. I will let everyone know that you are away on pilgrimage."

Dana reached out and clasped her friend's hand. "Thank you again for covering for me."

"As if I could ever say no to you." Olga squeezed Dana's hand in return. "Safe travels."

Dana watched her friend walk away, then looked at the city again. She hated this sinking feeling in her stomach. Her visions, Adol, all that was going to happen millennia from now, she told herself firmly. And in the meantime, Eternia would live and prosper, enjoying the riches they'd built.

Her path from here led down to the gate, through the guard tower, into the lower city. The same path Adol and the others had taken in her vision. It felt surreal walking it now, seeing it in two different realities through two different pairs of eyes. All the destruction in Adol's time. What could have possibly happened to cause it?

Customers in the market plaza were in good spirits, cheering Queen Sarai and the Maiden of the Great Tree with the wine they'd just bought. Merchant Mussdan's stall had already drawn a crowd with another sale they were having. Ten barleys for the price of one. Even at the discount, the barleys were not worth it, but the pile was melting away in front of Dana's eyes, as if everyone's life depended on grabbing as many as they could. Dana continued past, up the stairs leading to the palace.

A little girl stood at the edge of the plaza, sniffling, her face swollen with tears. Sia, the daughter of a local artisan. In the good old days, Dana often played with Sia and her twin sister, Mia, during her forays into the city. She rushed toward the girl.

"Sia? What's wrong?"

"M-maiden..." Sia blinked her tears away. "I was playing hide-and-seek with Mia and another girl. But I can't find them anywhere. What if a bad person kidnapped them?"

"I'm sure that's not the case," Dana said. "Who is this other girl?"

Sia lowered her eyes, her expression miserable. "We just met her this morning. Io. She's got fluffy pink hair, and she's really nice. I think she might be a year or two older than me." She sniffled. "If anything happens to Mia and Io, it'll be all my fault."

Dana smiled and patted the girl's shoulder. "Don't worry, Sia. I'm going to help you find them."

Sia looked at her in disbelief. "You are?"

"Of course. After all, if two people are hiding, then two people need to look for them. I'm sure we can find them if we look together."

"M-maiden... Thank you so much!" Sia wiped her eyes with the back of her hand, a smile dawning on her face.

"Tell you what," Dana said. "You stay here in case they show up. I'm going to go look for them"—she reached out with her Essence—"here. In the Stupa building." Her eyes widened as she said it. Had Mia and Io really hidden on the palace grounds? Well, she supposed the kind and generous Queen Sarai wouldn't really mind, would she?

The tall Stupa crystal filled the chamber with its soft glow, rising out of sight through the opening in the ceiling. Essence Maester Odo stood at the side, watching his assistant, Reince, working on the pedestal at the Stupa's base. They both bowed to Dana as she passed by on her way toward the exit into the gallery and the Aerial Corridor.

The sight of the royal palace of Eternia took Dana's breath away every time she saw it. But today, she also remembered the gaping hole in its place she'd seen in Adol's era. Once again, she wondered what could have happened, mentally reaffirming the solemn oath she'd made to herself to avert this event with every bit of her power.

In the octagonal garden halfway down the Aerial Corridor, Council Darius stood talking to his secretary. His voice was loud enough for Dana to overhear the conversation, all about construction plans around the kingdom. The Queen had approved the request from the north to build a flood wall along the river, as well as three new Essence towers. The Council looked extraordinarily pleased—so much so that he hadn't even noticed Mia hiding behind the stone urn housing the elaborate royal flowerbed.

"There you are, Mia," Dana said.

The girl spun around. "Maiden? You surprised me. I'm playing hide-and-seek."

"I think," Dana said, "you picked your hiding spot a bit too well this time. Sia's in tears out on the palace plaza."

Mia sighed. "Why is Sia such a crybaby? It's only a game. Not my fault she's so bad at it."

"She's better at different things than you," Dana said. "It happens, especially when two people are as close as the two of you. And this is what makes you both stronger. For example, there are things that High Priestess Olga and Queen Sarai excel at, but I can't do. But because we're each good at different things, we can help each other out."

Mia nodded. "I understand. But..."

"What?"

"We were playing with that other girl. Io. She was the one who suggested we hide on the palace grounds. But then she said, 'I'm gonna hide at my favorite spot!' and ran off. I tried to chase after her and find her before Sia did, but..." She hung her head. "I couldn't find her anywhere. And then I had to find someplace for me to hide before I ran out of time."

"It's all right," Dana said. "I'll find her for you. Palace grounds are not the best hiding spot for children."

"I know," Mia said.

Dana looked around. Where could this other girl, Io, have disappeared to? There weren't many places to hide north of the Stupa building—unless, of course, this girl was hiding inside the royal palace itself. It seemed very unlikely, given that the guards at the palace entrance tended to be much stricter than the ones outside.

Now that she thought about it, she remembered sensing a strange presence at the Stupa. It might be worth checking out.

"Mia, could you go back to Sia?" she said. "You two should at least make up, all right?"

Mia nodded. She looked just a tiny bit guilty. "I know. That means it's up to you to avenge me, Maiden."

Dana laughed. "I won't let you down."

Mia ran off along the Aerial Corridor, and Dana followed her back into the Stupa building.

Odo and his assistant were nowhere in sight. She hesitated, looking around the chamber. She definitely felt a presence here, faint but persistent. Someone with a strong but unusual flavor of Essence had passed through here recently, leaving behind this phantom trace.

Dana scanned the room, searching for the source of the sensation. Four stylized Saurian statues lined the sides of the chamber on the palace side, each holding a half-sphere carved in stone. It took her a moment to realize that one of the spheres emanated a faint, nearly invisible glow. Essence, so subtle that only a very powerful person could detect it. Strange. In all the times she'd passed these statues, she'd never noticed anything like this. What was going on?

She examined the other statues. Their globes weren't emanating Essence light, but as she leaned closer to examine them, she sensed it, a concentrated ball of Essence trapped just under the surface of the stone. Odd. She reached over with her mind and released it, so that the half-sphere now glowed just like the other one. She had no idea what she had just done, but she felt compelled to continue, repeating the action until all four were glowing. And then...

A section of the floor at the base of the Stupa sunk downward, revealing a spiral staircase that descended into darkness.

A hidden passage? She definitely needed to investigate.

As she started down the stone stairway, she realized that it wasn't actually as dark as she had initially believed. Blue lanterns set into the wall sconces filled the narrow corridor with a mysterious Essence light. The Essence was so strong here that the air hummed with its power, making her feel energized. A secret sanctuary, built right under the Stupa? How was it that she, the Maiden of the Great Tree and the supreme Essence user in the kingdom, had never heard of it before? Did Odo know about this place? Did Queen Sarai? Questions crowded in Dana's mind as she followed the staircase into a large underground chamber.

The hall in front of her ran into the distance, its walls carved with ornaments and symbols she didn't recognize. She could see a faint outline of an open doorway in the shadows at the other end.

"Someone help!" The distant voice sounded like a child's. Io? It didn't seem possible that a simple street girl could use this sanctuary as a hideout, but whoever it was, they definitely needed help. Dana rushed through the doorway into the next room.

The chamber looked empty—at first. But as her vision adjusted, she detected a bluish glow wavering in midair. Another trapped spirit? She reached out with her Essence to dissolve the invisible cage. A small glowing orb floated into view.

"Finally," the spirit said. "I know not who you are, but I thank you all the same." The orb bobbed up and down in front of Dana. "Whaaaat? An Eternian?"

This spirit seemed different from Jenya, the Spirit of Life, its speech less archaic and audible right away.

"My name is Dana," she said. "I'm glad you're safe."

"I'm Amy," the spirit said. "I am known as the Spirit of Possessions."

Dana nodded. As she recalled, one of the beliefs had it that spirits could dwell in powerful items and Essence equipment to give them special properties. Amy was probably one of those.

"Have you by any chance seen a little girl around here?" She knew it was a long shot, but she was running out of options. If Io was indeed down here, she needed to find her at once. This wasn't a safe hiding spot for a child.

"No," Amy said. "Such mundane things don't interest me. However, if you seek possessions, you can always find me by the Essence crystal near the entrance." She bobbed down the steps and off into the next chamber.

The Essence crystal. Dana nodded. She had seen one near the entrance, somewhat different from the ones above ground but filled with the same power. She could use it as a transportation point. The Essence here was probably strong enough to warp to it from anywhere.

She proceeded through a string of rooms, dodging animated suits of armor that moved on their own, obviously left here to guard the place. They reacted to movement, so she avoided them by keeping to the shadows and hiding behind walls. Questions continued to swarm in her head. Who had built this sanctuary, and why? What were these creatures guarding?

A smaller room up ahead was a dead end. A black stone slab rose in its center, gleaming with a mirror-smooth finish. An archival monolith, a device for storing vast amounts of information. It looked quite old. She approached and used Essence to activate the jewel at the base.

Dana was surprised to see a glowing hexagonal tablet form in mid-air. So, despite its age, the monolith still worked. Impressive. She peered at the text and images running across the ethereal page.

In the beginning was the Sage. The Sage, a wise man of enduring intelligence, embarked on a long journey, when he discovered a colossal tree. Seating himself at the foot of the tree, the Sage began to meditate. And in his trance, a mysterious power was revealed to him. The Sage could read the wind as easily as a bird. He achieved mastery over the elements of Fire and Water. He could even see future events yet to occur in distant lands. The Sage had tapped into that power, which governed the very laws of nature, and he saw fit to call it Essence.

When the Sage returned to his homeland, he used Essence to drive out the Saurians that threatened his people. Freed from the threat that had plagued them for so long, peace had finally come to the Sage's homeland. The people honored the Sage, learned from him the art of Essence, and with it achieved untold prosperity. With his newfound influence, the Sage assembled his people and established a nation. So it was that His Radiance, Light King of Alchea, became the first King of Eternia.

Dana stared at the text. This account of the founding of Eternia seemed a bit different from the one she and the other trainees had learned. She'd always thought the Light King had lived in harmony with the Saurians and came from the area near the Great Tree.

Laughter rang through the room. A girl with pink hair came out from behind the monolith.

Io? She looked familiar, Dana realized. She'd seen this girl somewhere. The Temple, on the day of the Arboreal Awakening? Not possible. It'd been over three years, but this girl didn't look a day older than the one she'd seen on that day—around eleven or so.

"Hello, Lady," the girl said. "Did Sia send you to find me?"

She seemed eerily calm for a child stuck in an underground crypt, with animated suits of armor patrolling around, but Dana was determined not to let herself be swayed.

"You must be Io," she said. "And you shouldn't be in here. This place is too dangerous for children. Come along, I'll take you home."

"Home?" Io pouted. "But... I wanna play more."

"Next time," Dana said firmly. "And somewhere more suitable."

Io appeared to consider it. "Very well. If you're gonna be all pushy about it, then I guess I'll go with you. After we've checked that out." She pointed into the shadows at the end of the room.

Dana peered in that direction. "A door?" How could she have overlooked it before?

Hiding in a deep niche behind the monolith, the tall stone door was carved with the Great Tree symbol, done in bronze and almost as elaborate as the one in the Great Tree Garden. She pushed. Locked, of course. She tried harder, but the door didn't budge.

Dana examined the surface more closely. Only now did she notice a line of text engraved on it, carved skillfully into the ornaments. Old Eternian, but luckily she could understand it well enough.

"*Only the Virtuous may Enter,*" she read out loud.

"Huh?" Io said. "I wonder what that means."

Dana shook her head. For a moment, she'd almost forgotten about the girl. "I'm not sure either. Maybe it will only open under the right conditions. Anyway, this is as far as we're going. Let's get out of here."

Io looked disappointed. "All right. Let's go back."

Mia and Sia were waiting on the palace plaza. They both beamed when they saw Dana and Io emerge.

"I didn't think I was gonna lose this bad at hide-and-seek," Mia said.

Io laughed. "Looks like I'm the champion today."

"I'm gonna challenge you again tomorrow!"

"Come now," Sia objected. "You both really worried me! I was this close to getting the guards to go look for you!"

"Sorry, I got a little carried away," Io admitted. "I didn't think it'd end up being such a big deal."

Dana smiled. "Still, you're lucky to have people who worry about you. Don't ever forget that."

The girls nodded, and once again it struck Dana how different Io looked from the other children. As if she were older than her apparent age. As if she possessed deeper knowledge that made everything Dana said seem trivial. She shook the feeling away. Dreaming about Adol was making her see things that weren't there.

"I must be off," she said.

"All right," Mia said. "Time for us to go back to our mom. Come, Sia, I'll tell you a scary story."

"Mia," Sia protested.

Mia laughed as she ran on ahead. Sia laughed too and followed.

Dana turned to Io. "What about you? Do you want me to escort you home?"

Io shook her head. "I'm not that little, y' know. Besides... I'm in the middle of looking for something."

"Looking for something? I can help you if you'd like."

"No need. I think I've nearly found it. I'll just wander around this area for a bit. You don't need to worry about me." She ran off.

Dana stood for a moment, looking after her. What a strange child. She still had no idea what to make of their conversation. But she knew she wasn't getting any answers, at least not today. She shook off these thoughts and followed the road she'd seen Adol take toward the Temple.

In her vision of Adol, the highway had collapsed right before reaching the Temple's Mountain Gate. Even though she didn't expect it to be in ruins in the present, she felt ridiculously relieved to see the road intact. She tried to convince herself that the events in Adol's era took place very far into the future, but these thoughts did nothing to ease the cold grip of worry that continued to seize her heart.

The road was lined with pilgrims, and she maneuvered around them toward the place where Adol had been stopped by the collapsed road. Here, the glowing Essence crystal loomed next to a bas-relief of an ancient Saurian rider. She searched for a patch of soil next to it and took out a tiny prayer tree sapling, digging its roots gently into the dirt. She used Essence to have it take hold and strengthen, then knelt next to it and closed her eyes.

"Please, open a path for Adol," she prayed.

Her vision faded, consumed by overwhelming white light.

DANA

Just like before, Adol woke up lying on the ground with everyone leaning over him. He should have learned the routine by now. Still, it felt embarrassing to see everyone's concerned faces, as if he'd just had a fainting spell.

"Are you all right, Adol?" Laxia asked.

"Did it work?"

She nodded.

Adol hastily got to his feet and looked.

The chasm they'd faced when they arrived here was now covered with the protruding roots of a giant tree, running horizontally across to piece together the ruined stone bridge that previously lay in shambles down below. It looked wide and sturdy, almost like the original road.

"Incredible," Thanatos said quietly. "It's like the tree is consciously trying to prevent the bridge from collapsing." He turned to the party. "It's one thing to hear you guys describe this, but it's another thing entirely to actually see it."

"Told you." Ricotta looked proud, as if she personally carried some credit in what had happened. "Now we can keep going."

"I still don't understand," Hummel said. "If Dana is deliberately trying to help us, it must mean she's aware of Adol's actions too. But how is that possible, if she's all the way back in the past?"

Adol had been wondering the same thing. It was difficult enough to come to terms with the fact that he was having dreams that revealed past events he had no prior knowledge of. But even if he accepted that, it still didn't seem possible for Dana's awareness of him to span the chasm of time—or for Adol to share her consciousness all the way back in the past. He felt so confused. Had the events he'd just witnessed happened right now? Or ages ago? He knew no amount of wondering was going to give him any answers.

"Let's go," he said.

Everyone nodded. They shouldered their packs and stepped onto the newly formed bridge.

Having just shared Dana's vision, Adol could easily compare the state of the city now to what it looked like then. It had been so magnificent back in Dana's era—elaborately built and perfectly maintained. It was run-down and ruined in the present time, but even with all this destruction, the fact that many of the buildings still stood was testament to the superb skill of the original builders. What could have possibly happened to destroy such a beautiful and advanced civilization?

Inside the familiar gatepost, two stairwells ran up, flanking a small alcove with an elaborate pattern carved into the wall. The symbol of the Great Tree. Despite the worn state of the stones around it, the symbol looked pristine, gold and green, just like it did in Dana's time. Set against the dark wall behind it, it seemed to float in midair, solid and ethereal all at the same time.

This appeared to be an altar. Empty stone braziers sat on either side, the walls above them still bearing the details of old carvings. Standing here, Adol imagined Dana stopping in this very same place to offer a prayer to the Great Tree of Origins.

They made their way through a gateway at the back of the building, onto the Temple grounds.

The Great Tree rose in the distance at the end of the valley, high enough to dwarf the Temple's main dome and partially obscure the mountain behind it. Its crown spread wide, like a roof over the world. A tranquil, quiet feeling of seclusion reigned in its shade, as if this Temple and its grounds were enclosed into a sheltered world of their own. Adol drew a long breath, soaking in the view.

They followed the stone walkway toward the Temple. Here it was easy to forget that they were in another timeline. Dana had followed this exact walkway over and over, and, save for some extra layers of moss and cracks in the stone, it looked almost the same.

Adol hoped that the Temple would be relatively intact too, but there was no such luck. Some of the walls had collapsed, filling empty chambers and hallways with piles of broken stone. Giant rats lurked in the rubble, scattering away as the party approached.

Ahead, two staircases flanked a deep alcove with the holy symbol carved into the wall—faded and crumbling, not nearly as well preserved as the one at the gate. But despite the disrepair, Adol felt the same reverence as he approached it. They were nearing Dana's sanctum. Even in ruin, it felt special.

Picking their way through the Temple proved difficult. Many of the hallways and passages were blocked, forcing them to retrace their steps and find a way around, deeper into the compound. They passed many collapsed doorways and stairways, following the bends of the corridor that, as far as Adol could tell, should eventually lead them into the main hall. But just before they reached it, a gaping hole in the floor blocked their way, leaving no possibility to proceed any further.

Adol recognized this place. Dana's room should be just around the corner. In fact, the wall on their left should be the one that separated this hallway from her chamber. He looked around. As far as he remembered, that dark niche beside the doorway they'd just walked through should harbor a secret lever that opened Dana's escape hatch. Did the mechanism still work? He traced his fingers along the wall until he found the familiar metal rod protruding out of the stone. He pulled, and a section of the wall slid noiselessly aside.

The party watched in silence as Adol approached the newly formed hole, just wide enough to squeeze through. He shrugged in response to their questioning looks, then led the way into the chamber beyond.

Dana's room. Here in this era, covered in dust and grime, it looked nothing like the cozy, peaceful place he remembered from his dreams. But all the furnishings were still here, amazingly well preserved. His heart raced as he looked around, identifying every familiar object. The bed, its bare surface stripped of all the sheets and decorations. The table in the center of the room, positioned to make the maximum use of the sunlight streaming from the ceiling window overhead. The stone basin next to the altar by the far wall—empty, now that the spring feeding it had dried out. The bookshelf beside the escape hatch they'd just entered, gaping with bare shelves. The pottery collection on the floor. In his mind's eye, he could still picture everything as it used to be in Dana's time. He could imagine her here too—sitting on this bed, praying at this altar, dipping her hand into the stone basin to cool off on a hot day. Memories overwhelmed him.

This was the place he'd been fighting to reach, struggling through all the obstacles, overcoming them with Dana's help. He had felt absolutely sure that her room, in the heart of the Temple of the Great Tree, would hold all the answers. And now that he was here, he had no idea what to do.

He couldn't have seriously expected they were going to find Dana here. She was gone, millennia ago. Yet the disappointment he felt almost brought tears to his eyes.

Perhaps they hadn't come far enough?

"Let's move on," he said.

"Move on to where?" Laxia asked.

"There's more of the Temple to explore. The door from this chamber should bypass that gap in the floor and lead us to the main hall and the sacred garden at the foot of the Great Tree." Perhaps that was the place that would hold the answers.

Now that he thought of it, a new purpose filled him. They needed to get to the Temple's main hall behind the double doors ahead, and then to the Tree. They had to find a way through. Quite possibly, whatever lay there was the whole reason he'd crashed on this deserted island in the first place. He had to find out.

Adol shivered as they entered the giant domed space of the main hall, so familiar to him from his dreams. The stone statues here were arranged differently from the way he remembered them in Dana's time. Most of them were pushed to the sides, except for the Saurian-headed Warrior, its multiple arms bristling with stone blades, that now blocked the path forward.

"Check out this weird-looking statue," Sahad said.

"What an odd spot to put it in," Laxia agreed. "Right across the path."

A rumble echoed through the hall.

Adol froze in his steps.

Had the statue moved?

Not possible. It had to be a play of shadows. Yet, deep inside, Adol couldn't feel convinced. In Dana's times, Essence-powered statues and suits of armor guarded secluded areas all the time. Could this be one of them?

He peered closer. Did this statue emit a faint Essence glow? He didn't think it was possible for him to see Essence, but he swore he could detect a faint halo surrounding it, just visible in the dim hall.

He drew his sword and edged forward.

The stone warrior shifted on its pedestal.

"What's happenin'?" Sahad whimpered.

"It's a moving statue," Ricotta explained, her trembling voice betraying a conscious effort to stay reasonable. "I read about that in a book once."

"That was just a story, Ricotta," Laxia said tensely. "Statues can't really move."

The stone warrior raised its head and lowered its blades toward the approaching party.

"Then why is this one moving?" Hummel asked.

"How should I know?" Laxia snapped.

Sahad drew his hammer.

As if on cue, the statue leaned forward and swiped its arms at the group. Its blow connected with Sahad's hammer and sent the large man scattering back along the floor.

The stone blade should have broken against the orichalcum, but the magic that held the statue together was clearly stronger than the legendary metal. Another stone blade whizzed past Adol and crashed into the floor at Laxia's feet. A blow this strong would smash a person flat. How many arms did this statue have? Six? Eight?

Dancing between the flailing stone blades, dodging the statue's blows, Adol spotted a crack running along one of its arms, just above the elbow. He aimed the point of his sword, wedging it into the crack just as Sahad's hammer crashed down on one of the blades the statue was swinging. The stone arm broke off and fell to the floor, where it shattered into pieces.

"Finally," Sahad panted. He stumbled back as two blades swept at him from opposite directions, tripping over the debris and skidding to a halt just out of the statue's reach. "One down. How many does the sucker have?"

Adol measured up their opponent. Missing one arm didn't make the statue look any less capable than before.

"We need to coordinate," he shouted. "Sahad, let's aim for the one on the bottom left. Ricotta and Hummel, go for the one on the right. Laxia, try to keep it distracted. Ready?"

Nods came from all around. Hummel aimed his gun, while Ricotta darted forward with her clubs raised. Her blow, paired with a gunshot, took off another arm. Adol and Sahad attacked on the opposite side, hacking and stabbing. Laxia danced in between them with her rapier.

They didn't stop until the Warrior had no more limbs left. Ricotta emitted a triumphant shriek as she jumped up on the pedestal, landing a massive blow to the statue's head. The rest of the party joined her, swinging and hitting with deep resolve.

Piece by piece, the entire statue reduced to a pile of stone rubble at their feet. The Essence glow faded. The ancient magic powering the automaton was gone.

"Whew." Sahad sheathed his weapon and wiped his forehead. "Glad that's over."

Ricotta jumped down from the pedestal. Her face was caked with dust and sweat, its smears resembling elaborate warpaint. Strange how, despite that, she still looked so innocent and cheerful.

"It's like magic from the stories I've read," she said. "Did the people who lived here use magic?"

Adol nodded. "Dana and her people wielded a mystical power. They called it Essence."

"Essence." Ricotta appeared to taste the word.

They skirted the remains of the statue and crossed the hall toward the open doorway on the far end.

Adol's heart quivered as he stepped through the doorway into the Great Tree Garden.

The world around him receded to the background. He could no longer hear his companions' hushed conversation, or register any details of the scenery around him. His eyes were drawn to a cradle of twined branches suspended at the base of the Tree.

Somehow, he knew exactly what he was going to find inside this basket-like cradle. Yet, as his feet carried him toward it, as he got close enough to see what was inside, he felt as if he had just lost connection with solid ground, tumbling into a freefall.

A young woman lay inside the cradle, curled up in a deep sleep.

His breath caught. Even though he had never seen her face-to-face, he recognized her at once.

Dana.

He reached toward her, but an invisible force repelled him, preventing his hand from touching her. The movement caused a ripple of energy, echoing in a tremor that shook the entire structure.

Her eyes fluttered open. For a moment, they looked dazed, unfocused. Then her gaze found his and stirred with recognition.

"Adol?" she whispered.

A wave of warmth washed over him. Something inside him that had been restless all this time settled into a calmness, deeper than anything he ever experienced before.

"Dana," he breathed out.

The tree branches entwining her wove apart. She slid out of her cradle, and Adol rushed forward to catch her into his arms.

Did you say . . . Dana?" Laxia asked.

They all gathered around, looking at the young woman curled up in Adol's arms. She was awake, but seemed dazed, her unfocused gaze drifting unseeingly around the group.

In his dreams, Adol had seen her enough times to become familiar with her features, but none of this knowledge prepared him for encountering her in the flesh for the very first time. Slender and tall, she wore a soft blue tunic and breeches, the plain outfit she favored for most occasions. The cloth draped loosely over her slim, elegant form, crossed by the straps of the crescent blades sheathed at her back. A mass of dark hair spilled over her in waves, their lush blue-black shine offsetting her distinct eye color—aqua-blue, like the morning sky meeting the sea right at the horizon.

Carefully, he lowered her onto the moss-covered ground and knelt beside her.

"We need to take her back to the village," Laxia said. "She looks unwell. Perhaps Licht—"

"She doesn't look fit to travel anywhere," Thanatos protested.

Dana sat up, leaning on Adol's arm, and ran her eyes around the party. Strange how she didn't look in the least bit surprised to see them all.

"We can use Essence crystals to travel," she said. "Your village has one, doesn't it?"

The question was directed to Adol. He blinked. The Essence crystal. Right.

"We have one," he said. "But I am not sure it's—"

"Here." Dana held out her hand. A ring set with a watery blue stone glinted on her finger, emitting the same glow as the Essence crystals they had seen throughout this island. "Think of the destination." She clenched Adol's hand and closed her eyes again.

Adol's skin tingled. The feeling that enfolded him felt similar to the times when he'd touched the crystals to transport to Dana's time.

Except this time, he didn't fall to the ground or pass out. Instead, he felt light, as if flying. And then...

The scenery around him changed. Instead of the cool tree shade, sunlight hit his face, fresh breeze carrying the familiar smells of sea water and campfire smoke.

"Adol? What the hell..."

Dogi?

Adol opened his eyes.

They were back in Castaway Village, the entire party kneeling around the crystal with dazed looks on their faces. Dana was still leaning into his arms, except that now she seemed truly unconscious, her eyes closed, her cheeks so pale that Adol's heart raced with worry.

"What in the blazes..." Sahad said.

"We're in Castaway Village!" Ricotta announced. "Wow. That was really fast travel!"

Dana was the only one who could offer any explanations, but she hadn't regained consciousness since the entire party had inexplicably zapped all the way across the island. While Licht crouched by her bedside, fumbling with pouches and elixirs that seemed to have very little effect on his patient, Adol paced around the cave chamber that served as the women's sleeping quarters, trying to enfold everything that had happened. The rest of the party gathered nearby, watching the scene with puzzled looks.

"Maybe the Kingdom of Eternia existed more recently than we thought," Laxia said. "How else could a person like Dana survive all this time?"

Hummel shook his head. "I don't know about that. Her kingdom is reduced to ruins. It had to have taken longer than a few years to bring it to that state."

"She's got a symbol on her shoulder," Ricotta said, pointing.

She was right. As Licht leaned over to rub an ointment into Dana's temples, her sleeve folded away, exposing a tattoo in glossy red ink over her upper arm. It looked like a depiction of an eye, adorned with spikes that made it appear hostile, evil. The image made Adol feel uncomfortable.

"What kind of a symbol is it?" Ricotta wondered.

"An aspect of Eternian culture?" Hummel suggested.

"I don't think so." Adol had no idea how he knew it, but the symbol seemed foreign. Wrong.

"Now, gentlemen," Laxia said sternly. "I think that's quite enough leering for today."

She was right. Yet when they all left the room, Adol couldn't stop feeling concerned. He had so many questions, so many things to understand. Now that he had found Dana, he didn't want to separate from her.

The mysterious bond they shared had transcended millennia to bring them together. And now that she was here, he felt a strange mix of contentment and worry. There was some higher reason behind all this—and while he hoped for the best, he couldn't escape the feeling that he and Dana had been united to face some sort of a trial that neither of them could survive on their own. Or maybe he was just overthinking this whole situation. Dana was here. He hoped she was going to be all right.

The sun was already setting as they all gathered around the fire. Only now did Adol realize how tired he felt. In this one day, they had traveled all the way though the ruins of Aegias and the Temple of the Great Tree, and then transported back to Castaway Village in the blink of an eye. On top of that, he'd also experienced not one but two flashbacks into Dana's time. He felt overwhelmed.

"The ruins of a lost civilization," Dogi said. "And the girl who's been appearing in your dreams. I never imagined you'd find all that on the north side of the island."

Euron nodded thoughtfully. "If you hadn't brought her back, I would've said you guys were losin' it."

"None of you seem all that surprised though," Thanatos said.

Dogi laughed. "Hang around Adol long enough, and you'll build up a tolerance to crazy things happening. Or, in my case, complete immunity."

"Stories or not," Laxia said, "it's obvious that a great mystery lies at the heart of this island."

"Yeah, certainly looks that way," Dogi agreed. "And even though we've got blueprints and are using them to build a ship, we're not out of the woods just yet."

Adol felt too exhausted to participate in the conversation. He needed a break to process everything that had happened. As soon as he finished his meal, he stumbled into the lodge, sank into his hammock, and fell asleep.

DANA

Adol woke up at dawn to the sound of a gong ringing at the edge of the camp. The alarm system Dogi had installed around the barricades protecting the village to warn of intruders. He grabbed his sword and rushed out of the cave, joined by Dogi, Euron, and the others.

The outer camp barricade was under siege. The attacking Primordials were thankfully not large, but there were enough of them to make Adol worry. Could the villagers fend off so many? He led the way as he jumped the barricade and rushed into battle.

It didn't take Adol long to realize that, orichalcum weapons or not, the villagers were badly outnumbered. The Primordials kept coming, lizards taller than humans running on two legs, not very strong but incredibly aggressive. Every able-bodied person was fighting by his side, using blades and clubs or hurtling rocks from behind the barricades. They killed a few beasts and fended off some of the others, but the enemies just kept coming.

"They're gettin' more aggressive," Sahad panted.

Hummel aimed his rifle and put down another one with a clean shot through the eye. He was running out of ammunition though. Without it, he would be left to using his bayonet at close range, no better than a regular pike.

"They'll overwhelm us," Laxia said.

Adol knew she was right. There were too many of the creatures. They needed to fall back to the cave, and then—

A spinning circle descended from above, cutting the air with a whistling sound that seemed almost musical. It looked like a rainbow closed in on its own tail—a multicolored gleaming disk, sharp and deadly. It sliced into the group of Primordials, hacking them down. The animals fell back, collapsing left and right.

Dana.

She stood on the rocks above. As Adol looked up, she reached over and caught the spinning circle, separating it into two crescent blades. *The Eldersphere.* Now that he saw it in action, he finally realized the reason for the name.

The Primordials scrambled away, as if intelligent enough to realize that this new addition to the party had irreversibly tipped the balance against them. Dana jumped down from the rocks and spun into their midst, her blades blending into two sheets of air in her hands. The beasts scattered and ran.

Dana stopped at the edge of the rock and turned to face the villagers. The halo of rising sunlight highlighted her slender shape, so graceful as she sheathed her swords behind her back in a single fluid move. Her eyes met Adol's, and he felt a surge of warmth rushing down his spine.

Wow, was all he could possibly think. But even that thought left his head as Dana approached.

"Adol." She smiled. "I'm Dana. I guess this is the part where we both say 'Nice to meet you'."

Her voice, soft and musical, made his stomach do a funny somersault.

"Nice to meet you," he managed.

THE ROAD OUT OF THE CITY

Rising sunlight poured over the landscape as they all gathered around the fire to have breakfast and reflect on the recent events. The cries of seagulls accented the rhythmic splash of the waves on the beach. Smells of pine and wild roses blooming on the upper terrace wafted through the air. No matter where he went next, Adol was going to miss these gatherings, sitting together next to the campfire sharing a meal.

But today was different. Dana was here, the focus of all the attention. She kept quiet, sitting on the log next to Adol with her knees pulled up to her chest, staring into the flames.

"So," Dogi said. "Basically, the Kingdom of Eternia existed in an era where Primordials flourished."

Dana nodded. "We called them Saurians. In our time, they used to be far less aggressive."

"I can't believe people actually lived alongside Primordials. That literally contradicts every last scholarly paper written on the subject." Laxia's face lit up with fascination, as if contradicting scholarly papers was a major achievement everyone should be proud of.

"How long ago did Primordials exist?" Ricotta asked.

"No one knows for certain," Laxia said.

Hummel turned to Dana. "I know your memories are fuzzy, but do you remember anything else?"

Dana shook her head. "I remember my name, and I remember I was the Maiden of the Great Tree. I also remember sharing my consciousness with Adol through dreams and the crystals. But I don't remember why I'm here in this era. Or why I was asleep at the base of the Great Tree. I can't remember what brought me here."

"What's the last thing you remember?" Laxia asked.

Dana closed her eyes briefly. "Let me see...I was planting a prayer tree in order to guide Adol to the Temple, and...And then—" She gasped, pressing her hands against her head, as if in pain. Adol hovered over her, unsure what to do.

"Are you all right?" Ricotta asked.

Dana took a breath. "Y-yes, I'm sorry. I just felt lightheaded all of a sudden. The more I try to remember, the worse it gets." She glanced up at Adol. "I'd like to remember more though. Maybe if I can accompany you in your explorations—?"

Adol met her gaze. The question felt strange. Of course Dana was going to accompany them. It seemed odd to even consider any other possibilities. The mere idea of not having her by his side seemed unthinkable.

It was their bond, he tried to tell himself. Nothing to do with how good she made him feel when she was sitting next to him like this. Or maybe this was part of the bond too? A connection through dreams, sharing each other's past, had to make people feel special about each other.

"I was hoping you can accompany us," he said. "Absolutely."

"Yay!" Ricotta exclaimed. "More family. You can be my big sister, Dana!"

Dana laughed. "I would be delighted."

"Good," Euron said. "And while you are exploring, we will focus on building the ship—now that we have the blueprints."

"Speaking of ships," Dogi said.

Euron shook his head vigorously. "Dogi...Now's not the time."

"Wait, what about ships?" Ricotta asked.

Dogi glanced at Euron. "A strange fog has been rolling over the ocean the past couple of days. And whenever that fog rolls in..." He paused. "A ghost ship appears."

Adol stared. "A ghost ship? You aren't serious, are you?"

"When I first saw it, I thought I was goin' nuts," Dogi admitted. "But then other castaways reported seeing the same thing." He kept his eyes on Euron as he spoke.

"Ghost stories," Euron rumbled. "You should know better than believe this sort of thing."

"Do you have any better explanation? All the castaways—"

Euron tossed his head. "I know. Somehow, people love getting themselves spooked. But we have no concrete proof. Honestly, Adol,

I don't think you guys need to worry about that right now."

"I agree," Hummel said. "We have more important things to deal with. The Primordial that sank the *Lombardia*. Even if we build a ship, we can't leave the island without clearing that obstacle."

"Good point," Euron agreed. "Even with a ship, we can't go anywhere with that tentacled beast roaming free."

"But how do we deal with a creature that has domain over the sea?" Thanatos said.

Dana lifted her head. "A tentacled creature than sank your ship ... Are you talking about the Oceanus?"

"What?" Thanatos blinked.

"The Oceanus was a monstrous tentacled beast that threatened ships in Eternia as well. Extensive research was carried out in order to establish safe passage by sea." She paused. "Records of the Oceanus's ecology might still exist."

"Where?" Dogi asked.

"I would start at the Baja Tower, a research facility east of the capital. All our historical records and other valuable information are archived there. If these archives are still intact..." Dana's voice trailed into silence again. She did this a lot, speaking in half sentences, falling into deep thought in mid-phrase. Fighting for her memories. Adol hoped she would regain them without going through any pain.

"A tower of Primordial research." Laxia looked wistful.

"I'm not sure if the tower is still standing though," Dana said.

"Why don't we return to Eternia and find out?" Adol suggested.

Dana nodded. Adol couldn't tell for sure, but it seemed to him that the prospect of returning to the ruins of her world pleased her.

It took the party no time to gather their packs and meet in the village center again. Dana looked like a proper member of the group now, outfitted with a pack from Dina's supply stand, her crescent swords strapped across her back. A born adventurer, with a lot of knowledge about the area. The mere idea of exploring the island with her made Adol feel energized.

"When we found you," he said, "you did something to transport us all here."

Dana nodded. "It's called warping. The Essence crystals, like the one in your village, have been built for this purpose throughout the realm. All you need to do is wear a ring with a piece of Essence crystal in it. Every time you discover a crystal, the ring tunes in to it. It works like memory, enabling you to instantly transport yourself from any location to one of these warping spots. All you have to do is touch the crystal in the ring and think of one of the crystals you've previously visited." Dana held out her hand for all of them to see.

The ring was plain, the translucent stone set into it carved into a faceted oval that seemed to change color, shifting between blue-green and orange-purple as Dana moved her hand. Adol recognized the golden glow playing under the surface of the stone, just like in the large crystals they'd found throughout the island. They must be made of the same material, although Adol hadn't noticed the crystals on the ground exhibiting this kind of a color change. Warping spots. He wished they'd known how to use these transportation points all along, rather than braving the mountains and fighting the Primordials.

"Can I have a ring like this too?" Ricotta asked.

Dana smiled. "Of course you can. It doesn't have to be the same style. We can just find some crystal shards to set into rings. There should be a lot of them scattered around."

"Euron can make the rings," Dogi said. "He's quite a handyman."

They walked around the beach and the terraces, looking through rocks and pebbles covering the ground. Before long, Dana reached down, pulling out a piece of gleaming bluish stone that had fallen between the pebbles at the side of the rock cliff. Almost at the same time, Ricotta on the other end of the beach squealed in delight and straightened out, holding a larger piece in her hand. Unpolished, they didn't look as shiny and transparent as Dana's, but Adol could now see that they were made of the same mineral.

Soon they were in possession of a large handful of crystals in different sizes and shapes. They brought the stones to Euron's workshop, where Dana explained to him what to do.

"Give me few days," Euron said. "We should make enough rings for everyone, as well as for the new castaways we may still discover."

"In the meantime," Dana said, "the search party can all use my ring to travel together to the Eternia ruins."

They picked up their gear and gathered around the crystal.

The pulling sensation felt more familiar this time. Adol didn't feel as disoriented as before as he felt drawn into a swirl and then emerged into a completely different setting.

They were standing in front of the gap that had replaced the royal palace, staring at the giant whirlpool beyond.

"The palace." Dana kept very still, watching the falling water. "I...I should remember what happened to it, shouldn't I?" She turned away abruptly before anyone could respond, and walked down the Aerial Corridor toward the Stupa.

No one spoke as they proceeded through the Stupa building into the palace plaza and down the stone highway leading out of the city toward the east. Adol looked around curiously. This wasn't the area familiar to him from his dreams about Dana's era. The view of the water gardens looked different from here, the greenery partially obscured by at the row of giant stone statues lining the way. They all depicted the same woman, wrapped in thick garments that covered her head to toe, leaving only the face to stare at the passersby with blank stone eyes. A goddess of some sort? Adol wanted to ask Dana, but her determined look warned him off.

Adol could relate to her state. It had been hard for him to handle the change between the beauty of Eternia's past and the desolation in the present day. For Dana, seeing her own world in ruins for the very first time had to be a lot. Every building they passed was a reminder of the times gone by, of the destruction of her civilization. She needed time to deal with the shock.

After a while, the walkway they were following ended with a locked gate.

"A dead end," Hummel observed calmly. "Just like the one back at the Temple."

"The Temple?" Dana blinked.

"The Mountain Gate," Adol explained. "When we approached it from the trail descending down the mountain, we couldn't open it, no matter what we tried. I hope this one won't turn out to be the same."

"I see." Dana nodded. "This one is exactly the same, actually. These gates can only be opened with Essence." She stepped forward and folded her hands under her chin, as if deep in thought.

Standing behind her, Adol couldn't see what exactly she was doing, but after a moment the massive stone gate clicked and swung open on its own.

"Holy cow," Sahad whispered. "Did ye see that? She didn't even touch it."

Dana turned to face the group, her expression calm, as if nothing out of the ordinary was going on. "Let's keep going."

As they passed through the gate, Adol ran a stunned look up the massive frame—still intact, as if the intervening centuries hadn't happened at all. The gate had looked fused together when Dana first approached it. How was she able to open it so easily?

They were in the countryside now. No more buildings, or even ruins, could be seen in the grassy foothills ahead, where the remains of an old road ascended in a wide coil around the cliffs. A tall tower rose in the distance, leaning precariously to one side.

It was the same tower they'd spotted from the other end of the plains on their initial approach to the ruined city. But now, from up close, they could fully appreciate its size. Aside from the Stupa, Adol had never seen a structure this tall. No one in his world even had the technology to build something like this. How advanced had the Eternian civilization been, exactly?

"That's Baja Tower," Dana said. "I'm relieved it's still standing, even if it is leaning quite a bit."

Laxia tore her eyes from the view. "So that's where your people conducted research on Primordials?"

"Among other things, yes. Our research on Essence was actually far more fruitful." Dana looked into the distance ahead. "There used to be a road here, part of the overland trade route. It used to lead to foreign lands."

And now, there's only water. Adol shielded his eyes from the sun, looking in that direction. It was hard to imagine this place was once covered with land, where people lived and prospered. The cataclysm that destroyed Eternia must have reshaped everything, allowing whole parts of the Earth to be swallowed by the sea. The idea was mind-boggling.

The range ahead of them curved around this side of the bay, the cliffs on the left overlooking the chasm that gaped in place of the royal palace. Halfway up the hill, the road looped in that direction, allowing a good view. They stopped at the edge of the cliff, watching water cascade down into the misty hole that churned and boiled, as if a giant creature at the bottom was trying to suck up the sea.

"What an incredible view," Laxia said. "Seawater is pouring down that chasm like a waterfall."

"What *is* this place?" Ricotta asked.

Dana moved to respond, then gasped and swayed, sinking down to the grass. Adol rushed over and knelt in front of her, unsure what to do.

After a moment, she straightened and drew a shaky breath. "I'm all right."

"Are you sure?" Adol had his doubts. She still looked pale, her face contorted as if in pain.

"Yes." She slowly relaxed, then grasped his hand and pulled up to her feet. "When I saw that chasm...my head...it just suddenly started hurting."

"Let's get away from it then," Adol said.

She hesitated, then nodded.

The party continued uphill to a shallow plateau at the top, with the Baja Tower looming just ahead. At its side, a few hundred melye away, two Primordials milled around the base of a cliff, looking up. Chasing prey? Rocks and debris showered down on them, as if a large creature up there were scrambling away from the edge.

The Primordials paid no attention to the travelers, and Adol was about to pass them by, when he heard a scream from that direction.

"Someone! Anyone! Help me!"

The party froze in their tracks.

"That's a person," Ricotta said in disbelief.

They drew their weapons and rushed toward the cliff.

The Primordials didn't pose much of a challenge. Faced with six humans holding weapons that could inflict actual damage, they quickly retreated out of sight. Adol approached the vines leading up the cliff and peered upward.

"You can come down now," he called. "They're gone."

A head appeared over the edge of the cliff.

Adol's mouth fell open. "*Katthew?*"

"Adol?" The *Lombardia*'s first mate hastily scrambled down and gathered Adol into a long hug, then retreated, looking at the rest of the group. He looked bruised and disheveled but otherwise unharmed.

"I—I can't believe it," he said. "Are these survivors from the *Lombardia?*"

Adol introduced everyone, leaving out the details about Dana's origin for now.

"How did ya end up there?" Sahad asked.

Katthew shrugged. "Long story. Are there any other survivors?"

"There are," Laxia said. "Quite a few, actually. Captain Barbaros was among the first we found, and with his help we've established a village—"

"Captain Barbaros!" Katthew beamed. "That's great news. Can't wait to see him. With the captain in charge, we're all in good hands."

"Well..." Laxia looked at Adol uncomfortably.

"Let's sit down and take a break," Adol suggested.

They found a few flat rocks to sit on and shared their rations with Katthew, who wolfed them down before everyone in the party had a chance to settle down. Clearly, he hadn't fared that well in the wilderness all by himself. Adol detailed everything that had happened in the months since their arrival on this island. The foundation of Castaway Village; their plans to build a ship; the unfortunate events that had led to Captain Barbaros's death.

Tears stood in Katthew's eyes by the time he had finished.

"I... I can't believe it," he muttered.

"We're honorin' his last wish by makin' sure we all get off o' this island alive," Sahad said.

Katthew nodded. "You can count on me. I may not be as skilled as the captain, but I still know a thing or two about ships."

"I can probably use my Essence to warp him back to the village by himself," Dana said thoughtfully.

"*Warp* me?"

"We'll explain later," Adol said. "Prepare to meet Dogi and the others." He nodded to Dana.

She touched her ring to Katthew's hand and closed her eyes.

For the first time, Adol saw how warping looked from the outside. One moment Katthew was sitting in front of them. The next moment he was gone, leaving only a shimmer of Essence behind. Adol hoped the experience wouldn't be too much for the man.

"Let's continue on, shall we?" he said.

The entrance to the Baja Tower was decisively blocked by a huge boulder. Another impassable obstacle. But even before Adol had time to contemplate how they were going to find a way around it and into the tower, he heard a low hum from the bushes at the edge of the clearing.

An Essence crystal—an active one, calling for the party to approach. Dana rushed toward it, and he followed close behind.

"It has responded to our presence," Dana said quietly. "There must be something that we can do back in the past to open the way." She glanced at Adol, then stepped up to the crystal and held her hand to it, just short of touching.

The pulsing intensified, and Adol saw light radiating from her palm.

He didn't need a prompt on what to do next. It felt so natural to step up to her side and raise his palm to the crystal too.

"We share the same consciousness in my world," Dana said. "You will experience the same things as I. But"—she glanced over her shoulder at the rest of the party, watching them from the edge of the glade—"I can also amplify the Essence with this crystal, so that everyone here will be able to see what we're experiencing too."

Her voice trembled. It must be hard for her—so tantalizingly close to her home world, knowing exactly what awaited it, but powerless to save it from its fate. Adol still had no idea how this worked, but he felt determined to do his best for her anyway.

"Here we go," Dana said.

Light pulsed in waves around them. The world shifted.

TOWAL HIGHWAY

Maiden, how's the calibration progressing?"

Dana looked up from the stone panel she was working on to see Essence Maester Odo approaching. She smiled. "It went off without a hitch. Some minor adjustments were necessary, but there are no major issues to report."

Odo bowed his head. "Brilliantly performed, as always. I stand in awe of your skill. I'm sorry to trouble you with this when you're only here on an inspection."

"No apology necessary," Dana assured. "After all, I insisted on helping."

"Well, just know that I appreciate it," Odo said. "This facility is integral to supplying Essence to the capital, so it's very reassuring to have you here inspecting it, my lady. Will you be returning to the capital once you're done here?"

"Not right away. I need to visit Baja Tower next. And you?"

"I must return to the Stupa," Odo said. "May I accompany you as far as the central district?"

"I'd be delighted to walk with you."

They continued to discuss Essence as they walked through the city together. At the market plaza, a crowd was milling, as usual, near Mussdan's stall. Dana didn't bother to look what he was selling this time. Mussdan had a gift of creating sensations out of nothing.

"It's Lady Dana!" a girl shouted.

The activity slowed, people turning and bowing deeply as Dana and Odo passed by.

"You're certainly very popular," Odo observed. "I don't remember your predecessor commanding quite as much devotion."

Dana looked away, trying to hide her embarrassment. She would never get used to the ceremony. The fact that people seemed to value her more than the previous Maiden didn't seem right. Perhaps her regular outings and conversations with citizen made them all feel closer to her, but in the grand scheme of things she'd done nothing to deserve this kind of worship.

She parted with Odo at the entrance to the Stupa building and walked on.

Beside a stall at the upper market to the east of the Stupa, the meat merchant, Barossa, hailed her.

"I just heard the news, Lady Dana. The war between the northern nations has finally come to an end. They brokered a peace deal, thanks to your vision."

Oh, that. Dana lowered her eyes. How did these things ever get out? "Queen Sarai is the one who brokered the peace. I was just fortunate to accompany her. I didn't do anything, really."

The merchant let out a knowing laugh. "Oh-hohoho! You're so humble! Regardless, we are all glad that dreadful war is finally over."

I hope you're right. Dana smiled. Sarai was indeed the one who'd done the talking, but it had come in handy when Dana told the delegates about the famine she'd read of in the Temple chronicles, the result of a previous war in the north. She didn't exactly mention where the description came from, leaving people in the room free to assume she was detailing her own vision rather than historical records. Amazing how such a small ambiguity could do wonders for their motivation. She and Sarai made an effective pair.

At another stall, Essence equipment craftsman Lakey was ranting about his daughter, Yuka. Apparently, he'd discovered just this morning that she also made Essence equipment...using his own tools, without his permission. Worse, the equipment was exquisite, but the merchant was selling it too cheap. Dana left him to contemplate the situation, winking to Yuka, who was hiding behind potted plants on the other end of the plaza. She felt tempted to interfere but knew she should let father and daughter sort it out.

At the entrance to the Towal Highway, she ran into a young guard. Tall and lean, he looked so familiar. She approached, peering into his face.

"*Rastell?*"

"Your Eminence." He stared straight ahead, stiff with effort.

You've finally become a guard. She ran her eyes over his gear, his graceful, muscular shape. A man grown. What a change from their last meeting. "You've really come into your own."

Rastell lifted his chin another notch. "Thank you, Your Eminence. I'm honored to receive praise from the Maiden of the Great Tree. How may I be of service to you?"

"Be of service?" She frowned. "Rastell, you don't need to be so formal with me."

Rastell lowered his head, finally meeting her gaze.

Her skin prickled as she looked into his eyes. After she became the Maiden, she'd made a conscious choice to abandon their friendship, knowing that it could never last. And now, all the regret she'd ever felt about that decision came back at once. Rastell, her loyal companion since her first days at the Temple, her devoted admirer, her knight and protector. Was she going to live with this regret of losing him for the rest of her life?

"I miss the old Rastell," she said quietly.

An emotion stirred in his gaze. It told her so much more than words. He missed her too. He also felt hurt at the way she had cast him aside. And he had every right to feel that way. How had they come to this, talking as near-strangers, about to lose the remains of a bond they once had?

"Your uniform has a loose thread." She stepped closer, plucking the invisible thread off his shoulder. Her hand lingered over his chest as she looked up at him.

Rastell's face lit up with color. Through their touch, she could feel his heat, his heartbeat, rapid like her own. She smiled.

"There's the old Rastell," she said.

His blush deepened. "Well, yes. But I'm trying to be more like my father. Otherwise..." His voice trailed into silence.

She knew what he wasn't saying. His father would never waver in his duty because of personal feelings. Rastell wouldn't either— but now that they stood so close, the temptation was so hard to resist. Being the spiritual leader of the realm, helping people with her Essence, meant being alone all the time, no matter how many people revolved around her. With Rastell, she didn't feel alone. He was one of the very few who saw her only as a person, without caring about her Essence skill or her high position in the kingdom. Was there any harm in allowing herself to dream, just for a short moment?

"I still remember your promise," she said. "You're going to be a great guard and protect me, right?"

"Ah." His gaze washed over her with warmth. "Yes." He raised his chin again. "That's right, Your Eminence. But...I still have a lot of work ahead of me."

"I look forward to that day."

He closed his eyes for a moment, then looked at her again. "So do I."

She should let him go—but it felt so hard to withdraw her hand, to step away. She reveled in the contented feeling she always had when they were together. In all these years, she had almost forgotten it. He'd come such a long way from the child she first met on the Temple's training range. If he proceeded at this pace, she was going to fall behind.

She couldn't stop herself from running her hand up his shoulder, swiping away another invisible thread.

"I'll see you again soon, Rastell," she whispered, then stepped away and continued onto the road, summoning Essence to calm herself and force her mind away from the encounter.

The guard tower at the end of the Towal Highway looked more crowded than usual. A line of pack beasts pulling loaded carts waited at the bottom of the stairs, with a small crowd gathered nearby. The guards on duty directed the traffic with restrained looks that suggested the arguments here had been going on for a while and showed no sign of stopping.

"...need to have patience," the lead guard was saying.

The crowd of merchants rumbled in protest.

"Freshness is key to seafood. They don't understand..."

"...will take us about two months to travel back home if..."

"No danger could possibly compare to..."

"We can't let it run wild." That came from one of the guards. Dana strained her ears to hear more, but the merchants were louder.

"My paperwork is in order, so why haven't they let us through yet?"

"No need to be impatient, I suppose." The voice rang with sarcasm. "We're traveling to the southern nations, so we have all the time in the world. They have no concept of time here in the south."

"If they don't hurry up, it's going to be night soon."

Good point. Dana wove her way around the angry crowd and through the gate to the outside.

More carts were lined up here, and more guards. They already looked on edge, but they tensed up even more when they saw her. The nearest one—a young man, only a bit older than Rastell—approached her with a resigned look.

"Your Eminence," he greeted.

"What is going on here?"

The guard threw a nervous look over his shoulder. "Excuse us, Your Eminence. A vicious Saurian was spotted nearby. It's uncommonly large and aggressive. One of our guards wounded it on its snout, and this made the beast even more uncontrollable. In the interest of public safety, we closed the highway for the time being."

"But I'm on my way to Baja Tower."

The guard stiffened. "I'm terribly sorry, Your Eminence. We can't possibly let you through. At the moment, we have no idea where that Saurian might be hiding. We're dispatching a squad to track it down."

Dana nodded. "Commendable. The Temple of the Great Tree cannot turn a blind eye to what's happening here. I will help you track down this Saurian."

The guard hesitated. He clearly didn't like the idea but was luckily experienced enough to realize that contradicting the Maiden of the Great Tree herself was far above his pay grade. Good. Dana hated the kind of arguments that forced her to pull rank.

"Th-that would be very helpful, Your Eminence," the guard said. "If you need anything, please let me know."

"Thank you." Dana nodded dismissal, then stepped to the side, surveying the scene. Agitated merchants, carts, beasts munching grass, guards milling around, blended into a disorderly crowd. Essence Maester Reince, Odo's assistant, stood at the side, watching the activity. Running Odo's errand at the Baja Tower? Or sneaking out on his own? She had no time to question him.

Up the road behind the nearest cliff, a faint glow of Essence glimmered in the grass. She would have passed it by without notice if not for her recent experience with trapped spirits that had enabled her to see it clearly. Wondering why so many of them were being trapped now, she reached out with her Essence to unravel the glowing cage.

A ball of light popped out, surrounded by dancing images of green leaves. A male voice, filled with raw power, rang in her head.

I thank thee for rescuing me, stranger. Knowst thou that my name is Wagmur, Spirit of the Wood.

"My name is Dana," she said. "Dana Iclucia."

The spirit bobbed in place, as if considering something.

"Thou art most peculiar for an Eternian." As with Jenya, his voice became audible after she spoke, to match hers. "Thou hast a seeming connection to our kin."

"You can tell?" Dana felt genuinely surprised. Until recently, she hadn't realized herself how much of a connection she had to the spirits.

The ball of light spun around a few times. "Indeed. How fortuitous. Pray lend me thine ear. Due west, thou wilt find the misty wood I call home. A fellow spirit ventured forth from the wood, never to return. Thus did I embark on a quest to find my companion... but I was set upon by a Saurian most foul!"

A Saurian? Dana frowned, thinking of the commotion at the guard post.

"Beset by madness," the spirit continued, "the Saurian gave chase in hopes of devouring me. What a foul that those detestable creatures possess enough connection to the spirit world to consider us prey."

What a foul indeed. Dana had no idea about this either. Could Saurians use Essence too? This would certainly explain why they posed so much more threat than other wild beasts.

"Though I managed to elude the Saurian," Wagmur said, "I then found myself trapped in a rift. T'was truly vexing."

"Was it a large Saurian?" Dana asked.

"Indeed. A remorseless creature, eyes brimming with malice."

"Did it, by any chance, have a fresh wound on its snout?"

"I must say, thy powers of deduction are most—"

A loud roar thundered through the ravine. A giant bipedal Saurian crashed through the passage ahead and thumped onto the path.

It looked bigger and tougher than any Saurian Dana had ever encountered. She stared. No wonder it had caused such a commotion.

"Aahhh—that's the very same one!" Wagmur wailed. "Oh fie!"

Dana drew her swords.

"Those weapons would do naught to it," Wagmur said. "Such minor wounds as thine blades inflict would only anger it."

The Saurian lunged. Dana slashed at it, but just like Wagmur had predicted, her blade slid down the Saurian's skin with only minimal damage. The creature reared, angling for a new blow.

Wagmur edged closed. "I shall grant thee my power, Dana Iclucia. I trust thee shall make good use of it!"

A light enfolded Dana, for a moment hiding everything in sight. Her body felt different—heavier, more grounded. Her weapon changed too, a heavy staff with a bulging head that made it look like a giant club.

She could tell that it was only an illusion, a new ability that shifted her existing weapon and skills rather than truly transforming them, but the effect was compelling anyway. She swung her club. It connected with a massive thud, sending the Saurian a few steps backward.

As she advanced, the creature staggered under her blows, retreating farther along the road—then turned and ran, raising a cloud of dust in its wake.

Dana lowered her club. Amazing how she didn't even feel out of breath.

"What kind of power is this?" she asked. "Such pure, calm Essence."

Wagmur laughed. "Thou wield my power most excellently. So long as the wood exists, thou may continue to wield it. I hope it serves thee well."

"Thank you, Wagmur," Dana said. "I will use it carefully."

"We spirits have a long history with the Maidens of the Great Tree," Wagmur said. "Thou may yet cross paths with others of my kin soon enough. I am pleased to have met thee."

"As am I." Dana had no idea how Wagmur recognized her as the Maiden, but she assumed the spirits had their ways.

"I think I shall take my leave now," Wagmur said. "Should fate will it so, I do hope we meet again, Dana Iclucia."

As Wagmur faded out of sight, Dana had an unexpected vision. The mysterious door in the underground sanctuary crypt, the one previously shut, now stood open, as if beckoning. *Only the Virtuous may Enter.* Had her actions, freeing Wagmur and defeating the Saurian, somehow cause her virtue to increase enough to be able to open that door?

She had no time for any delays. She needed to help Adol, to clear the way to the Baja Tower. But she simply had to find out. That sanctuary contained versions of Eternian history not taught anywhere above ground. The knowledge may well hold the key to her purpose, to the fact that she somehow existed in two realities at the same time.

She reached out with her Essence, seeking the warping crystal she'd spotted inside the crypt.

A familiar tingling sensation surged through her. Next thing she knew, she was standing beside the archival monolith, facing the mysterious door.

Unlike in her vision, the door stood closed. But as she approached it and reached out to it, the door came alive under her touch, its massive stone halves sliding apart smoothly to disappear into the walls on either side.

A wide staircase ran down into the gloom, descending to the next level of the Sanctuary Crypt.

A large chamber opened in front of her, brightly lit with Essence that filled brass sconces suspended on chains from the tall stone pillars. The place looked both ornate and massive. Mind boggling, to think that this place had existed underneath the Stupa and the royal gardens, and she'd had no idea about it. Who could have possibly built it? And who else knew about it?

With her newly acquired power of the Wood Spirit, the animated suits of armor in her way didn't feel like a challenge at all. One swing of her heavy club could destroy several of them at a time. Even the biggest ones crumbled under her blows. She knew they would rematerialize again after she left the chamber, but doing this made her progress faster, without having to hide in the corners to let the golems pass.

The path ahead led her through several chambers where she needed to climb rocks, destroy golems, and pull different levers, some of them Essence-powered, to find her way ahead. In her mind, she called this area the Hall of Stone—maybe because the stonework here was especially massive and elaborate compared to everywhere else.

As she suspected, another archival monolith waited for her at the end. She activated it, running her eyes through the ethereal lines that appeared in mid-air in front of her, continuing the text from the previous monolith.

Thus, by vanquishing Saurians and cultivating the Earth, did the kingdom expand its domain. In time, the Kingdom of Eternia grew to become the mightiest nation in the land. With its expansion came a Golden Age of Prosperity for Eternia. It was during this Golden Age that the Light King of Alchea issued the Edict of Southerly Migration. With this Edict, the kingdom set forth migrating its capital to the site of the Great Tree, where the Light King discovered Essence.

And so, at the site where the Light King first gained the knowledge of Essence, where the Great Tree of Origins, Giver of Knowledge, stands tall to this day, the Eternians devoted themselves body and soul to the establishment of a capital worthy of the Great Tree and their King. A grand capital, housing an enormous crystal with which to amplify Essence, was unveiled to the world. In this way, the new capital was more than the center of the kingdom; it was the very heart of the land itself.

Dana finished reading and watched the glowing hexagon disappear. Well, she hadn't learned anything of immediate use, but this version of Eternian history was definitely different from the one she she'd been taught before.

As she was reading, she couldn't escape a feeling that someone was standing behind her, watching her. But now that she finished and turned around, she couldn't see anyone. The hallway was empty, visible all the way through its Essence-lit depths.

Just like in the previous monolith chamber, this one had a door at the end, tightly shut. It didn't budge as Dana tried to push it open, but this time she knew for certain that if she came back later, after accomplishing more virtuous deeds, she would be able to walk through. It wasn't time to open it yet, that was all. She focused her Essence and warped back to the guard tower at the end of the Towal Highway.

The commotion here was over, probably due to the fact that, with Wagmur's power, Dana had successfully banished the Saurian. The guards still looked baffled, but they offered no objections as she walked through and set out on the road leading to Baja Tower.

In Adol's timeline, a massive boulder was blocking this path right in front of the entrance to the tower. Nothing in this timeline resembled it, so she had to use her best guess in choosing the spot to plant the prayer tree sapling, using her Essence to start its growth. She stood back, watching it for a while. So fragile, yet it was going to grow so powerful in the distant future.

She hoped she'd planted it correctly and it was going to do the job.

THE BAJA TOWER

The scenery was the same in Adol's time, except for the color of the sky—morning-blue in Dana's timeline when she planted the sapling, sunset-red here in the future. It was such an odd feeling, to awaken from a momentary trance to this kind of change. Dana looked over the familiar faces of her party members. Another era, no less real than the past she'd just left. She would probably never get used to this time travel.

She looked at the place where the boulder had been. A giant tree now rose in its place, its roots wrapping around the rocks at the side of the passage, pushing them aside to create a wide path to the foot of the leaning tower. Even though she had expected this, the mere idea of a tree planted millennia in the past changing things in the present with such finality was difficult to comprehend.

"The way is open now," she said.

They all looked stunned as they continued to stare at her. Of course. This time, she had used Essence to bring them along with her into the past. Like Adol, they had seen and experienced everything as if physically present, looking out through her eyes. It had to be a lot for unprepared minds.

"Thank you for showing us your world," Laxia said quietly.

Adol kept his silence, watching Dana with wonder. No one since Rastell had ever looked at her this way—as if she were a marvel of nature, not a confused young girl suspended between timelines and eras. For a moment, she allowed herself to revel in the feeling.

"I still have no idea what's happening," she confessed. "Much as I enjoy spending time back home, this shouldn't be possible at all."

"There's a reason you're here," Adol said. "And we'll find out what it is."

She nodded. She wanted to say so much, but she had no words left.

"It's gettin' late," Sahad said. "We should set up camp."

"Right," Hummel agreed. "Staying up late diminishes the quality of one's work. Plus, it's bad for the skin."

Skin? Seriously? Dana looked at him. Well, maybe Hummel had a point. His skin was smooth and unblemished, like a baby's. Besides, after a day in her era, she felt exhausted—not only from all the events, but from too many emotions tearing her apart. All the people so dear to her in her time. Olga. Sarai. Rastell. She had no idea what had happened to them. But seeing Rastell in her past had stirred it all up. And if she hadn't met Adol, if he hadn't awakened the kind of feelings she had tried her best to stay away from for most of her life, would she have really made that advance toward Rastell today? She felt too confused to think about it.

"Hummel's right," she said. "We should rest for today."

They set up the tent with a view of the city below. In the gathering dusk, Dana could almost imagine it to be intact, as if she were back in her own timeline.

Somewhere between the chores, Hummel managed to set up some bird traps, while Ricotta and Sahad scoured around in search of edible plants. The result was a meal of roast quail and baked yams, luxury food that somehow tasted even better when served at the campsite.

Sahad polished off his share and burped. "Whew. That surely hit the spot."

"I'm stuffed," Ricotta agreed.

Dana leaned against the stones at her back, watching them absently.

"Are you all right, Dana?" Laxia asked.

Dana smiled. "Fine. I just haven't done something like this in a long time. It brings back memories."

"Memories?"

She nodded. "When I was a child, my father and I would sit by the fireside after dinner and just talk. It was..." She paused, trying to find the right word. *Calming. Comforting.* No, that wasn't quite right. In all this time, she had almost forgotten what it felt like to have a real family. To belong. And now, in this era, she found herself remembering it.

"Your father?" Ricotta asked. "What about your mother?"

Dana drew a breath. Only an innocent child could hit so precisely into such a painful spot. "My mother . . . She passed away when I was little."

"Then we're the same," Ricotta exclaimed. "I grew up with my father, just like you."

Not quite the same. Dana didn't say anything as she stared into the fire. Perhaps this was the true reason for her existence in this era—so that she could understand the meaning of family. She found herself wishing that was it. But she knew things were probably more complicated.

Adol had felt a change in Dana when she'd emerged from her timeline the previous night. She seemed pensive, absorbed in her thoughts. Had any of her memories come back? Or was it the fact that visiting her past had sharpened her awareness that her world, the people she knew and loved, were no longer there? He wanted to ask her, but he knew she needed to share information at her own pace. And then there was Rastell. What had ended up happening between them? He did his best to distance himself from this question as he emerged from the tent, ready for a new day.

It promised to be a fine one. The sky was clear, with not a cloud in sight. In the light of the rising sun, the leaning tower above them threw a long shadow across the grass. The massive prayer tree Dana had planted last night in her timeline curved around its base, keeping the way clear. They walked past it and into the tower.

The entrance hall was vast, with carved stone columns rising into the gloom overhead. A spiral ramp in the center wound around a glowing pillar. Essence-based power source? Adol guessed so. This much Essence had probably helped to keep the tower from collapsing for all these millennia. He wished people in his era could figure out how to use this kind of resource.

Ricotta skidded up and down the floor, laughing. "Check it out, everyone! The floor is all slanted!"

"I think the tower might be leaning more than we realized," Dana said. "We should tread carefully."

As if in response, they saw a movement off to their side, and an empty suit of armor walked into view. It paced right past them and disappeared into a doorway on the opposite side.

"What was that?" Ricotta's voice sank to a whisper.

"A golem," Dana said. "An animated suit of armor. They've been left behind to guard this place. They can be defeated, but we should probably do our best to stay out of their way."

Ricotta nodded, quiet now as they made their way up the spiral ramp.

The tower had many levels, each accessible by ramps and staircases. Some of them stood intact, while others had crumbled and partially collapsed, forcing the party to look for ways around. In one chamber, they found a large chest holding a wing-like charm on a gleaming metal chain that looked to be made of orichalcum. Dana picked it up.

"Archaeopteryx Wing," she said. "That's a piece of Essence equipment."

"Essen zee kwip mint?" Ricotta asked.

Dana laughed. "Close enough. It's a tool that has a great amount of Essence sealed within it. Equipping one will grant you special powers, depending on its intended use."

"What does this one do?" Adol asked.

"Its wearer should be able to jump higher than usual. Go on, try it."

Adol slid the chain over his head. He immediately felt lighter. As he jumped, it felt as if an invisible force bounced him higher into the air, then held him in place to enable him to grab a ledge far out of his normal reach and pull himself over it. He stood there for a moment looking down at the stunned group, then stepped over the edge and floated down to rejoin them.

"Wow," Sahad said.

They all took turns with it. Passing it from one person to the other made their progress through the tower much faster. They were now able to navigate broken stairways and reach high ledges to ascend the tower.

The top floors were much better preserved. Different types of columns supported the ceiling here, glowing with pink rather than green light. Dana approached a small stand at the base of a glowing column semicircle.

"What is this?" Laxia asked.

"An authentication device powered by Essence," Dana said. "It prevents people from entering the upper floors without permission. I should have permission though." She closed her eyes and extended her palms overt the device. It spun, and the columns by its sides lit up with intense blue light.

A rumbling echoed in the distance. A staircase slid out of the rock wall, opening the way upstairs.

They ascended several more levels this way, until they reached a hexagonal platform surrounded by a low stone rail that sat next to a blue glowing crystal.

"An elevator," Dana said. "It will take us the rest of the way to the top. Assuming, of course, that it's still working."

"How would we know?" Ricotta asked.

"Just step on it."

They did, and the platform came alive, rising up through a stone shaft to another chamber. Adol wasn't sure if Dana was moving it or it moved on its own, but it was still very impressive.

This had to be the very top of the tower. They could finally see the ceiling overhead.

Four alcoves surrounded the platform they stood on, each housing a large slab of black stone, with a glowing crystal set into its top.

"These are archival monoliths," Dana said. "They are used for storing and delivering information."

"But it's just a piece of rock." Ricotta frowned. "Where's the information?"

"If you offer up Essence, the information you seek should appear." Dana stepped over to one of the monoliths and raised her hands.

Nothing happened. After a moment, Dana relaxed and turned back to the group.

"This monolith is wrecked. Let's check the others."

Adol followed, swallowing the obvious question. If the monolith with the information about the Oceanus were nonfunctional, they would have come all this way for nothing. They may never find a way off this island. But for the first time in his life, he found himself wondering if staying here forever would really be so bad, as long as Dana were here too. The thought was surprising—and scary—but it kept returning to his head as he watched her explore.

Most of the monoliths remained silent when Dana used her Essence on them. But just when they were considering giving up, an Essence glow rose around a monolith in the back, folding into an image of a hexagonal tablet covered with symbols.

Adol's eyes widened. He hadn't expected to be able to read the text, of course. But the way the symbols were arranged made the tablet look like a page of a book, with sections and chapters, and even some illustrations, depicting vaguely familiar shapes. Were these...Primordials?

"Let's see." Dana ran her eyes over the lines. "Saurian Directory...Aquatics...Oceanus..." More ghostly tablets were appearing around her as she spoke, some covered with text, others containing drawings and images.

"There it is!" Ricotta exclaimed, pointing to a tablet in the middle showing a tentacled creature that did indeed look familiar. "What's it say?"

"Hold on." Dana kept her eyes on the tablets. "Um...*Oceanus*... *An aggressive species of Saurian. They attack anything that enters their territory, including ships. They must be exterminated if they claim territory along a naval route, but doing so is extremely difficult. They swim remarkably fast, and they are very powerful. However, they do construct nests within their territory and periodically return to them to rest. The best opportunity to defeat an Oceanus is when it is resting in its nest. But...*" She paused.

"What is it?" Adol asked.

"The record ends here. It looks like the rest of it was either damaged or never logged."

The panels around her started flickering, new windows of text popping and disappearing too fast to follow.

"It's malfunctioning. Hold on a second..." Dana turned back to the display, then went very still as a new set of panels appeared around her.

"What information is it displaying now?" Laxia asked.

"The Great Tree of Origins..." Dana's voice trailed to a halt.

"What does it say?"

"*The purpose of the Great Tree of Origins,*" Dana read, "*is to foster evolution in all living creatures.*"

"Huh?" Sahad said. "Wait a minute...I've heard that word, 'evolution,' before."

"Laxia explained it to us once," Ricotta said. "Isn't it the process by which living creatures change over a long period of time?"

"Yes," Dana said. "My people were the protectors of the Great Tree of Origins. Maidens such as myself would pray to the Tree to receive its blessings. Through the blessings of the Great Tree, we Eternians evolved from Saurians."

"Hey...Aren't Saurians an' Primordials

pretty much the same thing?"

"Yes. Why?"

"Your ancestors were *Primordials*?"

Dana laughed. "Yes, actually. That's why Eternians were so large and powerful."

"You're not that large," Ricotta protested. "Powerful, yes. But— you're not even quite as tall as Adol."

"I was always shorter than anyone else," Dana explained. "Most Eternians would tower over all of you."

"So that's the reason the buildings in the city all seem to be built for taller people..." Laxia paused. "I do find it very surprising, though, that Eternians evolved to be so remarkably similar to humans. Evolution can be mysterious."

Indeed it can. This new information didn't quite fit into Adol's head. Evolved from Primordials? This made Dana a completely different species. Yet was she really all that different?

THE GHOST SHIP

When they warped back to Castaway Village, they found it shrouded in thick fog that clung to the skin with sticky moisture, reaching into every nook and crevice around camp. They made their way toward the campfire, where Dogi stood, looking up the watchtower.

"What's the situation, Euron?" he called. "Did you see it?"

"Yes, unfortunately," came Euron's voice from above. "As much as I hate to admit it, this looks like the real thing."

Dogi glanced at the approaching party.

"Adol's back," he yelled up to Euron.

"Tell him to get his ass up here then."

Dogi turned to Adol. "No time to explain. Just climb up."

Adol ascended to the observation platform. Wordlessly, Euron handed him the binoculars.

A large three-masted ship was sailing a few cable lengths off the coast. It was moving incredibly fast. As Adol stared, unable to believe his eyes, it disappeared behind the cape.

"Did you see it?" Euron demanded.

"The ship?" Adol lowered the binoculars. "Yes, I did."

"Noticed anything unusual about it?"

Adol considered the question. Besides the obvious—the fact that a large ship had just passed through these cursed waters where every known vessel had crashed before—nothing really came to mind.

"Anything about its rigging? Sails?" Euron prompted.

Adol brought up the mental image in his mind.

"The sails looked a bit ragged." Now that he thought about it, he remembered more. "And the glow?"

"Bluish and eerie, right?"

"Right." Was it Essence? Did this ship originate from ancient Eternia? It seemed unlikely. A ship like this could have come from nearly any large port in the Gaete sea. Well, maybe its bow was a bit more curved, similar to the ships that sailed a hundred or so years ago, but, as far as he knew, shipbuilding hadn't really changed all that much in the last century. Imagining that similar ships also sailed in ancient Eternia, however, seemed like too far of a stretch.

"That's the ghost ship everyone here's so spooked about," Euron said. "Now you've seen it with your own eyes."

They descended the ladder and joined the group arguing down below.

"Thanatos." Sahad's voice seemed on edge. "Ya mind runnin' that crazy idea by me again?"

"I *said*, maybe we could hijack that ghost ship and use it to get off this island. I don't know why you made me repeat myself. I know you heard me the first time."

"That's a crazy idea," Laxia said.

"Yeah," Sahad roared. "That's what I just said, wasn't it?"

"He's right, though," Hummel said. "If we take that ship, we won't need to build our own."

Ricotta jumped up and down. "I wanna sail on a spooky, scary ghost ship!"

Adol looked at Dana, standing aside from the group, watching them curiously as if observing a problem-solving exercise by a group of young children.

"What do you think?" he asked.

She shrugged. "Seems like a reasonable idea."

"Y'all can't be serious," Sahad protested.

"Before we sign off on anything," Euron said, "are we sure we're even dealing with a real ship? Sure, it looks like a ship...but it's also covered in eerie blue fire. How do you know it won't 'poof' and disappear as soon as we reach it?"

"Maybe we could start by finding out where it docks," Adol suggested.

"Hah!" Dogi slapped his hands together. "Knew it. I told you Adol would grab a chance to explore this ship. Should've made that bet with you, eh, Euron?"

Euron grumbled something unintelligible and turned away.

"How the hell do we do it?" Sahad demanded. "From what I just heard, the ship always just shows up outta the blue and disappears too darn fast. Not like we can swim to it or anything."

"When I saw it just now," Adol said, "it disappeared behind the cape on the southeast edge of the bay."

Euron nodded thoughtfully. "Come to think of it, it always does."

"I don't believe we've explored that side of the cape yet," Laxia said.

Adol nodded. "We haven't. Let's head out there first thing tomorrow."

Another surprise awaited them in the lodge. Alison was not at her usual tailoring station. As Adol and his party entered the common room, they almost ran into Licht rushing out of the women's quarters.

"What happened?" Adol asked. "Is someone ill?"

"Not ill, exactly." Licht rummaged in his medical bag as he headed outside.

They sprinted into the bedroom.

Alison lay in bed, a wet cloth across her forehead. She smiled faintly as she saw them. Dana, Laxia, and Ricotta knelt by her side.

"Alison, what—?"

"Alison's pregnant," Licht said from the door. He crossed the room and set his instrument bag on a small stool by the bedside, ushering Ricotta out of the way.

"Pregnant?" all of them exclaimed in unison.

Licht nodded. "She was hiding it from everyone, but this afternoon she fainted after overworking herself, and I had no choice but to put her on bed rest. She could give birth any day now."

Adol opened and closed his mouth a few times but couldn't quite find his voice. Pregnant. She did seem to be getting plump lately, but somehow the possibility had never occurred to him.

"Perhaps you could give her a chance to sleep," Licht suggested. "You can talk to her later."

Adol returned to the common room and lowered himself to the bench next to the table. After a while, Ricotta, Laxia, and Dana joined him, deep in conversation.

"...not easy," Laxia was saying.

"I'm worried too," Ricotta agreed.

"If only there were something we could do to help her feel better," Dana said.

Laxia let out a sigh. "I just wish her husband, Ed, were by her side. But we have no way of knowing if he even made it. We haven't found him so far. Let's just do what we can for now."

"What about flowers?" Ricotta suggested. "A nice bouquet of her favorite flowers ought to cheer her up."

Laxia nodded. "I remember something Alison told me earlier. Her hometown has a beautiful flower garden. It sounded like it was a memorable place for her husband too. Apparently, her favorites were purple bell flowers. But they're very rare and can only be found in Greek."

Dana cocked her head. "Is it a flower with purple petals, arranged in the shape of a bell?"

"Yes," Laxia said. "The name's kind of self-explanatory."

"I saw them during the Eternian era. They were rare back then, so they might be even harder to find now. But it's possible that they're still around."

"Let's try to find some," Adol said.

The three girls stopped talking and turned to him, as if only just now noticing his presence.

"We haven't seen any so far," Laxia pointed out.

"Are you sure?"

"I think I would remember such rare flowers, Adol."

Of course you would. Even though Laxia no longer carried that book of hers everywhere, she did pay inordinate attention to wildlife.

"We're about to explore a new area," Adol said. "Who knows? We might get lucky."

Access to the cape on the southeast of the bay was blocked by rock cliffs too steep to climb, which had previously prevented them from exploring it. But now that they'd found the Archaeopteryx Wing, they had no trouble jumping over the obstacles into the area.

The first thing they saw as they entered the beach was a ship graveyard. Pieces of ship carcasses stuck out of the sand and piled along the rocks at the tip of the cape. Most looked very old, covered by layers of barnacles, kelp, and coral. The victims of the Oceanus. Adol hoped they could find a way to get rid of the creature, once and for all.

Dana stopped at the edge of the beach and looked up into the low hills ahead.

"The soil up in those meadows should be very sandy," she said.

269

"The flowers we're looking for like sandy soil."

"Are we seriously goin' to stop and look for *flowers*?" Sahad rumbled.

Hummel adjusted the sling for his rifle over his shoulder. He looked calm, but a side glance he threw at Adol held a subtle question.

"It's for Alison," Laxia protested. "Don't you want to make her feel better, Sahad?"

The fisherman shrugged and looked away.

"Let's check it out," Adol said.

They walked up the shallow hill and onto a grassy meadow at the top, then stopped to admire the view. The cape jutted out to sea, surrounded by water on three sides. A gentle breeze touched Adol's face. The sea looked so tranquil from up here.

A patch of deep purple beckoned from the meadow ahead. Flowers? Ricotta ran over.

"I've never seen this kinda flowers before," she exclaimed. "Sooo beautiful!"

"Purple and bell-shaped." Laxia paused as if recalling the pages of her book. "Seems correct, doesn't it?"

"Yes, these are the purple bell flowers," Dana confirmed.

They rushed forward, but Hummel shot up his hand in a warning gesture. "Someone's here."

A slim dark-haired man emerged from behind the rocks on the other side of the glade. He froze as he saw the travelers. "Y-you're ..."

"Survivors from the *Lombardia*," Adol said. "You wouldn't be Ed, by any chance, would you?"

The man's eyes widened. "How did you know my name?"

"A lucky guess. Besides, I had a very good description of you." Adol quickly explained the situation and told Ed about Castaway Village.

It was amazing that the man had survived here all this time, alone, only a short trip away from the village. Apparently this was one of the few spots on this side of the island, from which one couldn't see the campfire. With the rock slides and beasts roaming around, Ed had never dared to venture far from this place. He'd camped alone next to the patch of purple bell flowers, Alison's favorite, because they reminded him of his lost wife.

Somehow, he was convinced these flowers would bring them back together. And, in a way, they had.

Laxia and Ed carefully picked some flowers, and Dana used her Essence to warp Ed back to the village. Adol wished he could be there to witness the happy reunion, but in Alison's condition she would probably appreciate the privacy. He hoped everything was going to be all right.

The cape they saw the ghost ship sail toward was just ahead. A barely perceptible path clung to the face of the cliffs and wound around into a cave opening, covered by a curtain of hanging vines.

"This looks jus' right for a pirate hideout," Sahad remarked.

"Ghost pirate hideout?" Hummel suggested.

No one responded as they made their way into the cave.

The passage from the entrance wound down, illuminated by dim but natural light, suggesting that somewhere below, this cave must have an opening to the outside. As the passage widened, they came across wooden scaffolding and platforms piled with old barrels and crates, similar to the deeper areas in the Waterdrop Cave at Castaway Village. Could the same pirates have built both?

The path brought them to a secluded cove, gaping with a distant opening leading out into the sea. But it wasn't the sea view that brought Adol and the rest of the party to an abrupt halt.

A ship was docked in the middle of the cove.

It looked old and run-down, its sails torn to shreds, masts and rigging coated by barnacles and dried seaweed, as if at some point this ship had spent quite a bit of time underwater. Holes and cracks gaped in its hull. The bow, shaped like a giant toothy jaw, leered at them ominously.

"The ghost ship," Adol said in disbelief.

Except for the seaweed and shredded sails, the ship didn't look all that ghostly. If they hadn't seen this very same ship sail yesterday afternoon, they would have discounted it for an old piece of wreckage.

A boardwalk ran across the water, connecting to the path on the other side and eventually to the ship's dock. At some point, these structures had been sturdily built. Parts of them had collapsed here and there, sagging into the water, but most of the boards were still strong enough to walk on.

At the side of the ship, the boardwalk ended abruptly in a jagged broken line. Deep water separated them from the barnacle-encrusted hull that sat in the water high enough to obscure the deck view.

"There's a name engraved on the hull," Laxia said. "*Eleftheria*."

"But how are we supposed to get on board?" Ricotta wondered.

"Let's search the area," Adol suggested.

The dock was built in two tiers, with the upper level obviously used for ship access before it had collapsed and the lower level holding some chests and crates. Most of them were broken, but one was intact, with a lid fitted on snugly, as if someone had taken extra care to prevent water from getting in. Inside lay a neatly folded parchment, sealed in a waxed leather pouch. Adol unfolded it and read.

Ship's Log, Day Three since leaving Atlas Port—

The Eleftheria *is handling the journey well. We should soon make land on the Isle of Seiren, ominous as it is. It is imperative that I reach the island and return safely. Indeed, they must be exposed and shown for what they are. I must do this. Should I fail, I will forswear my own rank and name, and be Captain Reed no more.*

"Cap'n Reed?" Sahad blinked.

"You've heard of him?" Hummel said.

"'Course I've heard of him! Everyone in Greek has heard o' the dread pirate Reed."

"Dread pirate?"

"Yeah. The Scourge o' the Gaete Sea, they used to call him. Accordin' to the tales, he was around a hundred years ago. Let's see... He had long ruddy hair and was missin' an arm. He burned down whole villages on different islands. Not even women an' children were spared."

"That's horrible." Laxia looked at the ship in wonder.

"Yeah, he was a monster," Sahad agreed. "The Greshuns hate him to this day. Won't even say his name."

"And yet, here's his ship," Dana said.

Sahad shook his head. "Not possible. No way. They say Reed was captured by the Greshun Navy an' executed at their headquarters. I never heard anythin' 'bout him goin' to the Isle of Seiren."

Before anyone could respond, a rumble shook the cave. A section of the dock's upper level slid out across the gap to bridge to the ship's main deck.

CAPTAIN REED

"All right, let's board the ship." Adol kept his eyes on Dana as he spoke—the only person here who had any idea about magic and supernatural powers. She seemed curiously unfazed as she stepped forward and tested the planks with her feet, as if the solidity of the wood was her only safety concern. He followed her onto the ship, with the rest of the party behind them.

The main deck was strewn with skeletons. They looked frozen in mid-movement, scattered around the various stations where the deck crew would normally be working their shifts. One held a mop and a bucket; another had a coiled line clutched in his bone fingers. It was as if the entire crew had been struck down by a sudden ailment in the middle of their duties.

Sahad darted his eyes around. "I don't like the feel o' this, guys. We should get off o' this ship now."

The ship's bell rang overhead.

The ramp behind them slid in, cutting off the way back to the dock.

"Look!" Laxia said sharply.

All around them, the skeletons were rising. They didn't seem interested in the newcomers as they resumed their posts. The sails flapped, filling with wind Adol couldn't feel in the depths of the cave. The ship moved, heading toward the cave opening and out into the bay.

"What in the world is going on?" Laxia whispered. "How is this possible?"

It wasn't. Yet was this really harder to accept than the existence of Primordials? Or Dana's presence in this era? Adol tried to keep up with adjustments in his mind as he watched the activity on deck.

"These pirates are pretty hard workers for a bunch of dead people," Ricotta observed.

"Yes, they're very professional," Hummel agreed. "I could learn much from them."

"How can y'all be so calm at a time like this?" Sahad protested. "Me an' Laxia are practically wettin' ourselves in terror over here..."

"Speak for yourself!" Laxia snapped. But she did look badly shaken.

"They don't seem to mind us," Adol said. "Why don't we explore the ship?"

"Fine," Sahad grumbled.

Most of the doors and hatches were jammed, leaving only one way open, down to the lower deck.

"I have an awesome creepy feeling about this place!" Ricotta announced as she hopped down the ladder into the gloom below.

"Why do ya seem so happy 'bout that, squirt?" Sahad wondered.

She made a face at him, then ran ahead of the group as if having trouble containing her excitement.

Some doorways and passages on the lower deck were blocked by walls of blue light that repelled any attempts to get through. Others stood open, seemingly unobscured. As the last member of the group descended the stairs, another wall of blue light rose behind them, sealing off the way.

"And now we can't get back on the main deck," Sahad whimpered.

Dana nodded thoughtfully. "Essence barriers. Not sure how they were placed—and by whom—but they seem to be directing us to proceed through this ship."

"*Directin'* us?" Sahad looked terrified.

No one responded.

Just like Dana said, as they walked forward through the gloomy space, Adol had a feeling that they were being guided, that whatever forces were behind this wanted them to explore the ship in a certain order and find something important. He kept his eyes open for clues as they proceeded.

The first clue presented itself in the form of an open chest containing a rolled-up piece of parchment similar to the first one they had found on the docks. Laxia picked it up and unrolled it.

"It appears to be another entry from Captain Reed's log," she said.

"What does it say?" Ricotta prompted.

"Before I reach the Isle of Seiren, I must reveal the truth regarding the scouring by fire of the archipelago's villages. None were spared . . . certainly not the men, but women and children fell victims just as surely. The people curse the name of Captain Reed and blame me for these heinous acts, but I tell you, I am innocent. The Eleftheria *is crewed mostly by victims of the slave trade . . . including myself. It seems the authorities did not appreciate us banding together and fighting to emancipate other slaves so that we could all stand free. The people of the archipelago accepted us, and even took to calling us the Pirates of Justice. Truly kind folk, they were. And just as truly, it was the men of Greshun Navy that put the villages to the torch. Word later reached my ears that they did this to draw us out, to purge the Gaete Sea of our ilk. I'd sooner wallow in horse manure for a hundred days than obey those of so twisted sense of justice. But the people have suffered enough, and I would trouble them no further. After giving it much thought . . . I have decided to go to the naval headquarters and turn myself in."* Laxia lowered the page. "The entry ends there."

"No way." Sahad shook his head vigorously. "Can't be."

"What?" Adol asked.

"This isn't what really happened . . . Is it?"

"Why are you surprised, Sahad?" Ricotta said.

"The name of this ship . . . *Eleftheria.* It means 'freedom' in the Greshun tongue. Why would the dreaded Cap'n Reed name his ship 'Freedom'?" Sahad paused, staring into the distance.

"He sounds like an honorable man," Hummel said.

The blue light covering the hatchway flickered and faded, opening the way to the lower deck.

"Is this what we are here for?" Dana wondered. "To discover the truth about Captain Reed?"

"I can only tell you one thing," Ricotta said. "That creepy feeling is gone now. I guess it means we must be doing something right."

"Shall we continue on then?" Dana suggested.

They descended to the next deck, where another chest held a new piece of parchment. Sahad leaned over and picked it up.

"This looks like more o' Cap'n Reed's log," he said.

"Read it, read it!" Ricotta exclaimed. "I wanna know what happened to Reed!"

Sahad lowered his eyes to the page.

"I am held captive. The Navy has sent a strange bearded pig to visit me. I'd not think the Navy to keep a pet for themselves, nor defer to it as 'Captain'. For all its brutish smell, it spoke with words like a man and

told me that it wanted to negotiate. It instructed me to investigate an island that none have been able to safely approach. Yes, the infamous Isle of Seiren. In exchange for investigating the island and returning alive, it would graciously release my entire crew from incarceration. I've always had a gift for spotting a liar by observing faces. And I don't trust that grotesque swine to keep its promise for a moment. But had I refused, I believe it would have kept its other promise—to hang my crew. Truly, we live in mad times. I reminded myself that I want to be a good man, and agreed to be the pig's lickspittle. And so I find myself before the Isle of Seiren."

"So, Captain Reed did come to the Isle of Seiren," Laxia said. "Aside from the obvious evidence of finding his ship here, of course."

Sahad nodded. "Yeah, that's what it sounds like."

"It's so unfair," Laxia said. "He genuinely cared for his crew, and for other people as well. And all he got as reward was being made the scapegoat for crimes he never committed, then used as a pawn."

"The people responsible for this atrocity are a disgrace to the Greshun Navy," Hummel said.

Another wall of blue light faded from in the hatchway ahead.

"Let's move on," Ricotta said.

The wood on the lowest deck was waterlogged. An open hatch gaping in its center led to the cargo hold, flooded all the way up. Water lapped at the edges of the decaying floor boards, the space below too dark to see into. Evidently, the ship had a big hole below the water line. How in the world was it staying afloat?

They proceeded past the gap to the ladder at the far end. Another doorway blocked by blue light loomed ahead of them, with another chest standing nearby. This time, Dana picked up the page from the chest and read aloud:

"I have escaped the tentacled titan and set foot on the island to begin investigating. Unfortunately, the Eleftheria *is crewed this time by naught but rabble, barely worth their own weight in horse manure. The Navy picked this lot. They are criminals to a man, and inexperienced besides. Obviously, no seasoned sailor would agree to come near the Isle of Seiren, but that changes nothing of this madness. One of the fools thought to mutiny and take my ship, but I put the boot to him and sent him into the water. I have too many rebellious men to contend with, to say nothing of the beasts of this island. I've not seen their like before. I'm continuing to investigate, but my progress is held back by some malady. I am tired, and I believe a fever has taken hold of me. Loath as I am to admit it, I may be in peril. Once I am done with my writing, I will take to my bed and attempt to rest."*

"This is where it ends," Dana said.

Sahad scratched his head. "Tentacled titan... The Oceanus. He must've been one hell of a sailor to make it ashore with his ship in one piece."

"Still, it seems like things took a turn for the worse after he arrived," Hummel pointed out.

"Yes, he contracted an illness," Laxia said. "I wonder what happened to him in the end?"

The blue flame disappeared from the doorway, and they heard the creak of a hatch opening above. They ascended the ladders, once again finding themselves on the main deck.

The ship must be sailing in the open waters now, yet Adol couldn't see anything through the thick fog enfolding them. An ethereal wind filled the sails but didn't touch the skin, making Adol feel as if the entire ship were floating in a void.

The skeletons kept clear of the center of the deck as they went about their tasks. As the party stepped forward, a swirl of dark flame wavered in the empty space, and a chest materialized in front of them.

It held another page from the ship's log. Adol picked it up and read:

"My health grows worse by the day. I am overcome by some unusual sickness. It appears that this fever is something only found on this island. I've received word that my family has escaped and taken refuge on a small island in the Gaete Sea. But my mates... The real crew of the Eleftheria *still await my return. It's entirely possible that they're all dancing the hempen jig already. But I will not give up. Not so long as I believe I have a sliver of a chance of succeeding. In addition, some of those here have come to admire me, fools that they are. I'd like to see them returned safely as well. So I must stay the course. Worthless fool that I am, I've never been known to surrender or accept defeat. Not even if I should wither to bones and dust—"*

The increasingly illegible handwriting abruptly cut off before reaching the end of the page.

"It looks like the entry ends there," Adol said.

Laxia leaned over the chest. "No, look, there's a second page." She picked it up and unfolded it. "A map?"

Sahad peered at it. "Huh? No way... This is a sea chart of the waters around the Isle o' Seiren."

"That map be useless t' me now," a deep voice said. "Why don't ye lubbers put it t' good use?"

They spun toward the voice.

A stately man stood in front of them. He wore a triangular hat, a long coat, and tall leather boots—an old-fashioned seaman's attire like Adol had seen in historical drawings. A cutlass was strapped at his belt. His straight hair draped down to his shoulders, its loose strands blowing across his tall forehead and dark, piercing eyes. Tattoos covered his left cheek, chin, and upper arms—double wavy lines that resembled the patterns Sahad adorned himself with. Again, they made Adol think of old drawings. He believed this was the way sailors of old depicted water, the tattoos a ward against the storms.

The man's left arm ended in a hook, strapped to the elbow with a wide leather band.

It took Adol a moment to notice that the man wasn't completely solid. The faint outline of a mast was visible through his form.

Sahad gasped. "A ghost! A-a-and your arm..." His mouth fell open. "Are you...?"

"Aye." The ghostly man nodded. "I were once th' man known as Cap'n Reed." His face turned bitter. "Jus' a fool of a freebooter, made th' scapegoat by th' Navy an' set adrift t' die like a dog."

"But...you're supposed to be dead," Ricotta blurted out.

Captain Reed chuckled, but his eyes held no laughter. "Ye read me log, didn't ye? Ye be knowin' the fate wha' befell me. A bloody fever took hold o' me, and I died with anger still festerin' in me 'eart...'Cause o' that, me soul lost its way an' began roamin' the world of the livin'...And with it, the *Eleftheria*."

"How is this even happening?" Laxia whispered.

Captain Reed slid his eyes over her. "I got a hold o' meself again, all 'cause ye lubbers were crazy enough to find yer way aboard. Ye 'ave me thanks, ye do."

"I'm happy to hear that," Adol said.

Captain Reed bowed his head. "Aye, now I can finally face me crew on the other side. I 'spect 'em to give me no end o' grief, fer bein' late by a hundred years. You an' yer crew still got a rough sail ahead o' ye. I made that sea chart back when I was still tryin' to escape the isle. Should prove useful ta ye." He pointed at the map Sahad held in his hands.

Sahad nodded. "Aye, this chart has all kinds o' detailed information. A lot o' work went into puttin' this thing together."

A smile of approval creased Captain Reed's ghostly lips. "Sounds like ye know a thing or two 'bout the sea yerself..." He peered closer. "That hair color o' yers...Ye be hailin' from Creet, seadog?"

"Yeah, I do."

"Gah-haha...Mus' be fate. Well, pay it no mind. Now then, I suppose I'll be takin' ye back to shore, then. One last voyage for the *Eleftheria*."

The ship's bell rang overhead.

Captain Reed saluted them with a hand to his hat, then ascended to the quarterdeck, giving orders to the crew. The *Eleftheria* turned and sped back to shore, bringing them smoothly into the cove. The board slid out to bridge the ship to the dock.

As they made their way ashore, Captain Reed stood at the rail, watching them all line up to face him.

"S'ppose it be time now," he said.

Ricotta shook her head. "Are you saying goodbye?"

"Aye, 'fraid so, lass." He turned to Sahad. "Avast, ye seadog! Don' be lettin' the wind fill up yer sails jus' 'cause ye 'ave that map there. We best not be crossin' paths in the underworld any time soon, ye hear me?"

"Yes, sir." Sahad looked at him uncertainly, as if trying to figure something out.

Captain Reed moved his gaze further into their group. "Adol, was it? I'm sure ye've seen many a sight on this 'ere isle. There be all manner o' beasts, ruins, and hidden wonders buried here, waitin' to be found. I weren't able to uncover all this isle's secrets, but I've a hunch that ye'll be able to find 'em all." His eyes shifted to Dana, standing by Adol's side. His lips twitched. "Seems to me ye've found yerself a fascinatin' crew member already, eh, lad?"

Adol exchanged glances with Dana. She smiled.

"Rest in peace, Captain Reed," Adol said.

Captain Reed chuckled quietly. "I dunno 'ow much peaceful restin' I'll be gettin' down in the locker. Though an ocean of time separates us, we be part o' the same crew, fightin' to escape this isle's clutches. So batten down yer hatches, all o' ye...Ye'll weather this storm...an' survive. Farewell."

He faded.

The docking board slid inward, and the ship sank down, settling into the bottom of the cove with the main deck less than half a melye above the water. The magic that was holding it together despite a hole below the waterline was gone.

"I wish Reed could have stayed longer," Ricotta said. "He probably could tell us a lot of fascinating tales."

"I feel like he kept singlin' me out fer some reason," Sahad said thoughtfully. "As if—"

As if you're his kin. Adol didn't say this out loud. But now that it had come up, he was beginning to notice the similarities. The way they spoke, softening the vowels in a distinct sort of way only people who grew up in the same region would. The singular hair color, dark with a greenish tint as if stained by seaweed. He knew this wasn't the time to talk about it, but he should probably have a chat with Sahad if the man didn't figure it out on his own.

"The sea chart he gave us will be very helpful," Laxia said. "I think we've taken a major step toward getting off this island."

"Yeah," Sahad agreed. "Let's head back to the village an' let everyone know."

A WALK THROUGH THE CITY

Alison had given birth while they were gone. A healthy baby boy slept peacefully in her arms. Ed, the proud father, was sitting by the bed with a shaken look. He stood up as he saw the party enter.

"Congratulations," Adol said.

Ed blinked, and Adol realized that the man was fighting back tears. His lips trembled as he took a moment to steady himself.

"No matter how long I live," he said, "I will never be able to thank you enough. For saving my family. For finding me in time. For..." He paused, looking at his wife and son with such love that Adol felt his own eyes tingle.

He stepped forward and patted Ed on the shoulder.

"I'm very glad we found you," he said. "Alison was one of the first castaways we rescued, and she never stopped talking about you. Seeing your family reunited is one of the happiest things that's happened since we landed on this island."

Ed nodded, clearly at a loss for words. They stood together for a while, looking at the sleeping mother and child.

"We decided to name him Luke," Ed said finally. "The light. The fact that he was born healthy after everything that happened is a miracle. May another miracle like this lead us all to escape."

Adol nodded. "Good name. And yes, we will escape. We'll all get out of here soon, to resume our regular lives." Despite the map they'd found, he still didn't have any idea how they were going to accomplish that. But he had to keep the promise he'd made to Captain Barbaros.

Outside, a group of castaways were gathered around Captain Reed's map, spread on the table in Euron's workshop. Adol approached them, catching shreds of the conversation.

"Where did you say it was?" Dogi asked.

Thanatos pointed. "Right here, north of the capital."

Adol stepped up to the table.

Unlike the map of Seiren they had been working on in Castaway Village, this one had fewer details of the island itself. But it captured a great deal about the surrounding waters. The currents, the underwater reefs, the complex shoreline, were all drawn with intricate care, as if the person who made this map had been exploring the island from the water rather than over the land. Only a ghost ship could avoid the Oceanus long enough to accomplish a task like this. Had Captain Reed worked on this map in his undead form, hoping to benefit travelers in need?

It took Adol a moment to realize what the discussion was about. The dotted lines around the island were not an indication of ship routes. They couldn't be, with the way ship traffic was all but impossible around these parts. As a further clue, a small drawing of a tentacled creature marked one of the lines...The Oceanus's migration paths?

Laxia and Dana were tracing them with their fingers, bending over the map with the concentration of scholars translating an ancient text.

"According to this chart, it seems to have multiple travel routes," Laxia said. "But look at this."

She was pointing at the center of the bay off the Aegias shore. The giant whirlpool, the place they'd labeled on their own map as the Archeozoic Chasm.

Dana nodded. "True. This is the only area where all the Oceanus's routes pass by. It has to be the place."

"Inside that giant sinkhole?" Thanatos asked in disbelief. "That's not very useful, is it?"

"It's the exact information we were looking for," Dana said. "Now we know where to find the Oceanus."

"Oh, right." Thanatos's voice brimmed with sarcasm. "Inside a magical whirlpool that shouldn't even exist. Deep underwater too, I assume. How exactly does this information help us defeat the creature?"

They all exchanged glances. He had a point. None of them could breathe underwater. And even if they could, how would they be able to defeat a monster larger than a ship inside that gaping chasm?

"You must know at least something about that whirlpool, Dana," Euron said. "It had to have been created by some Eternian magic."

"Well, I—" Dana paused abruptly. Blood drained from her face, and she swayed, clasping the edge of the table for balance. Adol rushed to her side, but she recovered quickly, heaving a few deep breaths. "Sorry. Every time I try to remember... That place must be really important to give me such a splitting headache."

"Don't push yourself," Adol said.

Dana lifted her face to him. "But I must. I can't just accept the way things are right now. I want my memories restored, more than anything."

Adol understood. But watching Dana strain herself was painful. He wished he could do something to help her.

"Perhaps you should stay behind when we go out and investigate the chasm," he said.

She shook her head. "No. I need to go with you. Whatever is out there, it should give us some answers."

"It looks like the answers we seek are inside the chasm itself," Hummel pointed out. "But how are we supposed to cross the water to get to it?"

Sahad sighed. "True. We'll end up like that stuffed shirt Carlan if we try to get there by boat."

"Maybe we should have hitched a ride on Captain Reed's ship," Ricotta said.

"Maybe we should have," Sahad agreed. "But it's too late now."

"I got it," Dana suddenly said. "The memory I was looking for. That chasm is exactly where the royal palace of Eternia used to be. Not just in the same area, but in the same exact spot."

They all looked at her.

"Can't be," Adol said. "The royal palace stood on land, didn't it?"

She shook her head. "I think this is what has been eluding me all this time. *Part* of the palace was built on land, but the rest extended to sea. Not everyone knew about this, even inside the palace, but its underwater substructures extended into the bay and led directly to the ocean floor. The royal family used a special passage to access it, and they had Essence Equipment they would use to move about freely underwater. I heard of a secret royal treasury located in one of those chambers."

"And now it's all gone," Hummel said.

She shook her head. "That's the thing. It's not exactly gone. The *palace* isn't there—but the space it used to occupy is still holding the same shape, keeping the water from filling the gap it left behind. *That's* what creating the chasm. I have no idea how, but—" She paused, staring into the distance. Adol could see her mind working, as if she'd just had an idea, but she didn't say anything.

"I wonder," Laxia said. "Could that chasm be connected to the palace's disappearance?"

"I can't say." Dana seemed distracted again, her face paler than usual.

"Then there's no point in discussing this further," Hummel said. "We should just go see the place for ourselves. A professional transporter must always know the lay of the land."

"We're not all transporters," Laxia corrected. "But otherwise, I agree."

After donning their gear, the party gathered at the crystal in the village center. Each of them now had their own warping ring, crafted by Euron from the crystal pieces they'd gathered. They all touched their rings and focused their thoughts, the way Dana had taught them.

A wave of light swept them, and they found themselves in the center of the Eternia ruins.

No matter how many times they did it, Adol would never get used to this mode of travel. The pulling sensation, the thrill of a freefall, the instant change of scenery. Instead of sea salt, campfire smoke, and wildflowers, the wind touching his face now smelled of lichen and stone. The tall shape of the Stupa rose ahead. He blinked, forcing himself back to reality.

They stopped on the terrace overlooking the royal gardens and the Aerial Corridor, staring at the gap where the palace used to be.

Through the mist swirling over the bay, Adol couldn't make out many details, but the empty space inside the gap looked prominent, as if invisible walls inside were holding back the water. Curiously these imaginary walls didn't prevent the water from cascading down into the gap, or the thick fog of droplets from swarming over it, filling the view.

How in the world were they going to descend into that chasm and face the Oceanus?

As soon as the question formed in Adol's head, he heard a chime coming from the walkway ahead. The blue crystal rising at the edge of the gap was glowing, as if inviting them to approach.

Before anyone could say anything, Dana rushed forward and touched it.

"What is it, Dana?" Olga said.

Dana blinked, looking down the valley at the distant city view. From the overlook at the Temple's Mountain Gate, she could see all the way to the harbor.

"The sunlight seemed to dim for a moment," she said.

Olga shook her head. "You must be seeing things. The clouds are nowhere near the sun."

Dana heaved a breath. Traveling timelines like this was so disorienting.

"Sarai and I have spent our entire lives in the capital," Olga said. "You can see why it's difficult for us to accept that such a terrible thing will come to pass."

Dana swallowed. It was difficult for all of them. Unbearable, really. If before she had harbored some hope that the disaster could be averted, after visiting Adol's time she had no hope anymore. The only possibility that seemed even remotely positive was that the future she'd seen wasn't going to happen for a very long time.

"I'm also concerned about that chasm down in the harbor you've mentioned to exist in Adol's era," Olga said. "Why does that appear in the place where the royal palace used to stand, and why—"

A booming voice from the side gate interrupted her. "Let's move it, people! We must finish before the day is done."

Dana and Olga turned to see Chief Dran enter through the gate, heading a procession of beast-driven carts loaded with goods, with merchants and guards in attendance. To Dana's disappointment, Rastell wasn't among them. They all stopped, bowing respectfully.

"Lady Dana. High Priestess Olga," Dran greeted.

"Blessings of the Great Tree be with you." Dana smiled as she met his gaze.

Out of the corner of her eye, she noticed Olga's disapproving frown. Ever since excelling at his sword lessons, she'd thought of him as a friend—but somehow a personal friendship with the chief guard wasn't on Olga's list of acceptable qualities for the Maiden.

"What are you and your men going here, Chief?" Olga asked.

Dran glanced at the procession in his wake with just a touch of exasperation. "We are storing food, High Priestess. By decree of Her

Majesty, Queen Sarai. Lady Dana is said to have received a vision of a poor harvest this year."

"That vision came to her just yesterday," Olga said in disbelief. "How impressive of Queen Sarai to take action so soon."

Dran bowed his head solemnly. "Indeed. Even if this year's harvest is poor, we have nothing to fear. The kingdom of Eternia has faith in both Queen Sarai and Lady Dana. After all, they have brought about the most prosperous age in Eternia's history." His eyes slid over Dana again, and she felt her cheeks warm with a blush that would certainly earn another measure of Olga's disapproval. Even after all these years, a praise from Chief Dran still felt special.

"Of course," Olga said. "Forgive me for distracting you from your duties, Chief Dran."

Dran's lips formed a more definite smile this time. "It's always a pleasure to speak to you and Lady Dana, High Priestess." He signaled, and the procession resumed their walk to the gateway on the other side of the area.

Dana followed them with her gaze. She could see Olga's pale cheeks flare with pink too, a curious reaction for someone of her character. Even in his older age, Dran tended to have this effect on people.

"We probably should have told him the truth," she said.

"There's no reason to cause unnecessary confusion." Olga straightened, all businesslike again. "Now then, Dana. We should be on our way as well. You said this man, Adol, was headed down the Aerial Corridor toward the palace last time you visited his time line, yes?"

Dana nodded. "That's right."

"Let's get moving then."

They walked down the stairs.

"Maiden! High Priestess!" Cleric Cecile rushed toward them at the bottom landing. She seemed flustered.

"What's wrong, Cecile?" Dana asked.

"Are you two leaving so soon after the Harvest Festival?"

"Yes. Why?" As always, Olga appeared affronted at a question from a subordinate.

"N-no reason. It's just... You both seem rather preoccupied of late." Cecile looked from Olga to Dana, then shook her head. "Let me express myself better. I don't know what you two are so busy investigating, but I can tell just by looking at you that it's something serious. I want you both to remember that you are not alone. If you ever need help...Please let us do whatever we can."

Olga looked more surprised than Dana had seen her in a while, seemingly at a loss for words.

"Thank you, Cecile," Dana said earnestly. "We're very grateful for your offer. At the moment, we cannot share any details, but when the time comes, we will call upon you for help."

"Lady Dana..." Cecile bowed. "Thank you. You and the High Priestess carry the burden for all of us. Whenever you need to leave, please don't worry about a thing. We can handle things here."

"Thank you, Cecile." Now that she was over her surprise, Olga seemed unexpectedly moved.

Dana parted with Olga at the gate. Before setting out on the road to the capital, she paused to take a look around. She wanted to remember everything just like this. Sunlit landscape, peaceful groups of pilgrims on their way to the Temple, priestesses standing at the top of the gate, looking at the view. Nothing to foreshadow the horrible future she saw in her visions.

She wished this moment could last forever.

Beside the Stupa building, at a merchant's stall, Dana noticed the familiar pink-haired girl. Io. She was eating a honey cake. When she saw Dana, she hurried to stuff it all into her mouth, as if afraid she wouldn't be allowed to finish it if Dana got closer.

"Don't rush." Dana studied her curiously, realizing she knew nothing about this child's background. Were her parents poor? Did she often go hungry? Unlikely, given the way Io ran around all day, as if she didn't have a single care in the whole world. Yet the way she devoured the honey cake made Dana wonder. She turned to the merchant woman, standing at the side, head bent, hands folded in a respectful greeting.

"Maiden." The merchant bowed deeper, then straightened, following the direction of Dana's gaze. "I've seen this child a lot lately," she said quietly. "She looked hungry, so I gave her some food."

"Oh, thank you. Please, let me pay you for it."

The merchant shook her head. "No need, Your Eminence. You've been such a great help to us. This is no trouble at all."

Io finished chewing and wiped her face with the back of her hand. "Whew, I'm stuffed." She looked at Dana. "Alright, Lady, let's go!"

"Go?" Dana frowned. "Where are we going?"

Io grinned. "I'm going wherever you're going, duh!"

"You can't do that," Dana protested. "I have things to do."

"Awww, fine. I guess you have been pretty busy lately. Take care of yourself then." Io giggled and ran off.

"Thank you, you too." Dana stood for a moment, looking after the child. What a perplexing girl Io was.

At the side plaza, the twins Mia and Sia were arguing again. Their mother, Ansia, watched them with a mix of fondness and irritation. Dana walked past them, through the crowd, to the other side. She was sensing something unusual... An Essence glow? Another trapped spirit? She reached out with her mind to release the disturbance.

A tiny glowing orb floated into view from a dark alley between the buildings. It bobbed in place, and Dana had a feeling it was surveying its surroundings.

People continued to hurry around as if nothing unusual were going on. Could no one else see the spirit?

"Hello," the spirit said. "T'would seem I'm visible to thee. How delightful! Might thou be...? Oh, never mind. Let us merely agree that a mysterious event has transpired. My name is Plau, Spirit of the Raindrop. I make my home in the river due west of here. Yet for some reason, I was inexplicably drawn to this location. Hmm... What power beckoned me? T'would seem the other spirits did not succumb to it as I did. The loss is theirs, of course—for I have finally met someone who can see me!"

"Is this so rare?" Dana felt genuinely curious.

"Indeed, it is!" The spirit glimmered. "Naturally, I do not desire to rush into a serious commitment, but might thee by any chance wish to be my... friend?"

Dana smiled. "I'll be delighted to be your friend. My name is Dana."

"Dana... Thou art a kind person, Dana. Please accept this as a token of my gratitude."

A surge of warmth flowed through Dana as the spirit filled her with new power. For a brief moment, she sensed the smell of a rainforest, a clean, fresh scent that made her feel energized.

"Thank you," she said.

Plau bobbed in place. "Anything for thee, friend Dana." Her glimmer paused. "Oh? Could that be... Do I sense my brother? I... I apologize. I must hide now. Farewell, Dana! Until we meet again!"

A brother? Hide? Were spirits playing hide and seek? Dana blinked. Some spirits certainly seemed more eccentric than others.

A vision floated up in her mind. The door behind the monolith in the Sanctuary Crypt, sliding open with a silent invitation.

She paused. Was this a memory? Or a sign that she was now free to proceed to a new area of the Sanctuary? Had her virtue increased since she'd last visited the Sanctuary? Well, only one way to check.

As she focused her Essence to warp into the Sanctuary, she tried to tell herself that she was doing this for Adol's cause, that the knowledge she gathered from each new monolith could hold critical information that would help solve the mysteries they were facing in Adol's timeline. But deep inside she realized this was only an excuse. She was doing this for her own sake, hoping to get the answers she was looking for. Or was it merely to satisfy her curiosity? In the end, it didn't really matter.

The door behind the monolith slid open easily this time, admitting her to the new level of the Sanctuary Crypt. She navigated through, avoiding the golems, using her Essence to find her way through the maze of chambers and stone blocks to another room with another archival monolith.

On the images of old drawings, a man wrapped in a toga had a star in place of his head. The text read:

There will always be those who, in the presence of glory, seek to claim it for themselves. Thus did weaker nations seek to wage war against Eternia and usurp its Golden Age for themselves. With its Essence and its powerful military, Eternia was in no danger of falling. But civilian casualties mounted along Eternia's borders, threatening the peace and security of the people.

Amidst the fog of war, one man stepped forth and ensured his place in Eternia's history: Urianus. Though he appeared to be an unassuming traveler, he possessed calm Essence and a powerful will that could withstand any hardship.

Urianus was a peaceful man above all else. He preached his word to all who would hear, tended to the poor, and healed the sick. Whilst traveling through a region ravaged by war, Urianus was set upon by bandits. A young woman, believed to be the leader, drew her sword from its sheath. As she made ready to cut him down, Urianus, ever tranquil, said thusly: "Wrath will not calm your wrath. You need not feel wrath, you need not feel fear. Embrace tranquility. Only when you abandon wrath can you walk a new path."

She did not understand Urianus at first, but when his meaning dawned on her, she wept. Thus did the bandit leader become his disciple and traveling companion.

With each passing day, Urianus drew more disciples. Even the beasts of the Earth began to follow him. With his tranquil demeanor, he later became known as the Saint of Salvation for his role in saving the people of Eternia from a great cataclysm.

Dana paused as she finished the text. She'd heard of Saint Urianus, of course. He had been very important to the establishment of the kingdom. But she'd never learned all these other details. Saving Eternia from a great cataclysm. Converting a bandit leader into one of his disciples. Even animals followed him. He seemed truly fascinating.

Laughter echoed behind her.

This time, she didn't need to turn and look to guess the owner of the voice, however impossible it seemed.

"Did you follow me, Io?" she asked.

Io stepped up to her side. "I tried my best to be super sneaky, but you looked so stunned just now that I couldn't help laughing."

Dana sighed. "I told you before, this place is dangerous, and you should stop coming here."

"Aw." Io screwed her face, as if about to cry, but Dana could tell it was pretense. "Don't say things like that. How come you're so interested in the history of Eternia, anyway?"

"If these records are genuine, they contain lost history. It's important to understand our roots."

"I see."

For a moment, Io looked much older than her age. Dana shook off the impression. It had to be a trick of the light.

"Didn't you say you were looking for something?" she asked. "Is this why you keep sneaking down here?"

Io appeared to hesitate. "In a way, yes."

"Can I help you look for it?"

"I think I might have found it," Io said. "But then, maybe I haven't. In fact, it might be better if I don't find it just yet."

Dana shook her head. "I don't understand what you mean. In any case, I have to give you a good scolding for disobeying me."

Io turned around. "Oh, I just remembered. I still have chores to do at home. Bye!" She ran off.

Dana paused for a moment looking after her, then headed out of the Sanctuary Crypt.

Rastell stood guard at the entrance to the royal palace—another testament to how rapidly he was advancing through the ranks.

"Lady Dana," he greeted.

"Rastell!" She smiled. "I see you got a big promotion. Guarding the palace now, are you?"

He smiled too, a glimpse of the boy he used to be that filled her with warmth. "Only temporarily. I'm filling in for my father while he's away on the outskirts."

Dana nodded. "They don't allow just anyone to guard the main entrance to the palace, even as a fill in. I'm so proud of you, Rastell."

"Th-thank you, Your Eminence."

She looked up at him. Guarding the palace meant he had already achieved the honor he was striving for, joining the elite ranks that were also assigned to the Temple. As she met his gaze, her mind swirled with the possibilities.

"You might find yourself guarding me sooner that I realized, Rastell," she said.

"I—I—" Rastell's cheeks lit up with color. "I'll strive to achieve this honor, Maiden, so that I can make my father and my superiors proud."

She had to stop her hand from reaching over to touch his arm. It wasn't a good idea. With her memory loss, she had no idea what, if anything, ended up happening between her and Rastell. Until she remembered more, she should be taking example from the restraint he showed around her. Besides, she needed to focus on her mission.

"I will see you later, Rastell. May the blessings of the Great Tree be upon you." She gave him a quick smile, then walked past him to the crystal at the palace entrance.

Yes, this place seemed about right. And here it was—a patch of fertile land, perfect for the prayer tree sapling. This one needed to grow particularly strong to survive what was coming.

She knelt down and planted it, then prayed for a while, summoning all the Essence she could. She had no idea what disaster was going to befall the palace, but this was the least she could do.

THE ARCHEOZOIC CHASM

Hოw the hell is this possible?" Sahad demanded.

Adol stared. Where a moment ago a giant whirlpool had swirled in the middle of the bay, a majestic domed building now rose by the shore, entwined in a giant tree that supported the massive stone structure. The royal palace looked damaged, but still whole. *The Pearl of the Gaete Sea. Here, as if it never disappeared anywhere.* Adol let out a sigh.

"Did you do this, Dana?" Ricotta asked.

Dana kept her eyes on the sight. "Yes. If I remember correctly. I planted a prayer tree sapling at this spot so that it would support and protect the palace."

"Protect it from what, exactly?" Ricotta insisted.

"From..." Dana gasped and swayed, breathing heavily. Adol rushed to her side. After a moment, she steadied herself. "Anyway, we should be able to approach the chasm from the subterranean levels of the palace."

She seemed to have forgotten Ricotta's question.

The doors to the palace stood open. The hallway inside was adorned with a grand staircase at the far end. Most of the decorations here were gone, making it difficult for Adol to recall this place at the height of its glory, as he had seen it in Dana's visions. Back then, the side doorways opened to long hallways, each beautiful in its own way. In the present time, all these doorways were blocked by stone rubble, piled high enough to conceal the view. Only one passage was still open, leading off to the right and down into the depths of the palace.

The winding stairway brought them to a partially collapsed chamber that Adol didn't remember seeing in his visions before. One of its walls was broken, with a gaping hole leading outside. The gap breathed with moisture. Falling water roared outside.

The Archeozoic Chasm. Adol's heart quivered as he stepped through the gap.

The massive waterfall curved around the giant circular hole, falling endlessly into the abyss. A rock wall creased the closer side of the chasm, with a path running around it in a descending semicircle and disappearing behind the wall of water. The rest of the chasm was hidden from view by the wall of mist, the air infused with cool salty droplets. After only a few steps Adol's clothes and hair felt damp, sticking to his wet skin.

Taking this path was one of the most frightening things Adol had ever done. He could see fear on everyone's faces, yet no one said anything as they started their descent. The wall of water falling into the dark abyss below gave him a sense of vertigo. He could see no explanation for what was holding it back from flooding the place. Only after the path took them into a cave behind the waterfall did he allow himself to heave a sigh of relief, marveling that he could still breath air. From everything he knew, they should be deep underwater, yet the cave looked no different from the other ones around the island, except for the roar of water streaming outside the window-like openings along the cave wall.

The path wound steadily downward as it looped around the chasm. The rock wall gradually gave way to more regular stonework that definitely looked man-made. They were entering the underwater recesses of the royal palace, the subterranean levels Dana had spoken about.

Dana looked at the symbol carved into the stone above the entrance to a side passage. "According to this sign, this passage should lead us into the treasury room. Let's check it out."

They followed a narrow stone corridor into a chamber at the end.

The floor here was arranged in sections, placed at different heights—like very large shelves in a storage. Each section was surrounded by a low stone rail, but the one in the center of the room also had taller pillars running around it, as if designed to hold something more precious than the others. This was also the only area that wasn't empty or flooded. A large chest rested in its center, surprisingly well-preserved.

"This chest must hold Essence equipment," Dana said. "These

pieces tend to be powerful enough to protect the container. And this lock—" She reached out with her palm, just short of touching, and Adol heard a barely perceptible click. The lid popped open.

Inside the chest, a set of blue teardrop-shaped iridescent ornaments gleamed against the dark wood. The translucent pieces seemed delicate but sturdy, each threaded with a flexible metal chain crafted so finely that its links blended together into a continuous smooth line. Royal jewelry? Adol reached forward to touch one, then paused. Essence equipment could be dangerous. He looked at Dana for guidance.

"I believe this is what we were hoping to find," Dana said. "The charms the royal family used to breathe underwater. They're called hermit scales." She reached into the chest and pulled out one necklace, sliding it on.

It looked exactly like a piece of jewelry. Adol had no idea how something like this could possibly help anyone breathe. Still, he lifted out several more and passed them around to the rest of the group.

"How lucky," Dana said. "There's enough for all of us."

Adol adjusted the scale over his chest. "How does it work?"

"It channels the Essence to create a layer of air around you when you're underwater," Dana explained. "Enough to breathe, and to keep dry."

"For how long?" Laxia asked.

Dana shrugged. "As long as you need, really." She headed back along the passage, and the rest of the party followed.

A pool of water opened at their feet. Tall weeds wavered in its depths, their long stems descending out of sight. Dana, walking ahead, stepped off the edge right into the water and sank in, surrounded by a silvery gleam. Air trapped around her? Adol couldn't wait to find out. He exchanged glances with the other party members and jumped in too, splashes behind him telling him that everyone followed.

The sensation was unlike anything he'd experienced before. Adol could see the water around him, sense its weight, except that it didn't seem to restrict his movements, enabling him to walk as easily as he did on dry land. The hermit scale emitted a glow that penetrated the gloom, illuminating the way. Each of the party members looked like a silvery light source, shining softly among the gloom. They hurried to catch up with Dana.

The path ran level for a while, then ascended again, bringing them to another submerged section of the royal palace. Inside, water stood only waist deep, held back by the same magic that had created the Archeozoic Chasm.

Columns lining the hall looked like trees, their twined branches forming a ceiling with weeping garlands of small green leaves hanging down like elaborate decorations. Adol couldn't tell if they were real or merely crafted from some unknown powerful material to look like living plants. It seemed impossible for trees to grow so deep underwater without any sunlight, but Adol was past being surprised.

A gap at the end of the hall led underwater again, into a deep cave that descended steeply toward a platform with a blue Essence crystal rising from the floor. A warping point they could now use if needed to transport in and out of this otherworldly place. Adol felt relieved. He didn't like the idea of traversing the chasm again.

The floor here was strewn with debris that looked mostly man-made. Wooden boards—some nearly whole, studded with rusted nails, others decayed and misshapen—scattered around the space, heavily overgrown with coral and weeds. An old anchor leaned against the wall. The thick tube protruding out of the silt at the edge of the platform had to be an old rusted cannon. They walked over to it and found themselves at the edge of a steep drop. Adol paused, staring into the depths of the water.

The vast space stretched into the distance, threaded by scattered columns of eerie bluish light—sunbeams, piercing through melye and melye of water. Tall reefs formed a rugged circle with decayed ship carcasses stuck in the deep crevices between them.

"This must be the bottom of the chasm," Dana said. "But we didn't see the Oceanus's nest as we—"

"Wait." Laxia rushed forward.

Adol's eyes widened as he realized what she was pointing at.

The board lying at the very edge of the rock had letters on it, partially concealed by silt and sand. Laxia bent down and swept it clean, until the word written on the board become clearly visible to everyone.

LOMBARDIA.

Adol gasped.

They had found what they were looking for. The Oceanus's nest.

He stared at the *Lombardia*'s nameplate. This couldn't be the place where she sank. The shipwreck happened all the way on the other side of the island. He could think of only one explanation for how this plate had found its way here. The creature that sank the ship must have ripped it off the hull and dragged it here as a trophy, displaying it on the edge of its nest along with all these other man-made objects it took from the ships that fell victim to it.

Destroying the Oceanus suddenly felt far more personal than before. It wasn't only about their escape. They owed closure to Captain Barbaros, to all the people who'd traveled on the *Lombardia* and hadn't made it to shore, to all those who'd perished in these waters during the past centuries and beyond. How long had the Oceanus been living here? Adol didn't really care. They were going to put a stop to it, once and for all.

"There is no telling when the Oceanus will return," Dana said. "It must be roaming the sea somewhere. But it looks to me that we may need to prepare better before we face it in battle. Now that we know where its nest is located, we can always warp back here. Let's return to the village for now."

They gathered around the Essence crystal in the depths of the cave, touching it to feel a familiar pulling sensation.

Despite tuning in to the village as they warped, the group found themselves in a different place—near Eternia's royal palace, in the same spot from which they'd started their descent into the chasm earlier today. Adol wasn't sure what went wrong. Maybe warping from deep underwater didn't work over long distances.

Their eyes were drawn to a large set of ripples in the bay ahead. A giant creature brushed the surface and dove out of sight. Adol thought he could see tentacles trailing in its wake.

Sahad's face twitched. "Damn monster, swimmin' without a care in the world."

"It seems to be returning to its nest," Hummel remarked.

Laxia glanced around uncertainly. "What should we do?"

"Hey, Adol!" Dogi and Thanatos rushed up to them and stopped, looking out into the bay.

"Dogi! Father!" Ricotta ran over and threw her arms around Thanatos. He smiled and patted her head.

"We found the Oceanus's nest," she announced proudly. "It's right here, under this palace."

Dogi and Thanatos exchanged a glance.

"Looks like we got here just in time," Dogi said.

"In time for what?" Laxia asked.

"We warped here earlier today to check out the city," Thanatos explained, "and we came across some pictograms in one of the buildings with more information about the Oceanus. They give details about how people used to hunt it back in the day."

Dana frowned. "I wasn't aware such sources existed in Eternia. Pictograms, you say?"

"More like stone carvings," Dogi said. "We found them inside a house, just off the market plaza. Must've belonged to some rich guy, to have his own personal artwork carved into his wall."

"Merchant Mussdan," Dana guessed. "His house was right next to the market plaza. He and the meat merchant Barossa ran a standing bet that someday one of them would be selling Oceanus meat at his stall. Barossa actually claimed victory at some point, but I don't believe he was truthful."

Dogi chuckled. "It looks like this Mussdan fella took the competition seriously."

"He didn't like to lose," Dana said.

"So how do we hunt the Oceanus?" Hummel asked.

"Trapping it in its own nest is actually a good idea," Dogi said. "Apparently, the Oceanus has more of an advantage in open waters. The Eternians would split into two teams to hunt it."

"That's right," Thanatos put in. "The first team would taunt the Oceanus from the shore, using arrows and catapults to drive it back into its nest, and the second team would wait for it down there and finish it off. The only thing we didn't quite understand is how they all managed to breath underwater. The pictograms—"

"Oh, we got that covered." Ricotta lifted the hermit scale off her chest and showed it to him. Dogi looked at it blankly.

"It's an Eternian artifact," Adol explained. "It uses Essence to create an air bubble that traps enough breathing air to last a very long time."

"Must be handy for fishin'," Dogi noted.

"I'll let you wear it some time," Adol promised. "For now, let's go get ourselves an Oceanus."

THE OCEANUS

The entire Castaway Village spent the next few days preparing to hunt the Oceanus. Under Kathleen's supervision, they made bows and catapults and prepared loads of ammunition. Dana used her Essence, aided by the crystals, to warp everything to a vantage point above the bay on Eternia's side of the island, overlooking the royal palace. An ideal position to taunt the Oceanus with arrows and rocks as it swam in and out of its nest. With the amount of people they had, they could probably even deal the creature some damage before engaging it at the nest.

Sun blazed in the clear morning sky, illuminating the bay and the reefs flanking it on the outside. The water was so clear that from the grassy plateau they'd chosen for their attack position they could see under the surface, to the reefs descending out of sight into the clouds of the wavering kelp. They should see the Oceanus before it emerged, aiming their weapons to do the most damage. Adol's skin prickled in anticipation.

The tension was high as they stood at their posts, primed and ready. Even Alison and her baby were here, sitting in the grass beside the catapult manned by Ed and Licht.

"There it is." Dogi pointed.

A giant creature glided up from the depths, taking shape against the forest of kelp. It looked enormous. The surface of the sea rippled, the creature's hide gleaming as it cut through the surface and disappeared again with a mighty splash.

"It's undulating up and down," Laxia said. "I think it's about to come up again over there, between those rocks."

They watched in tense silence. Licht, at the nearest catapult, trembled slightly as he craned his neck to see the water below. He noticed Adol's look and stilled, turning away.

From here, the Oceanus looked like a giant ship moving under the surface. It was coming up in nearly the exact spot Laxia had pointed out.

Dogi raised his hand. "Take aim, and . . . fire!"

The catapults creaked and thudded. Bows sang. Arrows and rocks cascaded down, showering the Oceanus's exposed hide.

The creature shook and buckled, splashing wildly before it dove out of sight. Adol thought he saw a trail of turbid liquid. Blood?

"Yes, excellent!" Thanatos roared.

"Everyone, brace for the next the attack." Dogi turned to Adol. "I think we got the sucker's attention. Another blast or two, and it'll be headed to its nest for sure."

"Right." Adol turned to his team. "It's time."

They all crowded around him and touched their crystal rings to warp to the Oceanus's nest.

T he underwater space in front of them looked huge. The party lined up at the edge of the platform, weapons at ready. This seemed to be the best starting point that would enable them to face the Oceanus at the head level rather than attacking from below. Adol narrowed his eyes, surveying the battleground.

"It's coming," Hummel said quietly. "I can feel the current."

Adol could feel it too, a movement of water that could only be made by a very large object propelling toward them at great speed. After a few heartbeats, a giant shape materialized in the distance. It grew as it approached—until it filled the entire space, drowning out the sunlight.

Even though Adol had been preparing for this moment, he felt a chill run down his spine as he looked at their enemy. The Oceanus was enormous. Its large cone-shaped head, crowned with massive fins, rose up level with the stone ledge they were standing on. Two gleaming yellow eyes, each as large as a ship's wheel, stared down at them. They looked surprisingly intelligent—cold and malicious, cruel. As the creature surveyed its enemies, readied at the edge of the platform with weapons out, Adol had a distinct feeling that it was smiling, as if delighted with the anticipation of a kill.

The party attacked.

Adol first aimed for the eyes but quickly realized that the creature would never let him land a blow. The Oceanus was very effective at evading these attacks, tilting its head just out of reach. Its tentacles swept over the rock, forcing the group to run and jump between them to avoid being swept down onto the sea floor. Ink spread out of a jet hole at its side, clouding their vision. For a while all they could do was dodge and swerve, focused mostly on avoiding the tentacles while also keeping their footing in the inky-black water.

After the ink cleared, Hummel was able to aim a few lucky shots that forced the creature to recede to the bottom of the pit. When it recoiled, Adol saw an opening on its back—an oozing wound, probably made by the arrows and the catapults aimed by Dogi's team. A minor advantage, but they'd take anything they could get.

The currents here rose in steep streams from the sea floor, so that one could jump and float up and down as needed. Adol used one of these streams to leap on the creature's back, showering blows into the vulnerable spot, ripping the wound open, deepening it. Aiming for the heart. Somewhere in there the creature should have one, shouldn't it?

Another person landed next to him. Dana. Her blades whirled, slicing through the enemy's body. A tentacle descended on them, but Adol was able to sever it with a quick and powerful blow. The Oceanus shuddered.

They redoubled their attacks. Blood fountained out of the wound, clouding the water until Adol could see nothing but the gleam of their blades. And then even that faded, drowned out by the blind rage he felt. This was the creature responsible for so many deaths. It killed for enjoyment, its very existence an ancient curse that had plagued these waters for millennia. It was up to Adol and his team to put an end to this monster, once and for all.

He had no idea when it ended. Suddenly, the creature under them was no longer moving. The rest of the team were all around them, Ricotta brandishing her clubs, Sahad sinking his anchor into the creature's side, Hummel aiming his rifle at its head. Dana grabbed Adol's shoulder and pulled him back. He steadied himself against her.

"It's dead." Dana's voice was uneven as she looked down at the mess of the creature's hide, the deep stab wounds, the severed tentacles. Adol looked too. He should be brimming with anger, with the animal triumph that lit up Sahad's and Ricotta's faces. This was the ultimate enemy that had destroyed the *Lombardia*, the nemesis that had kept them from leaving this island. Somehow, though, he could no longer feel any of this rage. All he could think of was the intelligent eyes that had faced them at the start of the fight. Such an ancient creature, advanced enough to dominate these waters for countless ages. Did they really have a right to take its life?

They used the flow of currents to float up to the stone platform where they had started their fight. From here, the body of the Oceanus, sprawled on the sea floor, looked hideous and pitiful, broken. Schools of scavenger fish were already gathering for a feast that would last many days.

Adol bent over the *Lombardia* name plate and picked it up. It seemed not right to leave it here. They should take it back, in honor of Captain Barbaros, who had given his life for his ship and all its survivors.

Castaway Village's celebratory feast lasted well into the night. Miralda had outdone herself with the cooking, using a variety of supplies to create true culinary masterpieces, with many of the villagers working under her supervision. Dogi brought out a bottle of rum, salvaged out of the pirates' reserves. After they ate and drank their fill, they sat around the fire, chatting.

"I wish Captain Barbaros could've been here to see this," Dogi said.

They all nodded. Adol wished he could believe that the captain's spirit was still here somewhere, smiling on their victory that finally made it possible to leave this island behind. He looked across the fire at Dana, who was sitting with Laxia and Ricotta on the other side. She met his gaze, then turned away as all three of them stood up and walked toward the lodge. Turning in for the night already? Adol looked after them. He had hoped to talk to Dana, but with all the excitement, he hadn't gotten a chance.

"Say, where'd Sahad wander off to?" Euron asked. "I haven't seen him in a while."

Thanatos laughed. "I think Sahad already drank himself to sleep."

"He'd better take it easy." Euron looked in the direction of the cove. "We still have work to do. I'd say, another two weeks before the ship is finished."

"Yeah," Dogi agreed. "We also need to make sure we've found every last castaway. Not to mention prepping food and water for the trip."

"Still." Thanatos sighed. "It won't be long before we're bidding fond farewells to our lives as castaways. I must admit, I think I'm actually going to miss living like this."

"Would you rather stay here?" Euron asked.

"It's not a wholly terrible idea." Thanatos paused. "I wouldn't mind staying here longer, but I decided long ago that I'd leave this island if I could. I want Ricotta to see the world. That daughter of mine has a lot of potential."

"Say, Adol." Dogi looked at his friend keenly. "What are you planning to do about Dana? Even if we escape this island, she's...well..."

"I was wondering about that myself," Euron agreed. "She hasn't fully regained her memories yet. Wouldn't she regret leaving?"

Adol didn't hurry to respond. These questions had been troubling him too. Now that the Oceanus was defeated and they could safely navigate the local waters, their departure was imminent as soon as they finished building the ship. Would Dana agree to leave the island with them? He hoped with all his heart that she would, but he also realized this decision wasn't a simple one.

He planned to talk to her about it once they'd recovered from the day's excitement. Tomorrow, probably. But even though she'd left the fireside, there was a chance she was still awake, wandering around camp. She may not be in the mood to talk, but he should at least make sure she was all right.

He mumbled an excuse, then got up and walked off into the darkness.

Somehow, he knew exactly where to go. Dana's favorite spot in the camp's mid-level meadow, overlooking the sea. As he made his way up the path, he felt certain he was going to find her there. And he was right.

Dana was standing at the edge of the cliff, her silhouette clearly outlined against the gleam of the sea in the light of the rising moons. She turned around as Adol approached, her face unreadable in the darkness.

"Quite a celebration today." She paused. "I thought, with all the excitement we had, you'd be off to sleep by now."

He sensed an edge in her voice. Was she upset? He shifted from foot to foot. "I thought the same about you. We all had quite a day."

Dana nodded. "Yes. You all must be happy you can finally leave this island."

You. The distancing word hurt more than he expected. They had all come to think of Dana as one of them, but in this one word she'd just separated herself, showing him beyond doubt that in her mind their interests lay apart.

"I was hoping we all could," he said. "Together."

She shook her head. "You know I can't."

"Why?"

She didn't respond at once, looking at the view. "You, of all people, should understand this, Adol. I still have no idea why I'm alive in this era, or what happened to the Kingdom of Eternia. I'm certain, though, that there is a purpose to all this. I can't leave until I find out."

"I do understand," Adol said. "But we're in this together. You and I are—"

"Gah-hahaha! Heyyy, you two! What're ya doin' here?" Sahad stumbled into the glade, coming toward them unsteadily.

Sahad. Impeccable timing, as usual. Adol sighed.

The fisherman stopped a few paces away and plopped down to the grass, hiccuping loudly. For a moment he looked like he was about to throw up. Adol and Dana rushed toward him.

"I think you drank a little too much, Sahad," Dana said soothingly.

"Gah-hahaha! Today was such a great day!" Sahad lifted his face into the wind. "What a nice breeze... Reminds me o' the winds on Creet." He lay down on his back, arms out. "Damia... Tetty... Just wait... Daddy's... comin' home soon..."

His eyes fell closed. In just a few moments, a loud snore announced that he was asleep.

"We shouldn't leave him here," Dana said. "Let's carry him back to the lodge."

Adol leaned forward and hooked Sahad's limp arm around his shoulder, lifting him off the ground with Dana supporting him on the other side.

He needed to talk to Dana more. But the moment was lost. He hoped they could continue this conversation tomorrow.

THE FATED DAY

Dana knelt in front of the Great Tree.

She could sense the vision coming, the familiar disoriented sense as the world around her changed color, for a moment folding the scenery into a swirl.

Scarlet.

Even the sky turned blood-red, the sun a black disk looming above. She saw herself standing on the terrace above the water gardens, beside the royal palace. A large object took shape above her, growing as it descended at an enormous speed. She gasped, watching it slam into the ground, raising a cloud of dust and debris, leaving a gaping chasm in the spot where the royal palace used to stand. The vision melted away as fast as it had come, morphing into a peaceful sunny day.

A scarlet vision.

Dana shuddered as she tried to wrap her mind around the information. Scarlet visions foretold events that would definitely come to pass, that couldn't be averted no matter what. Usually, though, such events clearly fit into Dana's reality, making it possible to find workable ways to soften the damage—like that time when she, Sarai, and Olga had prevented the Temple from burning down in the forest fire. The vision she'd just seen was different. A star falling from the sky to destroy the royal palace of Eternia? It seemed impossible. It didn't make any sense. If she hadn't seen the ruin with her own eyes in the distant future, she would have had serious trouble believing it. A feeling of dread seized her, worse than anything she'd ever experienced before.

A scarlet vision this clear normally foreshadowed events that were going to happen very soon—hours to days, at most. Even if she had no idea how this was going to happen and what she could do to protect the city, she wasn't about to just stand back and let it unfold. She had to act fast.

Are you certain of this, Dana?" Olga asked.

Dana swallowed, running her eyes around the throne room. It was hard to imagine that this majestic hall was going to be destroyed.

"Yes, I'm certain," she said. "Between the dreams I've been experiencing, and my scarlet vision, there is no doubt in my mind. I was thinking, with your and Sarai's help—"

They both looked at Sarai, who sat on her throne staring absently into space. Dana had an eerie feeling that the Queen wasn't surprised at the news. Had she had a vision too?

"Sarai?" Olga prompted.

Sarai shook her head. "Forgive me. To think that such a disaster awaits us..." She turned to Dana. "Thank you for bringing this to my attention."

"There isn't much we can do about it." Olga locked her gaze on Dana. "Scarlet visions can't be averted. You should know this better than anyone, Dana."

Dana swallowed. "I do know. But we can't just sit around and do nothing, can we?"

"What do you propose?" Olga looked at Sarai, but the Queen still seemed distracted, as if her thoughts weren't entirely there. Dana and Olga exchanged glances. Sarai had always been the fast thinker, the decisive one. Even a scarlet vision shouldn't sway her. Why was she acting so strangely?

"The Stupa at the center of Aegis," Dana said. "It provides Essence to the entire kingdom. Perhaps we can use it somehow, draw enough Essence to at least ease the blow. Even if the royal palace is destroyed, the rest of the city could still be saved." She paused. Perhaps if they drew enough Essence, they could avert the destruction of the palace too. Even scarlet visions had to have a weakness somewhere. Maybe the belief that they couldn't be averted existed only because no one had ever tried hard enough before.

Sarai lifted her head, meeting Dana's gaze. She looked composed again, the decisive leader back in place. "Yes, the Stupa. We could use it to erect a giant Essence barrier over the kingdom."

"Are you mad?" Olga protested. "That crystal pillar is the lifeblood of Eternia. If you use it in this manner, the entire kingdom will be drained of Essence. And how do you think the neighboring nations will react once they learn of this?"

"We can worry about the neighboring nations later," Sarai said. "The Essence stores can be replenished too. It's much more important to avert the disaster now, isn't it?"

"I suppose," Olga conceded.

Sarai nodded. "Very well, then. I will begin the preparations to create a barrier in the sky. All Essence Maesters throughout the kingdom will be assembled here for an emergency meeting."

Dana let out a sigh. She had a very bad feeling about this. But as long as the three of them worked together, they were going to succeed. She wanted to believe it, with all her heart.

From the elevated garden terrace, Dana had a perfect view of the royal palace and the city below. The giant crystal column of the Stupa loomed in their direct view. The scene looked exactly like it had in her scarlet vision, a terrifying thought Dana pushed far to the back of her mind.

The Essence Maesters formed two sizeable groups on the opposite sides of the Garden, with the Stupa in the center. Chief Dran and his guards positioned themselves in between, relaying signals between the groups to coordinate the efforts. But would even this assembly of the kingdom's most powerful people be enough to avert the disaster? Dana turned to the Queen, standing on the elevated platform at the side.

"We're ready, Sarai," she said.

Sarai nodded. "And so it begins." She lifted her head and gestured with an outstretched arm. "Commence barrier deployment."

A glow rose from the Stupa and spread, gradually enfolding the city. In the bright sunlight it was nearly invisible, but if Dana squinted her eyes just right, she could see the dome stretching overhead. Pure Essence, crackling with power, covering everything in sight. Along with all the Maesters, she lent her entire ability to the task, strengthening the barrier until she felt sure nothing could penetrate it anymore.

She didn't expect the blow to come so soon. Just like in her vision, a giant fiery ball materialized in the clear sky, growing rapidly as it descended straight toward the royal palace.

"Brace for the impact!" she screamed.

The ball hit.

Dana felt the energy hum and bounce as the falling star collided with the barrier, the impact point radiating with a chain of cracks erupting across the sky. The giant rock, the size of a minor mountain, slid down to one side and rolled into the jungle outside the capital.

"Clear!" she shouted.

Everywhere in sight, the Essence Maesters were lowering their hands, staring at the sky with dazed looks.

"Did it work?" Olga asked.

"I cannot say for certain," Sarai said. "But it seems to have protected us."

Dana briefly closed her eyes. "No..."

Olga rounded up to her. "What's wrong?"

"There's more than one. It's not..." Dana heaved a breath. "It's not over yet. The next wave is inbound!"

"*What?*"

"Chief Dran!" Sarai snapped. "Signal the Essence Maesters on the other side to maintain the barrier!"

"Yes, Your Majesty!" For the first time in her life, Dana sensed fear in Dran's voice. He was frantically giving signals, guards under his command running all over the place.

She was afraid too, but there was no time to dwell on her fear. Fiery balls took shape against the clear sky, cascading onto the city. *So many.*

There was nothing they could do. No matter how much Essence they all channeled, they couldn't possibly deflect them all.

"I'm going to the Stupa. More chance to maintain the barrier from there." Dana turned and ran. Olga rushed down the steps in her wake. The ground shook with a blast, a falling star that had definitely penetrated the power dome. It seemed much too close.

The sun was no longer visible. As they rushed though the Aerial Corridor, thick fog rolled in, swallowing everything in sight. Dana was having trouble seeing her way. She slowed down and looked around.

Where had this fog suddenly come from?

"Olga?" she called.

No response came. Strange. Olga must have changed her mind and returned to the palace garden. After a moment, Dana resumed her run.

The path seemed much too long, the other end of the corridor invisible through the fog. As she sped forward, an otherworldly voice echoed in her head.

Help me, it pleaded.

Another trapped spirit? She saw a glow through the mist ahead, confirming it.

"Hold on. I'll free you." She reached out with her Essence.

A glowing orb rolled out, its light cutting through the fog, melting the nearest layers away.

"Thou hast my gratitude, Eternian," the orb said. "But the wroth stars hath rent asunder my celestial garden. A rift hath been torn from the Earth...'Tis too late, I fear. If this continues, the world will—"

"It's not too late," Dana said firmly. "We can still stop it. There must be something we can do."

The spirit hesitated. "Thou art..."

"What?"

"Forgive me, 'tis nothing. I am Astios, the Spirit of Light. Like you, I, too, wish to forestall the end. Please use this."

Energy flowed into Dana. She felt lighter—translucent somehow. Luminous. It was hard to find words for this feeling.

"What is this power?" she asked.

"The power to see that which remains unseen," the spirit said. "But even with that power, I lost sight of my path. In thy hands, however...I sense a troubling presence in this fog, to say nothing of the stars themselves. Please continue to open new paths, for as long as thou hast life."

"I will," Dana promised.

The spirit faded.

With the new power, Dana felt energized and renewed. The walkway finally ended, and she ascended the steps to the Stupa building.

A giant creature emerged from the fog, blocking her way.

A Saurian?

It had to be, even though it looked like no Saurian she'd ever seen. Huge, with horns that curved forward alongside its narrow face, it had tree branches growing out of its body, twining into wing-like protrusions at its shoulders and forming a tall contraption over its back. Half-tree, half-animal? Dana had no time to wonder. The creature roared and lowered its head, stampeding toward her.

She drew her swords, calling on the new Luminous power the spirit had granted her. With this power, she felt so light, faster than she could possibly be otherwise. It felt easy to dodge the creature, to avoid its outlandish horns. She advanced, slashing at it with her blades. The creature roared and trembled, then fell to the ground. Its massive shape faded away into thin air.

Dana knelt down to catch her breath. She should be feeling amazed, terrified. Creatures like this didn't exist in real life—nor were they supposed to simply vanish after they were defeated. But she had no strength left to feel surprised. She heaved a few breaths and lifted her head, watching the fog around her dissipate, as if it had never existed in the first place.

The encounter with the strange Saurian seemed too surreal even for a vision. And now there was no trace left to prove that it had even happened. The area looked normal, just like it did before she'd run into the fog. Could she have imagined all of this?

"Dana?" Olga ran up to her. "What happened? I lost sight of you after that thick fog rolled in ... Are you all right?"

"I don't know," Dana admitted. "But right now, we need to—"

Another blow shook the ground.

"Oh no! The barrier!" Olga gasped.

They stared in horror as another fiery ball tore through the sky and collided with the barrier.

Cracks of light erupted across the sky as the force dome buckled and shattered into pieces. The falling star plummeted through, straight through toward the royal palace.

Just like in her vision, Dana watched the majestic building fold inward, the sea below it opening like a giant maw to swallow it. But before the palace could completely collapse, a mighty tree rose out of nowhere and wrapped itself around the building, holding it in place.

How had it grown so quickly? Had it transcended here all the way from the future? Dana felt too confused to find an answer. For the first time in known history, a scarlet vision had been averted—and that gave them all hope.

"The prayer tree you planted," Olga said. "It's protecting the palace ... Still, if another falling star should arrive, the capital is in no condition to withstand it."

"I think it's over." Dana paused. "But ... " She thought back to her vision. "What I saw ... " A crimson flash, an exploding building. She gasped in pain. "Not again ... I can't ... save them?"

"Dana?"

A searing pain pierced Dana's shoulder. She yelped.

"What's wrong?" Olga darted forward and knelt beside her. "Dana! What's happening to you?"

"My arm . . . It burns!"

"And so it begins," a new voice said. "Selection and Rejection."

A veiled figure materialized in front of them.

Hooded and gloved, the newcomer was wrapped in a long black robe, covered by a silvery gossamer mantle that glimmered as it moved. A large amulet on a long chain—a circle with a depiction of a tree inside—hung down the front.

"Who are you?" Olga demanded.

The newcomer ignored her. "Dana Iclucia." The voice coming from beneath the veil was genderless, devoid of any expression— as if it were an automaton speaking, not a person. Yet Dana could sense this wasn't the case. The strange figure breathed with emotion, knowledge . . . anguish. This wasn't how this person normally spoke. Dana wasn't sure what gave her this impression, but she felt certain of it.

"Venture west of the capital," the figure said. "To the forbidden Valley of Kings."

Olga stepped forward, shielding Dana protectively. "I'll ask you once more. Who in the world are you?"

Again, the person ignored her, as if she weren't there. "In the depths of the tomb rests the true purpose of the Great Tree, unknown to even the chosen Maidens."

"What?" Dana blinked. The Valley of Kings? The tomb? That place was off limits to everyone except the royal family—even to the Maiden. How could this person—

A glimmer enfolded the figure. And just like that, it was gone.

RUNAWAY

Contrary to the usual trend, Adol wasn't the last one to wake up this morning. As he sat up in his hammock, he saw Hummel and Sahad sitting in their beds with dazed looks.

"Did ya see it, too, Adol?" Sahad said. "Th-that was Dana's . . ." He glanced at Hummel, who nodded.

"Did we all have the same dream?" Adol asked in disbelief.

"Yeah," Sahad confirmed. "At least us here did. Not a dream, I think—it was just like that time, with the crystal, when Dana—"

"Adol!" Laxia ran in and stopped, panting. "It's Dana. She's gone."

Adol leapt up from his bed, grabbed his sword, and rushed out of the room.

The entire village searched everywhere but could find no trace of Dana. Her pack was gone too. She must have gotten up earlier than everyone else and left while they were still sleeping.

Thinking of last night, Adol felt miserable. They hadn't had a chance to finish their conversation. The dream they all shared must have restored more of her memories—and she'd left to search for answers alone, because Adol hadn't had the time to convince her last night that he was part of it too. Was he only fooling himself when he imagined the unbreakable bond they had?

It turned out that everyone in the village had dreamed the same dream, so the conversation at the fireside over breakfast naturally revolved around it.

"So the kingdom of Eternia was destroyed by falling meteors," Euron said.

Laxia looked up thoughtfully. "I wonder though. Even after the meteors fell, Dana and the others were still alive. What happened afterwards?"

"Did you manage to talk to her last night, Adol?" Dogi said. "What did she tell you?"

Adol swallowed. Dogi didn't exactly imply that he had messed things up, but he felt this way anyway. "She was...worried." He could find no better way to put it. Worried about her fate, the reasons she was here. Adol had been so consumed by his desire to keep her by his side. Why couldn't he have done a better job of persuading her that they were in this together?

"I felt it too," Laxia said. "She watched us celebrating our victory last night, while her problems continue unresolved."

"Well, I don't think Dana's the type to hold that against us," Euron said.

"Of course she's not," Thanatos agreed. "Still, the fact that she left...I think we've been taking her for granted, ignoring how complicated her past is. We have to help her find the closure she needs."

"Assuming we can find her," Hummel said. "With the way she knows this island, with her ability to warp—" He broke off.

"Maybe Dana left to see that robed person?" Ricotta suggested.

Laxia shook her head. "That happened so long ago. I doubt that person is still around."

Sahad clicked his fingers. "What was that place she was headed to? Some forbidden valley or such, was it?"

"Valley of Kings," Hummel said. "Any idea where it is, Adol?"

"West of the capital." Adol wouldn't have had an answer just a minute ago, but he suddenly felt certain, as if he'd known it all along. "It's a mountain valley where the Eternians buried their kings. Off limits to everyone except the members of the royal household...Of course, in our time those restrictions probably don't apply."

"Probably not," Thanatos agreed. "But physical restrictions can be just as powerful. As I recall, the bridge leading west out of the capital is collapsed. That leaves just one possible route, through the Mountain Gate at the Temple of the Great Tree."

"Protected by an impassable wall and a gate sealed with Essence," Hummel reminded.

"Not if Dana already opened it," Laxia said.

Adol nodded. If Dana had indeed unsealed the gate to head that way, she wouldn't waste time and Essence to seal it again. They would be able to follow her. She couldn't have gone too far. Hope quivered in his heart as he strapped on his gear.

Would they be able to convince her to rejoin them?

Adol was determined to do everything in his power to try.

The Mountain Gate's west entrance stood ajar, admitting them to the city overlook followed by a few descending stairwells that led them out to the road. To their north, the ruins of Eternia lay open all the way to the sea, with Baja Tower leaning in the distance. The road wound down along a crest, with steep drops on both sides, gradually descending into the jungle.

It took them about two hours to reach the tree shade. The air here was infused with moisture, carrying smells of decaying plants, flowers, and mud. They skirted around a deep murky pond that looked to be just the right kind to house some nasty monsters, and followed the muddy ground deeper into the jungle.

A blue Essence crystal greeted them in the clearing ahead—a mark, suggesting that at some point in Eternian history this had been an important place. Beyond it, a tall pile of moss-covered rocks blocked off the way into a narrow canyon—the only way forward.

"We should look for tracks," Hummel said. "Anyone passing through here is bound to leave footprints in this mud."

"Unless they're trying not to be followed," Adol corrected. The area had plenty of rocks and fallen tree trunks that could help an experienced traveler avoid leaving tracks on the muddy ground.

He looked around. The pile of boulders they were facing was wedged firmly between the rising rock cliffs, decisively blocking any possibility of proceeding. Superimposing the geography of this place onto his memories of Eternia told him this was the only way toward the Valley of Kings—which meant that Dana had to have been stopped by this obstacle too. Did that mean she was still around here somewhere? Or had she already warped away to another area of the island? They scouted around, but failed to find any clues.

"I don't understand," Ricotta said as they gathered back at the crystal. "I thought Dana was part of our family. She was going to leave the island with us, right?" She looked at Adol.

"It's complicated." Adol averted his gaze. If only he could have talked to Dana sooner. If only he had expressed himself clearer and hadn't acted like such an idiot last night.

"She *said* she was my big sister." Ricotta seemed near tears.

Laxia put a comforting hand on her shoulder. "She is. But she's dealing with a lot. Her world has perished. All her people are gone. And she doesn't even remember what happened. It must feel terrible not to know. We need to do our best to help her find the answers she seeks. Maybe then—"

"Then she will come with us?" Ricotta brightened.

"I'm sorry, Ricotta. That would be difficult for me."

Dana.

Adol lifted his head. His heart skipped a beat.

She was standing on top of the rock barricade. In the deep forest shadows, she seemed to glow. Or maybe it was the relief of seeing her again that had created the impression.

"Dana!" Ricotta shouted.

Dana gave her a brief smile, then ran her eyes around the group. "What are you all doing here?"

"Tryin' to find ye, duh," Sahad grumbled. "What does it look like?"

"You ... came for me?" She seemed surprised.

Of course we did. "We—" Adol began, but Ricotta cut him off.

"Why did you run away, Dana? Why can't you leave the island with us? Do you hate us?"

"Hate?" Dana's expression softened. "Of course not." Again, her eyes swept over Adol, leaving him with a feeling that whoever she was addressing at the moment, she was really talking to him.

"You've been such a help to us, Dana," Laxia said. "Now it's our turn to repay you. We want to help you regain your memories."

Dana's gaze became distant again. "Thank you. But this is something I need to do on my own."

Hummel crossed his arms over his chest. "You don't have to be acting so stubborn."

"Hummel!" Laxia protested. "How could you—"

Dana shook her head. "He's right. I'm acting stubborn. But I have a reason for it. I had a scarlet vision."

"What?" Adol blinked.

She stepped closer to the edge of the rock pile, looking down onto the group.

"The inevitability of the events I foresee varies depending on their hue. A scarlet vision shows events that will come to pass, that cannot be avoided."

"Then ..." Laxia began.

"Yes." Dana nodded. "I had a scarlet vision of the future, after we defeated the Oceanus. And that vision told me I couldn't be with you. One way or another, we will part ways. It's destined this way. I want to accept this destiny with a smile and be true to myself when I bid you all farewell. So don't worry about me. The sooner you get off this island, the better."

Adol shook his head. "Your scarlet visions don't matter."

"Don't *matter*?" Dana stared at him. "These events cannot be altered through sheer force of will. If that were possible, my people would not have—" Her voice cut off.

"You were able to do it once," Adol said. "The tree you planted saved the royal palace. This *proves* scarlet visions can be altered."

"I was able to do it once," she admitted. "But I still don't fully understand how."

"I think I do," Adol said quietly. "You did it because you resolved to. And you can do it again. If we act together, we can avert your vision and set things right. And even if we fail, this doesn't mean we should just play along and help the vision fulfill itself, do we?"

She hesitated.

"Adol's right," Sahad joined in. "Even if yer vision's true, so what? One way or another, we'll part ways, is that what ye saw? Well, I have news for you. Any one o' us could say that. Once we get off o' this island, we're all gonna part ways an' go back to the lives we had before we met. But we're still gonna be family. We will still cherish the good times we had. At least that's what we're all thinking, deep down at the bottom of our hearts. An' I think you're thinkin' the same thing too, Dana."

"Yes, but... My circumstances are different from yours."

"No, they're not," Adol said.

"How could you—"

He shook his head. "We're all strangers who found ourselves cast away on this island. But despite our differing origins and stations, we banded together for the sake of survival. Yes, your circumstances may differ more than others', Dana, but you're a still castaway like the rest of us."

Sahad laughed "Gah-haha! Couldn't have said it better myself! You're part o' this crew, through thick an' thin."

Dana's gaze wavered.

"Why don't you come down?" Adol said.

She slid to the edge of the rock pile and jumped off, landing next to him.

The relief of getting her back, was overwhelming. Adol had always admired her, but only by losing her and then finding her again did he realize how much she had become a part of him.

A pulsing sound drew their attention, a high note ringing just at the edge of hearing.

The crystal.

Lifeless just moments ago, it now radiated waves of light, its surface rippling, as if made of water.

Dana's face dawned with understanding. "That veiled figure told me to go to the Valley of Kings, just up ahead. The way is blocked, but this crystal is our next clue." She held out her palms toward the crystal.

The glow enfolded her, then spread around to engulf the whole group. The world faded away.

BENEATH THE SULLEN CLOUDS

"Hey!" a man pleaded. "Let us through! Please!"

The guard blocking his way ran an indifferent gaze over the man's pack beast pulling a cart piled high with household goods, and a woman walking by his side. The sky over Aegias was covered with clouds, snow drifting down in a thin but steady curtain. It felt so cold. Dana didn't remember it ever being so cold before.

"Where do you think you're going with all that stuff?" the guard said.

"Where?" The man scoffed. "Anywhere but here."

"We haven't seen the sun in days," the woman joined in. "And the earthquakes and volcanic eruptions have yet to stop. We can't live like this anymore. We need to go somewhere safe."

"Just let us pass," the man insisted. "You have no right to stop us."

The soldier shifted from foot to foot. Even from this distance, it was clear to Dana that he and his fellow guards were just as scared as the fleeing family. Probably more, given their job to maintain order in the face of a disaster. Why had Sarai restricted citizens from leaving?

Beside her, Olga craned her neck. "The number of residents attempting to evacuate the capital keeps rising."

"You can't blame them," Dana said.

"Perhaps," Olga conceded. "But surely they must realize there's nowhere to go. The impact of the falling stars has caused a chain reaction of other calamities all over the kingdom, and beyond. All the dust and smoke blanketing the sky are causing abnormal weather. I understand the panic, but still, we need to think rationally." She frowned, watching the family and their cart retreating down the road.

Whatever they had done to convince the guard, Dana was glad they had finally been allowed through. Even though Olga was right about there being no safe places anymore, people still should have the right to make their own decisions.

"Are you really going to the Valley of Kings?" Olga asked.

"Yes, I am."

"You should talk to Sarai. The place is heavily guarded. She could—"

Dana shook her head. "I haven't seen Sarai since the palace was struck. Assuming she's all right, she must be staying away for a reason. I'm sure she's overwhelmed."

"But she—"

"There's no time, Olga. Adol should be heading there now. And . . . my future self has asked me to do this."

"I see."

They resumed their walk toward the stone highway leading out of the city. Low gray clouds swirled ominously overhead. White flakes circled down, melting as they touched the ground.

"The temperatures keep dropping," Olga said. "Is this because the sun is being blocked off?"

Always so rational, Olga. Always looking for a natural explanation. Dana looked at her friend fondly. Where would they all be without Olga's level head?

"I better hurry," she said.

Olga turned and met Dana's gaze. "It pains me to say this, but if the Valley of Kings holds some secret about the Great Tree, then it's possible that Sarai, as a member of the royal family, has known that secret all along."

"Yes, I know." Dana swallowed. "That's another reason I haven't spoken to Sarai. She might try to stop me. I must see for myself what's hidden out there."

"Maybe I should go with you."

Dana shook her head. "Not a good idea. The people will panic if they learn that the Maiden and the High Priestess are both missing."

"In that case," Olga said. "Please be careful."

"I will." Dana reached over and patted her friend's shoulder, then turned and strode away.

Down the road leading out of the city, two citizens stood talking. As Dana approached, she caught a piece of their conversation that froze her in her tracks.

"Did you hear?" one of the men said. "They still haven't found Chief Dran."

The other man sighed. "He was last seen protecting the women and children."

"I guess we can assume he didn't make it."

Dana's heart quivered. Not Chief Dran. The loss would be unbearable.

"On top of that," the first man continued, "the Queen hasn't shown herself since the day all of this started. Damn it, what the hell is happening to this country?"

Inadvertently, the memory of the falling star hitting the royal palace floated up in Dana's memory. *Sarai.* She had to be alive, somewhere in the ruins. After all, someone had been giving orders on her behalf.

The two men paid her no notice, so after a moment she moved on.

The air ahead wavered, emitting a mysterious glow. Another trapped spirit? She reached out with her Essence to release the disturbance.

A reddish glowing ball popped into existence.

"I thought I'd never get out," it said, bobbing uncertainly in place. "But where am I?"

Dana stepped closer. "Spirit, do you know anything about what's going on? What's happening to Eternia?"

"Oh." The spirit paused. "You must be the Maiden of the Great Tree or some such. Sorry, didn't notice you there. I am Orvis, Spirit of White Nights. I reside in the southernmost mountains."

Dana looked at him curiously. This spirit talked differently from the others. Like Amy, the Spirit of Possessions, his speech was more ordinary and less archaic.

"My name is Dana," she said. "The southernmost mountains...I think I know what you're talking about. That huge mountain range at the edge of the continent, far south from my homeland. But then, why are you here?"

"I haven't the foggiest," Orvis confessed. "A great commotion occurred in the mountains, and one by one, my kin began to disappear.

I was powerless to stop it. All I could do was watch. Before I knew it, I was here. Alone. I'm scared just talking about it. What's happening to us?"

Dana only shook her head. The spirits fed off Essence. If they started disappearing, did it mean the world's Essence was coming to an end?

"I apologize," Orvis said. "I forgot to thank you. I don't have much power left, but I would like you to have it. The blessings of my birthplace—the Great Mountain beneath the southern sky."

Dana felt the tingling sensation that was becoming familiar by now. For a moment, she felt stronger, more grounded. The spirits were granting her strength. But would it be enough to set things right?

"Thank you, Orvis," she said.

"And now, I must go," Orvis said. "I would like to find the rest of my kin, while I still have my wits about me. Safe travels, Maiden." He floated away.

A vision of the Sanctuary Crypt's door opening formed in her mind. By now, Dana had a fairly good idea what this meant. Every time she committed a good deed—released a spirit, or helped someone, her virtue increased. Only the virtuous one could pass through those doors. And now it was time to discover another chamber, to gain another piece of knowledge about the history of Eternia. She knew it would delay her from her quest, but it also might provide some vital clues about their current predicament. She had to take this chance.

She focused her Essence and transported to the Sanctuary Crypt, where the previously locked door behind the archival monolith opened easily under her touch.

The path led her through a new set of chambers, so cold that she could see her breath in the air. While Essence kept her warm, the desolation reminded her of the events above ground. Was this chamber cold because everything was turning cold in the world? Or had it always been like this?

After a maze of passages and hallways, some of them ending with sheer drops gaping into the dark abyss, she arrived in a small chamber with another archival monolith. She activated it and read:

The Capital's relocation was progressing without delay. The energetic Light King did not shirk a single duty during the transfer. He focused on paving highways to other nations, and other infrastructural endeavors. One day, while the King was deeply focused on making history, a woman came to visit him. A beautiful princess from a provincial nation, who brought with her a letter. Princess Baja was as lovely as a summer peahen and sang more beautifully than an Orsun harp. Her beauty so enchanted the King, that it would come to be chronicled in the Tome of Five Histories. He fulfilled his royal duties while courting the princess in equal measure, before finally deciding he would make her his Queen. The two were wed on the same day that the capital's relocation was completed.

The wise King's marriage was celebrated throughout the entire nation. On the outskirts, a great spire called Baja Tower was erected in honor of their new Queen. The Queen asked that the Tower be dedicated to the research of Essence and medicine, which quickly gathered her much admiration.

She was dedicated to her people, and their well-being was never far from her mind. But she was a frail woman and often confined to her bed due to illness. Because of his Queen's condition, the Light King ordered the construction of a villa near the capital. It was to be built by a beautiful lake in the western region of the kingdom. Unbeknownst to the Light King, this decision would bring about unmitigated disaster.

The record ended here—and of course, the door at the back of the chamber was firmly locked, blocking the way forward. Dana paused, contemplating the information she'd just learned.

Outwardly, the record didn't seem important—just some information about the Light King's personal life: not surprising, even if quite a few historians she knew would be shocked to read this chronicle. But the mention of the villa made her wonder. The lake in the western region of the kingdom had to be where the Valley of Kings was located. There was only one building there.

Why had the villa become a tomb?

And what was this disaster it had brought?

A laugh echoed behind her.

Io?

Dana's eyes widened as she watched the girl step out of the shadows toward her.

Where had she come from? How was it she appeared here each time Dana visited the place? Did she *live* down here? Not possible. Not unless she was a monster, or an automaton left behind to guard the place. Dana dismissed the ridiculous thought. The girl looked so cute and innocent.

"Hi there, Lady," Io said. "It's been a while."

"Io," Dana managed. "I'm glad you're safe."

"Yeah, me too," Io agreed. "Can you believe this horrible disaster?" She narrowed her eyes. "But you knew something, didn't you? About what just happened . . . About what's going to happen. So the real question is, what are you gonna do now?"

Dana heaved a breath. Was this childish blabber, or had Io just revealed a knowledge of Dana's visions? With everything that had happened, she could no longer assume that Io was just a regular girl. She should probably be scared out of her mind—but whatever Io was, Dana could sense no danger emanating from the child. Why not pretend this was a normal conversation and speak her mind?

"Nothing will change," she said.

"Huh?"

"No matter what difficulties await me in the future," Dana said. "I want to help those in need until the very end."

Io looked at her with quiet curiosity. "So you *are* the one."

"What?" Dana blinked. She had no idea where this conversation was going or what to make of it.

"I actually came here to say goodbye," Io said.

"Goodbye?" Another unexpected turn. "Why?"

Io frowned. "Didn't I tell you? I was looking for something. Well, I finally found it."

"Wait." Dana shook her head. Her mind was working too slowly to keep up with the conversation.

"Wait for what?"

"I am not sure. This is so sudden."

"Well," Io said. "Goodbyes usually are. But you gotta promise to see me one more time."

"But—"

Io laughed. "Don't look so surprised. When the time comes, I'll find you. Then you'll learn the rest."

"All right, I'll wait." In the next monolith chamber? Dana knew this decision wasn't up to her.

"Thanks, Lady. See ya!" Io turned around and walked away.

A glow formed around her as she walked. Before she reached the end of the room, she had melted into thin air.

Dana stood for a while looking at the spot where Io had disappeared. She had no idea what this girl was, or what she had been talking about in this enigmatic conversation, but she knew that she wasn't going to find answers until their next meeting—which would be possible only if she managed to become even more virtuous. But before that, she needed to return to the surface and help Adol.

She warped back to the city highway where she'd encountered Orvis earlier today and proceeded onward to the Valley of Kings.

A pair of guards stood flanking the entrance to the next mountain valley. They would stop her if she tried to get through, but she didn't need to. Instead of alerting them, she used her Essence to put them to sleep, then bent down and planted a tiny prayer sapling near the spot.

The Essence crystal glowed nearby. It was time to return to Adol.

THE VALLEY OF KINGS

S ometimes you act in very surprising ways, Dana," Laxia said.

Ricotta laughed. "She's like the main character in a book."

They're talking about the guards. Dana did feel guilty about putting them to sleep like this. She didn't like using her Essence to subdue anyone. She turned toward the newly formed path created by the massive tree she'd just planted in the past.

"Let's keep going," she said. "The Valley of Kings is up ahead."

The path ran through another stretch of the jungle into a maze of rising cliffs with grassy areas in between. Without a defined road to follow in this era, Dana had no idea where to go. All she recalled from her timeline was the historical record she'd just read that mentioned the royal villa built near a lake. They circled the only body of water they could find, a large, murky pond with a curtain of vines hanging over it, but found no signs of any structure.

The sun was already beginning to set when they finally spotted a passage winding between the tall rock cliffs. They followed it into the valley beyond and stopped, gaping.

The ruin spread right in front of them, perfectly positioned in the center of the valley.

The first thing that drew the eye was a giant headless statue crouching over the flat rooftop of the main building, holding stone blades in its many hands. The Warrior was usually depicted with a Saurian head, crested and horned, grinning with a row of monstrous fangs, and even though the statue's entire head was missing, Dana could easily imagine all these features as she faced it.

The building itself, square and low, gaped with the dark opening of a doorway directly below, with the Warrior's stone blades fanning over it. Goddess statues rose on the sides, framing the paved walkway lined by double rows of stone columns partially concealed under the blanket of vines. Sunset peeking through the low clouds painted the scene into a palette of ominous dark reds.

The ruin evoked a mix of fear and awe. Dana felt sure something horrible was lurking beyond the gaping doorway in the tomb's dark depths. A villa turned tomb that held the secret of Eternia's demise. What was it, waiting inside?

"Let's set up camp," Adol said. "It's too late to explore it today."

The rest of the party nodded, throwing down their packs.

They chose a friendlier-looking area on the outskirts of the ruin. With the lush vegetation, there were plenty of materials here to build a tent, and enough dry branches and twigs to start a fire. They cooked a warm meal out of the supplies from their packs and sat around, talking.

"So even Maidens weren't allowed to come here, huh?" Sahad said. "And yet, you came here anyway."

"I believe I did, yes." Dana stared into the fire. She must have come here at some point, in her era. Why couldn't she remember?

"Graves spook the hell outta me," Sahad said. "How could you even think of going here alone?"

"Dana is full of surprises," Laxia said. "For someone who seems so reserved, she often takes a rather . . . bold course of action."

"So you're saying she's reckless." Hummel's lips twitched.

"Hummel!" Laxia snapped.

Dana laughed. "It's all right. Olga used to say that about me too. But I wasn't always like this."

"Really?" Ricotta asked.

"Yes. When I still lived with my family . . . When my mother was still alive . . ."

A memory hit her without warning.

"My sweet girl. You had a vision again?" Mother's voice was so sooth-ing. The night outside was dark, the only light coming from the flickering candle on the bedside table. As she sat on the bed beside Dana, she emanated safety and comfort, scaring the vision away. Dana cuddled up to her, feel-ing Mother's hand under the blanket find her finger and slip a ring over it. A gift? Wasn't she too young to be given jewelry? Her head filled with questions as she traced the elaborate metal carvings, their curves calming, like Mother's touch.

She wanted to bring the ring out and look at it, but the calmness that enfolded her felt so good she didn't want to move just yet. Her mind became so peaceful as she lay cradled in her mother's arms, her vision forgotten, like a bad dream.

"I had this ring made for you," Mother said. "I want you to wear it all the time. Promise me that you'll never take it off."

"Why, Mommy?"

"This ring seals Essence. It will stop your visions from ever bothering you again."

Dana nodded, cuddling up to her as she drifted off to sleep.

"Dana?"

Ricotta's voice brought her back to reality. She swallowed. "Sorry. My mind drifted for a moment."

"I was asking about your family," Ricotta said. "What was your life like, when you were a little girl?"

Dana heaved a breath. "I wasn't exactly a normal child. Ever since I remember, I've had these visions. I had a gift to see things that were going to happen."

"That's amazing," Ricotta said. "I wish I could—"

"No, you don't." The words came out with unnecessary force.

Ricotta looked at her in surprise.

"You see," Dana explained, "more often than not, the future I saw wasn't a happy one. It showed pain. Suffering." She paused. "I wish I'd never seen most of it. When I was still little, I became withdrawn and depressed because of these visions."

Memories carried her as she spoke. Mother and little Dana, forehead to forehead, smiling. She forced the image away.

"My mother could tell something was wrong," she went on. "So she tried to help me by giving me a ring. That ring blocked my connection to Essence and sealed away my power to see visions. After I received it, I was finally able to have a normal childhood, just like the other kids. I never felt safer than I did at that time, surrounded by my parents' love. Then one day . . ." She paused.

"What happened?" Ricotta prompted.

"A fire broke out in the shed while my father and I were away. It took my mother's life. Had I not sealed my powers, I would have foreseen the accident. I would have heard my mother's voice crying for help." No matter how long she lived, she would never stop blaming herself. She'd been so selfish, sealing her power away for the sake of protecting herself, choosing the easy way out. "From that day on, I vowed to use my Essence to serve others, to prevent as much suffering and sadness as I could. I never wore that ring again."

A silence hung heavily over the fire.

"How awful, Dana," Laxia said.

Dana nodded. "I've always felt like I would fade away if I didn't prevent enough suffering. I'd get so scared of it that I acted without thinking sometimes. And then, I just caused more problems for Olga." She swallowed and turned away.

Sahad scratched his head. "That's heavy. I dunno what to say, really."

"It's all in the past now," Dana said. "And here and now, we have a busy day tomorrow. We should all get some rest."

The large entrance hall stretched away into the gloom, its floor littered with stones and debris. Here and there, armed skeletons sprawled on the ground, as if the guards patrolling this place had all died on their posts and remained here all this time. For all Adol knew, this could well be what really happened, even though none of them would probably ever know.

At the far end, a maze of stairways and passages ran out of sight. Adol's head spun as he tried to count them, figuring out where to go. How were they ever going to find their way into the depths of the tomb?

As the party proceeded, they soon discovered that the skeletons weren't merely part of the scenery. They rose and attacked when approached, seemingly intent on preventing any progress into the depths of the compound. Luckily they proved to be poor fighters, easily defeated, but they never died completely—just collapsed to the floor and then rose and attacked again if the part was still in range. But even these skeletons were far less annoying than the Essence-powered auto-shooters stationed at every intersection. They sensed motion, emitting a series of blasts every time the party came into sight. Destroying them seemed impossible, so the best strategy was keeping away.

The path eventually brought them to a large stone chamber with a massive chest resting on a pedestal at the end.

"There must be Essence equipment inside." Dana reached out with her open palms. A click of a lock echoed in response. She reached into the chest and lifted out a hand bell, small but clearly heavy.

"Purifying bell," she said. "So, that's where the royal family kept it."

"Oh?" Sahad lifted his eyebrows. "What does it do?"

"We used to use it during the Requiem Ritual, to purify tainted souls. I believe it can help us defeat the undead that roam this place."

"Oh, nice." Sahad sounded uncertain as he glanced around the chamber. Even with the bell, it was hard to feel safe in a place like this.

The tomb continued deeper underground. With the help of the bell, they were now able to defeat their enemies for good, even the larger automatons that populated the lower levels of the compound. These automatons emitted glowing balls as they fell, which floated over the floor to fill a set of spherical cages hanging in the center of the main hall—an elaborate lock mechanism that responded to Essence, until they gathered enough to trigger the doors leading into a new area.

Adol couldn't stop marveling at the way this part of the building seemed completely intact, as if untouched by the flow of time. The underground chambers looked glum and dreary, but not a single crack marred the elaborate stone carvings, and no rust touched the ancient gear mechanisms setting the doors into motion. As they descended through three more chambers into a larger area beyond, doors slid apart with clockwork precision to open the way.

An Essence crystal glowed near the doorway ahead. They were nearing the heart of this place—one where, Adol hoped, the answers they were seeking lay waiting. Still, as Adol and his friends walked through the doorway into the next chamber, he wasn't prepared for the sight that greeted them inside.

This chamber looked like . . . a garden? An abandoned garden that once must have been magnificent, despite being hidden so deep underground. Terraced arrangements of dry plants cascaded down its sides, coalescing near the central area, where a dead tree rose, stretching its slender branches toward the distant ceiling. Bottomless trenches that must have once held water ran along the walls. Despite the fact that they were deep underground, soft, suffused light filled the chamber, as if somewhere high above it had access to daylight. They stopped at the entrance, gaping.

"I think I may have been here before," Dana said quietly. "I don't recall all the details, but there should be a room farther back. It holds something important."

They cautiously made their way forward. Dry plants rustled under their feet. Amazing how they hadn't disintegrated after all these millennia. As they passed the dead tree in the center of the chamber, Adol couldn't get rid of the feeling that the key to this place's preservation lay within the tree itself.

The next chamber was much smaller and resembled one of the Temple areas, with two staircases on the sides and an altarlike structure in the middle. Except that this altar did not bear the Great Tree symbol. Instead, a giant mural depicting a tree loomed over it, covering the entire back wall.

"Is this the Great Tree of Origins?" Laxia said.

It did look like it—a simplified version, clearly painted very long ago. Adol recognized the massive trunk, composed of intertwining wavy lines, the circular crown that stretched over the top. Sawlike leaves protruding along the edge of the crown were accurate too, but in this depiction their jagged edges made them look a bit like blades, pointing at the ground below.

The artist who had painted this mural didn't lack in skill. Every detail looked deliberate in its placement and execution. He lowered his eyes to the bottom of the mural.

People underneath the tree cowered in terror. Some were kneeling, others running or tumbling down, trapped between a wall of fire on one side and a line of jagged rocks rising from the ground on the other. Not the peaceful image of tranquility Adol had come to associate with the Great Tree, both in his era and in Dana's memories.

"This depiction..." Laxia frowned. "One could interpret it as the Great Tree destroying the world. But it wouldn't make sense, would it?"

The air at the side of the chamber shimmered, and a figure materialized out of thin air beside the wall.

The veiled person they had all seen in Dana's time, the one that had first told her to visit the Valley of Kings.

How was this possible?

Up close, the figure looked even more ominous than in the dream—a head taller than Adol, clad in black from head to toe. A disembodied mechanical voice echoed through the chamber as the person spoke.

"I've been expecting you. I knew you would come here one day."

Dana narrowed her eyes. "You... But how?"

The veiled figure disappeared from the top level and reappeared again right in front of Dana. The rest of the party backed off.

"It's been a long time, Dana Iclucia. It seems you have not yet fully restored your memories. You must have been surprised to see that mural."

"I—"

The figure chuckled bitterly. "How did those texts go? '*The Great Tree of Origins evolved Saurians into Eternians and brought forth prosperity.*' A lie, propagated by a fraction of Eternians to instill reverence for the Great Tree."

"A lie?"

"Yes. The purpose of the evolution fostered by the Great Tree is not to develop a species. Rather, it selects species that can withstand the environmental changes and rejects those that cannot."

"What does that mean?" Sahad demanded.

The figure regarded him for a moment, as if deciding whether he was worthy of an answer. "As the mural depicts, the Great Tree will periodically bring about cataclysmic events. Those who manage to adapt and survive receive its protection. The rest are culled accordingly. This cycle of Selection and Rejection is the true purpose of the Great Tree."

"But why?" Laxia looked appalled.

"It is necessary," the figure said, "to sustain the world's continued existence. We call this culling of life the Lacrimosa."

"The Lacrimosa?"

Tears. The word had the same root—Lacrimosa, an event that brings tears. Was this how the word had originated?

The veiled figure nodded slowly. "Yes. Eternia's extinction was but a single Lacrimosa."

Dana peered into the veiled face. "Assuming you're telling the truth, who are you, and why are you here?"

The figure shrugged. "Who I am is of no consequence. The rest should be obvious, I hope. I am here to observe your current actions, in light of your refusal."

"My ... refusal?"

"I can see you haven't fully remembered. No matter. Today I have only come to greet you. From now on though, I will be watching you. I look forward to witnessing the full extent of your obstinacy." The figure shimmered and disappeared, fading into the semidarkness of the chamber.

"Wait," Dana called out. "I still need to know ... "

"They're gone," Hummel said.

Sahad spread his hands. "The Great Tree destroyed Eternia? That's gotta be a lie."

Dana turned toward them. Her eyes looked glassy, her expression reminding Adol of last night, when she'd talked about what happened to her mother.

"We're not in a position to reliably assert that," she said. "There is so much we still don't know. Perhaps the best thing to do right now is reexamine the situation."

"Dana—" Ricotta began.

Dana shook her head. "We should leave this place for now. Let's warp back to the village."

VISTA RIDGE

The castaways were finishing dinner when Adol and the others returned to the village, but there was still plenty of soup in the pot to share around, along with herbal tea and delicious honey cakes Miralda had whipped up from some local root, powdered into flour. They told their story as they ate, with everyone listening intently.

"A mural in the Valley of Kings," Thanatos said. "To think that the true purpose of the Great Tree . . . " He paused.

"Yeah," Sahad agreed. "It sounds like a spooky fairy tale. No, even crazier than that. I dunno what to make of it, really."

"And what about that robed individual?" Dogi joined in. "I thought this person was from the past. Does that mean other Eternians survived besides Dana?"

"I have no idea," Dana said.

Ever since they'd entered the dried-up garden in the Valley of Kings, she seemed detached, as if her mind wasn't entirely in the present. Adol longed to ask her more about what she remembered. But there was never a good moment for it.

"So what do we do now?" Sahad asked.

Everyone looked at Adol, as if this decision were up to him.

"We need to gather more information," he said. "Maybe in the parts of the island that are still unexplored." He took out his map with newly sketched areas and spread it on the ground for everyone to see. "Here." He pointed to the area south of the one they'd just visited. "This ridge runs above the marshes we've just traveled through. It might have another ancient ruin that holds the next piece of a puzzle."

Euron nodded. "True."

"I don't know about y'all," Sahad said, "but I feel wasted. Time for a good night's sleep. We can explore that ridge tomorrow." He rose and walked off in the direction of the lodge.

"I should turn in too," Dogi said. "There's a lot we need to do at the dock. We plan to have an early start."

As they warped back to the marshes that led up to the Valley of Kings, Laxia couldn't help feeling resentful. She hated the place. The heat and humidity alone made the task of ripping through the thick jungle undergrowth feel almost unbearable. But there were also the giant mosquitoes that swarmed around, as if completely unafraid of people—not to mention the mud that covered her outfit in no time, making her look like one of the swamp newts that roamed in the jungle on the other side of the island. Of course, she'd long given up the idea of trying to look like a proper lady, but she strived to maintain at least the minimum standards.

After climbing some vines, they finally ascended above the jungle. Fresh wind swept her face. She paused, enjoying the view above the tree crowns, all the way to the Aegias ruins.

The path became steeper as it climbed to the top of the hill and into a small ruin that must have been an Eternia-age villa. There didn't seem to be enough of the building left to hold any secrets, but they explored it anyway, tracing the old foundation toward a broken stone wall at the back that stood to about a man's height, gaping with a hole that led into a small herb garden.

Laxia went through the gap in the wall first, jarring to a halt as she saw a man standing among the ruins.

Franz.

Her breath caught.

She had been picturing this moment for such a long time, ever since she'd convinced herself that there was absolutely no way he could possibly perish in the shipwreck—and right up to the time when she'd pretty much given up hope. In these visions, she'd imagined him wearing his impeccable butler suit, holding a cup of tea in his hands. It was ridiculous, of course, to imagine a castaway from a shipwreck in this manner, but...

That was exactly how she saw him now.

She blinked.

This had to be a figment of her imagination. Blame it on heat and humidity that were making her see things. But even as these thoughts swept through her head, her feet continued to carry her toward him.

Franz. Even when she reached him and stopped right in front of him, even after she finally convinced herself that he just might be real, her lips seemed unable to form the word. Or was it the lump in her throat that prevented her from talking, swelling until it became painful?

He looked unharmed, with no visible signs of hardship from surviving for two months all alone. Perhaps he grew just a touch thinner and more muscular, his face more tanned than before. His hair looked different too—longer, draping down his neck in a neat curtain, as if he had just combed it. She was sure she looked like a fright next to him, muddy and sweaty, her hair a mess. Strange how the thought didn't bother her at all.

"Lady Laxia." His voice trailed to a whisper, as if he also were having trouble speaking.

"*Franz.*" She wanted to say so much. How she'd missed him. How miserable her life had been when she'd thought he was lost. How glad she was to find him alive. How annoying he had been for following her on an adventure that was meant for her alone. How grateful she felt to him for doing that. Ever since she was a little girl, Franz had always been around, growing up in the same household, playing the same games. But only now that she'd almost lost him and then found him again did she realize how much he meant to her.

A swirl of emotions in his gaze told her he felt the same way. The thought made her knees dangerously wobbly. He was looking at her as if everything around them was utterly unimportant, as if she were the only person in the world.

Tears filled her eyes. She sniffled and drew herself up. This wouldn't do for Lady Laxia von Roswell. Wouldn't do at all.

"You had me worried, Franz," she said. "How could you get yourself lost like that?"

His smile washed over her like a breath of warm wind. "It was very careless of me, my lady. I am so very sorry." He wasn't looking remorseful at all. The tenderness in his gaze sent another lump into her throat.

"You—you—" She sniffled again, wiping her cheek with the back of her hand. She was probably smudging mud all over her face, but for once, she didn't care. "You tried to save me on the *Lombardia* and ended up falling overboard. How could you act so irresponsibly?" Oh, drat. This wasn't what she'd wanted to say, not at all. She felt angry at herself.

He bowed. "It was misguided on my part, my lady. I should have done a better job. You see, I know how to swim—unlike you—so I was never in any danger of drowning. You, on the other hand..."

"I..." Gosh, why was she being so tongue-tied? All these weeks she'd been imagining this conversation, thinking how she would scold him for disobeying her orders like any proper lady should. But none of those words came to mind now. "You risked your life for me, Franz...It was my fault you were on the *Lombardia* in the first place. I—I'm so sorry my stubbornness put you in danger."

Franz cocked an eyebrow. "Did you just call yourself stubborn and apologize to me?"

"Don't push it."

"Duly noted, my lady." His smile faded. "There hasn't been a day since the shipwreck when I wasn't hating myself for failing you so badly. Lord Roswell tasked me with a duty to protect you, and I—"

"It wasn't your fault that I fell overboard. The ship was sinking, for heaven's sake!"

He shook his head. "Even on a sinking ship, it was my job as your loyal servant to stay by your side. I made you feel so resentful, you kept away from me. If I had been near you when you fell—"

She met his gaze. There was probably truth in it. If they'd fallen overboard together, they wouldn't have spent all this time on opposite sides of the island feeling guilty and mourning each other's deaths. As for the blame—

"I've been an idiot, Franz," she said.

He measured her with his gaze, and once again she felt warmth spreading over her.

"You've changed," he said softly.

She felt a blush creep into her cheeks. If they continued like this, she was definitely going to do something inappropriate—like throw herself into his arms, an utterly unacceptable behavior for a lady.

"Like I said, don't push it." She lowered her eyes to the teacup in his hands. "What are you doing with this silly teacup, anyway?"

He looked at the teacup blankly, as if just remembering he was holding it.

"Silly indeed," he agreed. "It's much too large. The tea would turn cold before I even finished filling it." His gaze trailed past her to the group standing at the side of the ruin.

Gosh, how had Laxia managed to forget all about her companions? Only now did she realize that all this time a conversation had been going on behind her.

"...another survivor," Sahad was saying. "Did he say he was her servant or somethin'?"

"I guess," Ricotta replied. "But they act like they're really close friends."

"His clothing looks impeccable for someone who washed ashore and spent so much time in the wilderness," Dana observed.

"Plus, he's been wandering the northern region of the island all by himself," Hummel added. "He must be very skilled to do that."

Skilled. That, he was. And many more things. When Franz got settled, Laxia fully intended to ask him all about it. For now, though, seeing him alive and unharmed was a relief so big that she was having serious trouble containing it. Perhaps it would be best if she finally pulled herself together and started acting in accordance with her station.

"Franz," she snapped. "You will return with us to Castaway Village at once."

"Yes, my lady." Did his lips twitch when he said it? She couldn't tell for sure.

"Gather your belongings, if you have any."

"Right away, my lady."

"You'll be a big help at Castaway Village," Ricotta said. "Welcome aboard!"

Franz turned to her. "You honor me. For my mistress, I will gladly offer my services to your village." He bowed.

For my mistress. Not just empty words, not in Franz's case. Everyone stranded here would help each other out, of course, but Laxia knew that he truly meant it when he said he would be helping the village just for her. She felt as if a gaping hole in her soul had been filled up, leaving her balanced and content like never before.

Close friends, Ricotta had called them. Yes, they were. The best friends in the world. She didn't want to spend another day without him, ever again. Ever since they were children, she'd always thought it inappropriate to think this way, but now, after everything that had happened, she had no trouble admitting it to anyone.

Even to Franz.

Franz proved to be extremely capable, good at almost any task. Adol marveled at how this man managed to stay in the background while everything around him clicked magically into place, whether it involved cooking, cleaning, or shipbuilding. It seemed as if everyone in the village had become more competent and efficient with Franz around.

It was also curious how Franz changed when Laxia was in sight—from a quiet but powerful man that could calmly challenge even such alpha personalities as Euron, to a dazed youth who couldn't take his eyes off her. He treated her words so reverently, as if each was a precious gift—even when she snapped at him, which tended to happen a lot. Knowing Laxia well by now, Adol suspected that this was her way of dealing with her feelings for him. In time, they were going to figure it out, or so he hoped.

That morning, Adol had just finished his breakfast and was collecting dishes, when Franz approached him from the direction of the lodge.

"Adol. May I have a moment of your time?"

"Sure." Adol looked at him curiously. Despite the calm façade, he had a feeling the man was nervous. Was something going on?

"I understand that you call yourself an adventurer," Franz said.

It didn't seem like a question, nor did the statement come through as an entirely friendly one. Inadvertently, Adol remembered how Laxia had referred to this occupation when they first met—with distaste, as if calling yourself an adventurer was a bad thing.

"I still have a lot to learn," he admitted.

Franz appeared to hesitate. "I have a favor to ask. I recently discovered tracks not far from the village that appear to have been left by a Primordial. The creature may still be in the vicinity. However, I see no need to involve the rest of the village. Will you join me in tracking down this beast?"

Adol frowned. A Primordial so close to the camp was alarming. An investigation was a good idea—and he did agree that there was no need to alarm the whole village just yet. But why had Franz called it a favor? And why had he approached Adol so personally, as if this was a secret meant only for the two of them?

"All right," he said.

Franz's gaze briefly trailed away to where Laxia stood talking to

Miralda. "Naturally, I expect you to fight the Primordial should we find it. I'm not much of a swordsman. But as I heard it, you are."

A challenge, Adol decided. Or rather, a test. Was Franz trying to determine if Adol could be trusted with Laxia's safety?

Under ordinary circumstances, he may have refused. But tracking Primordials in the vicinity of the village was important. After they'd defeated the Oceanus, these beasts were among the very few forces on this island capable of thwarting their escape plans, not to mention dealing serious damage if they chose to descend on the village in force.

Besides, even if fighting Primordials was only an excuse for arranging a conversation alone, they probably needed to have it sooner or later. Even though Franz never said anything, it didn't escape Adol how he looked at any man who came into Laxia's vicinity. It was a good idea to clear the air.

"Lead the way," Adol said.

Franz nodded solemnly, then turned and walked out of the camp.

They made their way across the stream toward the bayside beach, where Franz stopped and surveyed the ground carefully.

"I saw the tracks around here," he said.

Adol looked. By now, he half-expected Franz had made it up, but here they were—three-toed footprints of a mid-sized bipedal Primordial, joined by two other similar tracks that led off across the beach.

Franz frowned. "I only observed one set of tracks when I first came here. I hope—"

A roar interrupted his words. Three Primordials stepped out of the rocks ahead and faced them.

Franz swallowed. "Please forgive me. I fear I may have bitten off more than we can chew."

"No problem," Adol said. "The two of us can handle them all."

Franz drew a long knife from a sheath at his back. Oh, so he did have a weapon after all. Adol had no time to wonder. They stood back-to-back as they readied for the attack.

Franz fought well. Adol had enough to handle on his side, but he thought he recognized some of the moves. Franz and Laxia must have had the same teacher, and he suspected the butler had been practicing in his spare time. While Franz's blade wasn't infused with orichalcum, he acted in concert with Adol, engaging the beasts and delivering them to Adol's sword. Perfect teamwork. With the right weapon, Franz could be invaluable on the exploration team.

It took no time before the lead beast reared, emitting a wail Adol had learned to recognize as defeat. The three Primordials turned and hobbled away before the humans could finish them off, leaving Adol and Franz standing over the bloodstained sand.

Franz took a moment to steady his breath, then wiped his blade and put it away.

"Well done," Adol said.

Franz shook his head. "Please accept my apologies."

"You really don't need to apologize. Your bladework was superb."

"Not that. I shouldn't have lured you here like this. I put your life in danger because of an error of judgment."

"You're being too hard on yourself," Adol said. "We've all run into Primordial traps. These beasts are more intelligent than we realize."

"You are most kind."

"Look," Adol said. "We're all equals here. Besides, I'm not even a noble in the first place. You don't have to talk to me like that."

Franz's gaze wavered. "Acknowledged. The truth then?"

"Please."

"You and Mistress Laxia—"

"Are friends," Adol finished. "She was the first castaway I found. During this time, she became like a sister to me. And if you really want to know, the thing that preoccupied her the most all this time was finding you. She rarely spoke about it, but it was easy enough to tell."

Franz looked at him in wonder. Dear gods, was this man, so smart and capable at nearly everything he did, really that blind?

"Now that we found you," Adol went on, "she's changed. She looks so happy."

"Happy?" For a moment, Franz's face became dreamy.

"Yes, happy. How could you possibly not see it?"

"Perhaps," Franz said quietly, "it's because I have no reference point. I wasn't here all this time."

Adol sighed. "In that case, you'd better take my word for it. You can ask anyone, by the way. But if you really want to know how she feels, you should ask her."

Franz lowered his eyes, then raised them again to meet Adol's gaze. "I'm afraid I must ask you for another favor. Please don't reveal the details of this incident to Mistress Laxia."

"Why not?" Adol felt genuinely curious.

Franz averted his gaze. "Lord Roswell gave me one final order before his departure. He released me from my duty to serve him, so that I could serve his family from that day on. In his honor, I have kept a watchful eye on Mistress Laxia over the years. If she learns that I..." He paused.

That you care for her so much? She would be beside herself with joy. But Adol didn't say it. Franz and Laxia had to find their own way to resolve their feelings for each other.

"My lips are sealed," Adol assured him. "But if you ask me, the two of you really need to have a conversation."

Franz didn't respond. He looked thoughtful as they washed in the nearby stream before heading back to camp. The man took an inordinate amount of time to straighten his clothes and hair, until he looked as impeccable as before. Almost. On a deserted island, no one would mind a few tears in his shirt, ripped by the beasts' claws, or a long scratch on his arm, which he had hidden carefully beneath his sleeve after applying some herbs to stop the bleeding. Adol was much less careful about his own appearance, but he had to admit that this experience, and Franz's request to keep it a secret, made the two men feel more bonded. In this one short encounter, he had learned more about Franz than during the last few days.

"Adol! Franz!" Laxia rushed toward them as soon as they entered the camp. "Where have you been? I was worried about you."

Franz bowed from the waist—a butler's bow. It looked so odd here in the wilderness.

"My apologies, Lady Laxia," he said. "Our business took longer to resolve than anticipated."

Laxia narrowed her eyes. "You don't sound like you're about to tell me what exactly is going on. What have you two been up to?"

Adol held a pause, noting the way Franz's lowered eyes darted to him briefly. Laxia must have noticed it too. She stepped up to Adol.

"Look at you, Adol. You're covered in dirt, and your collar is bent out of place...My word. What on Earth did you get yourself into?"

With a huff, she began to primp Adol's clothes. Franz stood beside them, eyes fixed on the ground. Adol couldn't escape a feeling that this was all a show on Laxia's part, made entirely for Franz's benefit. He felt uncomfortable.

After taking her time with Adol, Laxia finally turned to Franz, who immediately pulled up straight, staring ahead.

"That goes for you too, Franz," she said. "Your shirt is ripped.

And...Hey! Are you listening?"

Franz forced a smile. "Yes, m'lady. And might I say, you two make the ideal image of a devoted husband and wife."

Color rushed into Laxia's cheeks. "Ah...Wh-what...Um... Franz! How dare you say something so...so...unnecessary!"

Adol kept his eyes firmly ahead. Why did people insist on tormenting each other? He didn't like the idea of being an instrument of such torment, but he didn't want to interfere. These two would just have to figure it out on their own.

Later in the day, Adol found Franz standing at the base of the watchtower, looking into the distance. He stopped beside the man. For a moment, they just stood there in silence.

"Thank you, Adol," Franz said. "From now on, I will redouble my efforts to handle any issues by myself. And," he added quietly, "do take care of my lady."

"I will," Adol said. "Her, and everyone else here. But you should remember what I said."

Franz didn't reply at once. His eyes trailed past Adol to the sea view. The wind was picking up, the surface of the water rolling with angry white crests that foreshadowed an upcoming storm. If they were at sea, they would be working double shifts right now, preparing for the worst. But here in Castaway Village, they were well protected from almost any weather. When had this place started feeling so much like home?

"I wanted to ask you a question," Franz said. "Do you believe we will survive this experience?"

"Yes, I do," Adol said.

Franz let out a short laugh. "I am relieved to hear you say that so confidently. But..."

"What?"

Franz hesitated. "I will lay down my life, if needed, to keep her safe. If the worst happens to me, please look after Mistress Laxia in my stead."

"In your stead?" Adol turned to him again. "You'd better not get yourself killed. There could never be anyone to replace you, Franz."

Franz shook his head. "You exaggerate. She is used to me being around, yes. Eighteen years ago, Lord and Lady Roswell took me in after my parents were killed in a war. They treated me like family, but you see, I'm not a noble. Serving House Roswell as a butler is the highest honor a man like me could achieve. As far as my life is concerned, I live only to serve them. But...I believe the time will soon come when Mistress Laxia no longer requires my service. She has grown wiser, thanks to you. I believe her pride and determination will prove to be invaluable when she fulfills her destiny to restore House Roswell to its former glory."

"You have a duty to see that through too," Adol said.

Franz's lips twitched. "Duly noted. I do. But from observing everything that's going on, it may not be me that she needs."

"Not you?"

Franz laughed. "I see through your feigned ignorance. You are so much like Lord Roswell."

Adol shook his head. "Have you been listening? She cares about you. Not just as a butler."

"Oh, no. You are surely mistaken."

"Not in this case." Adol held his gaze. "And there's something else I wanted to say. Here on this island, boundaries between nobles and commoners don't exist anymore. We're all one family. Some of us became like brothers and sisters. That's how I will always feel about Laxia. Acting as a brother, I will tell you again. You're special to her. There will never be anyone like you."

Franz held a pause.

"You don't have to be a butler all your life," Adol went on. "Now that her father's gone, she needs you, more than ever. But even if her father is found, this won't change anything. You and she are bonded. I wanted to make sure you know that."

He didn't wait for a response as he turned and walked away.

THE FOG

The next morning, Adol and Sahad ventured out to a more distant beach in search of a good fishing spot. It had become a tradition for the two of them to have a swim before breakfast and bring some fresh catch to roast on skewers over the fire. But this time, as they entered the area they hadn't visited for a while, they found a new type of wreckage stuck in the sand.

A small rowing boat.

"Does it look familiar to you?" Sahad asked.

Adol walked around it. Of course he recognized it. Some of these chip marks on the hull were probably his own handiwork, as Dogi was teaching him to hand-carve the driftwood they recovered. This was the boat that Sir Carlan had taken on his fatal escape attempt. It must have drifted all the way here after the incident. Had it really been that long since they'd come to this particular beach?

"That's our boat," Adol confirmed.

"Well, it would be a waste just to leave it here," Sahad said. "Can we fix it up?"

"We probably could," Adol said. "But now that our ship's almost finished, what use would it be?"

Sahad shrugged. "We haven't explored every spot yet. Fer instance, that islet over there." He pointed at the lone rock crowned by a giant tree rising in the middle of the bay.

Adol looked too. It seemed unlikely that tiny islet held anything of interest, but Sahad was right. The boat was in relatively good shape. With some patching, they could definitely take it out there and have a look.

It took the villagers no more than a couple of hours to fix up

343

the boat. The craft was large enough for six, so Adol and his party hopped in and rowed toward the islet.

A small bay with a sandy beach greeted them. The water here was calm and clear. Large fish darted in the depths just off the shore, suggesting that this was a good fishing spot.

A small cave opening gaped at the foot of the tree. Inside, scattered debris suggested the place had been used as a shelter. They couldn't tell how long ago though, or what kind of creatures had used it. Perhaps the Eternians? The idea came up when they found an old chest in the back, holding a black stone fragment Dana identified as a piece of an archival monolith. It was heavy, but Adol collected it and stuffed it in his pack, just in case.

The islet was tiny, just a strip of land around the tree that ran into rocks on the other side. A spring trickled from underneath the large tree. The ground around it was strewn with yellow fruit that emitted a sweet scent. They looked a bit like apples, but larger and more elongated. Edible? Probably. Adol was about to pick one when a shape next to the rocks on the far end of the small clearing drew his attention.

At first he took it for a large brownish mound. Then it moved, crawling around as if searching the ground for food. Was that...a pikkard? A giant one by the looks of it. Or was it a...

"I—I'm so famished," the shape moaned. "I can hardly move... Need food...Need...food...Grghgrghgrgh..."

"Sir Carlan?" Laxia exclaimed in disbelief.

It was indeed Sir Carlan. He looked ragged and mud-stained, and definitely thinner than the last time they'd seen him. He watched the approaching group without any surprise, a bitter smile spreading over his face.

"Ha...The hallucinations have set in," he said. "At long last, the end has come for me."

"Sir Carlan..." Laxia knelt in front of him.

Adol joined her, peering into the nobleman's face. "It's really us."

Sir Carlan's gaze wavered, and after a moment Adol saw reason dawning in his beady bloodshot eyes.

"What? Have you truly come to rescue me?" Tears streamed down Sir Carlan's face. "I nearly died when that monster sank my boat. I've been stuck on this island for weeks, with hardly any food except those disgusting fruits and naught but filthy water to drink!" His gaze drifted to a hole in the ground, filled with spring water, with leaves and twigs floating over the top. "If you're not a hallucination, then please! Rescue me at once!"

"Sounds like ya been through a lot," Sahad said.

"But you've done well to survive this long," Dana added soothingly.

They loaded Sir Carlan into the boat and rowed back to Castaway Village.

Sir Carlan recovered from his ordeal in only a few days, quickly returning to his usual ill-tempered self. He took offense at nearly everything around him, starting with the fact that the villagers hadn't erected a monument to him next to Captain Barbaros's grave when he was believed to be dead, and ending with the fact that the village had grown in his absence, adding a bunch of other rude and uncultured people he couldn't possibly tolerate. Even Austin and Reja, the two other nobles in the group, seemed beneath his standards somehow.

It felt like a welcome change from all the grumbling to continue exploring the Eternian side of the island. To Adol's great surprise, they were able to rescue two more castaways. Silvia—a retired gladiator from Romn, an impressively muscled woman in her fifties—turned out to be the one whose campfire they'd discovered in the plains on their initial approach to the Aegias ruins. But even more surprising was finding Griselda, Adol's acquaintance from one of his previous adventures and none other than the Governor General of Celceta, who was fending for herself on one of the ridges not far from the area where they found Franz. Both women had done well surviving in the island's northern reaches, but they were delighted to join the village.

Except for the mysterious veiled figure that stayed hidden for now and had the ability to appear and disappear into thin air, Adol could say with certainty that no living humans were left to rescue. Their search of the island was complete. They could now focus their efforts on finishing the ship as they waited for another vision from Dana's past.

The Primordials around the camp seemed to multiply, becoming bolder and more cunning. One morning, when Adol and Sahad went to a stream outside camp for a quick round of morning fishing, they found themselves facing a giant beast they'd never seen before, with a spiky body, bat-like wings, and giant curved claws, each nearly as long as Dana's blades. Luckily, they'd brought their weapons. The sounds of the fight drew out the other villagers, and they managed to chase the beast away.

"Is it just me," Sahad said when they were back by the campfire, "or are these beasts gettin' uglier?"

"Uglier and nastier," Dogi agreed. "And definitely more numerous. I'm beginning to feel as if we're under siege."

"Where the hell are those damn things even coming from?" Euron wondered.

"Something's going on around the island." Adol met Dana's gaze. "Any ideas?"

He wasn't sure why he addressed her so specifically, as if he somehow knew she would have an answer. She nodded slowly.

"I've had some visions. Too vague to tell for certain, but there is a disturbance I sense, just like the time when..." She paused, but Adol understood her without words. The Lacrimosa that had destroyed Eternia. A chain of natural disasters of catastrophic proportion, capable of wiping out entire species. But surely there was no real connection between such cataclysmic events and what was happening now.

"If we only knew where the Primordials were coming from," Laxia said.

"True," Thanatos agreed. "Maybe we should focus on figuring that out before anything else. Thanks to Dana, we have the ability to warp."

"Given the circumstances, we must choose our destination carefully," Dana said. "We need to warp somewhere that will allow us to effectively assess the island's situation."

"Gendarme," Adol said. "There's a spot at the very top that gives you the best view of the entire island. If I remember, it has a warping crystal."

Thanatos nodded. "Good idea. We'll use Little Paro to keep each other posted in case one side needs reinforcements."

They gathered their gear and warped to the Gendarme summit.

The sun shone so brightly here it took Adol a moment to adjust his eyesight. Cool air filled his lungs. He glanced over the sweeping view, remembering how much effort it had taken them to reach this summit the first time. Warp magic was truly amazing.

At a first glance, everything around them looked the same. On the southern side, the bay spread in a near-perfect circle, with a column of campfire smoke from Castaway Village rising on one end. To the north, the ruins of Aegias lay gleaming in the sunlight, spreading from the jungle in the east to the plains in the west.

It took Adol a moment to notice the unusual amount of bird-like Primordials circling in the sky. There were definitely more of them than he remembered from their previous visits to this area. They also looked like different species, even though from this distance he couldn't tell for sure.

"Something's wrong," Dana said.

"What?" Sahad asked.

"Look down. The Great Tree of Origins..." She paused.

They looked, but the only thing they could see was a giant swirling cloud that covered the entire area.

Adol blinked. The massive tree crown should be directly below them, adjoining the mountain on one side and the Temple on the other. What could have possibly happened down there?

"Is that...fog?" Sahad asked.

Laxia narrowed her eyes. "Whatever it is, it's centered around the Great Tree—and it has a remarkably sharp boundary, almost like a cocoon."

"A fertile cocoon," Hummel pointed out. "It's swarming with creatures, as if the fog is birthing them."

He was right. The swirl around the crown of the Great Tree moved with shadows. As they emerged from the fog, they became recognizable—leathery wings, scaly tails, toothy maws...

"Primordials?" Ricotta asked.

"They look like the new kind that attacked the village this morning," Sahad said. "There surely's a lot of 'em flyin' around."

"I've never seen these species before today," Dana said quietly. "They must predate the Eternian era."

"Is the *Tree* spawning them?" Hummel wondered.

"We can't determine anything from up here." Dana turned and met Adol's gaze.

Adol's skin crept at the resolve in her face. She was sensing something. Something bad.

"Let's head to the Great Tree," he said.

Their first idea was to warp, but they quickly discovered that any warping attempts in the area were being blocked, as if the mysterious swirl around the Tree were interfering with Essence somehow. Whatever it was, the only way to proceed was by walking, so they set down the winding length of the mountain trail that descended toward the Temple grounds.

The path brought them to their earlier campsite at the Temple approach, right to the fog boundary. Its swirls covered the Temple ruins, hiding them from view. The meadow up ahead apparently served as a launch area, where the Primordials flying out of the fog landed on the grass and ran away. Thankfully, none of them paid any notice to the travelers as they stood at the side of the road, watching.

"Is it just me, or is this fog gettin' thicker?" Sahad asked.

They all kept silent for a while.

"We have no choice but to enter it if we want to get closer to the Tree," Dana said and led the group into the cocoon.

Inside, it looked like a very foggy day. As they followed the walkway through the guard house at the Mountain Gate and toward the main Temple building, they couldn't see anything at all up ahead. Worse, nothing around them seemed to change, as if they were walking in place without covering any distance.

"Strange, we should have reached the Temple by now," Hummel said after a while.

"Yeah," Sahad agreed. "I don't remember the path from the gate to be this long."

"I have a bad feeling about this," Dana said.

Adol had a bad feeling too. The Temple should be right there. A few more steps and they should find themselves right at the entrance. He sped ahead, but saw nothing.

The fog engulfed him. He suddenly noticed that he was alone. Had the others stopped behind him? He called, but no one answered. Fog and silence filled the area.

Eerily, the scene that floated into his mind was one from Dana's past, when she and Olga had been rushing along a stone walkway amidst the falling stars and got separated by a very similar fog. He refused to dwell on the parallels between the disaster that hit Eternia back then and the present events, but what if—

His foot hit a stone step. The Temple entrance, finally. He ascended a short flight of stairs, but instead of the gaping doorway he'd expected to find, he came face-to-face with an enormous beast.

It looked like the same one Dana had faced on that fated day when Eternia was bombarded by falling stars—a monstrous version of a horned bull with a contraption made of tree branches rising on its back. It lowered its head, ready to attack. He drew his sword and rushed into battle.

The beast was massive but slow, especially on the turns. Adol took full advantage of this, dodging and swerving, attacking from the sides. It took extra effort, even for his orichalcum-infused blade, to pierce the skin and inflict significant wounds. The beast reared each time he connected a blow, flailing and thrashing from side to side.

In her timeline, Dana had faced this beast equipped with a new spirit power that made her lighter and faster than before. Adol had no such advantage. All he had to rely on was his sword skill and the orichalcum. He hoped it was enough.

When the beast finally collapsed on the ground, Adol collapsed too. He felt so exhausted he wasn't sure he would ever be able to stand again. Panting, he watched the beast's carcass dissipate into the fog, as if it had never existed. The ground shook, and for a moment the image of the Great Tree floated up in his mind.

Had this fight been a test imposed on him by the Tree?

Shakily, Adol rose to his feet and stumbled back along the walkway.

Almost immediately, he ran into Dana, Hummel, and Laxia, gathered near an Essence crystal.

"Adol." Dana rushed toward him. "I'm so glad you're safe." She sounded relieved but not surprised, as if she knew exactly what had happened to him.

"Looks like we somehow ended up back at the Mountain Gate," Hummel observed.

"The Great Tree seems to be resisting our attempts to approach it," Dana said.

"How could it do that?" Laxia wondered.

Adol had no idea. But after everything he'd seen, he didn't have any room left to feel surprised.

"Where are Sahad and Ricotta?" he asked.

Laxia cleared her throat. "Well . . . "

A scream pierced the fog, and Sahad and Ricotta emerged, running up the walkway toward them.

"It's no use . . . " Ricotta panted.

Sahad leaned his hands on his knees, breathing heavily. "I ran as fast as I could, but—"

"I tried to stop them," Laxia said. "But they were determined to see if they could get through the fog by sprinting."

A sudden burst of searing pain pierced Adol's shoulder. He sank to his knees and grasped the spot, groaning despite himself.

"Adol!" Dana rushed to his side.

The pain enfolded him, shooting up his arm and into his body, until he felt as if he was burning, with no way to stop the agony. Then, just as suddenly, it was gone. Only a spot on his upper arm continued to burn, as if seared by hot iron. Adol heaved a few long breaths.

"I'm all right," he said through clenched teeth.

"What's going on?" Sahad demanded.

Adol rolled up his sleeve.

A red mark gleamed on his upper arm, a stylized depiction of an eye done in glossy red ink that seemed permanently fused to his skin.

"The same symbol as Dana's?" Ricotta said weakly.

Adol and Dana locked gazes.

This couldn't be a coincidence. The fog. The fight with the giant horned Primordial. The eye mark, burned into the shoulder in a fit of agonizing pain.

The Lacrimosa.

No.

"The cocoon of fog surrounding the Great Tree is expanding," Hummel remarked.

"What's going on?" Laxia demanded.

"The evolution of the world, begun anew by the Great Tree of Origins," a new voice said.

Four figures stepped out of the fog.

THE WARDENS OF EVOLUTION

The newcomers approached in solemn steps. The veiled figure from before walked in front. Behind it loomed three larger shapes. Not human, or any species Adol had ever seen.

The tallest one, blue-skinned, and broad-shouldered, had the head of a seahorse rising on a long neck, flanked by two long skin protrusions that hung down to its shoulders. A golden crest decorated its head—all flesh, not jewelry or adornment. It was easier to imagine meeting this creature at the bottom of the ocean than here, on dry land.

The one standing next to the blue being looked like a burly muscular man, except that his thick neck was topped with a bull's head, rimmed with two sets of horns—the smaller ones sticking up, the larger ones extending horizontally out to the sides.

The last one was slender and insectoid, its long, thin arms covered by wide sleeves that looked a bit like dragonfly wings. Its triangular head was greenish-yellow, tapering sharply from its large, faceted eyes down to a small, pointed chin.

"Monsters!" Ricotta gasped.

"A thousand pardons for bewildering you," the seahorse-headed creature said. "Let us begin by introducing ourselves. My name is Hydra."

"I am Minos," the bull-headed creature said, in a deeper voice. "Upon closer examination, you humans are far more frail-looking than I expected."

"My name is Nestor," the insectoid said. As it turned, Adol saw its tail, a triple-layered arrangement of the same material as its wing-sleeves. "I do not require that you commit my name to memory.

Nevertheless, we are well met."

"And I am Ura," the veiled figure supplied.

Ura. A genderless name, to match the voice. Yet, more and more, Adol wondered if all these veils concealed a woman, perhaps not that different-looking from the rest of them. He ran his eyes over the others. Hydra and Minos, male. Ura and Nestor, female. It wasn't important, but he felt more comfortable referring to them in his mind with distinct pronouns.

"We wish you no harm." Hydra fixed his eyes on Adol, as if more curious about him than the others.

"Really?" Sahad's voice rang with doubt.

Laxia sheathed her rapier. "I am skeptical, but I suppose we should hear them out."

Hummel put his rifle away too. "So, who are you?"

"Selection and Rejection," Ura said. "As I mentioned before, this process is the means by which the Great Tree fosters evolution. We are the Wardens of Evolution—beings tasked with overseeing that process."

"The . . . Wardens of Evolution?" Dana asked slowly.

Laxia's eyes narrowed. "Ura, right? You said something earlier, back in the Valley of Kings. I memorized it, actually. 'The evolution of the world, begun anew by the Great Tree of Origins.' What does that mean?"

"It is beyond your ken," Nestor said. "The Lacrimosa has visited this world many times over the ages. The fact that humans now claim dominion will not forestall the inevitable. The same fate that befell the Eternians will befall you. Humans have been rejected for the coming evolution."

"You mean we're all gonna die?" Ricotta whimpered.

"Unfortunately, yes," Hydra said. "The Lacrimosa will bring forth a cataclysm, the nature of which varies in accordance with the era." He gestured overhead. "In this case, the resurgence of the prehistoric world unfolding before your very eyes. That is, in fact, the Lacrimosa of this era."

"The effects are currently confined to this island," Minos said. "But in due time it will spread across the world. So it has been decided since time immemorial."

Adol looked up. The stream of Primordials spawning from the fog around the Great Tree flowed steadily, with no sign of slowing. If they continued like this, there would soon be enough of these creatures to kill every human on Earth.

"I refuse to accept this," he said.

"So do I," Laxia agreed. "How can you say we've been rejected when we don't even know the reason why?"

Hydra nodded knowingly. "These are understandable reactions. I sympathize with your plight. But there is nothing we can do."

"Not once in the entire span of existence has a species thrived forever," Nestor said. "By necessity, the species must be renewed to maintain the world. Simply put, the Lacrimosa is the natural law of the world. All living creatures must accept its judgment."

"No..." Ricotta's eyes widened.

"What is it?" Sahad asked.

"They all have the same symbol as Dana and Adol."

To Adol's horror, they did. He could see them now, tattooed on different body parts, but clearly visible in each case, as if displayed on purpose—all except for Ura, whose body was completely covered.

"What does this symbol mean?" he demanded.

Dana gasped beside him, briefly closing her eyes. The Wardens observed her with interest.

"It seems you've finally remembered." Ura turned to the rest of the group. "When the Lacrimosa comes, a single individual is selected from the species facing extinction. That individual will then witness the destruction of their own species. In doing so, the cycle of Selection and Rejection will be perpetuated for all eternity. We, the Wardens of Evolution, are those chosen."

"You, Dana," Minos said, "are the chosen Warden of the Eternian Era. It is only right that you be by our side."

Dana's gaze turned glassy as she looked at him.

"Dana? Then..." Laxia's eyes drifted to Adol. Everyone else was staring at him too. The mark on his shoulder throbbed again, as if disturbed by the intensity of their gazes.

Hydra nodded. "The symbol on your arm, Adol, is proof that you've been selected to be the Warden for your era. That is why we have come to greet you."

"Why was Adol chosen?" Sahad demanded.

"Only the brightest soul among the species facing extinction is selected to become a Warden," Nestor said. "As the selected soul, you are beholden to this fate. Now cease your resistance and join us, Adol."

"No," Adol said.

Laxia stepped forward. "I stand with Adol. I refuse to accept this."

The rest of the group stepped forward too, watching the Wardens grimly.

"Hmm..." Nestor's cold eyes drifted over the party. "What a pity."

"They are merely overwhelmed by the gravity of our sudden revelation," Hydra put in. "Nothing more. For now, we will take our leave."

"You will see us again," Minos added. "Steel yourselves."

"Until we meet again, Dana," Ura said.

The Wardens turned and walked away into the mist.

"Wait!" Laxia called after them.

"They're gone," Ricotta said.

Hummel crossed his arms on his chest. "The Wardens of Evolution, huh?"

Adol glanced at Dana, who still looked dazed. He didn't blame her. This was a lot to process.

Sahad scratched his head. "I dunno what's goin' on, but like hell we're gonna curl up an' die just 'cause they're tellin' us to."

"Maybe humans can be selfish and arrogant at times," Laxia said, "but I believe we have much potential and a bright future ahead of us. No one can just go and mark us all for elimination."

They looked at the sky again, watching the winged Primordials circle in the fog.

Dana shook her head. "Too many things about this are still unclear. If I'm a Warden, why am I not with them?"

"Good point," Sahad agreed. "That *is* weird. They came to see Adol, but they didn't seem very concerned with you, Dana."

"Perhaps something happened in the past between you?" Laxia suggested.

"I wish I could remember," Dana said.

As if in response, the Essence crystal next to them suddenly came alive, glowing and emitting sound waves.

"The crystal," Adol said. "Do we—"

"Yes." Dana met his gaze. "The next clue we've been waiting for. We need to view the past. This could be our answer about what happened between me and the Wardens."

Adol nodded. "Go. We will be right here, watching."

GLOOM

A dark sky loomed over Eternia, snowflakes slowly circling down toward the ground. They formed a thin white sheet as they fell, still melting but not as quickly as before. If it continued this way, the whole realm would sink into snow very soon.

Two men stood in the center of the market plaza, talking. Dana crouched behind a nearby building to listen.

"Are you serious?" one of the men said. "Lady Dana was the one who summoned those falling stars?"

"I don't know if it's true or not," the other man admitted, "but the ones who believe it are trying to capture her. They're telling people that the witch who summoned those evil stars deserves no mercy."

The first man spread his hands. "How could this happen? And how long is the royal family going to ignore this?"

"You didn't hear?" His companion scoffed. "The wise and virtuous Queen Sarai has vanished from the palace."

"I-is that true?"

"They say the entire royal family abandoned the country and ran away. We're on our own now."

The first man sputtered. "What the hell... The city is all but defenseless these days, and the sky is covered in dark clouds."

"Yeah, it keeps getting colder and colder, and it's getting harder to find food. How could this happen to the glorious Kingdom of Eternia?"

They stood together for another moment, then walked away in different directions. Dana looked over to Olga, crouching behind a stone rail on the other side of the alley.

"Glad you weren't followed," Olga said.

Dana nodded. "Yes, that's a relief. I guess wandering through all those alleys as a child really paid off."

Olga's lips twitched. "I'm grateful for how unrestrained you were back then."

They both smiled at the distant memories. They'd been so carefree back then. If only they'd known in those days what they were headed for. If they had, would they have been able to change anything?

"So what have you uncovered?" Dana asked.

"My colleague finished translating the document this morning," Olga said. "It took him a while, but he managed to locate Seren Garden. Apparently it was created in secret by those who rebelled against the providence of the gods." She let out a laugh. "I never expected to find a clue to stopping the Lacrimosa in a children's song. We must hope this lead bears out."

"Where is the garden located?"

"Exactly where you expected," Olga said. "The only restricted area of the kingdom. The Valley of Kings. It seems the royal family passed down their knowledge of Seren Garden over generations. Perhaps that's why the place has always been under such tight security."

"I knew it."

Olga sighed. "As a member of the royal family, Sarai had to have known about this. Where has she gone, and why didn't she tell us anything about it?"

"I don't know," Dana said. "Either way, we must hurry to Seren Garden."

"Seren Garden is said to be located in the depths of the tomb."

"The depths of the tomb?" Dana hesitated. "But in Adol's era, the only garden we found inside the tomb was long dead..." She paused. If the garden was magical enough to hold the key to saving Eternia, how could it have turned into such desolation? A cold grip seized her heart. Were all their efforts for nothing?

Olga patted her shoulder. "Perhaps there is a reason the garden doesn't exist in Adol's time. Either way, it exists in ours."

Dana nodded. It wasn't like her to give up hope.

"You should have an easier time entering the tomb now that the royal family has fallen from power," Olga said. "Still, there was a riot recently that destroyed the west bridge leading out of the capital. The only other way to get to the Valley of Kings is through the Mountain Gate."

"Then I'll head to the Mountain Gate at once."

Olga squeezed her hand. "Yes. Please be careful."

Snow continued to fall over the plaza as Dana stepped out into the open and made her way across. According to the conversation she'd overheard, there was a mob of citizen out here somewhere, looking for her. But she couldn't afford to worry about them now. Time was precious, and they didn't have much left.

At the side of the plaza, the clerics from the Temple had set up a field clinic, a few benches and cots protected by a large piece of sailcloth stretched overhead. A woman in one of the cots was coughing uncontrollably, with two clerics hurrying around her. From their faces, Dana could tell the situation wasn't good.

Many of the streets and passages were blocked, piled over with rocks and fragments of collapsed buildings. Eventually Dana found one staircase that still seemed intact and led to where she needed to go—the upper city and the central district. As she was about to ascend, Council Darius emerged from a side street and rushed over to her.

"Lady Dana." He glanced up the stairs nervously. "There are guards stationed in that direction. I suggest you find another path."

Dana's eyes widened in surprise. "Council Darius...Where have you been?"

Darius averted his gaze. "Surely you've realized why the palace has shut its doors. The day the stars fell upon us was the day Queen Sarai vanished."

"Vanished?"

"Disappeared. Into thin air, or so it seems. She didn't die, I'm certain of it, but she is nowhere to be found. We had no idea what to do."

"But the royal decrees—"

"I know. Hiding the truth and issuing false decrees was my idea. We had to do something." He sighed. "I grow weary of this façade. I can no longer stand the lies and deception I've been party to."

Dana frowned. "You're leaving too, aren't you?"

Darius laughed bitterly. "Criticize me if you'd like. I've committed terrible crimes." He turned around to glance at the ruins, then leaned closer and lowered his voice. "The east Essence tower has fallen, opening a path to the central district. You should be able to enter from there." He turned to leave.

"Council," Dana called out. "There's still hope. We can still—"

Darius paused without turning. "Do not lie, my lady. Lies help no one. My actions are proof of that." He walked away.

I'm not lying. I never do. Dana stood for a moment, watching his retreating back. She was going to get to Seren Garden and save her people, no matter what.

The market plaza looked more lively than other areas. A group was gathered near a merchant's stall. At the side, a little girl lay on a stone table, her head bandaged. A Temple cleric sat beside her.

The girl lifted her head when Dana approached. With a sinking heart, she recognized Sia, one of the twins. She rushed toward the girl.

"Sia? You're hurt... What happened to you?"

"I..." Sia's words turned into a sob.

"When the building collapsed," the cleric said, "she managed to survive, but her sister..." She shook her head.

"No." Dana's chest felt heavy, and for a moment she struggled for breath. Mia. The stronger, more active twin, always cheerful, always leading in all their games. "Why?" she whispered.

"Don't cry, Your Eminence," Sia said weakly. "Mia, she... she saved me."

"Oh, Sia." A lump in Dana's throat made her voice sound hoarse, crooked.

Sia smiled. "Deep down in my heart, I always knew I wanted to be more like Mia. She was so full of life. But before she died, she told me... that she'll always be in my heart. So... I know I'm gonna be all right. For Mia."

Dana wiped her eyes. She felt ashamed of her tears in the face of this little girl's bravery. To think that she, Dana, was supposed to be the strong one. "Yes, I understand. Truly, I do. Please rest, Sia. You have to get better."

"Haha..." Sia's laugh was weak, but in that moment she looked so much like Mia that tears filled Dana's eyes again. "I will. And... Maiden? Please forgive my mother. I'm sure she knows it's not your fault. But she... If you meet her in the city..." She paused helplessly.

Blaming me then. I see. Dana didn't feel surprised. She glanced at the cleric, the way her shoulders drooped tiredly as she tried to summon more Essence to heal the little girl. Dana knew she would keep trying. She smiled and patted the other woman's shoulder, then moved on.

Beyond the healing station, a pile of rubble and stones rose high, towering over the waterway and forming an impromptu bridge toward the central district. This must be the place Darius had mentioned. Glancing around to make sure she hadn't been followed, Dana climbed discreetly up the rocks and over to the other area of the city.

Everything here looked even more ruined. Or maybe it seemed that way because there were much fewer people around. Farther ahead, Dana could see a gap where the bridge leading out of the city used to be, now collapsed and impassable. That left only one way—south, toward the Temple. Just like in Adol's era. She hoped she wouldn't encounter any unexpected obstacles that way.

In contrast to the rest of the area, the plaza in front of the Stupa building looked surprisingly intact. Even the flowers were still growing in their urns, frosted over by falling snow. Dana paused, taking in the view.

A sudden ringing in her ears echoed with a splintering headache, sending her to her knees. Another vision. This area in ruin, dead bodies scattered among the snow. She whimpered, the pain of destruction in her mind's eye far surpassing the physical pain, then took a deep breath. This was no time for despair. She couldn't possibly stop, no matter what.

"Hey, look!" a voice rang from ahead. "That's her, isn't it?"

"It's the Maiden of the Great Tree!" another voice joined in. "Stop her!"

Oh no. Dana clambered to her feet and found herself face-to-face with a group of angry citizens. Ansia, Mia and Sia's mother, strode at the front.

"Where do you think you're going, 'Your Eminence'?" a muscular man said.

"Running from your guilty conscience, is that it?" an older man on the side of the group joined in.

"I remember I used to see you gallivanting around town," the first man went on. "Without a care in the world. Playing with children. Wandering around the market. You treated your position like a joke. That's why this calamity happened!"

"That's right," a man at the back of the crowd agreed. "You invited the wrath of the stars! You're no Maiden to us, witch!"

Ansia stepped forward. Her eyes were swollen with tears, burning with such hatred that Dana's breath caught. "Give me…Give me back my daughter! Give me back Mia, you murderer!"

Dana raised her hands, even though the effort of calming this crowd seemed futile. "Everyone, please! Just calm down. I didn't..." She stopped. What could she possibly say to them? Everyone here had lost their loved ones, their homes. They were likely going to die. How could she possibly reason against this?

Footsteps clattered over the pavement behind her.

"So you're saying you didn't do any of this?" a new voice said.

Dana turned to see another group approaching, led by...

"Rastell?"

He looked disheveled but seemingly unharmed. At least not physically. His cold expression as he stopped in front of her stabbed like a shard of ice. No. Not Rastell too. She couldn't bear the thought of Rastell turning against her.

"Please tell me why this happened, Your Eminence," he said. "Why didn't you protect Eternia? Why didn't you protect your people?"

"Rastell," Dana said quietly.

He paused, looking down on her. Slowly, his posture deflated, the cold fire fading out of his eyes. His gaze wavered. "They found my father's body...Near the crater, where the falling star landed."

"Chief Dran?" Dana felt a weakness in the pit of her stomach. "Oh. I...I didn't know." Oh, but she did. She'd heard the rumors. She should have known that the Chief wouldn't be so prominently absent at such a time unless something terrible had happened to him. She paused, at a loss for words.

"Tell me these people are wrong," Rastell said. "Tell me you had nothing to do with this. I—" His lips trembled as he abruptly looked away.

"Rastell..." She paused. Seeing him like this hurt beyond measure. Knowing that he blamed her felt unbearable. But this wasn't about her pain. She met his gaze. "I have foreseen some of this. But not to this extent. I did everything in my power to avert this disaster. Did I fail my people by being unable to prevent this? Maybe. But some things in life are simply beyond our control. Even mine. And now..." She raised her voice so that the rest of the crowd could hear. "I will devote my entire power to finding out what happened. I cannot bring back those who died, but I believe I can still save Eternia...my people. All hope is not lost. I am Dana Iclucia, Maiden of the Great Tree, protector and leader of the people of Eternia. I never have, and never will, forsake my duty. I will learn the truth of what happened, no matter what. I will find a way to save us all. Now let me pass!"

Rastell watched her, wide-eyed. Around him, the growing crowd looked more like a mob. They stood their ground, some doubtful, some determined, others chuckling as if Dana's speech were a great joke.

"You really expect us to believe a word comin' out of your mouth?" a man said angrily.

"Yeah!" came the shouts from the crowd. "Get her!"

A rock flew at Dana. She side-stepped it, but more rocks followed, forcing her to dodge and swerve to avoid them.

"Listen!" she shouted. "I understand why you are angry, but—"

A larger stone flew straight at her head, but before it connected, a spear swept by, brushing it aside. Rastell stepped in front, shielding her as he faced the advancing crowd.

"Go, Your Eminence," he said over his shoulder.

"Hey! What're you doing?" someone from the crowd shouted. "You're siding with *her*? She's the reason your father's dead!"

Rastell stood his ground. Dana couldn't look him full in the face, but she could see his profile, his narrowed eyes, his mouth set into a determined line. He looked so much like his father. She wished Dran could see him right now.

"There are things I'll never be able to tell my father now," Rastell said. "But I know, with all my heart, that he died upholding his sworn duty. So I will honor my father's memory by living my life as he lived his. I will keep my promise and protect the Maiden at all costs."

"You traitor!"

"Get him!"

"You must hurry," Rastell said over his shoulder to Dana. "I don't know how long I can hold them off."

"But Rastell..." She paused. Leaving him here would certainly mean his death. But if she stayed, she would suffer the same fate. She would be trampled over by the angry mob and never make it to Seren Garden.

She couldn't afford for that to happen.

"Don't worry about me," Rastell said. "Just let me keep my promise to you."

"I promise," Dana said. "I will find out why this happened and come back!"

"I know you will."

They both knew he was going to die. Dana couldn't let his sacrifice be in vain. She turned and ran.

"You face Rastell!" the young man bellowed at the crowd behind her. "Son of Chief Guard Dran! And I will not allow any of you to pass!"

"The Maiden's getting away!"

"Out of the way, you!"

Dana ran faster, until the sounds of the battle no longer reached her ears. She ran all the way to the guard post marking the Mountain Gate. Only then did she pause to catch her breath. It brought no relief.

Please be safe, Rastell, she prayed, knowing all too well that her prayer was unlikely to make any difference.

A PAINFUL DECISION

A crowd was gathered inside the guard post at the Mountain Gate. Many of them looked sick, dying. Dana's heart quivered. *So many. At this rate, we won't be able to last long.*

"My lady!" Handmaid Alta rushed toward her from the depths of the building. Her eyes slid over Dana with worry.

"I am unharmed," Dana said. "But I must hurry to Seren Garden at once."

Alta nodded. "Everyone from the Temple is gathered on the upper terrace. We are waiting for your orders, my lady. And . . . there's something we need to tell you."

Dana nodded and followed her upstairs to the city overlook. Clerics and priestesses were gathered there—but instead of the city view, they were all looking in the direction of the Temple. The Great Tree. Its all-familiar form loomed reassuringly ahead, its crown ascending in circles into the mists above.

"It was reported that the Great Tree was glowing with golden light during the stars' assault," Alta said. "At the time, we thought that light was the Great Tree displaying a negative reaction to the falling stars. But we now know that the Earth's Essence surged abnormally before each star fell. And at the center of this Essence surge . . ."

"Was the Great Tree of Origins," Dana whispered. She knew this to be the truth, no matter how it shattered her heart.

"Yes," Alta said shakily. "It would appear that the Great Tree of Origins somehow caused the stars to fall to Earth. It can only mean . . ."

Dana swallowed. "The Great Tree of Origins is the cause of these terrible cataclysms. Perhaps people are right to lay the blame on me for this disaster."

"Your Eminence, no. You can't think like that!" one of the younger clerics protested. She seemed near tears.

"I don't believe it," another one said firmly. "You are our protector. We trust you with our lives!"

"You are an extraordinary Maiden," Alta said. "We believe in you." Advisor Urgunata stepped up to her side.

"The sole significance of the Temple's existence," she said quietly, "is now lost forever. What are we to do now, Your Eminence?"

More than the significance of the Temple is lost, I'm afraid. Dana took a breath and turned to face the group. "We'll learn the truth. But in the meantime, if people lose faith in the Great Tree, the kingdom will plummet into chaos. That's why we must stay our course and help everyone suffering from these cataclysms." She hated the idea of lying to her people, but being a leader meant she had to make these decisions without hesitation. Inadvertently, she remembered the Arboreal Awakening, how she'd concealed the truth about her disturbing vision. It had been the right decision then, and it felt right to do the same thing now too, no matter what.

Advisor Urgunata nodded. "We have an arduous road ahead of us. And yet, I have never been more proud of you, Dana."

Proud? Dana's eyes widened. Ever since she was a little girl, she'd always thought of Advisor Urgunata as a disciplinarian—never satisfied with her progress, always punishing her harshly for any mistake. Later, the woman became a voice of caution that spoke against many undertakings she proposed. To hear her say that she was proud—

"Yes." Urgunata smiled. "Your rambunctious nature vexed me to no end on many occasions. But if it was all leading to this moment, then all is forgiven." She chuckled. "I suppose I chose wisely when I nominated you to become the Maiden."

Dana stared again. Nominated? She'd always thought Urgunata was in favor of Olga.

"We accept our fate," Urgunata said louder, so that everyone in the gathering could hear. Many heads nodded as they all crowded closer. "As you said, we must save our people, Your Eminence. Even if our faith wavers, our duty never will."

"Lady Urgunata... Everyone..." Dana paused, a lump rising in her throat. She felt at a loss for words.

"Go," Urgunata said. "We'll handle things here."

"I know you'll come back to us," Alta said.

Dana's eyes stung with tears. "Yes, I will. Thank you all. And . . . please be safe, everyone." She turned and set out on the west road.

As she descended the stone stairwell cascading along the mountainside, she felt a tug in her mind.

Olga.

She opened the link.

I know you'd want to know, Olga said. *The people at the Temple are fine. But Rastell . . .* She paused.

Dana's heart skipped a beat. *Tell me.* Even in her mind link, the words came out as a whisper.

He is barely breathing. But I will do my best.

Alive. Thank the spirits. Dana heaved a long breath. As long as she lived, she would never forget the sacrifice he'd made for her. *Please take care of him, Olga,* Dana begged. Please don't let him die. She couldn't say this last part, not even to Olga. She had to have faith in her friend's healing skill.

The gate toward the Valley of Kings stood unguarded. Dana stepped through and followed the winding path between the rising cliffs to the familiar passage leading toward the tomb.

In this era, the building stood intact, far more impressive than the ruins she saw in Adol's time. The Warrior statue sat on top of it, its Saurian head resting its heavy stare on her as she approached the entrance. For a moment she felt afraid that this was one of the guardian golems, animated by Essence to destroy intruders. That would have been one good way to protect the royal family's secrets hidden in the depths of this tomb. But luckily, the statue remained seated as she approached the gaping doorway and entered the large hall inside.

A blue glow shimmered in the air near the entrance. Another trapped spirit? Dana reached out with her Essence and released it. A small glowing ball popped into view.

"Ah, thank you!" it said. "I can't believe you rescued me, Dana Iclucia, Maiden of the Great Tree."

"How do you know my name?" Dana asked.

The spirit laughed. "I'm sorry to alarm you. My name is Selene, Spirit of Covenants. I was birthed in this sealed land. Due to the proximity to Seren Garden, Essence disturbances are more frequent here. Ever since my birth, I have been observing the history of Eter-

365

nia."

"You must know the true purpose of Seren Garden, then," Dana said. "Please tell me what I must do."

"I'm sorry..." Selene bobbed in place. Was this how spirits shook their heads? "I don't know the answer to that. All I can do for you is form this covenant with you. Please accept my power."

A wave of warmth flowed through Dana.

"A dark path lies ahead of you," Selene said. "One of pain and misery. Someone is very concerned for you too. Please allow us spirits to grant you our protection."

"Thank you," Dana said. "I'm very grateful for the spirits' protection, but you don't need to worry about me. I have people supporting me. They're the reason I can keep going."

Selene bobbed again, differently this time. Nodding? "I'm glad you are exactly who I hoped you to be. It's not every day that a spirit finds itself rescued by a mortal. I, Selene, Spirit of Covenants, commit everything to you. Please don't lose."

"I won't," Dana promised.

A vision of the opening door in the Sanctuary Crypt floated up in her mind. She paused. Should she make a detour to see if she could assess another monolith in the new area just opened to her and perhaps learn something about Seren Garden before proceeding? It seemed wise. Now that she'd discovered the way, she could always warp back here using the local Essence crystal looming beside the entrance. She warped to the Sanctuary Crypt, into the monolith chamber, and opened the door to proceed.

This area of the Sanctuary Crypt was dominated by fire. Walking over the hot stone floor, with rivers of magma flowing in between, Dana had to summon her spirit-powered Luminous form to withstand the heat. The way was guarded by semitransparent spirits that only became substantial when she used her Luminous skill, but with her new spirit powers, Dana defeated them all easily as she made her way to the next monolith.

As she touched her Essence to the control panel, it came to life immediately, as if it had been waiting for her arrival. The text formed in the air in front of her.

During construction of the villa, an ancient ruin was unearthed. While exploring this ruin, researchers found old records in areas they named "The Wall of Truth" and "The Garden." When these records were decoded, a terrible truth was revealed. The Great Tree of Origins, giver of Essence, was the harbinger of the world's doom. This revelation undermined all that Eternia had done to achieve its prosperity.

Upon notifying the King, he ordered that the ruin be concealed from the public. Unfortunately, an errant nobleman had also learned the truth and took matters into his own hands. "The Great Tree will bring about a terrible calamity that threatens all of Eternia!" Gathering his most loyal retainers, the nobleman set forth to burn the Great Tree to cinders. Flaming arrows were loosed upon the Great Tree, and the Heavens cried out, and the men who loosed those arrows were swiftly turned to dust. The cataclysm had begun.

Bolts of roaring lightning carved terrible scars into the land, tearing the Earth asunder. The Eternians had believed themselves above reproach. That they faced no threats due to their command of Essence... Within their new capital, the cataclysm worked the citizenry into a panic. Yet amidst the horror, there was a group of people who roamed the Earth unabated. Urianus ventured across blasted lands, saving many, until he finally arrived at the roots of the Great Tree.

"Calm your heart, for this time of tribulation is when the heart is tested most." With these words, Urianus led all who would hear him in prayer. And as they prayed, the inexorable march of time continued. Only when they heard the sound of bird songs did the people notice the wind's gentle touch and the soothing kiss of the sun's light. The cataclysm had ended, leaving behind a vast, deep scar in the southern lands.

Dana stood contemplating what she had just learned. If the Valley of Kings was the place where they'd tried to build the villa, then the Wall of Truth must be the mural in the depths of the tomb, and the Garden the chronicle spoke of must be Seren Garden. The people who built this Sanctuary and created the record stored in this monolith had to have known that the Great Tree was the cause of disasters. And that meant... She paused, her mind struggling to cope with all this information.

This room looked unlike any other monolith room in the Sanctuary. Instead of ending with a locked door, it continued to a stone platform, its sides dropping off into bottomless depths. The Great Tree Symbol was carved into the floor, centered inside a giant circular seal.

There was no obvious way forward, so she returned to the monolith room and warped back to the Valley of Kings, making her way through passages and down stairwells into the underground garden.

She was relieved to find none of the desolation she'd seen in Adol's era. The garden looked radiant, filled with Essence light that poured over the lush vegetation. Water flowed around the chamber, cascading down the tall, ornate pillars in the corners to form ponds and picturesque waterfalls.

For the first time since the cataclysm, Dana felt calm. Her eyes rested on the slender tree growing in the center of the garden. It looked both delicate and strong, reaching its smooth branches up toward the distant ceiling.

A stone plate was embedded into the floor in front of the tree. She didn't remember seeing it in Adol's era—it may have been destroyed or buried in debris. But now the words were clearly visible.

In every Era exists Seren Garden, into which the collective psyche of species does flow, providing herein nourishment to this Tree. Stored within the collective psyches of species is the very will to live. The collective psyches of species across Eras are amassed, producing power beyond reckoning for the Transcendent One. Thus, when the Tree of Psyches reaches maturity, disrupting Providence and the natural order, the Days of Weeping shall come to an end.

The Days of Weeping. The Lacrimosa. Dana looked at the tree. Did it really contain collective souls—psyches—of species that had the power to stop the Lacrimosa? It looked so young, so far from maturity. Was there a way to speed its growth?

"So you came here after all," said a calm voice from behind her.

Dana turned, watching four figures materialize out of thin air. The Wardens of Evolution. So she *had* met them in the past. And now she was going to learn what had happened.

Nestor folded her long, slender arms, glancing around the chamber with her insectoid eyes. "Ah, Seren Garden... I've not seen this place in ages." She turned to Dana. "As you have come here, I can only surmise that you are not ready to join us yet."

"You've been here before?" Dana asked.

"Of course," Hydra said. "I am the architect of this garden."

"What?" Dana stared.

Minos inclined his head. "Take notice. The water bridges represent each species of a given era. The weak flow from that water bridge is the collective psyche of the Eternians."

"Far stronger psyches are required to disrupt the providence of the Lacrimosa," Ura said. "Look upon the Tree of Psyches. See how young it is. The collective psyches of species past are not sufficient to spur its growth."

"Was it not made clear to you in your scarlet vision?" Nestor asked. "You have no means by which to save your doomed species."

"You have shown remarkable fortitude in the face of this adversity," Hydra said. "That is why I think you understand. The Lacrimosa cannot be stopped."

"But..." Dana lowered her head. This garden had been her last hope. Could it truly be insufficient to save anyone? Deep inside, she knew the answer. She just wasn't ready to accept it.

Ura crossed her arms over her chest. It was hard to guess her expression under the heavy veil, but the set of her shoulders softened as she looked at Dana.

"We shall take our leave of you, Dana," Hydra said. "Should you change your mind, please seek an audience with us. We will not turn you away. After all, you are a fellow Warden of Evolution."

The four figures vanished.

"No," Dana said. "It's not over yet. The time will come for this garden to play its role."

She approached the tree and planted a prayer sapling next to it.

THE END OF ETERNIA

Months had passed since the last of Dana's species had frozen into oblivion. Or years. She couldn't really tell. It had been too long since she'd spoken to any living soul.

Everything was covered in snow. Its thick blanket smothered the ground, weighing heavily over the remains of once-lush vegetation. Even the buildings stood white under their snow shrouds. Dana could see no other colors left in the world.

She spent most of her time in the Great Tree garden, sitting in front of the altar, sustaining herself with Essence. After all, there was nowhere left to go.

Footsteps rustled behind her. Somehow, she didn't need to turn to know who it was.

Ura.

"How long will you continue this folly?" she said in her strange mechanical voice. "The cataclysms have wiped out all Eternians. Even your best friend, Olga, is gone."

"Olga." Saying the name hurt, but it also brought warmth—like a gush of warm blood over a fresh wound. Finding her friend's frozen body, along with the others who'd found their last refuge in the palace and fought the cold until the very end...She swallowed. Olga was a hero, but there wasn't anyone left to carry her name through ages and tell stories about her. Only Dana.

"Far be it from me to ask you this," Ura said, "but why not allow yourself to feel a measure of peace? Why are you still doing this?"

Dana stood up. She still didn't turn around to face the Warden, but closed her eyes instead, facing the Tree. "Because..." A crimson image of a burning barn flashed in her mind. *The past. Mother.* That incident had shaped her forever. She had to be true to the oath she took that day. "Because there are still people I can save."

"What do you mean? The Eternians are no more."

"Not them. Adol and his allies, who are defying the Lacrimosa in the distant future. And the Wardens of Evolution, all of you, enthralled by its curse." She finally turned to face the veiled figure. "I can still save you too. So please let me help you... Sarai."

Ura stood back, the set of her shoulders tense, as if Dana had struck her. Then she reached up and removed her headdress and veil.

"So you've figured it out," Sarai said.

Dana looked at her, the familiar features of her best friend in a distant face she could scarcely recognize. Sarai. A Warden of Evolution. Was this what she had been all along?

Sarai's lips twitched. "It's a foolish notion to think that we could ever be freed from this curse. Do you even understand what you are saying?"

"I see the way you Wardens look at me. I think I remind you all of the people you used to be."

Sarai scoffed, but no words came.

Suddenly, Dana knew what she had to do.

It wasn't a spur of the moment decision. No. Deep inside, she had known it all along. Wasn't this why she had been sitting here, day after day, after witnessing the demise of everything she held dear? Wasn't this why she had sustained herself with Essence, holding on instead of succumbing to despair? Far in the future, Adol and his friends were waiting. If she joined him, she could still save his species from extinction. She had failed to help her own kin, but knowing that there was something she could still do gave her hope.

Her entire existence, from the moment she'd discovered her gift of Essence and up to now, had been devoted to this one thing. She may not have realized this before, but this was it, the entire purpose of everything she'd gone through.

And now, she was finally ready to fulfill her destiny.

Dana put her hand to her head, gathering Essence.

Sarai's eyes widened. "You wouldn't... Why?"

Dana didn't respond as she released a blast of enormous power into her head. It flowed in, enfolding her, sending her into a deep, magical sleep that could last for thousands of years.

Softly, she collapsed on the snow.

"I ... I don't understand ..." Sarai whispered.

The other Wardens materialized beside her.

"What happened here?" Hydra demanded.

Minos frowned. "Don't tell me you've let her take her own life. Was the burden of the Lacrimosa really too much for her to bear?"

"She should already know that she is immortal," Nestor protested. "What an impulsive, pointless gesture."

"No, it wasn't," Ura said quietly.

Sprouts broke through the snow and wound around Dana, lifting her off the ground.

"What is she doing?" Minos asked.

No one spoke.

The sprouts wove around Dana like a cradle, then rose up to form a basket suspended in the lower branches of the Great Tree.

She lay in there, curled in a peaceful sleep, snow slowly falling to the ground around her.

"I see," Hydra said. "So this was her intention. She must have realized that once she succumbed to her despair, she would have no choice but to join our fold. Instead, she is refusing to become a Warden by sealing herself away."

"Really, now," Nestor said.

Ura—Sarai—stared up at her sleeping friend. "She will awaken when the next Lacrimosa comes to pass. And she will defy us then too."

Minos frowned. "Is she mad? She is bolder than her countenance would suggest. But how will she find the next Warden if she is slumbering here?"

"So long as the Great Tree continues the cycle of evolution," Hydra said, "her time will come eventually."

Nestor's faceted eyes twitched as she studied Dana closely. "How curious. Does this insignificant child really believe she is free to choose to defy the Lacrimosa?"

"Somehow, she was able to communicate with the next species," Ura said. "In hindsight, such a power has never been permitted before."

"Are you suggesting she is privy to knowledge that we were not?" Minos rumbled.

Hydra lowered his head. "At this time, I cannot say anything. Either way, she has chosen for herself the endless uphill path of rebellion. I hardly expect anything to change before the almighty

Lacrimosa."

"Our duty is to bear witness to the events as they unfold," Nestor said. "All we can do is watch over her as the next species takes root."

Ura looked at Dana, cradled peacefully in her hammock suspended under the Great Tree. Then all the Wardens turned and walked away, fading as they stepped over the snow.

THE CHOICE

Dana stepped away from the crystal and turned to the group, standing beside her on the misty bridge. They all watched her in stunned silence, but it was Adol who drew her gaze. His face bore the special kind of resolve that could only stem from an understanding deeper than words could convey. He *knew* what was coming. And he was determined to fight it, no matter what.

"You've seen everything now," she said. "And my memories are finally complete. I've sealed myself away to wait for the next species, so I can bring hope to the world."

One by one, the members of the party stepped up to her, patting her shoulders, nodding, smiling to her. For a while no one spoke as they stood around, their silence a bond that held them together. They all understood now what they were facing. And they were determined to see it through.

"Thanks to you," Adol said, "we have hope. We know what we must do."

She nodded. "Let's go to Seren Garden."

Everyone huddled together and joined hands, touching their crystal rings.

The garden looked so different now from the way they'd seen it before in this era. Instead of the dark, desolate place covered with dry remnants of vegetation crumbling away into dust, the chamber glowed with Essence that illuminated the large space down to its distant corners. Lush greenery covered everything in sight, cascading waterfalls filling the ponds and stone trenches running around the chamber. What a change from the last time they'd visited this place. Dana walked knee-deep into the grass and heaved a long sigh, absorbing the fragrance—richer here than in any other place she ever visited.

The sapling she had planted way in the past had done its job. She wasn't sure how, because no prayer tree was visible here in this era, but the fact that her actions had made all this difference left no question in her mind. Back then, she'd had no idea what exactly would happen if she restored the garden. She just knew that it needed to be alive, harboring the only power that had the ability to stop the Lacrimosa.

The Tree of Psyches.

Her gaze trailed to the middle of the room.

The tree looked beautiful, fresh and lively as it raised its slender branches toward the sky. Its glowing bark seemed transparent, so that one could see substance underneath, flowing up the tree's veins into its crown. Psyches? Could she actually see them flow? For the first time since the start of the last Lacrimosa, her heart quivered with real hope.

"The garden is alive," Adol said with wonder. "And the tree... it's grown so much."

Dana reached out with her palms and closed her eyes, searching for the tree's core. The power of the psyches worked differently from Essence, but her ability to bond with nature and draw strength from the Earth enabled her to sense the tree's growth.

She let out a disappointed breath. The tree was still too young. Even all these millennia, absorbing all the psyches that had existed since the Eternian era, hadn't been enough for it to reach maturity.

"Not enough, I'm afraid," she said. "Sorry I've gotten your hopes up."

Adol paused, running his eyes between Dana and the tree. A mix of sympathy and disappointment stirred in his gaze.

"Is there another way to make it grow?" he asked.

"I don't know." She swallowed. Moments ago, she'd felt so hopeful. And now...

Were they going to fail after all?

"Well," Sahad said, "we gotta try somethin'."

Ricotta raised her hand. "I've read about this in a book! Just give the tree more fertilizer. Then it will grow."

Laxia scratched her chin thoughtfully. "In this case, more fertilizer would mean more psyches."

Glowing spots glimmered on the grass, and the four Wardens materialized ahead, across a narrow canal.

"Well, well." Minos crossed his arms on his chest. "What's going on here?"

"The reservoirs supplying this place should have dried up because of the tectonic shifts that predated the human era." Hydra looked at Dana. "The garden should be dead. Preserving it this way is your doing, no doubt."

"No matter," Nestor said. "Restoring the garden was an exercise in futility."

Dana turned to Ura, the only one of the group who didn't say anything.

"Sarai..."

Ura removed her veil. "So you've regained your memories."

"Yes, I have." Dana's gaze wavered. The last time she'd seen Sarai without her veil was in the deserted, snow-covered Eternia, right before she put herself into a magical sleep. What had Sarai been doing all this time? What was her life like as a Warden?

Was anything about their friendship real? It was so hard to fit all this into her head.

"So," Adol turned to Hydra. "You created this garden, didn't you? Why would a Warden of Evolution create a means of defying the Great Tree?"

Hydra shifted his gaze between the group. "I understand now. You are sharing Dana's memories among yourselves. Well, that saves time explaining, I suppose. Surely you remember by now that only the brightest soul among the species is worthy of being chosen as a Warden." He glanced at Adol as he spoke. Dana looked at Adol too. A worthy choice, from everything she knew about him.

"In my time," Hydra went on, "I was deemed to be the brightest soul of my species—compassionate, selfless, righteous. When I learned about the Lacrimosa, I tried to do exactly what Dana is attempting. I defied it, in hopes of saving my people."

"Did you all do that?" Ricotta ran her eyes around the group.

"Yes," Nestor said. "Though our species and eras differ, that one commonality runs through us all."

"I extensively researched the Lacrimosa," Hydra went on, "forgoing food and sleep, digging up all resources I could possibly find. I discovered that it could be stopped, but only by amassing a vast number of psyches. Thus did I use all my knowledge and power to build Seren Garden. Even so, the psyches I amassed in my era were too few in number. And so, having done all I could, I watched my world die."

Dana's eyes widened. How could he be so resigned when talking about it? Spending millennia watching death and suffering, forced to stand aside as a silent observer must be what being a Warden was all about. Thinking of it made Dana was more certain than ever that she could never be one of them.

"I, too, tried to save my world," Minos said. "Using the same means as my companion here. But the outcome was no different. The span of time required to amass the number of psyches needed is beyond your reckoning."

"Our families and loved ones were taken from us," Ura said. "You know, Dana, what it feels like to be the last living member of your species. Faced with the power of the Lacrimosa, all we could do was succumb to despair."

Hydra nodded. "When psyches succumb to despair, they are captured by the Great Tree of Origins. By this process, the Great Tree creates a new Warden of Evolution."

Dana listened to them, entranced. She did know what it was like to be the last living member of her species. She would have succumbed to despair a long time ago if she hadn't managed to lock away a part of her soul that harbored hope. Was that why she hadn't ended up like the other Wardens?

Laxia frowned. "But if that's true, then you of all people should understand the situation we now find ourselves in. If there is even a chance of preventing the Lacrimosa, no matter how small, then we—"

"You have my sympathies," Hydra said. "But please do not misunderstand me. I have come to accept the necessity of the Lacrimosa. As a Warden, I have witnessed this world's iterations for a long time. Stagnation and deformation accumulate as long as a single species continues to claim unabated dominion over the Earth. These species must be refreshed periodically to maintain the integrity of the Earth. There is no reason why you humans should be an exception to this rule."

"We can't give up," Adol said quietly. "I won't."

"Perhaps it's selfish of us to feel this way," Laxia joined in, "but we can't surrender the memories we've made together, here in the present. Nor can we surrender the dreams we've entrusted to the future."

"Hmm..." Minos looked at her thoughtfully. "It would seem there are other humans whose souls are as bright as Adol's. I also selfishly defied the Lacrimosa until the very end. Your sentiment is not lost on me."

"Adol would not have been chosen to become a Warden if he were the type to give up now," Ura said. "This, too, must be the will of the Great Tree."

Nestor sighed. "The more hope you have, the more despair is created when that hope is finally crushed. Let's allow Adol to do as he pleases. It may hasten both his and Dana's ascension into our fold. I'm sure the Great Tree is eager to welcome back its disgraced daughter."

"So be it," Hydra said. "Our duty is to observe, not to interfere. We will provide you with as much advice as we are permitted."

"Really?" Ricotta asked.

"Yes." Hydra nodded. "Please listen very carefully to what I'm about to say. If you wish to defy the Lacrimosa, then you must grow the tree."

"But how?" Dana asked. "If it didn't gather enough psyches between my era and this one, how can we—"

Hydra's glance stopped her. "The psyches flowing into the tree belong to those who lived before the Lacrimosa appeared. The innumerable psyches of those who faced rejection and perished during the purge of their species are contained within the Great Tree itself. Should you release those psyches from the Great Tree..."

Dana's eyes widened. "Can we?"

"In theory, yes."

"But how?"

Hydra measured her with his gaze. "I've said enough for now. I will explain that process in greater detail once you are ready."

"*Ready?* What do you mean?"

"You must conclude all your other affairs. When you do, make your way to the Great Tree of Origins. Once this process is set in motion, you can't stop until you fail or succeed. From all I know, you are destined to fail. But if, by a small chance, you manage to stop the Lacrimosa, there's no telling what will happen. You must face this choice without any regrets. Make sure to come fully prepared."

"Wait!" Adol called, but it was too late. The Wardens had disappeared.

BEST FRIEND'S WILL

Conclude our affairs?" Sahad fumed. "How in the world are we supposed to do that, if our loved ones aren't even here?"

"I think Hydra meant our affairs on this island," Ricotta explained. "We could gather supplies, prepare our gear, ask Kathleen to up-grade our weapons. She told me this morning she found a way to infuse them with even more orichalcum. We can also spend more time with people in the village—get to know each other better."

Sahad frowned. "To what end?"

"The Wardens want us to change our minds," Adol said.

Everyone stopped talking and turned to him.

Dana nodded slowly. "Adol is right. The Wardens think that giving us this time will make us realize how futile our efforts are. But if you ask me, we should use this time well. If we face the Lacrimosa with any doubt in our mind, harboring regrets about something we could have changed but didn't, we are more likely to fail." Her eyes trailed over Adol. "We don't have much time though. Once the Great Tree started spawning the disaster, the end of your species is near. We must act without delay."

"As far as I am concerned," Hummel said. "I'm ready as soon as Kathleen finishes upgrading our weapons. I have no regrets."

"Neither do I," Ricotta agreed. "But I will spend this time talking to Father, telling him how much he means to me."

"I have no regrets either," Sahad rumbled. "At least not the kind I can do anythin' about. The way I see it, if we don't stop the Lacrimosa, I may never see my family again. If anything, I'll regret our course of action only if we fail."

No one else said anything. One by one, they rose from the fireside and dissipated throughout the camp.

Adol knew exactly what he needed to do. Two things, actually, and he started with the easier one.

He found Dogi sitting on the camp's upper terrace with a flask in his hand. Adol lowered down to the grass beside him, leaning against the sun-warmed rock at his back. The view from here was spectacular—one of Adol's favorite spots for watching the sea.

"Hey." Dogi handed him the flask. "I found some more liquor among the pirate supplies. Figured I'd give it a try before stashing it away. Good stuff."

"Thanks." Adol took a sip, the drink rolling through his body like fire.

Dogi took the flask back and brought it to his lips for a lengthy gulp. "Wooo! That'll put some hair on your chest. Man, that burned good goin' down. Haven't felt that in a long time."

"Slow down." Adol smiled. How long had it been since they'd sat around like this?

Dogi laughed. "Haha! It's gonna take more than one mouthful to put me under, so don't you worry. By the way, as far as wild adventures go, this one definitely takes the cake. You think you'll ever stop gettin' us roped into trouble all the time?" He handed the flask to Adol again.

"Beats me." Adol leaned back in his seat and took another sip. The stuff was vile indeed. It coursed through his body, making him feel more relaxed than he had in weeks. Dangerous drink, if only because of how good it felt.

"I guess," Dogi said, "we wouldn't have gotten into so many scrapes if you could stop, huh? Anyway, you just leave the village to me. I'll make sure it's still standing when you guys come back. Speaking of which..." He met Adol's gaze. "It's not like I'm really worried about it or anything, but... you are coming back, right?"

Adol shifted in his seat. He didn't hurry to respond.

"This Lacrimosa," Dogi said. "It might just be the craziest thing you've ever had to deal with. I've seen you head into danger more times than I can count, but I got a weird feeling this time, as if—"

"I'm coming back," Adol said. "With Dana. No matter what."

"No matter what?" Dogi frowned. "Uh... Didn't she have a vision about that being... impossible?" He sighed. "Man, you're such a... Oh well, it's not like I expected anything less from you. Whatever happens, you know I got your back all the way. But you gotta promise that you'll drink with me when you come back, alright? I intend to drink till my teeth start floating, so you better be ready."

"I will be," Adol promised.

They sat together for a while, enjoying the view. Then Adol got up and walked back into camp. He had other people he wanted to talk to before they left. One person, in particular.

Dana was sitting in a secluded spot on the mid-level terrace, tucked between two protruding cliffs that made her invisible to any passersby. As Adol approached, she turned and watched him, a smile creasing her lips.

Adol smiled too as he sat down next to her.

During his travels, he'd met people who had left a deep trace in his heart. He always moved on, until he had finally convinced himself that his only true love was adventure. But now, with Dana, he wasn't so sure anymore. He had so many things to talk to her about. But none of them seemed as important as just sitting together, enjoying her presence by his side.

"I was thinking about Olga," Dana said after a while. "How I wasn't there for her during her final moments. At the time, I was desperately trying to save what few people remained in the world. So we didn't even have a chance to say goodbye."

Olga. Dana's loyal friend until the end. Adol was lucky to have Dogi by his side. What would he have felt like if they separated, if Dogi perished out there somewhere without even a chance to say goodbye?

"Olga believed in you," Adol said. "She wouldn't have wanted you to do anything differently."

"I know." Dana paused again, looking at the view. "Do you know what was the last thing she ever said to me?"

"What?"

"When she was researching Eternian lore, she came across a character known as the Blue Bird. A bird that flew everywhere, doing unexpected things. It brought luck." She paused. "Olga said I reminded her of the Blue Bird. She also said she would always place her faith in me."

Adol nodded. From Dana's memories, he had come to know Olga as a strict person who always followed rules and imposed them on others. But he also realized Olga had another side. She loved Dana and supported her unconditionally, until the very end.

"I often wonder," Dana went on, "what she was trying to tell me. I still think about it to this day. One thing is clear, though. Olga is dead—and I don't feel sad, really. I just feel…alone."

"You're not alone," Adol said quietly.

She found his hand and squeezed it. He twined his fingers with hers. Her touch made him feel stronger. Together, they could accomplish anything they wanted—even stop the Lacrimosa.

"Let's find out what Olga's last words meant," he said.

Dana shook her head. "It happened so long ago. There's no point searching for answers now."

"It's never too late," Adol said. "Myths and legends are immortal. It's why I originally became an adventurer—just so I could search for their roots among the many cultures in the world. There's so much of Eternian history still intact among the ruins. I'm sure we can find the answer."

She leaned closer, until their shoulders touched. He put an arm around her. A brotherly gesture of two fellow travelers who'd been through a lot together—but Adol knew better than to deceive himself this way. He wanted to hold her close, now and always. He never wanted to let her go. It felt so good to sit like this, side by side, looking at the waves rolling endlessly toward the horizon.

"Let's do it then," she said. "It would certainly help me to minimize regrets."

Adol nodded.

They were still holding hands as he felt the familiar pulling sensation of a forming warp. The scenery around them shifted, the warmth of the sunlit terrace giving way to the gloomy chill of an abandoned hallway in the Temple of the Great Tree. An open doorway gaped in front in sinister greeting.

The last time they tried to reach the Temple, they'd run into the thick fog where Adol faced his trial. Today they found no obstacles, even though Adol had the feeling they would be blocked if they tried to proceed into its inner sanctum and the sacred garden—at least until they came here with the full party to talk to the Wardens.

"Olga did a lot of research in the Temple library," Dana said. "We had books and lithographs here, not the archival monoliths used everywhere else in the kingdom."

"I doubt any books would have survived," Adol said. "Maybe the lithographs?"

"Let's see."

They searched every intact area they could access, starting with Dana's room and ending with the large library on the second floor, gaping at them with empty shelves. They were about to give up when Adol noticed a corner of a stone tablet peeking from underneath a thick layer of dust on one of the tables. Carefully, he swept it clean, revealing rows of strange symbols carved into the stone.

"There's a lithograph here," he said.

"That's Olga's favorite spot. She could have been the one who left it here." Dana peered into the writing. "Wait, this description..." She frowned. "The legend of the Blue Bird."

Adol leaned over the table next to her. The text was illegible to him, of course. But Dana seemed to read it easily, her eyes flitting over the lines of ornate characters, so different from any writing he had ever seen.

"Listen." She leaned closer, translating as she read: *"The Blue Bird was one of the servants of Saint Urianus. The people once regarded it with suspicion and mistrust. They scoffed at its visions of rain on sunny days, and famine following bountiful harvests. But in time, everyone learned that its visions were accurate."*

"Sounds familiar, doesn't it?" Adol asked. "One could have said all these things about you."

Dana looked at the bottom of the page. "I wish there was more. The rest of the tablets with this record must have been destroyed. Maybe if we go to Baja Tower—"

Adol nodded. "Baja Tower it is."

Again, he let Dana do the warping. He could have used his own ring, but there was something special about warping together, feeling her magic enfold him. They only had this one day, and he was going to make the most of it.

The tower stood empty and desolate, just the way they'd left it after uncovering the records related to the Oceanus research. Most of the archival monoliths were unresponsive, and the few that remained functional proved to be irrelevant. Adol was beginning to wonder if they were ever going to find what they needed, when Dana stopped near a carved stone plate embedded into the wall on one of the upper levels. She frowned, looking at the carvings.

"This inscription is an account of the kingdom's history. There should be a description of Saint Urianus here somewhere..." She paused, reading. "Ah, found it! Listen:

"A wandering saint who existed during the foundation of the kingdom of Eternia. Through his teachings of compassion toward others, he was able to prevent many wars. Assisting with the construction of Aegias, he is praised as the capital's patron saint. The sculptures at the base of the Stupa depict the animals that accompanied him."

Adol frowned. The sculptures at the base of the Stupa. Was one of them a bird?

"I didn't know about this," Dana said. "The animals that accompanied Saint Urianus...A wise bird and a blue bird...Olga, did you...?" She didn't wait for a response as she grasped Adol's hand, summoning a warp.

Inside the Stupa building, Dana rushed to the row of animal statues in the center of the room. Adol hurried after her.

"There. I have no idea how I missed it before." She was staring at a statue of a slender bird, smaller than the other animals.

It took Adol a moment to realize that the delicately carved pendant around the bird's neck wasn't part of the stonework, as it had originally seemed. It was made of another stone, deep green and translucent—a knot of wavy lines that must have taken a great skill to craft. Jade?

"This belonged to Olga." Dana reached over and took it. Her breath caught as she cradled it in her hand.

"She must have left it here for you," Adol said softly.

"Dana...Can you...hear me?" The voice seemed to come directly from the pendant. As Dana unclenched her hand, the jade glowed, projecting a small hexagon with Olga's image in its center.

"If you're seeing this," Olga said, "that means I have died. My only regret is that I have left you alone in this world. For that, I am sorry. You always were so reckless. I never could guess what you might do next. You probably blame yourself for my death." She looked directly at them, as if she could actually see them. "Do you regret anything, Dana? Learning the truth about the Great Tree...Accepting all the blame...Trying to protect us...Becoming the Maiden of the Great Tree...Meeting Sarai and me...I'm sure you don't regret any of that. I don't regret it, either. So...please remember...As thankful as you are to have met me, know that I am just as thankful to have met you. I just wanted to say that before I go." She glanced around. "It's getting noisy outside. I must be going soon. Dana...believe in yourself. Never stop moving forward. I've stored my remaining Essence in this pendant. It's the least I can do for you. Don't lose,

Dana. Until we meet again...whenever, wherever that may be." She folded her hands and bowed. The image disappeared.

Tears filled Dana's eyes as she clenched the pendant in her hand, pressing it against her chest.

"I finally received it, Olga," she whispered.

She looked at the bird statue. It seemed to be watching her back, as if the ancient piece of artwork could recognize a kindred spirit.

They didn't hurry to return to Castaway Village, taking their time to wander around the ruins. Dana told Adol about the buildings and people who used to live here, adding on to some of the images he had from their shared dreams. When they got tired, they found a stone bench in one of the water gardens and sat side by side, absorbing the scenery. It felt so special to share this time in Dana's lost world, the two of them the only people here.

"I feel like I have some closure, finally," Dana said. "I haven't been able to mourn Olga since she died. Thank you, Adol...for coming with me all this way. For being here with me."

"There is no other place I'd ever want to be," Adol said quietly.

She looked at him searchingly, then slid closer, leaning her head against his shoulder. He put his arm around her, and she relaxed into his embrace.

Whether or not they stopped the Lacrimosa, Adol knew one thing. After wandering around for all these years, he had finally found his home. It was wherever Dana was. He would never give up his love for adventure, but for the first time in his life, he saw a future beyond that, something he could truly look forward to. It felt as if he'd found his other half, and he was never letting her go.

CONFESSIONS

Laxia had her own plans. If this was to be her last day in this world, if she wanted to face whatever was coming with no regrets, there was only one person she needed to talk to.

Franz.

She walked around the camp, eventually finding him in the lodge's common room, tidying up. Even here in the wilderness, he could never stop being a butler.

She stood in the doorway, watching him. He looked so neat, each of his movements so precise as the tasks seemingly accomplished themselves on their own all around him. Items scattered around in disorder clicked into place. Spots of dirt practically disappeared on their own. By overhearing Dogi's and Euron's conversations, she knew he had the same effect at the dock whenever they needed his help in the ship's construction. It was like magic—cozy, familiar magic that reminded her of home.

He seemed not to notice her as he moved around the messy shelves stacked with supplies, leaving behind neatly ordered arrays that looked almost decorative. She didn't mind waiting. Sooner or later, he was going to realize she was here. She wanted to let him have his time.

He finished the row and stopped without turning.

"Anything I can do for you, Lady Laxia?" he asked.

She stared. Had he known she was here all along?

"When did you notice me?" she demanded.

"As soon as you walked in." She sensed a smile in his voice, but when he turned around it was gone, the calm, polite face of a proper butler back in place. She heaved a breath. How in the world was she going to say what she planned to, with him looking at her like this?

"I—I came to see how you were doing," she said.

He raised an eyebrow. For the first time in a very long while, he seemed just a touch surprised.

"Why?" he asked. "Is anything wrong?"

"I have no idea why you find it so surprising," she snapped. "Am I not allowed to inquire about the well-being of my own servant?"

He bowed. "Of course you are, Lady Laxia. It's just that—"

"What?"

He didn't respond, watching her from the other end of the room with a strange expression. Apprehension? Resolve? She had no idea why she felt so flustered when he looked at her this way.

Or maybe she did know. Maybe she had known all along. After father disappeared on his travels, Franz had become so protective, as if she couldn't take a step without his oversight. This change in him was one of the things that had prompted her to run away. She'd been so annoyed when he followed her on this trip without permission. But hadn't she also felt secretly relieved? After she had landed on this island and had eventually given up hope of ever finding him alive, she'd finally realized it. No one in the world was as close to her as Franz. She couldn't imagine a life without him. And if this was her last day on Earth, she had to make sure he knew this.

"I need to tell you something," she said.

He bowed from the waist, a proper butler's bow that seemed so unnecessary in this conversation.

"I am at your service, my lady."

"Oh, stop it, Franz." She glanced around. "Can we talk somewhere else, actually? Somewhere more private?"

He seemed puzzled, but after a moment's hesitation, he bowed again. "Of course, my lady."

"I know just the place."

"After you, my lady."

Laxia held her head high as she made her way out of camp to a small beach where no one would disturb them.

Franz walked beside her calmly, as if he wasn't even remotely curious what this was all about. A normal outing for a lady and her butler. This calm attitude weakened her resolve. Perhaps he had no interest in what she had to say. The old Laxia would have turned and fled. But the person she'd become was determined to see this through, no matter what.

She led him into a secluded inlet at the side of the beach and stopped, facing him.

Now that she knew they were truly alone, saying what she wanted seemed even harder. She took a breath.

"Here's what I wanted to tell you, Franz. I've always known you as the most annoying, conceited, self-assured person who doesn't give anyone room to have as much as a shred of their own opinion." She paused. That wasn't what she had meant to say, not at all. And now that she'd blurted it out, she realized it wasn't even true. On the contrary, she was the one who often came across this way, especially with him. "I—"

She stopped again as she saw the way he was looking at her—intently, as if her words were some sort of a revelation.

"Forgive me for being so imperfect, mistress," he said. "My only goal is to serve you. If you consider me unworthy—"

"Unworthy?" Laxia scoffed. "Don't be such an idiot, Franz. That isn't what I am trying to say. Not at all."

"It isn't?" He peered into her face. His eyes lit up with wonder, as if he'd found something in her expression she wasn't aware of. Damn it, why was this so difficult? How did he always manage to be so proper, so composed, so perfect in every way, when she . . . she . . .

"No. I am the one unworthy of you." She stopped. That wasn't it either. What she was here to tell him wasn't about worth.

A deep emotion stirred in his gaze, making her heart race. She was aware that her next words were hugely important, that she couldn't possibly mess it up again.

"When you were gone," she said. "When I thought I'd lost you forever, my world went bleak. Thinking that it was my stubbornness that drove you to follow me on this ill-fated trip, that it was your attempt to rescue me when the ship was sinking that caused your disappearance, was killing me inside. I've been a terrible mistress—rude, demanding, ungrateful. You paid me back with nothing but loyalty, patience, and understanding. You deserve better than me. If you—"

She broke off as he lifted his face abruptly, locking his gaze on hers.

"Are you dismissing me from your service, Lady Laxia?" he asked.

"Dismissing?" She blinked. "Whatever gave you that impression? No, never mind, don't answer that. Of course I'm not dismissing you. I—I'm trying to say the opposite, actually."

His lips twitched. "You have a strange way of putting it—if I may be so bold, my lady."

"I know." She sighed. "The way I'm putting it—that's because I am an idiot too. Along with everything else I've just said—conceited, arrogant, the lot."

His grin widened. "We seem to be a perfect match then, don't we?"

Her smile faded as she held his gaze. "Yes, we are. At least I think so. But I want you to make your own choice."

"A choice?" His smile was gone too, the torrent of emotions in his eyes making her feel weak in the knees. He stood still, as if afraid to move.

"Yes," she said. "You have the right to choose too. It goes both ways."

His gaze wavered. "You aren't joking, are you?"

"Joking?" Now it was her own turn to look at him questioningly. The smile was back on his lips, but his eyes were in shadow, and this contrast made her even more confused. What was he trying to say to her?

"I made a promise to your father," Franz said quietly. "To take care of you in his stead. The way I see it, this duty also involves protecting you from putting yourself in a situation you might regret later on. Especially if it involves me. You are a lady, and I am your servant. This gap in our ranks—"

She shook her head. "After everything we've been through together, do you think I care about ranks?"

He nodded slowly. "Ranks are indeed blurred here, on this island. But if all goes well, we are eventually going to return home. What will you think then?"

"Ever since I was a little girl," she said, "you were the closest person I ever had. I always dreamed we could be more to each other than just a lady and her butler. I always did my best to suppress these thoughts. It took being stranded on a deserted island, thinking that I lost you, to realize how stupid I have been. People may frown on us. So what? They also frowned on my rapier lessons, on my habit of wearing breeches instead of gowns, on the way I spent time camping with my father, burying my nose in books about nature and creatures long gone. I don't care what they think. Does their opinion matter so much to you?"

"Not in the very least."

"Then," she said, "go on. Tell me I'm crazy. Tell me you don't care about me in any way other than a loyal servant cares about his mistress. I won't hold it against you. If you can honestly tell me these things, we will return to camp and act like this conversation never happened. Tell me—"

He stepped forward and took her hands, cradling them between his.

His touch made her stomach flutter. She felt dizzy, as if she were falling, his hands the only solid anchor in the world that was swirling out of control all around her.

"Ever since I remember," he said, "I couldn't dream of anyone but you. I never considered a possibility of acting on these feelings, but—" He paused, looking down on her. The tenderness in his eyes made her shiver. "When I thought I'd lost you in the shipwreck, I lost a piece of my soul. I thought I could never be whole. And when I saw you again—I—I felt alive. I will stay by your side in any way you will have me. But if you truly meant what you said—"

She tossed her head. "Oh, damn it, Franz. Yes, I do mean it all, many times over. Love is a big word, but I know it as surely as I know my name—I love you. And as long as I live, I never want to spend another day without you."

The world around them faded as he swept her into his arms.

OCTUS

When the party warped to the Temple of the Great Tree the next morning, Adol couldn't escape the feeling that they were expected this time. No mysterious forces prevented them from transporting straight into the fog cocoon or proceeding through the passages into the Temple's main hall.

The door leading to the Great Tree Garden stood open, as if inviting them to enter. Even the Tree itself seemed less ominous somehow, its leaves rustling calmingly overhead as they walked over the moss-covered ground toward it.

Adol had never noticed before that the Great Tree had a hollow, a circular area enfolded by the base of its massive trunk. A circle of light glowed on the ground inside the hollow, flickering with letters and symbols Adol couldn't recognize.

"That's . . . a warp gate?" Dana said in disbelief.

"A warp gate to where?" Laxia asked tensely.

"Wherever it is the Wardens want us to go," Hummel murmured.

No one else said anything as they approached the tree. They exchanged uneasy glances, then nodded to each other and stepped into the circle.

A pulling sensation enveloped them.

Adol's vision blurred for a moment during the transport. When he regained his sight, it took him a moment to orient himself.

The giant space around them had no visible boundaries. Light radiated from a glowing ball in the center. It seemed immeasurably far, but at times it also seemed close, almost reachable. Adol was unsure what created this effect.

Floating hexagonal platforms formed a path in midair, leading into the distance. Each had a glowing pattern of symbols covering the floor. As they stepped onto the first platform, the air shimmered, and the Wardens materialized in front of them.

Ura had her veil off. Adol saw Dana's eyes widen as she stared at her former friend, as if unsure how to regard her.

"Welcome to the Octus Overlook," Ura said. "This is a world within the Great Tree, where we, Wardens, observe the world's evolution."

"Sarai..." Dana paused, running her eyes around the giant space. "Is this also where the psyches captured by the Great Tree reside?"

"It is," Hydra confirmed. "But they are not confined to a single location."

"The Octus has four paths," Nestor said. "One for each era gone by. Once a new Warden assumes their place, a new path forms." She ran her eyes over Dana coldly.

No path for Eternia then. Adol assumed it was a blessing. He wasn't sure how Dana would handle it if she had to face the psyches of her own world. He wouldn't have wanted to enter this place and retrieve the collective psyches of the humans. Hopefully, nothing like that would ever need to be done.

"You must follow each path in turn," Nestor went on, "to find a crystal holding all the psyches from that era that have been captured by the Lacrimosa. You need to destroy these crystals and release the psyches to make the Tree of Psyches grow."

"You will face many challenges to find your way through," Minos said. "And even more to release the psyches." He looked at the group appraisingly, as if expecting them to give up.

Not a chance. Adol stepped forward. "It looks like we have our work cut out for us."

Hydra's eyes hovered on him with an expression he read as pity. "Should you fail, the crystal will be your headstone as your psyches are taken."

"We won't let that happen," Adol assured him. He felt strangely energized. The Wardens didn't believe they could succeed, but Adol didn't care what they believed. Maybe it was the advantage of being young and inexperienced compared to these millennia-old beings that drove his certainty. In his heart, he had no doubt that as long as he fought for the right cause, he couldn't possibly fail.

"There is a proper order to the paths," Ura said, "that follows the order of evolution. You must first take the Ocean Path."

"The entrance is over yonder." Hydra pointed to a distant crystal barely visible across the sphere. "If you can conquer the Ocean Path, you will receive instructions on where to go next."

Dana and Adol exchanged glances.

"We'd better get going then," Dana said.

The Wardens nodded and, in the blink of an eye, were gone.

The path across the floating platforms took them closer to the glowing sphere in the center of the giant space. From here, Adol could see that it wasn't floating in the air like he'd originally thought. An ethereal tree grew underneath, holding the sphere in its branches, its trunk threaded with glowing lines that twined together to define its shape. Below, a pool of light spread around the tree, feeding its roots. Darkness reigned overhead, endless like the night sky.

The passage over the labyrinth of platforms proved to be more difficult than they'd expected. Ghostly but powerful monsters blocked their way, and some of the new branches of the path only appeared after they were defeated. Adol felt exhausted by the time they finally reached the first crystal, a glowing elongated stone rising from the platform ahead.

"A portal to the Ocean Path," Dana said.

"I assume we need to touch it to warp inside," Laxia said.

Ricotta huddled closer to Sahad and Hummel, looking up uneasily.

"Let's do it together," Adol said.

They all stepped forward and placed their hands on the surface of the stone.

The next moment, they found themselves standing on a rock rising out of the water.

Around them, endless ocean spread to the horizon. The air was warm, infused with smells of salt and kelp that resembled the sea back home. Sun blazed in the clear, cloudless sky. A path of rocks protruding from the water led ahead.

"It's beautiful!" Ricotta exclaimed. "Look how big the ocean is!"

"Could this be the ocean of the past?" Laxia wondered.

"I think so," Dana said. "I believe the Lacrimosa is using these paths to re-create the eras it destroyed. Everyone, be on guard as we advance."

The rocks were slippery but flat and wide enough for them to proceed. Jumping from one rock to another, they could see the clear water below their feet descend into the bottomless depths. Looking down gave Adol a sense of vertigo. Somehow, he felt that swimming in this water would be a very bad idea.

A tall crystal gleamed in the distance. From here, Adol could see no supports, as if the massive object were floating in midair. The Crystal of Psyches? It had to be.

As they got closer, the waters around them began to churn with shapes darting around the rocks just under the surface. Occasionally, a sea creature jumped out of the sea and into their path, taking aim at the group with sharp fins, pincers, or teeth. They retreated quickly when confronted, but fighting them off made it more difficult to stay on the slippery path. Once Ricotta slipped off as the creature landed right in front of her, but Sahad caught her by the arm and pulled her back just in time to avoid another shape, larger than the others, rising from below. Adol caught a glimpse of trailing tentacles before the creature descended out of sight.

Up close, the Crystal of Psyches emitted a steady glow, visible even in the bright sunlight. The air around it felt thick with despair. It weighed heavily on Adol's soul.

So many psyches, consumed by the Great Tree of Origins. So many lives destroyed, trapped here in an endless torment. He felt even more motivated to make sure this never happened again.

"So what do we do now?" Ricotta raised her clubs. "Should we crack it open?"

As if in response, the crystal glowed and chimed. Waves of light radiated from it, coalescing in the water in front of them to form a giant creature.

It looked like Hydra, a Warden of Evolution. A huge, aggressive version of Hydra, armed with swords that pointed at the party as the creature assumed an attack stance.

"I thought he said he was just observin' us," Sahad protested. "Why's he gettin' in our way?"

No one had a chance to respond as the creature launched at them.

By now, the party worked well enough together, but even with this precise coordination, the battle was one of the most challenging they had ever faced. I took additional effort to avoid falling into the water as the phantom Hydra swam around them, propelling itself with enormous speed, slashing and stabbing from all directions. Sometimes the creature disappeared underwater, and they had to guess where it was going to come up again. Each time it surfaced, it jumped out of the sea to smash into the party with all its weight.

Adol wasn't sure how much damage their weapons were doing. He couldn't see any marks left by his blade, but after a while, their opponent seemed to slow. Its attacks became less violent. It seemed almost as if the creature was losing its spirit rather than succumbing to its wounds. The party pressed on, showering blows until the creature arched and roared, then fell backward into the water.

The group looked out over the edge of the rocks, watching the body sink out of sight.

The Crystal of Psyches shuddered and stilled. Its light faded. Adol thought he could see a faint glow streaming out of it and dissipating, but in the bright sunlight, it was hard to be sure.

"It seems we've successfully released the psyches." Dana closed her eyes. "I can feel it. They are flowing into Seren Garden. The Tree of Psyches is growing."

"I cannot believe you actually managed to do it." Hydra rose out of the water where his monster body had sunk a short while ago. They grasped their weapons, but the Warden seemed peaceful this time as he stepped onto the rock in front of them.

"Ye said ye were just gonna watch," Sahad complained. "Why'd you interfere with us?"

"It was not I who attacked you," Hydra said.

Sahad blinked. "It wasn't?"

Hydra slowly shook his head. "No. That was my psyche, captured by the Great Tree as I succumbed to despair. It has been the guardian of this crystal for millennia. Only by defeating the guardian can the psyches be released."

"So," Dana said. "We're not just releasing the victims of the Lacrimosa, but the psyches of the Wardens too."

Hydra nodded. He looked strangely content, as if the defeat he'd just suffered brought him peace.

"During the era in which my people flourished," Hydra said, "countless species that lived within our mother ocean were invited to the surface by the Earth Goddess Maia. Thus began the world's evolution by the Great Tree of Origins."

"The Earth Goddess Maia?" Dana echoed.

"Yes. She vanished after sharing with me the truth of evolution. I have watched over the Earth ever since."

Adol tried to imagine it. Hydra, alone and despairing, watching his species die, all efforts to save them going to waste. Knowing that the process would repeat itself again and again, until the end of time. Such torment must have been unbearable. How could he possibly emerge from it so calm and composed, as if his duty of overseeing the evolution was a mere routine?

Perhaps this calmness itself could only be born from the kind of despair that went far beyond imagination. This being in front of them had literally seen it all.

"I will continue to observe you," Hydra said. "Perhaps you will come to accept the Lacrimosa as we did. Or perhaps you will find a new path, and escape the never-ending cycle. Know that my hopes go with you."

The warping sensation enveloped them, and they found themselves back in the Octus.

Another crystal glowed in the distance. They made their way toward it.

The winding path over the floating platforms took them halfway around the sphere, winding up and down, guarded by monsters at every step. When they finally reached the crystal and warped through, the world they found themselves in seemed nearly opposite to the one before.

The landscape around them looked desolate, a chain of dark mountains looming all around. The path creased their slopes and led over narrow bridges into the distant gloom. The air here was icy-cold. Their breath crystallized into vapor, tiny droplets of moisture freezing almost instantly. Low gusts of wind stung as they hit the skin. Not a very hospitable world. Which of the Wardens did it belong to?

They soon got the answer to this question. The icy bridges between the islands of rock were populated by mean-looking minotaurs whose fighting style seemingly consisted of concentrated attempts to push the travelers off into the abyss. It was annoying, but with enough agility it was possible to meet these attacks on solid ground to avoid a fatal fall.

At the end of the path, the giant glowing crystal floating in midair looked much more defined than the one on the Ocean Path, a focus of light against the surrounding gloom. Streaks of light swirled inside it. The psyches. The party made their way toward it.

The plateau separating them from the crystal stood empty. But when they started across it, a huge shape dropped from above, blocking their path. A muscular giant with a bull's head. Minos's psyche.

The minotaur attacked on sight, swinging its massive double-edged axe with shattering force. He seemed invincible to their blows, his skin so tough that even the orichalcum blades slid off it without doing any damage. After an exhausting melee, Adol managed to remember the tactics used by the minotaurs in this world. Could they lure Minos's psyche to the edge and push it off?

With the way the creature kept the entire party occupied, it seemed impossible to relay the message. But when Adol started dodging and skirting directionally toward the edge of the platform, the others caught wind of his intentions and followed. Even with the six of them, though, it took all their strength to accomplish the task without being dragged into the abyss along with their opponent.

They all felt exhausted when the minotaur finally overbalanced after Adol had successfully evaded his last vicious blow. The mighty axe hit the ground, splitting the rock at his feet. The creature hovered on the edge of the precipice, grasping the air in a vain attempt to keep his balance, then swayed and tumbled over into the void.

They stood at the edge, panting, watching the shape disappear into the darkness below.

"Did we do it?" Sahad huffed.

Adol looked up at the Crystal of Psyches. In the surrounding gloom, they all could see a faint stream of light flow out of it and dissipate.

"Yes," Dana said. "It seems to have worked."

Deep laughter echoed over the platform. Minos stepped out of the shadows and approached.

"Eh?" Sahad said. "The real one showed up."

"I never thought anyone would prove capable of releasing the psyches from this crystal," Minos said. "I found you creatures amusing at first, but you are much more remarkable than I imagined." He flopped down to the ground and crossed his legs, a gesture that reminded Adol of Sahad when he got tired of standing around. Perhaps the Wardens were not so different from humans after all.

"In a bygone era of ice and snow," Minos said, "my people conquered this land, and I ruled over them as king. You have defeated my psyche. I concede."

"You're a Warden, aren't you?" Hummel said. "Shouldn't you put up more of a fight?"

Minos shook his head. "I've done more than enough to fulfill my duty as a Warden of Evolution. Truth be told, I'm relieved that you have released my people's psyches. So long as they remained in that crystal, I'm certain they could not rest in peace."

"I didn't expect a Warden to be so compassionate," Laxia said.

Minos smiled. "Perhaps this is the effect of my psyche having been released by you all. I've not felt this mirthful in ages. But know this. Though you have accomplished much, defying the Lacrimosa is a fool's errand."

"We will reserve this judgment," Adol said.

"There is nothing you can do. But... I can already tell that you will not stop." Minos turned to Dana. "I'm beginning to understand why you have allied with Adol. His stubborn spirit complements your own."

"Thank you," she said, without a shred of a smile.

"The paths ahead of you are nothing like the ones you've faced so far," Minos went on. "I cannot help you, but I can at least pray for you. And when you finally know defeat, we can drink and watch the world unfold together."

Behind the calmness, Adol could now see the minotaur's broken spirit. Like Hydra, he too had lost everything despite his best efforts. And now, he seemed incapable of believing that someone else could actually succeed where he had failed.

"I'm not much of a drinker," he said. "But when I do drink, I prefer to drink to success."

Minos's eyes slid over him. "You had best be off then. Your time is dwindling. Stay the course until the very end."

With that, he vanished.

They warped back to the Octus. As before, the crystal behind them had gone dark, and a new path had opened before them. They followed it to the next portal crystal glowing in the distance.

If there were such things as opposite worlds, the Wardens' homelands were perfect examples of it. Hydra's Ocean Path seemed like a nearly exact opposite of Minos's ice age, but the new world they stepped into gave the whole concept of opposites a new definition.

Wild greenery rose all around them, humid air clinging to the skin with invigorating freshness. Moss-covered floor stretched among a dense growth of trees that spread their lush canopies overhead. Sunlight filtering through thick, fleshy leaves filled the forest with a soft emerald haze. Unlike the previous two worlds, this one seemed friendly, even cozy. Adol could imagine himself living in a place like this.

The forest path wound ahead, over moss-covered rocks and fallen tree trunks. Exotic flowers rising here and there filled the air with their subtle, elegant fragrance. Every once in a while, large and dangerous-looking insects swooped on them from above, but even with that, the place looked beautiful and lively, and so exotic. Had this world existed on Earth, in one of the eras long gone?

The Crystal of Psyches gleamed through the trees ahead. As they approached, the wall of trees around them receded, as if consciously moving aside to give access to the depository of the collective psyches of this world's inhabitants. The crystal's blue hues stood out sharply against the greenery.

"The third crystal," Ricotta said.

"Everyone, be careful!" Laxia warned.

A giant insect took form against the glow and swiped down at them. Nestor. But not the calm, reserved version they'd met before. This one was all legs and pincers, her faceted eyes shining with a cold, fierce flame.

Nestor attacked from the air, making it much more difficult to defend against her. Every time she landed, a hole opened in the ground, and once or twice Adol almost slipped into it. He gave it his all to keep up his side, slicing and stabbing at the impossible opponent with too many limbs lashing out all at once.

The moment the fight ended wasn't immediately obvious. One second Nestor's psyche was rushing at the party full speed. The next, she was tumbling down from the sky, dissolving as she fell, until nothing was left. Adol leaned his hands on his knees and stood, bent over, panting, so winded he felt he would never be able to take a normal breath again.

"Man," Sahad said. "It feels like these guardians keep gettin' stronger an' stronger."

They all looked up at the crystal, watching a stream of psyches wisp out of it, glowing against the dense forest shade.

"The Tree of Psyches has grown rather large," Dana said. "I can sense it." She paused, the unspoken question trailing in the air between them. They were succeeding so far—but would this be enough to stop the Lacrimosa?

"To suffer defeat at the hands of such a rudimentary species," said a calm voice, and Nestor materialized in front of them. "My psyche should be ashamed of itself." She ran her eyes over the group. "At its zenith, my colony numbered over one million, and I ruled over them as queen."

"Over one million," Laxia echoed in disbelief.

Nestor nodded. "Through our diversity of form and adaptability, my colony flourished throughout the world. And yet even our civilization came to accept the Lacrimosa. You humans, with your frail bodies and weak minds, have no hope of defying it."

"That doesn't mean we gotta accept it!" Ricotta exclaimed.

"Yeah!" Sahad agreed. "And you didn't have to accept it either. Didn't ya resist it for the sake o' yer people?"

Nestor averted her gaze. For the first time since they'd met the Warden, Adol saw uncertainty in her expression.

"I concede that I initially felt an impetuous desire for self-preservation," she admitted. "But in the end, my calm and rational demeanor won out. Instinctually, we understood the necessity of the Lacrimosa and willingly sacrificed ourselves. Thus did I accept my fate as a Warden of Evolution."

"Unbelievable," Laxia muttered.

Nestor looked at the group with interest. "Let me ask a question of you insolent humans. To defy the Lacrimosa is to defy the natural order. Your success would place the world in grave peril. Your actions—no, your very existence—poses a threat to the world. Not one, but two chosen Wardens of Evolution are among you, electing this futile defiance over doing your duty. What do you hope to accomplish?"

"You speak of duty," Adol said. "So let me answer this question. A duty isn't something anyone could impose on you. You must accept it willingly if you are to follow it for the rest of your life. It must be something you believe in, a reflection of your will. Something you are passionate about. Is this what you can say about yourself?"

Nestor didn't respond, looking at him intently.

"That's right," Sahad joined in. "We humans pave our own way through life. Men o' the sea don't shy away from danger. They accept it and coexist with it. Guess what I'm tryin' to say is . . . humans never give up till the very end."

Nestor inclined her head. "So be it. You humans are very different from your predecessors, that much is clear to me. Now go on."

"Huh?" Sahad blinked.

"I am but one of the Wardens. A judgment will be rendered soon. You will learn in due time whether your decision was correct or not."

She faded as they warped back into the Octus. The portal crystal behind them went dark and a new path glimmered ahead.

SARAI

This is it," Dana said. "The last portal."

Her heart quivered. She was about to face Sarai's world—the *real* Sarai, an ancient, immortal being who had worked her way into Dana's life and took roots there so firmly that it was impossible to separate from her.

Ura. Whatever she truly was, Dana would never be able to refer to Sarai by this other name. People changed, but they didn't change that much. Dana and Sarai had spent so much time together, it didn't seem possible that her friend's current manifestation could be an entirely different person. Of course, their entire time together had been but a blink of an eye compared to Sarai's endless lifespan— but however she behaved, whatever she said about herself, the Sarai Dana knew and loved had to be in there somewhere. And now she had the opportunity to find out if she was right about it. In this world, they were going to face Sarai's psyche, her inner core that made her who she was.

Would she turn up as an aggressive monster, like her fellow Wardens? Would she attack the party without remorse? Would she remember her bond with Dana in the end? Questions swirled in Dana's mind, so difficult to bear.

The path that stretched in front of them was composed of transparent tiles suspended in midair. Sun blazed overhead. White fluffy clouds floated peacefully underfoot. Dana couldn't see the ground below them, only the blue haze that stretched down and out of sight.

A sky world?

She hadn't expected this.

Walking here was more difficult than in the other eras they'd visited. The tiles paving the way were so ethereal that they wreaked havoc on Dana's senses. Every next step made her feel as if the surface under her foot was about to dissipate and send her into a freefall, plummeting all the way to the invisible ground somewhere far below. Here and there intense updrafts threatened to knock them off the path.

The Crystal of Psyches floated in the distance. Instead of standing out against its surroundings, like it had in Nestor's and Minos's worlds, this one blended with the sky, its boundaries nearly invisible, leaving only the glow to indicate its presence.

Was this the place where Dana's best friend had grown up to become the brightest soul of her species? Where had she lived? What was it like? As she proceeded, Dana was just beginning to realize that the gap separating her from Sarai was not limited just to time.

The tile in front of the Crystal of Psyches was much larger than the others. It stretched wide, its clear floor blending with the clouds below. Dana had time to reflect that fighting in these conditions would be especially challenging. In the heat of the battle, it would be easy to step off the edge without realizing it. Falling from this height would mean certain death.

She didn't have time to worry for too long. The crystal in front of them started to glow. Its pulsing light deposited a new shape in front of them.

Sarai's psyche.

Dana's breath caught.

Sarai had always stood out among her friends as the most graceful one, her movements breathtakingly fluid, her elegance and poise often making people stare. And now Dana understood why.

A beautiful maiden floated over the platform, her feet barely touching the floor. The glow emanating from her was so bright that it was hard to see her features. Even standing still, she looked like an embodiment of movement. Beautiful and cold—but deep inside, Dana knew that this coldness, this impenetrable light, were born of despair, not of the creature's true nature.

A sky dancer. Was this Sarai's true form?

The creature's shape was Eternian—or human?—even though twice as large as any Eternian Dana had ever met. Long wisps of fabric draped down Sarai's sleeves and the hem of her dress. Or were they really fabric? As the sky dancer took a step forward, they came into motion, lifting up her to sides.

Tentacles? Dana had no time to dwell on the terrifying thought as the sky dancer used them to lash at the group.

Adol jumped back just in time to avoid a tentacle strike. He brandished his sword, and the appendage retreated, but another swept in sneakily from the side, sending him rolling. Hummel shouted a warning as the fall brought Adol right to the edge of the platform. He was aiming his rifle, and Dana wasn't sure if even the orichalcum bullets could possibly do any damage to the sky dancer. She spun her own blades as she advanced. How ironic that these crescent swords had been given to her by Sarai, back in her time. And now Dana was using these weapons to defeat her friend's psyche.

As they fought, Dana's mind retreated to another dimension. She could no longer feel any pain as the light-infused tentacles, hard as ice, bit into her skin. She forgot the passage of time. Her thoughts focused on the creature they were facing, the essence of a person she once loved with all her heart. The only true friend left from the Eternian era—if she could ever reach that friend inside the layers of this ancient being before her that surpassed her understanding and everything she knew about the world.

Dana couldn't be sure if it was weaponry that eventually defeated the sky dancer. She couldn't see any actual damage inflicted by the party. She wanted to hope that the inner struggle of facing her best friend had at least contributed to weakening the creature that had once been Sarai. She certainly felt the effects of it. She felt exhausted when the sky dancer's movements finally slowed and the creature folded down, dissipating into thin air.

She panted, looking around the platform at the rest of the party, shaken but still standing—except Sahad, who was sitting too close to the edge of the platform, green in the face. Ricotta rushed to his side and pulled him to his feet, leading him away from danger.

Dana moved closer to Adol, drawing strength from his closeness to face what was coming. Together, they watched the crystal crack open, releasing the psyches. As they streamed out into the sky, a vision of the tree in Seren Garden rose up in her mind. It was growing, reaching full height, filling the chamber with its glorious form. All the streams around it flowed in full might, feeding it.

"So you actually did it. You managed to release all the psyches." Sarai's voice echoed in the air even before her form materialized on the platform in front of them.

"Sarai..." Dana began.

Sarai's gaze wavered. "Please stop. I have no right to be addressed by that name."

"But—"

"As I said before, my true name is Ura. My species descended to Earth from the skies, possessing the power of mimicry."

"Mimicry?" Ricotta asked in half-whisper.

"It's the ability to perfectly copy another creature's shape and features," Laxia explained.

Ura nodded. "Correct. With our power of mimicry, we claimed dominion over the land, and flourished. But we were eventually greeted by the Lacrimosa, and I was selected to be a Warden. When the Eternian era developed, I descended to Earth once again, in order to find the next Warden of Evolution among the Eternians."

Oh. Dana closed her eyes briefly. So this was why Ura—Sarai—had come to their world. This was how Dana had been chosen to be a Warden. It explained a lot. Ura. Perhaps it would be correct to refer to her this way after all.

"Then how'd ya become the princess of Eternia?" Sahad asked.

Ura's eyes drifted over the group. "To find the person whose soul burns brightest, I thought it best to insert myself among royalty. I snuck into the palace, where I learned that a young princess was deadly ill."

"Then..." Dana still couldn't quite speak, but Ura understood the question anyway.

"Yes. Princess Sarai. After she succumbed to her illness, I used my mimicry to assume her place. I reconstructed her personality and appearance and made it part of my own. Then, a few years later, at the Temple of the Great Tree...I met you, Dana."

"Then..." Dana tried again. "Then the Sarai I've always known was..."

Ura shook her head. "Dana...Don't make this more personal than it is. For the sake of the great Lacrimosa, I did what I deemed necessary to protect this world." Her gaze softened. "I didn't expect we'd become so close, Dana."

"I...We..." Dana paused. What could she possibly say to this sky creature, so distant despite its familiar form? Perhaps she'd do best to accept that her best friend was truly gone. Or maybe the Sarai she thought she knew never existed in the first place.

"I admit that what I did to you was unforgivable," Ura said.

Dana frowned. "If you know that, then—"

Ura kept her gaze. A new emotion stirred in her eyes. Warmth? Regret? The person that peeked at Dana from the depth of these large, dark eyes couldn't be some sky creature that entered Dana's world through the power of mimicry. It had to be...

"Sarai?" Dana whispered.

Their gazes locked.

A lifetime passed between them in a single instant. Then Dana rushed forward into her friend's arms.

"Dana..." Sarai shivered. "I...Ura...I'm losing control of my mimicry. I'm no longer..." A sob shook her as she leaned into the embrace.

"Sarai," Dana breathed out. "I...I'm sorry about your pain."

"I'm the one who is sorry, Dana. Sorry I couldn't stay with you until the end. Sorry about Olga..."

"No..."

They stood for a long moment, holding each other.

When they finally separated, Dana felt empty, disoriented. They had so much to say to each other, and so little time to say anything at all.

"Maybe—when it's all over—we'll have time?" she said.

Sarai shook her head sadly. "You still believe you can win."

"Yes, I do."

"Then go. If you win, I'll be waiting. And if not—"

We'll have all the time in the world. I know. Dana didn't want to think about it.

"We must go to Seren Garden," she said.

"Yes. And after you receive the power of the psyches, after you prepare, you must return to the Octus. Once you are back, I'll explain what you need to do."

A swirl of force caught them, and they found themselves back in the Great Tree Garden.

Through their bond, Adol could sense the emotions brimming inside Dana. The strain of the battle. The keen sense of loss as they fought and defeated her best friend. The joy at getting her back. He still didn't fully understand what had happened, but the change in Ura was obvious as she faded for a moment and then emerged as Sarai. Dana had this power, changing people around her to become better than they were.

In the grand scheme of things, it seemed like only a small token to add to their victory, but he knew how important it was. They had gained a true ally among the Wardens. At least one more person from the Eternian era was now alive. He hoped, when this was over, Dana and Sarai could reunite.

It crossed his mind that if they gave up right now, if they allowed the Lacrimosa to happen, he, Dana, and Sarai could all spend eternity together. But this bittersweet thought only reinforced his determination. If he had to give up everything to win this battle and save humanity, he was going to do it without any hesitation.

They warped to Seren Garden and approached the tree.

The change was dramatic. For a moment the party just stood there and watched, mesmerized.

The tree, once small and feeble, spread its mighty crown over them, its branches reaching up to the sky. Adol could *see* it growing—or was it the flow of psyches through its veins that created this sense of movement, expansion? Unlike in the Octus, the feeling dominating this place was not despair. It was hope.

"So how does one go about receiving the power of the psyches?" Hummel asked. "Does Dana receive it?"

Dana shook her head. "No. I understand this now. The power of the psyches conflicts with providence and natural law. It exists in direct opposition to the Essence wielded by Eternians. Therefore, it must be a human to receive it. The chosen Warden of this era." She turned to Adol.

"I'm ready," Adol said. "What should I do?"

"Face the tree and raise your sword."

Adol turned to the tree. As he raised his sword, he felt a torrent of power surge into it. The stream of psyches flowing up the tree intensified.

He could *feel* them, streaming up the trunk and into the branches and leaves, releasing their force into his blade. The air hummed with power as it filled the space around him and coalesced into the tip of his sword.

Mistilteinn, a voice said in his head. *We name your sword Mistilteinn, the liberator of souls.*

Adol lowered his hand. The power didn't infuse just the sword. It coursed through him too. He felt invincible. As he turned back to the group, it felt as if a glow radiated from him to envelop all of them, granting them all the power to defeat the Lacrimosa.

They all gathered around to look at the sword in Adol's hands.

The blade hadn't really changed shape, but it seemed more slender and fluid, light and powerful all at the same time. It hummed in Adol's hand, as if it possessed a will of its own, a mighty spirit eager to join him in battle. Fighting with this blade would feel different from anything he'd done before. He couldn't wait to try it out in action.

"So what do we do next?" Hummel asked.

"Like Sarai told us," Laxia said. "We must prepare, then return to the Octus. Let's warp back to Castaway Village to tune our gear and say our goodbyes."

THE WHITE MEMORY

The Essence crystal in the village was glowing, as if beckoning them to approach. Adol stared at it in disbelief.

Up until now, only a select few crystals among the Eternia ruins exhibited this glow, during the occasions when traveling into the past was necessary for the party to proceed with their ongoing task. Usually, these crystals also marked a location Adol or Dana needed to travel to so that they could perform a specific action—such as for Dana to plant a prayer tree sapling to clear the way. Adol had assumed these crystals were special, different from the others.

The crystal in the village had never called to them before.

He stared at it tensely. Now that they were so close to defeating the Lacrimosa, they had no need to travel to Eternia anymore. Besides, nothing important in the Eternia era should be located near this particular spot, too far away from Aegias or any other major settlements. Could this be some sort of a trick, meant to hinder their progress?

A warning cry escaped his lips as Dana reached out to the crystal. She paused, giving him a questioning look.

"There's no reason to travel to the past now," he said. "We've already seen all your memories, haven't we?"

"I agree with Adol," Laxia joined in. "I think this is a trap. Another attempt by the Wardens to stop us."

The rest of the party exchanged nods, looking at the crystal uneasily.

Dana closed her eyes briefly, then opened them again and met Adol's gaze. "We haven't seen all my memories yet. There's a specific moment in time we have yet to relive, so that I can share with you how it all ended. The truth of the Kingdom of Eternia—and of my feelings, as well."

Before anyone could stop her, she reached forward and touched the crystal.

The ruins of Aegias were covered in deep snow. Very few people were in sight, hobbling between the broken buildings. Wind howled among the ruins. The cold was bitter, even with the Essence protection.

Dana and Rastell stopped at the edge of the palace plaza, looking at the view.

"Watch your step. It's easy to lose your footing here." Rastell held out his hand, and Dana took it gratefully. The dark patch covering his eye made this side of his face look blank—the price he'd paid for defending her against the angry mob. It could have been much worse, if not for Olga's care.

"I can't believe how cold the kingdom has become," she said.

He lifted her over a pile of stone rubble, setting her down onto the pavement on the other side. "Yes. The chill has only intensified since we left three months ago."

Dana looked sideways at the view. "If this continues, the capital will..." She swallowed. "I hope everyone who has been evacuated to the palace is safe."

Rastell only nodded. Even though the ground was level here, they continued to hold hands as they walked, his touch giving her strength. She felt so lucky to have him by her side, the only good thing that had happened to her in all the desolation around them.

Seeing Rastell broken and dying after she returned from the Valley of Kings had destroyed a major boundary inside her. He'd almost died defending her. The world was ending. The rules and restrictions they both had been living by no longer applied. After she poured out all her Essence to nurse him back to health, she didn't want to hold back any longer. Ever since they were children, they had always been attracted to each other. And now, no one could stop them from acting on these feelings, allowing themselves to enjoy their time together before the end.

She paused as a strange sensation tugged her mind. Rastell stopped too, turning around to face her.

"What is it?"

She let out a breath. "I'm not sure. I just felt like we were being watched."

Rastell reacted in a flash as he stepped past, shielding her. His hand darted to the hilt of his sword.

A gust of wind howled in front of them, but no assault came. Rastell held his stance for a moment longer, then relaxed and turned back to her.

"I must have imagined it." Dana still couldn't get rid of the feeling that someone was watching, but she didn't want to alarm him anymore. The ghostly presence seemed familiar somehow. One of the spirits she'd rescued? She wasn't sure.

"The air is getting colder," Rastell said. "Even with our Essence equipment protecting us, temperatures this low are still dangerous. We should enter the palace. Lady Olga is expecting us."

"Yes."

They walked forward, through the Stupa building, down the Aerial Corridor, past the frozen aqueducts and the icy remains of the royal gardens. The palace doors were closed, but they rolled open easily under Rastell's hands, letting them into the hallway and up the stairs into the throne room.

It was warm here. Braziers set on the floor along the length of the hall glowed with hot embers, filling the large, vaulted space with a deep red glow. After the bite of the wind outside, Dana felt her skin pleasantly tingle as she stepped up to one of them.

It was staggering to think that this hall harbored all the remaining survivors from the entire city. People stood around talking in groups or huddled on the floor next to the braziers to take advantage of the warmth. Makeshift beds lined the walls, housing the sick and the dying.

Olga stood at the far end of the room on the elevated platform that used to hold the throne. Dana made her way toward her friend, catching shreds of conversations as she passed.

"I heard rumors that we're out of food. If that's the case, then maybe I should . . ."

"It's over. Eternia is over. We're doomed. Doomed, I say."

"Don't worry, my friend. I'll be with you soon." The sadness in the speaker's voice left no doubt he was addressing a loved one recently deceased. He and his group gathered around one of the beds, nodding solemnly.

"I'm cold . . . It hurts . . ." It took Dana a moment to recognize the young woman huddled by the nearest brazier. Kajura, a cheerful maiden who had been prancing around the town not so long ago, bragging how the famous Bard Sepa himself was teaching her harvest hymns for the next festival. She seemed half delirious. Frost fever, probably. Too many people in recent weeks had lost their lives to this disease, which had ravaged the population after the cold set in. Kajura's seemed to be in the early stages though. Dana reached into her medicine pouch and brought out a small bundle.

"I know it's not much, but I have some medicinal herbs here." She handed them to the young woman. "I hope you feel better."

Kajura lifted her head. "R-really? Uh..." She turned the bundle over in her hands. "When the herbs wear off, am I going to die? I don't wanna die yet...I don't wanna die!" She sank back into her spot.

Dana's heart wrenched in pain, but there was nothing more she could do for this girl. For any of them. After a moment, she moved on.

A little girl standing near one of the beds waved to her.

"Lady Dana!"

"Sia?" Dana's smile froze as everyone in the vicinity turned around at the sound of her name. None of the faces looked friendly. People eyed her cautiously, as if she were contagious.

"Ah, you're right," someone said. "It's Lady Dana. She's back."

"I thought she abandoned us. Just like Queen Sarai and Council Darius."

Dana ignored the sting of these words. These people had lost everything. Finding someone to blame was a healthy reaction. She pretended not to hear them as she hurried over to Sia.

The girl looked well, though thinner and paler than before. The group of beds here seemed denser, each of them occupied, with more people huddled on the floor around them. The clinic, Dana guessed as she spotted a few of the Temple clerics and priestesses working in the back.

The people in the beds were dying, but those on the floor didn't look much better. Merchant Barossa sat leaning against the wall, mumbling to himself. He didn't seem to recognize Dana. Further on, Cleric Cecile lay in bed, motionless. Dana's heart quivered.

"Welcome back, Lady Dana," Sia said.

Dana nodded. "It's good to be back, Sia. Thank you for taking care of everyone. But...you shouldn't push yourself too hard."

Sia's eyes trailed over the row of beds. "Oh, I'll be fine. Besides, I'm good at this. Me and my mom have survived so far, thanks to everyone...I gotta pay it back somehow."

She sounded so different from the little girl who could burst into tears over a game of hide and seek not so long ago. The disaster had matured her far too quickly.

Cleric Sienna stepped up to them.

"Lady Dana. I am so glad you are back." She lowered her head. "I have bad news, I'm afraid. About Odo."

Dana's heart sank. "Odo?"

"Yesterday he used the last of his Essence to protect us from the cold front. I tried to stop him. I told him not to overwork himself, but he—he—" She covered her mouth, stifling a sob. "Overnight, he just faded away. We couldn't do anything."

Odo. Dana swallowed. If she and Rastell had returned a day earlier, perhaps she would have been able to help. Odo could still be alive. It was but a small drop to add to the heavy burden of guilt she was already carrying, but a staggering one nonetheless. The Essence Maester was a dear old friend who had guided her since she was a child. It was just like him to die by spending the last of his Essence to protect everyone. But that didn't make the loss feel any better. A tear rolled down her cheek.

"Don't cry," Sienna said. "He wouldn't want that. I'm sorry to have to tell you this when you've only just returned..."

Dana couldn't find any words as she patted Sienna's arm, then stepped past her toward the platform.

Not that long ago, she, Olga, and Sarai had stood here next to the throne, talking about the upcoming disaster. The throne was now gone—probably used for firewood, like most of the furniture here. Olga stood in the center of the empty space, talking to two men. Dana recognized the one in the guard uniform—Sharl, Rastell's superior. The other man seemed unfamiliar, but the insignia and styling of his robe indicated an official position of a civil servant. Someone from Darius's office? It didn't really matter. She stopped near the steps, trying to catch the thread of the conversation.

"But our food supply is scarce," Sharl said. "The stockpile commissioned by the Queen is nearly empty."

"As things stand now," the other man said, "we may not outlast the cold. Do you think this winter will ever end? They say Lady Dana no longer receives visions. If she has lost her powers, as the rumors suggest, she has no right to lead us."

"Mind your tone," Sharl interceded sternly. "Lady Dana risked her life to travel north and investigate. Even if she has lost her powers, her dedication to her people is without question!"

"That's not what I meant," the other man protested. "I just—"

"Stop it, both of you," Olga snapped. "This argument is pointless. Regarding our food supply, we have potatoes stored in the underground sanctuary. We'll ask anyone who is able to bring them here."

"Oh, I see," the civil servant said. "Thank you, Lady Olga. I'll let the people know right away."

"Also," Olga went on, "I know there are still pockets of survivors in the city. I want you to investigate and tell any survivors you find to evacuate to this location."

"Good idea," Sharl said. "Anyone who's still out there won't survive the next cold front. My men and I will depart at once."

"Good." Olga nodded. "I'm counting on you both."

Dana ascended the platform. Olga's eyes widened, as if she'd only just noticed her—another testament to the extreme duress of being in charge here. In old days, Olga would have spotted her the moment she and Rastell came in through the main door.

"Dana," she breathed out. "I'm glad to see you're safe. You surprised me when you said you were leaving the capital to investigate the northern nations."

"I'm sorry, Olga. I hope I didn't worry you too much." It felt so good to be with Olga again. Even the reproach in her gaze felt comforting. Being scolded by Olga was part of the familiar routine, one they had both gotten used to ever since they were children.

"So what's the situation in the north?" Olga said.

Dana glanced around at the busy hall. "Perhaps we should discuss it in private?"

Olga nodded and led the way across the hall into the snowstorm outside. Rastell disengaged from a group of guards and fell into stride beside them. Of course he would never let Dana out of his sight. Dana's heart filled with warmth as she briefly caught his gaze.

They found an empty guardroom and left Rastell outside to keep watch. Dana felt guilty about it, but she had no other choice. She wanted to speak freely without being overheard—even by Rastell—as she described the situation.

"So the northern nations have been annihilated," Olga said after Dana had finished her report.

Dana lowered her head. "It gets even colder the farther north you go."

"That can only mean any survivors have most likely migrated south of the capital."

"I would assume as much. The surviving Saurians are migrating south as we speak. I hope we all make it through this."

Olga shook her head thoughtfully. "The southern nations are not so prosperous, but at least hope can still be found there. The real question is, what should we do?"

Dana raised her head. "This is what I wanted to talk to you about. I believe we should leave the capital and travel to the southern nations. We can even provide what resources we have here, as a way of helping."

Olga sighed. "I knew you would suggest that."

"So you're saying—"

"You do have a point, is all. But...let me think about it a bit." She peered into Dana's face.

"Anything wrong?" Dana asked.

Olga frowned. "There's a rumor going around that you don't receive visions anymore. But you still do...Don't you, Dana?"

"Y-yes." Dana hesitated. Her inability to see the future was only temporary. No reason to alarm Olga when so much depended on it. But even as the word left her mouth, she knew there was no fooling her old friend.

Olga's green eyes studied her thoughtfully. "I see...Then I need to think about this very carefully. Let's talk again tomorrow morning."

"Olga..."

Olga turned, all businesslike again. "I'm sorry, Dana. There is something I must take care of before nightfall." She swept past and out of the room.

Rastell entered as soon as she was gone.

"What did Lady Olga say?" he asked.

"She..." Dana took a breath. "She'll have an answer tomorrow."

"I see." He looked away, and Dana could tell she hadn't fooled him any more than she had Olga. Her shortcomings were leading them all into a stalemate. She didn't receive visions anymore, and Olga wasn't leaving. Even if it meant certain death.

"You must understand," Dana said. "Olga grew up in the capital, so the thought of leaving is a very difficult one for her."

Rastell scoffed. "I grew up in the capital too. It doesn't mean I want to stay here and freeze to death when there're people to be saved."

At least he still had his fire. She closed her eyes briefly, steadying her emotions.

"Dana?"

"I'm all right. Let's prepare as we planned."

Rastell nodded. "Understood. I shall take my leave then and begin the preparations."

"I'll catch up with you in a bit. I want to take a walk around the city."

"What? At this hour? In this cold?"

"Only a short one."

"Let me escort you then."

"No. I'll be fine. The city is so empty, there's hardly any danger. I just need to gather my thoughts."

Rastell bowed his head. "I understand. Just don't leave the city limits. And...Please be careful."

"I will." She found his hand and squeezed it, drawing strength from his touch.

Gusts of low wind blew snow across the city walkways. Even with the Essence charm she wore, it chilled her to the bone. Halfway down the street, she stopped, looking at the Great Tree of Origins looming in the distance against the gray cliffs.

Memories overwhelmed her. The Temple, the city, her home village, her friends...So many memories here—all blowing away like the dust of snowflakes flurrying over the ruined city. Some said snow could be beautiful. All she saw about it was death.

"Hey!" A shrill voice pierced the howl of the wind behind her.

Dana spun around. "*Io?*"

The little girl waved to Dana from the plaza beside the Stupa building.

Dana frowned in disbelief. Io seemed the same as always, as if she weren't strolling through the snowy ruins but taking a casual walk on a market day. She wore her usual light tunic but didn't look cold or uncomfortable at all. The girl must have come by a powerful Essence charm somehow. Dana rushed toward her.

"Hiya, lady!" Io's face lit up with a smile as Dana approached. Something about her expression seemed guarded though. Or was Dana only imagining it? In these harsh times, everyone felt guarded, really. It was much more of a wonder that Io was still here, apparently healthy despite walking around in this frost.

"Io..." she breathed out. "I'm so glad to see you."

"Me too, Maiden."

Dana shook her head. "I'm not the Maiden of the Great Tree anymore."

"You're not?" Io regarded her thoughtfully. "I'm not so sure about that."

"What do you mean?"

"It's not so easy for a person to stop being what they are."

Dana frowned. This girl always said the strangest things. A memory of their last meeting floated up in her mind. Back then, she had almost convinced herself that Io was a supernatural being. But here, on the frozen street, the thought seemed ridiculous.

"You need to evacuate to the palace, Io," she said. "Another cold front is coming. It's not safe here."

Io shrugged. "I'm fine. I only came here to fulfill my promise."

"Your promise?"

The little girl grinned up at her. "Yes. I promised to see you one more time, remember?"

"Yes, but—"

"I know it's sad, but it's time to say farewell."

"But—"

Io stopped her with a short glance. "Sorry. There is so much I need to explain. I'll tell you everything at the usual place. Come as soon as you can—I'll be waiting!" She turned and ran toward the palace.

Dana stood for a moment looking after her. The usual place. It had to be the Sanctuary. She couldn't wait to get down there and find out what Io had to say. But somehow she knew Io would wait for as long as needed. Before Dana could join her, there was another thing she needed to do.

IO

Dana made her way back into the palace. At the entrance to the throne room, Rastell was talking to Sharl—probably about departure. Both men looked tense. She veered away, into the hallway on the right and down the stairs.

Like the throne room, the chamber she entered had a glowing brazier in the center, but the air here was markedly colder—probably because most of this room was not occupied by the living. Coffins lined the walls, most of them closed and sealed, indicating the presence of an occupant inside. A few empty ones were stacked at the far side.

A small group of clerics were gathered around an open coffin at the back of the room, Handmaid Alta among them. Dana approached with a sinking heart.

Essence Maester Odo looked so peaceful as he lay there, eyes closed, hands folded over his chest. He would have seemed merely asleep if not for the paleness of his cheeks, hollow and frosted in a way that could never happen to a living man. Here in the back of the room the cold was likely sufficient to preserve the body for days, but Dana hadn't realized this kind of freezing could happen in only a few hours—probably because Odo had drained himself of all warmth before his passing.

Dana's heart sank as she approached and stopped beside Alta. The clerics edged aside to make room for her.

"He used all his Essence to protect us from illness and the cold." Alta's voice trembled. "We begged him to stop, but he just smiled and ignored us."

"If only . . ." another cleric began, then paused, wiping her cheek.

"If only we could offer him even one flower."

"Yes," Alta said. "He did so much for us. But where could we find a flower in this cold?"

"I'll find one," Dana said firmly. "It wouldn't be right to send him off without a flower."

She had no idea where to look. All the plants in Aegias were long dead. But it didn't matter. She had to do it, that's all. Odo had done his duty until his last breath, and she was going to do the same. She walked out of the palace and across the Aerial Corridor into the city ruins.

It was so empty and cold here, not a soul in sight. Climbing through the icy rock piles, Dana scarcely recognized these places, so lively and beautiful just a short time ago.

At the market plaza a mound of stone rubble created a shelter from the wind, with just a bit of grass still showing through. Dana's heart leapt as she approached. Here. A lone blue flower rose from the patch—frozen through, but still shapely and beautiful.

A Tyrennian blossom. These simple but elegant flowers were lovingly seeded throughout the kingdom. Even though this one was frozen solid, it still held the memory of that time. People used to give them to each other as symbols of gratitude—so appropriate in this case. Dana had so many things to be grateful to Odo for. His guidance. His friendship. His support. His devotion to her cause. Another tear rolled down her cheek, and she let it fall, melting a tiny well through the snow.

She bent down and carefully picked the flower, channeling Essence to preserve it as she headed back to the palace.

Alta's eyes widened as she watched Dana approach the coffin and lay the flower over Odo's chest. All around them the clerics were sobbing. Dana sobbed too, her tears falling freely as she tucked the flower into Odo's cold hand and stepped away.

"We lost Lady Urgunata on a day very much like today," Alta said at length. "She passed away shortly after you left, Lady Dana. She kept telling us to encourage you to press on, until the very end." She looked into the coffin. "Odo believed in you too."

Dana nodded. "Thank you, Odo," she whispered. "I hope now you can rest in peace."

They held a small funeral service for Essence Maester Odo and the others who had recently passed. All the able-bodied survivors helped to carry the coffins out of the room one by one, lowering them into shallow graves chiseled out of the frozen earth. Dana prayed silently for each person as their bodies were laid to rest.

It was getting dark when Dana finally entered the Stupa building. She felt only half surprised to find the door to the Sanctuary Crypt open, the familiar staircase descending into the gloom. Io must have left the way open to invite Dana inside.

The warping crystal at the entrance to the first chamber seemed intact. Dana used it to warp all the way across the crypt, to the platform with the Great Tree seal on the floor.

A green glowing ball was floating next to it, as if waiting. Jenya, the Spirit of Life? With Jenya's power now coursing through her, Dana couldn't possibly be mistaken. Her heart leapt. Seeing Jenya felt like meeting another friend from the better days.

"Jenya?" she said. "What are you doing here?"

"Jenya is not the only one here," another spirit voice said.

More glowing balls floated into view, surrounding Dana. The spirits she'd rescued during her travels. Their voices filled the chamber. Or were they echoing in her mind?

"Dana . . . "

"I haven't seen you in a long time."

"We are in your debt." This last one was Orvis, the Spirit of White Nights. Even though the spirits had no physical features, she recognized them all easily. Was it because all of them had once gifted her with their powers?

"The Great Tree hast begun the cycle of Selection and Rejection," Wagmur, Spirit of the Wood, said. "It will destroy all life in Eternia. Even we spirits are not exempt."

A chorus of voices rustled in response.

"Yes, for we were born of this Earth."

"Thus, we must one day return to it. Such is our fate."

"We're the only spirits that still remain."

"I'm sorry," Dana said. "And you all lent me your power too. I'm sorry I wasn't able to save you."

"I know how hard this must be for you," said Selene, Spirit of Covenants. "But please don't be sad."

"Yes, we are just disturbances in the Earth made manifest. We are simply returning to our original forms."

They swarmed in a circle around her.

"Goodbye, Dana."

"Thanks to you, we can face our fate with a sense of peace."

"We are thankful to you."

"Please do not forget us."

"I won't forget any of you," Dana said, from the bottom of her heart. "Not ever."

"Should we fade away," Wagmur said, "the protection we've granted thee will fade as well. Thou must make haste."

"Make haste? But...isn't this the final floor of the crypt?"

"Unexplored depths still remain. But thou must be careful...for a being of great evil awaits you."

"E-evil?" Dana frowned. She'd thought she was on her way to meet Io. What in the world did the spirits mean?

"Our last...gift to you..."

She felt a vibration at her back and drew her swords. They were glowing, humming with power.

"May your blades always ring true."

"May your hands be steady."

"Good luck."

"Farewell..."

The spirits dissipated.

Dana looked at her swords. The spirits had infused them with extra power, as if preparing her for a battle. What was it waiting for her at the bottom of the crypt?

Somehow, she knew exactly what to do next as she walked forward and stood at the center of the circular seal.

It had been unresponsive before, but this time the floor trembled under her feet and slid down into the chamber below.

An Essence crystal glistened in front of her. She climbed a stone stairway to a wide platform rising on massive supports out of the lake of lava down below. A rectangular slab of black stone carved with the Great Tree symbol loomed at the far end of the platform.

A monolith? Dana had never seen such a large one before. She ascended the stairs and crossed the floor, stopping in front of it.

"You finally made it." Io stepped from behind the monolith. "Dana Iclucia, Maiden of the Great Tree," she began solemnly, then laughed. "Just kidding! Hiya, lady! Nice to see you again!"

"Io..." Dana's skin prickled. *A being of great evil awaits you,* the spirits had said. No, not Io. But how...?

"I'm actually surprised you came here," Io said, "considering all that's happened. Another one in your place might have chosen to stay away. You're really trying your best to lead everyone till the very end."

Dana shook her head. "It's clear to me now that you're no ordinary Eternian. Are you...a Warden?"

"Hmmm." Io's eyes flicked to the floor and back to Dana's face. "Who can say? Sorry, but you're no exception, Dana. Before I give you any answers, I need to make sure you're worthy too. Even I can't stop the ritual that's underway in this sanctuary. Here goes..."

A circle of power formed around the girl's feet and rose like an opening flower, blowing up wind as it grew. Io spread her arms into the glow and laughed. "This is gonna be great. None of the previous Maidens ever gathered this many spirits. Yes...You are worthy of facing me, Io, as your final opponent."

The glow rose up to her shoulders now, drowning out her small shape. It momentarily flooded Dana's vision. And then...

A giant Saurian rose in the spot where Io had just stood. Fiery and winged, it raised its face into the air and roared. Before Dana could gather herself, it attacked.

Dana's blades, infused with the power of the spirits, came to life on their own, whirling so quickly they seemed directed by a separate mind. At times they seemed nearly invisible, streaks of light and power, not weapons she bore but extensions of herself. The spirits' last gift had filled her with strength and speed beyond anything she was ever capable of before. But Io—the Saurian Io—was her match...and more. This was by far the hardest opponent Dana had ever faced—and the most enjoyable one.

A being of great evil, the spirits had called her. But they were wrong. Even in her Saurian form, Io wasn't evil, just powerful beyond measure in this underground world. Dana's mind slid into a trance as she danced around the floor, facing the creature, using all the powers and all the spirit styles she'd ever learned. She wasn't fighting an enemy this time. She was fighting to achieve unity with this strange being, Io, that she sensed as a kindred spirit similar to her own.

They matched each other, form to form, blow to blow, power to power. Yet, after a while, Dana sensed her opponent weaken. Io took longer to recompose after each blow, lashing out weaker than before. She recoiled as Dana launched an attack using her Luminous skill, and at last the giant Saurian sank to the floor and lay motionless.

421

Light shimmered, enfolding the creature. When it dissipated, a little girl was kneeling in its place, huffing in exhaustion.

Dana felt exhausted too. She had spent every last bit of her strength. Both she and Io took a while to recover before they could speak again. Yet when the girl finally rose to her feet and turned to face Dana, a smile was playing on her lips, and her eyes gleamed with an excitement that Dana felt sure was mirrored in her own gaze.

They looked at each other and laughed.

"Well, this sucks," Io said. "You were strong enough to defeat my Saurian form. You have surely overcome many hardships to stand here as the final Maiden." She gestured to the giant stone slab. "Alright, don't be shy. I know you're dying to read the final monolith."

Dana nodded. She still felt entranced. In this new reality, things like a little girl turning into a vicious Saurian, then back into a girl, and continuing their conversation as if nothing had happened, didn't seem surprising at all. She approached the control panel.

The hexagonal reading pane popped up before she had a chance to touch it with her Essence. The text began in mid-paragraph, as if picking up right from where the previous monolith had left off. Dana tried to recall what it had said. Hadn't the last record been about Saint Urianus saving the people from the cataclysms of the Great Tree?

She read:

The King was bewildered. He believed the Great Tree brought blessings, when it was actually disaster incarnate. Having discovered the truth, the King found himself trapped in a downward spiral of terror. But Saint Urianus stood before the King.

"The Great Tree may be disaster incarnate, but it also gave life to Eternia. What does this make the Great Tree, if not the world itself? For the future of our people, we must accept this truth. The Great Tree can never be uprooted."

The Light King accepted the wisdom of the saint and placed the Great Tree under his protection. The Wall of Truth and the Garden, which depict the threat posed by the Great Tree, were sealed deep underground. As time passed, the Light King grew old, and Urianus, the Saint of Salvation, died as he lived—in total tranquility. Rain fell upon the capital for over a month, as if the sky itself was in mourning. But when a woman—a disciple of the saint—offered a prayer, the rain ceased, and sunlight shone down upon the capital.

She erected a temple south of the capital, where she would calm the Great

Tree, and reports of her exploits soon found their way to the King. The King approved of this, and Eternians received the blessings of the heavens as they entered a new era of prosperity. The woman remained in Eternia and became the first Maiden to devote herself to the Great Tree.

In time, the Great Tree became a symbol of prosperity for the kingdom. The King decreed that the Temple stood on equal footing as the palace, and this was how the Kingdom of Eternia was founded.

Dana looked around and met Io's gaze.

"So this is the final chapter of the lost history of Eternia's founding," she said. "I never knew the real history behind the Temple. The people would be shaken to their cores if they found out about this. But then... who built this sanctuary? And why?"

"There's more," Io said quietly.

Dana looked to where the girl was pointing. As if summoned forth, a reading pane appeared in front of her. The Great Tree symbol in this section was framed by text on each side.

As the people enjoy their prosperity, the threat depicted on the Wall of Truth will be lost to time. But it will return one day, like a bubble that must eventually burst. You Maidens who have come to this sanctuary, you Maidens who are my successors, you will know this truth and bear it on your soul forever. That is the true duty of all Maidens. The reason for their very existence. Until such a day that the final Maiden arrives.

"This message is for all the Maidens of the Great Tree," Dana said.

"Well." Io stepped forward to her side. "Don't you look surprised."

Dana turned to face her. "Io... Are you actually...?"

"Looks like you figured it out," Io said. "Yes, I am. Io, a disciple of Saint Urianus. The first Maiden of the Great Tree." She smiled. "You did a wonderful job overcoming my trials, Dana."

"But..." Dana paused. She had so many questions. The one that popped into her head first wasn't the most important one by far, but she asked it anyway. "Why do you look like that?"

Io's smile widened. "This form is just a manifestation of my soul. My power has weakened over all these centuries, which is why I look like a child now. I have no strength to maintain an adult form anymore. But finally, I'm able to fulfill my duty."

"Io..." Dana bowed. "I mean, Lady Io... What is your duty?"

"Lady Io, huh?" Io giggled. "I don't like formalities any more than you do, Dana. I prefer you keep calling me Io, like you've been doing. As for my duty, here is how I see it. I built this sanctuary as means to reveal the true history to every Maiden that came after me.

I've been doing it this way, so the Wardens wouldn't notice."

Dana stared. She couldn't imagine what Io must have gone through, knowing the truth all these centuries, unable to communicate it in any way except through the trials of this Sanctuary. Devising this method to evade the Wardens must have been hard, to say the least. The amount of skill and Essence that it took to build this place...She shook her head, unsure what to say.

"Not every Maiden could handle the truth either," Io said. "Some of them cussed me out, or accused me of being a heretic. Others just went mad from the revelation. But you are different. You were able to figure it out on your own, before I even told you."

"Why have you been doing this?" Dana asked.

Io's gaze trailed into the distance. "The Great Tree of Origins will destroy Eternia. Tomorrow is never guaranteed. Someday, you won't be able to do the things you currently take for granted. The world is a cruel place. At times, it even feels like a fleeting dream. Perhaps the same could be said of people's lives. No matter who you are, everyone meets death in the end. Whether you are a highborn noble or a lowborn bandit, everyone must return to the void of nothingness. Consider every action a person performs in their lifetime. Every decision that they make. Do you think they're meaningless?"

"I..."

"You'll have to face that day too, Dana. What will you think when it finally comes? Will you think your life was meaningless? Will you say to yourself: 'I shouldn't have become a Maiden. It wasn't worth all the suffering. I should have worn my mother's ring and kept my visions sealed away. Was I only helping people just to feel like I mattered?' Or maybe you'll think: 'I wish I had never been born.' Will you regret your life to that extent?"

"No," Dana said firmly. "I would never think that. All my experiences are the reason I was able to connect with so many people. If even one of those events were different, I wouldn't be the person I am today."

Io looked thoughtful.

"I think that's true of Eternia as well," Dana said. "The decisions made by you, the royals, and our ancestors, that's our inheritance. That's why we're alive right now. Even if Eternia disappears, whoever succeeds us will inherit our legacy. So even if Eternia is on the verge of extinction, I don't think my actions were meaningless."

"Wow," Io said. "I didn't think you'd actually have a response for me. Yes, you exist as you do now because of me. And your existence is proof that I once existed. I hoped your brand of determination would be the thread that ties all the Maidens together throughout the ages."

"So that's the reason you've been telling the Maidens the truth about the Great Tree?"

"Yeah." Io giggled, a little girl again. "Well, anyway. I was worried about how you'd handle the burden of being the final Maiden, but I see I was worrying over nothing."

Dana nodded solemnly. "Even if this work seems like a fleeting dream, no matter what happens, as long as the world goes on, so do our wills. So I will never give up."

Io measured her up and down. "I'm impressed. You know far more than I expected you to. I guess you have your own answers."

Dana kept her gaze. She did, but she still was so grateful for this conversation. She guessed she didn't need to tell this to Io. They understood each other without words.

"Looks like there's nothing left for me to tell you," Io said. "I'll leave the rest to the younger generation. I'm getting too old for this stuff anyway."

Dana smiled. "Thanks to you, I feel like I can see this through."

"Thank you too. Perhaps it's irresponsible of me to say this, but . . . Go get 'em, Dana!"

"I will," Dana said.

Early next morning, Dana and Rastell led the crowd of refugees out of the palace. Three dozen was all they could gather, those still strong enough to travel, those who hadn't given up hope. Dana was glad to see Sia and her mother among them, as well as many of the Temple clerics.

Olga walked with them up to the city gates. There she and Dana stopped, while Rastell and the others went on ahead.

"Must you leave so soon?" Olga said. "We still have provisions, you know."

Dana looked at the sets of footsteps through the snow. It's gotten so deep. Traveling would be difficult in this weather.

"The next cold front will be here soon," she said. "This is just the calm before the storm."

"I'm sorry I cannot come with you."

"It's all right." Dana met her gaze. She was sorry beyond measure to leave Olga behind, but she understood. Some people had chosen to stay behind. They needed a strong leader to survive here.

"I want everyone to make the decision that suits them best," Olga explained. "That includes the people who have chosen to remain in the capital. Their choice is not a practical one, but I understand why they have made it."

"Olga..."

"Some people still blame you for what happened. It's best if I stay behind to lead them through what is to come. Everyone must walk a path of their own choosing, so they can face their final moments with pride."

Dana sighed. "I would expect nothing less from you, Olga." She extended her hand for a shake. "This is not goodbye, is it?"

Olga stepped closer. "No, it most certainly is not." She took Dana's hand, then leaned forward and touched Dana's forehead with hers. Dana stifled a sob. This was what her mother used to do, a gesture of comfort and closeness, offering support at the hardest of times.

They stood like this for a while, then turned around and walked away in opposite directions.

THE LAST DAY OF THIS WORLD

Dana stepped away from the crystal and turned to the group.

"This is how it ended," she said. "Our move to the south wasn't enough to save all these people." *Rastell.* She closed her eyes briefly. "When I returned to Aegias a year later, alone, everyone was gone."

The only thing that had kept her sane at the time was the knowledge that, ages later, she was going to meet Adol. This thought had prevented her from succumbing to despair and being trapped by the Great Tree forever to end up like the other Wardens. And now, meeting Adol in person had made the wait worth it.

Rastell, Olga, Alta, Cecile, Io, everyone she'd ever known. The world they'd all wanted to protect was gone now. But this world here had inherited the same hope. She wished someday she could meet her friends' psyches, so that she could tell them about the true meaning of their sacrifice.

"I am ready, Adol," she said.

He met her gaze. "Let's finish this."

The party took another day to complete the preparations for the final battle. They all understood that it wasn't just a combat challenge they were facing. They had to throw their entire beings into the fight if they wanted it to decide the fate of humanity. Of course, no one knew if stopping the Lacrimosa was any guarantee that this world would survive, but Dana didn't want to think about it. Any alternative was better than watching everyone get consumed by monsters as she and Adol, the chosen Wardens, succumbed to despair and got swallowed by the Great Tree, leaving this place desolate and clear for the development of the next dominant species.

She searched the camp for Adol, eventually finding him on the small beach near the docks. The ship the villagers were working on was nearly complete. If all went well, they were going to use it to escape. Would Dana go with them and leave the remnants of her world behind? She dismissed the thought. If all went well, there would be time for this decision later on.

Adol's face lit up when he saw her approach. No one but Rastell had ever looked at her this way, as if seeing her was the greatest thing that had ever happened to him. Rastell was now gone. For the first time since she'd lost him, she felt closure. Somehow, she knew his soul had finally found peace, leaving her free to explore these feelings again with someone else.

"There's a place in the village I'd like to visit before we go," she said. "Would you like to accompany me?"

Adol nodded.

They climbed the watchtower and sat, leaning against the mast, watching the view. She felt so peaceful when they were together. If the world was ending tomorrow, this was how she wanted to remember everything.

"What's on your mind?" Adol asked after a while.

She looked at him sideways, then trailed her eyes to the endless flow of the waves running into the distance.

"Even if we manage to stop the Lacrimosa," she said, "we have no idea what will happen. We are about to disturb the natural order of things. Before we do... I have to confess something to you. Actually, I need to apologize to you."

"Apologize?" He frowned.

"Yes. You and I, we have a fascinating bond. We shared a consciousness, and through that we were able to travel together too. You allowed me a unique glimpse into your soul. It made me realize something. Your soul truly burns brighter than any other soul in the world. I think, somehow, I've known this all along."

He shook his head slowly. "I am nothing compared to you. If only you could see yourself... Every time I look at you, I just can't believe how perfect you are. Whatever happens tomorrow—"

She reached up and placed a finger across his mouth to silence him. He caught her hand and pressed it against his lips. Her toes curled, a surge of pleasure rushing through her body.

"You don't understand," she said. "I think I was the one who selected you to be the Warden of Evolution for humanity. I may be the reason you're forced to suffer in the future. I'm so sorry that I forced this burden on you."

He still cradled her hand in his as he shifted to face her more directly. His touch, the way he looked at her, made her melt inside.

"I'm honored that you chose me," he said.

Dana heaved a breath. "The honor is all mine. And I will fight by your side until the very end."

She reached into her pocket and brought out a ring, slipping it onto his finger, using her Essence to ensure the fit.

"I'd like you to have this," she said.

He looked at it in bewilderment. "Is this—"

"Yes. A keepsake from my mother. She gave me this ring to seal my ability to use Essence—and because of this, I failed her so badly." She swallowed. "I've always carried it with me as a reminder of my duty to everyone who needed help."

His eyes trailed over the intricate lines of the ancient design, a knot of silver threads forming a seal around a small circle of gold, a work of ancient craftmanship that could never be replicated.

"I remember," he said softly. "You spoke about this once. And . . . I can't take something so precious away from you." He made to remove the ring, but she cupped his hand to stop him.

"Normally this ring seals Essence," she said. "But I modified it somewhat, so that you could make use of it. It will aid the power of the psyches and your sword." *And if we must part, it will be a reminder of this time we spent with each other.* She didn't say this out loud. Her scarlet vision had told her that they couldn't be together. But they were set out to change the entire order of the world. On this scale, even scarlet visions didn't seem that important.

He twined his fingers with hers, looking at the ring, then flipped his hand over so that her palm was resting on top of his.

"Thank you," he said. "I will cherish this."

Did he mean the ring, or holding her hand? Both, she guessed. And yes, she too was going to cherish this moment as long as she existed.

It crossed her mind that if they failed, if Lacrimosa ran its course and she and Adol were forced to take their places as Wardens of Evolution, they were going to be together for all eternity. But even with this temptation, her choice was clear. She was going to put everything into the fight they faced. She was going to make sure they won.

She had no idea what was going to happen tomorrow, but it was possible that all they had left together was this one day. She wanted to make the most of it.

She reached up and cupped Adol's cheek. He leaned over and kissed her.

Adol felt unsteady on his feet when he and Dana climbed down from the watchtower. It was getting dark. They'd spent most of the day up there, and he didn't regret a moment of it. He didn't want to get back to the real world.

Griselda was sitting in the lodge's common room, studying a rock slab in front of her. At the other end of the table, Sir Carlan bent over the books, using a quill to take notes on the page. Adol looked over his work with interest. It had taken some frank and not altogether pleasant conversations to figure out the nobleman's superb talent with numbers, which had finally earned him a place as a highly useful member of the crew, in charge of keeping records and budgeting their supplies. Even Dina grudgingly accepted this new addition to her accounting system, forming a shaky alliance with the man.

Sir Carlan grunted as they walked by, as if the mere sight of them was a royal nuisance. Almost at the same moment, Griselda lifted her head, beckoning them over.

"Adol! Dana!" Her eyes slid down to their hands that had twined without Adol even realizing it. She smiled but didn't comment as she pointed at the stone slab in front of her.

Dana frowned as she leaned over it. "Is this...a fragment of an archival monolith?"

"I thought you'd know what it was. I found it while I was exploring the northern region of the island. As you can see, half of it is missing."

Dana leaned closer. "Well, the main section that stores the information is still intact. But without the missing piece, it cannot be activated. If we could only find the rest of it..."

"Wait here." Adol darted into the sleeping quarters and rummaged in the trunk next to his hammock, where he kept his spare supplies, as well as items they'd found during their explorations of the island that weren't of any immediate use. He emerged moments later carrying the rock piece recovered from the small islet where they'd rescued Sir Carlan recently. With all the excitement of the last few days, he'd almost forgotten about it.

"Is this it?" he asked.

Griselda's eyes widened as she took it from his hands and fit it to the other piece lying on the tabletop. The monolith looked whole now, the crack across it still visible but not as prominent as one would expect from a piece that old. Adol wondered if someone had deliberately broken this monolith into two, hiding the pieces on different parts of the island. It must have held something important and controversial.

What were the chances of uncovering it after all this time?

"It should work now." Dana stretched her palms over the monolith.

A glowing hexagon covered with symbols rose above the table.

"This is fascinating," Griselda whispered.

Dana ran her eyes over the text. "This is what's known as the Truth of Eternia... A lost scripture, said to explain the true purpose of the Great Tree of Origins. A version of it existed in the Temple library, but the original monolith..." She frowned. "Here:

"*All originated from an abyss—the boundless sky spreading in all directions. In time, rain fell from the sky, giving rise to the ocean. Fire spewed forth from the ocean, giving rise to the Earth and the Great Tree. By the power of the Great Tree, life was formed, evolved, and set foot on the Earth. And life is nurtured still by the Earth. One day, life must return to the sky through the Great Tree. Thus, life continues the cycle of evolution.*"

"Interesting," Griselda said. "There's a religion called Tritheism, which predates the Hieroglyph Church that currently dominates our world. It was centered around the worship of three gods: Horu, the Sky God, Grattheos, the Sea God, and Maia, the Earth Goddess."

"Maia?" Dana frowned.

"Hydra mentioned Earth Goddess Maia," Adol reminded. "Could this mean that Tritheism originated even before Eternia?"

"There's no way to prove that," Griselda said. "But... it's an interesting theory." Her eyes slid over Dana and Adol again. "But don't let me interfere any longer. You two should go ahead and spend more time together, right?"

Adol and Dana looked at each other and smiled.

THE SELECTION SPHERE

Sarai met them on the entrance platform inside the Octus Overlook. She looked calm, but knowing her friend well, Dana could sense the tension as Sarai glanced over the party, briefly meeting Dana's gaze. It was Adol that Sarai addressed though, as he stepped to the side of the group with his newly empowered sword in hand.

"It seems you have received the power of the psyches," she said.

Adol nodded. "We have. What do we do next?"

Sarai pointed behind her. "You must continue on to the Selection Sphere. With your newly empowered sword, you should now be able to cut open an entrance."

They looked at the sphere looming in the distance. It resembled a giant eye, watching them keenly, as if aware of their intentions.

"What's inside there?" Hummel asked.

"The Selection Sphere contains the foundational power that fosters the evolution of all living beings on this planet. The Providence of Evolution itself."

"No problem." Sahad rolled up his sleeves. "We're ready to face that Providence thing. We fought every kind of creatures before and defeated them all."

Sarai shook her head. "The Providence of Evolution is not exactly a creature, even if it may indeed appear to you in this form. You are facing the natural law of the world itself. I do not know what will happen if you interfere with it."

"You won't scare us with all that talkin'! We've been honin' our castaway spirit since we washed up on this island. So let's show 'em how far we've come! When it comes to survival, no one's more stubborn than us humans."

Nods came from around the group. Sadness stirred up in Sarai's gaze as she watched them.

"So you've truly decided then."

"We have," Dana said. "Thank you for everything, Sarai."

Sarai stepped aside. Was that pity in her gaze? Or hope?

"In that case, hurry on ahead," she said. "I can't help you where you're going, but I will be praying for your success."

The walkway ahead of them ended with a glow, so bright that it blinded. The party proceeded toward it, narrowing their eyes against the glare.

Adol weighed his sword in his hand, then thrust it forward in one mighty move. The blade sank to the hilt into the glow. Dana could see his arm tremble with effort as he held the sword in place, power radiating from the stab point all across the space.

The platform under their feet tremored, and two concentric rings radiated around from the sword, opening a gateway.

"Let's go." Hummel stepped through, followed by Laxia, Ricotta, and Sahad. Adol paused right before it and looked at Dana.

"Ready?" he asked.

She nodded and took a step toward him.

A high-pitched hum filled her ears. Images burst in her mind, freezing her mid-step.

A vision? Now?

It lasted only a brief instant. She saw a giant flash, an all-consuming blast of power, Adol's sword slashing through the flare. Herself falling into the void and receding out of sight.

Was this what she had to do?

"Did you just have a vision?" Adol asked. "What did you see?"

Dana heaved a breath. "Later. I'll tell you when this is all over." She knew she would never get a chance. But telling him the truth now would weaken his resolve. They couldn't afford to risk it.

They entered the sphere side by side.

A platform similar to the one they'd just left stretched under their feet. The two concentric circles they'd stepped through were projected onto the floor, with their party in the center. A low rail made of what looked like a coiling tree branch ran around the edge.

They looked into the glow ahead.

A giant creature looming against the distant light filled the entire horizon with its huge form. Tall and insect-like, with tentacled arms protruding from the sides of its long body, it appeared vaguely humanoid—calm, but also monstrous and terrifying.

"What in the holy hell is that?" Sahad asked.

"It's even bigger than the Oceanus..." Ricotta whispered.

"The Providence of Evolution," Dana said. "Don't worry. Everything will be alright." At least, if she did her part. She had no doubt she would do so without hesitation. This was also a goodbye. But her friends didn't need to know that.

A transparent winding walkway led down to the creature. Twining lines of energy glimmered and moved endlessly at its sides. It felt so disorienting.

As they approached, more details of the creature they were facing came into view. Or did it simply change shape, taking its time to decide on the best form in which to face its opponents? Its tentacles now looked more like tree branches, its eyes more faceted, its arms bristling with pincers as they sprouted from the creature's tall body. A blend of a tree and an insect, if that was even possible. Appendages protruded and retreated in constant motion. Only one thing remained unchanged—its size, enormous like an embodiment of the world.

The creature held no weapons, but it didn't need any. A lash from any of those protrusions could be deadly on its own, inflicting wounds that would be impossible to heal. Dana could only hope that the creature would be vulnerable to their orichalcum weapons. If not, what hope did they have of defeating it?

She braced for an attack as soon as the party finally approached, but the creature's first move came from an unexpected angle. A pouch on the front of its body opened, spewing a gleaming jewel that scattered shards everywhere. The party had to use all their skills to deflect and dodge them. This one maneuver instantly negated any attack plans they might have harbored, forcing them to scramble for their lives.

They'd faced and defeated many enemies together, but this one was unlike anything they'd encountered before. Beyond imagination, in fact. Dana supposed it was only right for the Providence of Evolution to be like that, but more than once she wondered if they had been delusional to think they could actually defeat it. But they had come so far. There was no way back.

If they had any chance, she had to do her part. Her vision told her that much.

The lashing appendages and limbs could be easily severed, but more sprouted in their place without delay. After a while it became clear that their only hope was to move up, toward the creature's head. They sprinted along the platform spiraling upward, dodging the lashing tentacles, attacking the creature on all sides until they reached the end.

Dana's skin prickled as she finally looked the creature straight in the face.

An ancient being stared at them—a pair of cold eyes, features that blended plant, human, and insectoid with too many other species at once. Dana couldn't read its expression. Remorse? Hatred? Forgiveness? Pity? Here at the top, no tentacles or crystals protected it from the attack. Nothing should stop them now from destroying it. But as Dana raised her blades, she paused.

Did they have any right to strike this creature down and destroy the natural order of the world?

Adol seemed to have no such misgivings. As he raised his blade to the sky, the power of the psyches crackled through it, coating him with an impenetrable glow. He turned and met Dana's gaze, and she felt his resolve, his power, enfold her too, a unity of souls that surpassed everything they had experienced before.

She cast aside her doubts and lent her entire being to it, raising her blades, joining with him into one mighty creature, more powerful than the divine providence that governed their very existence.

"Let's do it, Adol!" she shouted as she launched forward, answered by his cry:

"Let's do it, Dana!"

The world around them shattered into oblivion.

Dana knelt down, panting. Images floated up in her mind. The Great Tree of Origins, the Eternia ruins. Primordials running around, disappearing in flashes of light.

She opened her eyes.

The party was scattered around the platform, collapsed in exhaustion. Adol crouched beside her, leaning heavily on his sword. The creature they had been fighting was nowhere in sight.

She blinked in disbelief. Had they managed to defeat their enemy and survive?

A glowing circle lit up in front of them, slowly taking a human form. Sarai. She rushed up to the party.

"Is everyone alright?"

Dana and Adol held hands as they rose shakily to their feet.

"What happened?" Dana asked.

Sarai heaved a breath. "The Lacrimosa has been thwarted. But the island... The island is vanishing! And the world will soon vanish with it!"

Dana stared. They'd won the fight. How could this be happening?

The details of her last vision formed in her mind, some parts she hadn't fully understood finally clicking into place. She hadn't done everything she was supposed to. There was one more thing she needed to do to fulfill her vision and save the world.

And she finally knew for certain what it was.

She squeezed Adol's hand.

"This isn't over yet," she said. "I won't let everything we've done amount to a mistake."

Before he could respond, she raised her face into the sky and released her Essence, flinging herself into the void. A white glow enveloped everything.

THE ABYSS OF ORIGINS

When Adol woke up in his hammock the next morning, everything seemed all right. At first. He looked around the peaceful scene, the room with a row of empty beds, sunlight scattering reflections over the brook.

"Are you awake, Adol?" Laxia called out from the door. "How long do you intend to sleep? Dogi and the others have already begun to load the ship."

The ship? Adol frowned. "What happened to the Lacrimosa?"

Laxia scoffed, averting her gaze as he got out of his hammock and straightened his clothes. "Lacri-what? Adol! Are you still asleep? We leave this island in a week's time. You should get up and start helping the others."

"Where's Dana?" Adol asked.

"Dana...Who's that?"

"You know. Dana."

Laxia shrugged. "No idea what you're talking about. None of the castaways go by that name." She leaned closer. "Adol, are you feeling well?"

"I'm all right."

"If you say so. Try not to push yourself too hard today."

As Adol washed and changed, he noticed that Mistilteinn, the Sword of Psyches, had reverted back to a regular sword. He also noticed that the symbol on his arm marking him as a Warden of Evolution had vanished. Did that mean they had succeeded? Was that the reason for Laxia's sudden forgetfulness?

Outside, Franz was tidying up the shelves in the cave's common room. He stopped and turned as he saw Adol.

"Good morning, Adol," he said. "Are you feeling all right?"

Before Adol could respond, Laxia burst out of the women's quarters. "FRAAANZ! Shut that glib mouth and clean this mess up."

Franz briefly closed his eyes, a content smile sliding over his face. Adol blinked. A smile? In response to this kind of shouting? He looked curiously at Laxia, noticing the way her lips twitched as she met Franz's gaze, as if the two of them were sharing a private joke.

"Right away, mistress." Franz bowed, then stepped past her into the women's quarters. Laxia floated majestically after him.

Adol shrugged. Something about this scene didn't add up, unless... Unless Laxia and Franz... He turned away and hurried outside.

"What's wrong, Adol?" Griselda asked as she saw him. "Disappointed that no grand adventure materialized for you on this island? It's not always a bad thing, you know."

Adol stared at her. No grand adventure? Was thwarting the end of the world not grand enough? He considered asking the question but decided against it. Something was going on, and he needed to find out what it was.

Just as Laxia said, preparations to leave the island were in full swing. At the supply area, Adol nearly collided with Euron carrying a stack of crates. Farther on, Dina was packing her goods into bundles. Kathleen was sorting instruments around the forge. Everyone seemed far too busy, so Adol decided not to disturb them as he made his way toward Hummel, standing in deep thought beside the fire.

"Adol," Hummel said. "It's unlike you to sleep in."

"Right." Adol bent down to pick up a charred skewer of fish set out between two rocks near the fire. Sahad always left breakfast for the late risers. He bit into it, staring at the activity around.

After a moment, Sahad walked in from the direction of the docks.

"Adol," he said. "We just started loadin' cargo. Gah-haha! It hasn't been that long, but it really feels like we've lived the castaway life forever. Still, I've got some good memories of the six of us explorin' this crazy island." He blinked. "Did I say six? I meant five, not six. Oh, well. Ya wanna do some more explorin' before we shove off? Kinda doubt you'll find much to appeal to an adventurer, but ya can soak up the sights."

Adol looked at him thoughtfully. Except for the slip up about the number of people in their party, Sahad seemed to have no recollection of the events either. He had no idea what was going on.

He finished his breakfast and walked around, talking to other castaways. Everyone was preoccupied with departure and didn't remember anything about Dana, Primordials, Eternia, or the Lacrimosa. Bringing up any of these topics led to blank stares and polite inquiries as to whether he was feeling all right. When he asked Kathleen about the orichalcum, she laughed.

"Hey, Adol, everyone knows that orichalcum doesn't exist. You'd think I would remember if I actually worked it to infuse your weapons, wouldn't I?"

Finally, Adol couldn't stand it any longer. If he was the only one here who remembered what had happened, so be it. He wasn't about to leave the island without Dana. He had to find out what had become of her.

He approached the Essence crystal and took out his crystal ring, pressing it to the smooth surface of the rock. He felt relieved as the familiar sensation engulfed him. At least the warping still worked—and that meant he couldn't possibly have imagined it all.

By his calculation, the warp should have brought him straight to the Temple of the Great Tree. But the scenery didn't look familiar. He could see no ruins, no buildings, no trace of civilization. Even the Great Tree of Origins no longer loomed over him. Wild greenery stretched in every direction, as far as the eye could see. A jungle in its original form, untouched by any intruders.

Adol peered into the distance. Was this the insectoid world that the Warden Nestor had come from? Had he somehow ended up in the wrong era?

No, that didn't seem right.

"Hey, Adol!" a voice called from behind.

Ricotta? He turned to see her approach, followed by Laxia, Hummel, and Sahad. They all had dazed looks on their faces. By habit, he looked for Dana among them, but she wasn't here.

"What are you all doing here?" he asked.

Laxia shook her head slowly. "It's hard to explain. It felt like something was calling out to me, so I left the village and warped here. Surprisingly enough, I think that happened to all of us at about the same time."

"A strange coincidence," Hummel said.

Sahad scratched his head. "I'll say. I didn't expect to find ya here too, Adol."

Laxia frowned as she looked around. "Has this area...always looked like this?"

"No." Ricotta shook her head. "It feels different..."

"I sorta feel like somethin' big used to be here," Sahad said. "This place sure is pretty, but..."

They looked around again. Through the tangle of tree branches, they could see a waterfall cascading from the rock cliff above. Rainbows gleamed in its mist, hovering over the pond at the bottom, and the brook running through the secluded meadow. The waterfall, at least, was familiar. Was this meadow on the exact spot where the Great Tree of Origins used to stand?

A small tree with a reddish-golden crown rose out of the grass near the bottom of the waterfall. As soon as their eyes fell on it, it glimmered, forming a silhouette that slowly took substance in the center of the glade. A woman. Or, not quite a woman. Not a regular one, anyway.

Her dress was composed of intertwined tree branches that looked like they were still growing while also adorning her body. Her arms looked like tree branches too, her long, leafy fingers twirling around a glowing blue globe in her hands. A crown of leaves fluttered around her head—or was it her hair?

Adol barely had time to notice how the grass around the glade sprouted a carpet of blue flowers that looked like tiny stars among the greenery. Tyrennian blossoms, the gratitude flowers from Dana's memory.

Was Eternia in here somewhere after all?

"You answered my call." The woman's voice filled the space, melodious and deep, powerful. "May your lost memories of the forgotten world be yours once again."

A glow radiated from her, and when it touched Adol's face, it felt as if his head had been cleared. More memories flowed in, adding to the ones he had already retained, filling the void in his mind. It felt as if a boundary between him and this past, that seemed to exist only in his mind now, had been dissolved, granting him a new level of awareness.

Eternia. The Temple of the Great Tree. *Dana.*

Around him, his friends seemed to be remembering too. Their faces showed confusion, then brightened as they all looked at each other.

"How could we have forgotten all this?" Laxia said. "The time we spent with Dana. She..."

The woman shifted the glowing sphere in her hands. "These memories have no cause to exist. But I have restored them nevertheless."

Adol stared at her in disbelief. *"No cause to exist?"*

"Restored?" Laxia frowned. "Who are you?"

The woman smiled. "I am Maia. The goddess who created the Great Tree of Origins when the Earth was newly born."

"Goddess?" Sahad gasped.

"Maia..." Hummel touched his chin thoughtfully. "That name sounds familiar."

"I believe the Warden Hydra mentioned her," Laxia said. "Earth Goddess Maia...Creator of the Great Tree, and evolution along with it. But I heard that you vanished during Hydra's era."

Maia nodded. "I fell asleep that time, and I was dreaming. I dreamed...a never-ending tapestry of evolution throughout the eras. It was very comforting. But I've since awakened from that dream, and now that world has ceased to be."

"What'd ya mean by that?" Sahad asked.

"I dreamed every phenomenon that transpired in this land," Maia said. "Including the lives of all species, and even the Lacrimosa itself. Thus, when I awaken, the dream must end."

"End?"

"Are you saying we're just figments of your dream?" Hummel demanded.

"A dream that ended," Laxia echoed. "Wait, did it end when we...?"

"Yes," Maia said. "I was awakened when the Providence of Evolution ceased to be."

"Then...we destroyed the world?" Ricotta said.

Laxia glanced at her. "But...if that is indeed what happened, what is this world we're in right now?"

"This is a new world I reconstructed," Maia said. "Due to your actions, the previous world no longer exists. That Eternian girl who led you...She became aware that the world was a dream of mine. Through the act of awakening me, she stopped the Lacrimosa."

"Where *is* Dana?" Adol demanded.

Maia lowered her eyes. "At the moment the Providence of Evolution fell, Dana offered herself in exchange. In doing so, she relinquished her existence."

"Relinquished her existence? Does that mean she disappeared?"

Ricotta whimpered.

"Not exactly," Maia said. "When her own Essence combined with the power of the psyches, the two opposing forces caused Dana to sublimate into a higher concept of evolution. This act of self-sacrifice enabled me to reconstruct the world from the verge of annihilation."

Laxia's eyes widened. "Dana really planned that far ahead?"

"No. She acted without any knowledge of the potential consequences of her actions. By her own hand, she performed an act of God. As recompense, her existence was forfeit." Maia's gaze drifted around the glade. "In the history of this new world, Dana never existed. She is only a concept now."

"A *concept?*" Adol stepped forward.

Memories flooded his mind.

Dana. What was it she had once said? *If we're destined to part ways, I want to accept my destiny with a smile and be true to myself when I bid you all farewell.* Well. Perhaps she wanted to accept her destiny with a smile, but Adol was different. He met his destiny with a sword in hand, and he wasn't about to change.

"I won't let you say she's forgotten," he said.

"Adol—" Laxia began.

Maia chuckled. "Adol Christin... Brave child of humanity. So you still intend to search for Dana?"

"Till the end of my days, if need be."

Maia inclined her head. "I did not expect such an unprecedented situation to occur. The dream woven by you and Dana was rather wonderful. I reconstructed this world because I wished to dream of you again. If you intend to search for Dana, then I shall aid you."

Before Adol could respond, a glow rose behind her, opening a hole. Inside, the ghostly outline of a path showed through, lined by trees very different from anything Adol had seen in this world. The dark sky gleamed with a distant light, like a sunrise in the middle of the night.

Maia pointed. "I have opened a way to the Abyss of Origins. If you wish to see Dana again, you must pass through it."

Sahad shifted his weapon in the sheath on his back. "You heard the Goddess, everyone. Let's go see Dana again."

A dark forest stretched in front of them. A path wound through it, toward the distant light. Grotesque tree silhouettes loomed deeper in the darkness. Was this how the land had looked before the Great Tree of Origins? Or was this a place the gods had created out of their imaginations?

Walking along the path felt disorienting. Above and below, the night sky spread out into the distance, with wisps of vapor rising and disappearing among the stars. It felt as if the road they were following ran through the sky too, in addition to being part of a primaeval forest that seemed to have existed since the beginning of time. The light in the distance beckoned, and Adol focused all his attention on it. *Dana, I am going to see you again.* Walking became easier when he thought this way.

Some of the creatures lurking in the dark resembled giant slugs. Others looked like nothing Adol had ever seen before—floating balloons covered with spikes, pincers, and all kinds of other weird appendages one wanted to steer clear of. They avoided the creatures as they made their way toward the light glowing through the trees ahead, bright and cool like the core of a cold star. The road brought them out of the forest, across a sky bridge, and directly into the blazing radiance.

Adol had expected the path to end when they stepped through the light. Instead, a vast dark space greeted them on the other side. A primordial ocean, with no land in sight, stretched all around them. A shallow reef formed a platform under their feet. In its center, a wooden cage hung in mid-air, with a creature glowing inside.

Dana?

No. The ethereal being wasn't even fully humanoid—an embryo with a large head and dark eyes that looked both innocent and evil as they fixed on Adol and his group. The creature glowed with a purple light, and as the party started across the water toward it, hosts of other creatures, land and sea, formed directly from that light and fanned around to defend the inhabitant of the cage.

The party's weapons were no longer infused with orichalcum; at least, Adol thought they weren't. But here in this world they worked just as well, each as effective as possible against their enemies. But even with that, they had to lend their entire skill to the battle, slicing through the monsters that dissipated when struck, until there wasn't a single one left.

The cage broke. The creature inside spun through the air, spiraling slowly, as if supported by an invisible force. Or was it all Adol's perception? Here, outside the bounds of the known world, reality and time didn't seem to have the same meaning.

Before the falling embryo-like creature could hit the water, a giant shape rose from the depths and caught it, settling it in a new cage inside its back. This new creature looked nothing like the Providence of Evolution, but it had some of the same traits, a mix of tree and insect—maybe a scorpion, with a huge tail and too many legs to count. Blue energy flowed through its veins—Essence?

The Origin of Life. Adol wasn't sure how he knew, but this certainty settled firmly into his mind as he faced the creature. If this primal horror symbolized life, no wonder the goddess Maia was so keen on destroying each species that gained dominion over the land, making sure none of them had a chance to evolve to this creature's evil state. It was a strange thought as Adol watched the creature advance onto the group. He didn't want to fight it, but here, in this world, he seemed to have no choice.

Dawn broke over the ocean, outlining the silhouettes of giant trees with circular crowns, the kind Adol had seen reigning over Eternia before. The advancing monster looked dark against this light, menacing.

As he had done with the Providence of Evolution, Adol shifted his mind into a detached state and attacked. The team was by his side, and together, they were invincible. They had faced so many fights against creatures as frightening as this one. They had defeated the Lacrimosa. They were fighting for Dana. The stakes made it all worth it.

THE GODDESS OF EVOLUTION

When they finally defeated the creature, the scenery around them changed. They were no longer in the strange void-like place between worlds but back in the glade where they had met Maia. The goddess stood in front of them, looking at them curiously.

"You have returned," she said.

Sahad leaned his fists into his sides, stepping toward her. "What's going on? I thought you said we would see Dana again. Where is she? Did ya pull a fast one on us?"

Adol was pretty sure one didn't talk to goddesses like that. He was about to interfere, but Maia smiled indulgently, as if facing a temperamental toddler.

"As I stated earlier, Dana is a concept now," she said. "She no longer exists. She is everywhere and nowhere."

"A concept?" Sahad took another step forward. But before the conversation could get out of hand, a shimmer of air wavered in front of them.

A ghostly shape materialized in the glade, gradually taking substance until it was no longer transparent.

Dana.

She looked different. Instead of her Eternian outfit, a gossamer gown covered her head to toe, adorned with a Great Tree symbol on the front. Her hair had lost its rich color and turned pale and ghostly too, cascading down her back in a mass of loose waves.

Adol's breath caught as he looked at her.

"And now she is here," Maia announced. "The newest member of the pantheon. Dana, the Goddess of Evolution."

A goddess.

Was there anything of the real Dana left in this ethereal creature, beautiful and distant like the sky? Would she even remember Adol? He clenched a fist, reassured by the feeling of the smooth metal pressing into his skin. Dana's ring. It was still here, and therefore the events he remembered were real. He hadn't dreamt any of it. He would cling to this memory for the rest of his days.

Dana ran her gaze around the group. Her stunning aqua eyes singled out Adol, her smile echoing in his very soul.

"Adol," she said quietly.

She remembers. Hearing her voice speak his name made Adol feel weak inside. He longed to rush forward, to scoop her into his arms, never to let her go. But Ricotta beat him to it as she launched herself at Dana, throwing her arms around her. "Dana! It's really you!"

For a moment, Dana seemed stunned. Then she smiled and re-laxed into the embrace. The rest of the party surrounded her too, laughing, patting her. Laxia hugged her and leaned into her shoulder.

"The goddess Maia told us we can't really see you," Ricotta said. "But then she allowed us to fight this monster, and now—" She pulled out of the embrace and looked at Dana. "You are here."

Dana nodded. "I don't think you can perceive me unless you've made contact with the Origin of Life. Others may not be able to see me as you do."

"You've done a lot for us," Hummel said. "The Trabaldo family always pays their debts in full, but this might be too much even for me to repay."

"He's right," Sahad joined in. "I dunno how I could ever repay you either. The whole Greshun region is safe now, thanks to you, Dana. Heck, the whole world is safe. Can't even wrap my head 'round it."

"Hummel ... Sahad ... Everyone ..." Tears were standing in her eyes, but she turned away briefly and blinked them away.

One by one, the party exchanged words with her and stepped aside, until Adol was the only one left standing in front of her.

"Adol ..." Dana paused.

He swallowed. He wanted to say so many things to her. Why did he suddenly feel so tongue-tied?

"I wish there could have been another way," he said quietly.

She shook her head. "I'm sorry. I had no idea what else to do ... The world was disappearing. If I'd waited any longer, there wouldn't have been anything left. I did the only thing I knew to save us all. And then, I have become...*this*." She looked down at her form and back to Adol. "I'm so glad I got to see you again."

"It should have been me sacrificing myself," he said. "I fully intended to, if it came to that. I wanted to fight for you till my last breath. If I'd known what you were about to do..."

A sad smile twitched her lips. "I know. You would have tried to save me, and doing so would have destroyed the world."

Adol lowered his head. She was correct. And, despite her sacrifice, things did end well after all. Being a goddess had to be a good thing, right?

Why then couldn't he find it in himself to be glad things had ended up happening the way they did?

"At least we destroyed the Lacrimosa," he said.

"Actually..." Dana took a breath. "We didn't."

"What?"

"She speaks the truth," Maia said. "The phenomenon known as the Lacrimosa is not gone. For as long as I sleep and dream, the Lacrimosa's return is inevitable. But in the future, the Lacrimosa will be entrusted to the Goddess of Evolution."

"To...Dana?" Adol's eyes widened.

"Yes." Dana shifted from foot to foot. "In all honesty, I'm not confident in my ability to manage this. But this time, I'm not alone. I will have help."

The air next to her shimmered, and the Wardens of Evolution materialized in the glade.

"You...Are still here?" Sahad asked in disbelief.

"We are," Sarai said. "And by your actions, we have been freed from our duty as Wardens. From now on, we will assist Dana in overseeing the evolutionary process."

"I think we understand the people of this world better now," Hydra said. "If we can act in accordance with the era, and use the Lacrimosa properly, we can avoid the suffering and use evolution to make the world a far better place."

Sahad shrugged. "I dunno about all that. But I guess it's fine if you and Dana are handling the Lacrimosa now."

"But never forget," Nestor added. "Should this world rapidly fall into chaos, the Lacrimosa may come sooner than expected."

"We will be keeping a watchful eye on this world," Minos agreed. "We will not hesitate to come to its defense. Isn't that right, Goddess Dana?"

Dana nodded slowly. "Yes, that is the task we have been given by the Earth Goddess Maia."

"Guess we better not slack off then," Sahad said.

Maia stepped forward. "It is time, Dana. Time for me to sleep once again."

Dana turned to Adol. Again, as their gazes locked, the world around them receded. Was it her power as a goddess to do this? Or was it all in his mind? Every moment with her was so precious. He had to make the most of it.

"Adol," she said. "There is something I wanted to say to you before we go. Though you only came to know me after you arrived on this island, I've known you for a very long time. When I was all alone in this world, in the midst of despair, seeing how you and your friends lived gave me the strength to go on. Thank you from the bottom of my heart for giving me that strength. Thank you from the bottom of my heart for accepting me as your friend. And finally, thank you from the bottom of my heart for finding me."

She stepped forward and drew him into her arms.

He melted into their embrace.

Was saving the entire humankind worth throwing away an eternity with Dana? Yes, it was. He knew he would make the same choice, again and again. But this knowledge didn't make him feel any better about having to give her up forever.

"I'll never forget you, Dana," he whispered.

"I'll never forget you either, Adol."

Visions of Eternia, the place that never existed in this new reality, floated in his mind. He saw him and Dana among the ruins of Aegias, alone with each other, the way they'd spent that day together. He saw them walking the same streets in her time, with children playing around and merchants setting up their stalls in the market plaza. They sat together by the fountain in the water gardens, with winged Primordials circling far overhead. And more, things that never happened, even in the old world, things that he'd dreamed about all this time. He and Dana traveling together as adventurers, discovering new lands. Growing old together in his home village, fishing together on the beach, walking hand in hand to a house sitting atop a picturesque cliff. All this could never come to be, but he would never stop dreaming about it.

He knew that Dana shared the same thoughts too. She was a goddess, after all, able to see everything going on in his head. She could speak to him in his head too, and he heard her voice now, a conversation meant only for the two of them.

I will always be close by, Adol. You have but to think of me, and I will be right there.

I will never stop thinking about you.

Then I will never leave you.

You won't go to sleep for ages?

Not as long as I am in your thoughts. We can always create new memories together. We can always visit any place, experience things as if we are actually there. Even Eternia.

He deepened his embrace, images flowing in his mind. Put that way, this didn't seem like such a bad deal.

Too soon, she pulled away from him. Reluctantly, he let her go. She squeezed his hand then stepped away and looked at the whole group.

"Goodbye to you all," she said.

Laxia and Ricotta were sniffling. Even Sahad wiped a tear off his cheek.

"Thank you for everything," Hummel said.

White light flooded the world. And then Dana, the former Wardens, and the Earth Goddess Maia were gone.

The day of departure finally came. Adol, Sahad, and Thanatos stood together on the docks, watching the activity around the ship. She wasn't nearly as big as the *Lombardia*. A two-masted brig, she was just large enough to accommodate all the castaways for a trip to the nearest port.

"The weather's nice and the water's calm," Sahad said. "We should be able to leave the Isle of Seiren without any problems. I don't think we'll have any issues makin' it to Sounion Port."

Thanatos looked into the distance. "Never thought this day would come. For as long as I was a castaway, my time here felt remarkably short."

Sahad patted him on the shoulder. "You've been here longer than any o' us. It's probably just startin' to sink in now."

"Well." Thanatos tore his eyes away from the horizon. "Since this really is the end, I think I'll take one last walk on the island."

"You be careful now."

Thanatos nodded as he walked off.

"Hey, Adol." Dogi came down the path, carrying a heap of bedding and blankets in his arms. He set them carefully on a clean grass patch and stepped up to Adol's side. "You seem like you've changed a bit lately. Everything all right?"

Adol smiled, feeling the touch of a presence in his mind. *Dana*. A part of her had been with him all these days, emerging in his mind whenever he called her, so that the two of them could relive all his experiences together. With her so close, he would never feel alone anymore.

Dogi clicked his tongue. "Daydreaming, eh? Guess something nice happened ... Want to tell me about it?"

"Later," Adol said. "It's going to be a long story."

"Haha, I like the sound of that. We'll have plenty of time when we sail. Some rum too, just to pass the time." Dogi winked, then picked up a crate from the prepared stack and made his way on board.

Adol strolled through the village one last time.

Most castaways were still at their stations, finishing the packing and the preparations. Dina was rummaging among the crates. Little Paro sat on his favorite perch next to her, at the base of the watchtower. He clicked his beak and dipped his head when Adol passed by.

In the lodge, Franz moved around the shelves, arranging the items they were leaving behind. He smiled when he saw Adol. Come to think of it, in the past week or two Franz tended to smile a lot. The man seemed happy. Content. Perhaps Adol wasn't the only one who had a story to tell?

"Don't you think this is enough tidying up for a deserted island?" Adol asked. "No one is probably going to come here for years."

Franz nodded. "You're right. I should stop. Besides, before we leave, I was going to serve everyone a nice pot of tea."

Laxia and Alison walked in at this moment. Laxia cradled Alison's baby, holding it awkwardly but tenderly. The baby gurgled happily, tugging at a strand of her hair. Before she raised her eyes, Adol had a chance to catch Franz's expression as he looked at her—full of such tenderness that his heart quivered.

Adol was right, or so it seemed. He wasn't the only one to find his happiness on this island.

Laxia looked up and smiled. Her eyes met Franz's, and for a moment it seemed like they were the only ones here.

"I'm getting better with babies," she said.

"Much better." Alison reached over and took the baby from her. "Ready for your own, eh, Laxia?"

Again, Laxia looked at Franz, her cheeks lighting up with a deep crimson color.

"We, um, should finish up the preparations." She nodded to Adol and rushed past into the women's living quarters.

And then it was time to set sail. As Adol walked on board, he looked at the view of Gendarme, looming against the backdrop of the clear blue sky. They were finally saying goodbye to the Isle of Seiren. But, no matter where he went, he was always going to carry this place in his heart.

The Adol he used to be before this experience would be excited right now, planning his next big adventure. But for the first time since he became an adventurer, Adol felt as if he were leaving home, as if a part of him was staying behind. He vowed to himself to come back again one day.

To remember.

EPILOGUE

The castaways reached safety and went their separate ways. But from that day on, they always felt like family. In their travels, they visited each other whenever they could. Even Sir Carlan.

Hummel Trabaldo returned to the Romun Empire, where he quietly resumed his work as a transporter for the criminal underworld. Over the course of his work, he met the daughter of a wealthy noble who would eventually propose marriage to him, but he declined her offer and continued to work as a transporter, while also managing the orphanage where he spent his childhood.

Ricotta Beldine traveled the world with her father, Thanatos Beldine. A peace treaty was finally signed between the Romun Empire and the Kingdom of Altago, and the seas became safe once again. Soon after, Ricotta and her father traveled to another continent, and their current whereabouts are unknown.

Sahad Nautilus returned to his homeland, Creet, where he reunited with his beloved wife and daughter. Though the details are scarce, it is said that he lived the rest of his days in peace. However, tales eventually spread about the large, boisterous fisherman who helped his fellow castaways on the Isle of Seiren.

Laxia von Roswell fulfilled her promise of restoring her family to its former glory. She also followed her passion for science. While studying abroad at the Gllia Academy, she finally reunited with her father, who followed her back home to settle for his retirement. Garnering wide acclaim from both the public at large and other noble houses, Laxia became known as a capable ruler of her estate and one of the leading experts on Primordials. She married her butler in a large but informal wedding ceremony attended by all the *Lombardia* castaways, who traveled in specially for this happy occasion. The couple settled down at Roswell Manor, where they split their time between family life, estate governance, and scientific research.

Adol Christin and his friend Dogi parted ways with the other castaways after docking in Greek. Besides occasional visits to their old friends from the *Lombardia*, their travels took them on many exciting and perilous adventures, and their current whereabouts are unknown. Based on fragments of available information, it is believed that they eventually traveled west. Nearly one hundred travelogues, each chronicling Adol's adventures, have been recovered in his childhood home. Their full contents have yet to be revealed.

ACKNOWLEDGEMENTS

I am grateful to so many people for making this book possible.

First and foremost, I would like to thank Nihon Falcom Co. for creating the world of Ys and this beautiful game that has been so enjoyable to play and to write about. It has been my privilege and my pleasure to bring this project to life, while spending time on the Isle of Seiren and reliving the experiences of the *Lombardia* castaways and the ancient Eternians.

Many people worked behind the scenes on this publication. My editors, Kaelyn Considine and Paul Witcover, have gone above and beyond to make sure this book is as polished as it can be. Bernie Mojzes made key suggestions and edits that helped me shape the story and the characters. Sarah O'Donnell gave me a crash course on nautical terms and provided consultations and helpful feedback on everything to do with sail ships. Leo Korogodski, Yuri Wolf, John Jarrold, and Olga Karengina provided important comments and insights. Beverly Bambury and Mike Underwood guided and consulted our team on publicity, and provided support throughout the project. Modern Gladiatorial Arts, an amazing group of experts on martial arts and historical weapon styles consulted me on everything related to sword fighting and helped me to make sure the fights in this book are as believable and accurate as allowed by the genre. I feel so lucky to have worked with all these amazing people. This book would not have been possible without you all.

My very special thanks go to the team at Digital Emelas, especially to Limfinite, as well as Jeff Nussbaum, Jessie Brianna Cooper, Johnathan Sawyer, and Tom Lipschultz, for sharing their knowledge of the world and characters of Ys and their expertise on the Ys community and fans. Their support and advice not only ensured that this book conforms with the game's history and terminology, but also helped increase awareness of this publication and drove some of the important marketing decisions. But even beyond that, my interactions with Digital Emelas made me realize that there are other people out there who love *Lacrimosa of Dana* as much as I do, and this book really matters to them. Our conversations have been a pleasure and played a very special role in motivating and supporting me throughout the project.

Last but not least, I would like to thank my husband, for being a wonderful teammate and partner in all my undertakings, and my children, for being my first readers, editors, critics, and fans, who continue to keep me on my toes, and bring so much joy into my life.

ABOUT THE AUTHOR

Anna Kashina is a critically acclaimed award-winning fantasy author. Her novels, inspired by historical multicultural settings, fea-
ture adventure, swordplay, political intrigue, and romance. She loves
role-playing games and is a passionate fan of *Lacrimosa of Dana*.